NOTES A.
ACKNOW

CW01003878

This novel is a work of fiction. Some dates, individuals and events in the novel may be recognisable from historical documentation but they have been heavily fictionalised. The behaviour of any individual person or group identifiable from the historical texts cited below, or others, is fictional, and should not be interpreted as an assertion of fact.

Over the last 500 years, publications on the history and society of late Tudor London and Ireland, and the events and impact of the 16th century religious wars in Europe have proliferated. The diaspora and history of the French and Dutch Huguenots has also been documented. I have consulted the internet in addition to the sources below in preparing this novel and in chapter eleven I acknowledge a debt to the Sister Fidelma mysteries written by Peter Tremayne.

A Survey Of London by John Stow, (1598)
I am indebted to the staff of Tower Hamlets Local History Library and Archives for access to this volume.

A View Of The Present State Of Ireland by Edmund Spenser, (1595)

An itinerary, containing his ten yeeres travell through the twelve dominions of Germany, Bohmerland, Sweitzerland, Netherland, Denmarke, Poland, Italy, Turky, France, England, Scotland & Ireland by Fynes Moryson, (1617)

Fairy and Folk Tales of The Irish Peasantry ed. WB Yeats, (1888)

The Stranger In Ireland – from the reign of Elizabeth to the Great Famine by Constantia Maxwell (1954), Jonathan Cape

Irish Tales and Sagas by Ulick O'Connor (1985), Dragon Books

The Oxford Illustrated History Of Ireland ed. RF Foster (1989), OUP

Wicklow, History & Society ed. Ken Hannigan & William Nolan (1994), Templeogue Publications

Ireland in the Age of the Tudors by SG Ellis (1998), Longman

London: The Biography by Peter Ackroyd (2001), Vintage

LIST OF CHARACTERS

The Irish in Leinster

Lord Redmond MacFeagh, *Chief and Commander of the MacFeagh sept*

Lord Lorcan MacFeagh, *father of Redmond (died in 1581)*

Lady Eithne Kavanagh, *mother of Redmond (died in 1587)*

Lady Medb MacFeagh, *great-aunt of Redmond*

Lord Padraig MacFeagh, *great-uncle of Redmond and sept chief (died 1581)*

Lady Orlaith MacFeagh, *nee MacMurtagh, wife of Fergus, foster-mother of Redmond*

Lord Fergus MacFeagh, *uncle of Redmond (died 1592) foster-father to Redmond*

Niko MacFeagh, *son of Lady Orlaith & Mustafa Reis, foster-brother to Redmond*

Lord Fintan MacFeagh, *Redmond's disabled uncle & lieutenant commander*

Oonagh MacFeagh, *nee O'Toole, wife of Fintan*

Finn & Fionnula, *children of Fintan & Oonagh*

Ronan Kavanagh, *Squire to Redmond*

Dermot MacFeagh, *kin to Redmond and Squire to Niko*

Conan Kavanagh, *a Gallowglass, kin to Ronan*

Nuala O'Byrne, *a servant at Hurst Place*

Walter Grene, *a steward at Hurst Place*

The English Officials in Ireland

Thomas Hurst of Hurst Place *in The Pale around Dublin in the county of Leinster*
Sir Rowland Porter, *a Constable of Dublin Castle in 1597*
Master Gideon Goodyear, *the English Crown's Vice-Treasurer in Dublin in 1601*

The Londoners

Mistress Alice Plymmiswoode of Plymmiswoode Hall, *a cloth dealer, sister to Thomas Hurst*
Abraham Plymiswoode, *wool trader, husband of Alice (died 1596)*
Hope Polstead, *wife to Court cloth purveyors and friend of Alice Plymmiswoode*
Nat Gibson, *sergeant-at-arms retained by the Plymmiswoode family*
Sister Benedicta, *a former nun at the Somerset Abbey*
Christian Calvet, *a Walloon cloth finisher*
Dame Margery Calvet, *wife to Christian Calvet*
Edward, *stepson of Christian Calvet*

The Dutch in Amsterdam and Leiden

Hendrik Breydel of Leiden, *owner of a cloth finishing firm (drowned in 1597)*
Andreas De Hem, *his brother-in-law and business partner*
Pieter Heyden, *secretary to Hendrik Breydel &Andreas De Hem*
Susannah Breydel, *daughter of Hendrik Breydel. Susannah is a skilled weaver and cloth designer*

The English in Somerset

Lady Ann Templeton, *a landowner*
Sir Edmund Templeton, *son of Lady Templeton*
Dame Cecilia Walford, *sister-in-law of Abraham Plymmiswoode's 2nd wife Mary. Later, chatelaine of Somerset Abbey*

Seafarers

Alfonso Da Cuellar, *a ship's captain and a friend of Niko*
Captain Norris, *a ship's captain*

For my family

'Weave Truth With Trust'
the motto of the Medieval London Weavers Guild

CHAPTER ONE
Anno Domini 1597

Thomas Hurst, an official of the English Crown, entered the upstairs parlour. Still booted, he sat down heavily. He looked up at his sister who had been admiring a thick woven tapestry, not long arrived from England. Thomas had just returned from the north of Ireland to his manor in Leinster County, a large region lying in and around The Pale of Dublin.

He said, 'I have heard of a ship near the Head, wrecked in the fogs. Tell me what you know. He may stay.' Alice had glanced at the steward who had followed his master into the room.

'Light the candles Walter,' she replied, adding rapidly, 'The seas and rocky coast where the ship was wrecked had been thick with fogs, and were wild and near inaccessible. The Constable's men were unable to recover the vessel. They say that it was laden with trade goods, had come out of Bordeaux bound for London, and seemingly diverted to Waterford for some reason. It seems all have perished. When the Searcher of Customs finally reached the strand nearest the wreck – the fogs which had at first dissipated, had quickly returned - the cliff paths were dangerous. His riders found nothing except timbers, pennants and corpses. They searched for some leagues in each direction, but nothing was found. Lord have mercy on their souls.'

The dark waxed panelling glistened around the sconces and a candelabrum on an oak chest. Alice crossed herself with plump beringed fingers. The others did so too, Thomas saying with a frown, 'What – nothing at all?'

'Nothing.'

'Have you sent for the MacFeagh chief, or Lord Redmond, as he calls himself? This looting must be his doing.'

'I thought I would wait until you returned, Thomas.' She paused, liking to look at his profile, regal like a king on a silver coin. Both men and women still watched for his approach. 'We have no direct proof of their plunder as yet. You always tell me that they do not, at heart, acknowledge these lands as yours, so we have to treat carefully with them.'

Her elder brother had been an army officer, serving the English Crown with distinction in the Low Countries[1] and also in Ireland some twenty years previously during Earl Desmond's rebellion against the rule of the English Queen Elizabeth I. When the Earl was defeated, much land in the Irish counties was annexed. Thomas was granted territory belonging to the MacFeagh sept, and had been bound by oath to promote the Protestant Faith there. He was also required to keep his lands secure for the Crown and liaise with the surviving southern chiefs. After some years of peace, some of the mountain and forest areas on the edge of the sept's ancestral desmesne were given back to them.

'Anyway,' Alice continued, 'I doubt if they would have responded to a summons from me, rather than you.'

Walter, tall, with long curly hair and an unruly beard, had gone to stand behind his master's chair. He interposed, after looking at Thomas for encouragement to speak, 'Forgive me, mistress, but they are well aware that you have the ordering of the Hurst desmesne whilst he is absent.'

'And even when I am here,' said Thomas, smiling quizzically at the younger man.

'Well – I suppose Redmond's foster-brother, Niko, may have responded,' she replied, remembering the man's dark gaze proudly holding hers. Alice recalled meeting Niko MacFeagh and wishing that he was not so intriguingly handsome. 'As you know, he is the only civilised one of the MacFeaghs that I have met. He is smooth as silk. But I doubt if he would have given me anything but blandishments.'

Thomas raised himself, one slender hand leaning on his staff. His journey from the north had been arduous. He moved to the mantlepiece, impatiently dismissing Walter's offer of assistance.

'I do find his courtesies towards you too forward for my liking. You should show him his place. Asking him about his looting would have given you the opportunity to show our authority. And you underestimate yourself in thinking you could not get to the truth of the matter. Your questions are always apposite.' He sighed. ' I'm never quite sure where I stand with Redmond MacFeagh, although he professes loyalty. You will recall his visit soon after you arrived? You rapidly excused yourself on seeing his savage garb! He has a reputation for wiliness – and no-one knows where he is at any given time.'

He looked at Walter, who added, 'I am told that Baron Redmond largely stays in his re-assigned lands.'

Thomas continued, putting his hand on the small of his back, 'Although Niko and other envoys come here and communicate regularly with us, Redmond himself has rarely visited Hurst Place.' He decided to expand on his current difficulties as a Crown representative. 'Many of the Irish chieftains have never accepted us as Overlords, although much time has passed. I suspect Redmond is one of these. Others have turned their coats so often that we never know which side they favour. And they quarrel amongst themselves. There are so many, too many, barons for a small island!'

'I have tried to win the friendship of the MacFeaghs.' Alice nodded to Walter. 'You sent some of their men back with some supplies of meat and stored fruit whilst you were away. This last winter was as cold, if not colder, than the frosts we had to bear in England before I arrived here.'

Thomas snorted and looked irritable.

'I have no doubt they took them gladly. They want their fighting men to be well-fed!'

'I have heard, Thomas, that it is foreign and even English rogues arrived here, that are the worst plunderers, selling their services to the highest bidder. Surely, if we are neighbourly and help the clansfolk, they will maintain loyalty to our Queen and understand that the Protestant Faith is charitable and compassionate?'

'I doubt if they will consider that at all. Don't be too generous, sister. Their kerns raid cattle, poach deer and steal horses
and wheat whenever they can. And now, it seems they are looting
shipwrecks.'

Walter added, 'The Irish people here can live off the land.
They suffer no real hardship even if the harvest fails – there is
plenty all around: fish in the rivers, lochs and seas and boar and
rabbit in the forests.'

Thomas sat down again. 'Have we something to drink?' he
asked, looking round the room.

Alice gestured to Walter, who moved to pour some warmed
wine. Carefully carrying a Venetian glass goblet, she walked to
the window and peered into the gloom. The orchards, servants'
quarters and stabling surrounding the house were in shadow.
Some men were still weeding the gravel paths around the newly
laid knot-garden below. A crow could just be seen, stalking ungainly, on the lawns beyond.

Thomas and Alice were the children of a successful English cloth
wholesaler, Selwyn Hurst, who also owned farms and flocks. As
young people, they sometimes accompanied their father on his
trading journeys to Norwich and London. On one of these they
learned that their mother and all their siblings at their home in
Coventry had died of fever. When Selwyn re-married, his second
wife Mary and her infant son did not survive childbirth. Young
Thomas had been commissioned into the army to emphasise
loyalty to the English Crown, whilst Selwyn betrothed his small
daughter Alice to a Protestant fleece and wool dealer, one Abraham Plymmiswoode, a wealthy kindly widower slightly younger
than himself. In the negotiations around her marriage portion,
her father had willed some of his holdings to Alice's stepsons,
on condition that Alice, who had shown an aptitude for the wool
trade, would be allowed to assist if she so desired.

Alice turned and regarded Thomas, saying plaintively, 'It is good
that you have returned safely to me. I love to debate the Scriptures with you. And also poesie. Many such as I read those poets

who proclaim the virtues – but allegorically through the myths of ancient times.'

'Some would say allegory is heretical, Alice,' he warned.

'Only those zealots who would have the world forever literal would call it heresy,' Alice retorted, looking again at the vibrant tapestry she had been admiring earlier, and realising he had not yet noticed it. 'I rejoice in the subtle praise the poets give to our Gracious Queen Elizabeth. I model myself on her, whose knowledge of affairs, intelligence and subtlety is an example to all women.'

Thomas clutched the silver pommel on his staff, shaped like a wolf's head.

'If her Advisers would only persuade her to agree to reduce the burden of taxation, government here would be a deal easier,' he commented, shaking his head resignedly, then quickly quaffing his drink.

During his years in Leinster, Thomas had built a new manor he had named Hurst Place, and, following his sister Alice's husband's death the previous year, he had invited her for an extended stay to oversee further works there whilst he was away on Crown affairs. Selwyn Hurst had also died the previous year at which point Thomas sold the Plymmiswoode sons the remainder of his share of his father's estate, in order to keep a larger garrison at his desmesne in Ireland and make additions to his residence.

Soon after her arrival in Leinster, Thomas gave her local and recent news on the on-going rebellion against Queen Elizabeth's rule which had been instigated by the northern earls some four years previously. He knew that they constantly plotted, raided, and sought allies in the other counties.

'Indeed, I was not aware we were so hemmed in by thieves,' she had exclaimed. 'Are we well guarded and protected here?'

Thomas had then, somewhat hesitantly, reassured her. 'The Ulster Earl of Tyrone's campaigns against the Crown stop and start. When he is not fighting us, he sues for a truce or pardon – but on his terms only, and then breaching agreements with impunity. Neither we, nor other settlers, are forgiven for our Grant of fertile acreage, or for receiving the property of the dissolved monasteries, sister. Here in the south, we are not yet at war, and we try to keep trouble to a minimum. On my demesne, we trade with Redmond MacFeagh and his foster-brother Niko, giving up some of our profit. Their churls and ours labour together, cutting ships' planks and tanning hides. We can easily deal with raids and, if we can locate them, we always punish the malefactors severely.'

Now the gloaming had deepened. The candlelight accentuated the shadows on Thomas's lined face. He put down his tankard and signalled to Walter for it to be re-filled.

Alice asked, 'You are away more often than here, brother! For how long are you back with us?'

'A few days only. The Lord Deputy, Sir William Russell, is much preoccupied with the explosion of gunpowder at the Liffey wharfside in Dublin in March. I have been charged with some investigation into whether it was due to sabotage.'

'I have heard that upwards of two hundred folk have perished.'

'God rest their souls.' They crossed themselves. 'So for the moment I must continue to enquire and parley around the southern counties - although I am unlikely to be successful,' replied Thomas ruefully, 'and 'tis a pity that their impenetrable inheritance system has allowed some of base blood to become chiefs! It is very difficult to discuss matters, treat or negotiate with such men. Sometimes I think it would be better were they allowed to marry with us.' He drank deeply as Alice looked at him, noting his misshapen leg, and the way his face always softened as he regarded Walter's sturdy form and wheaten stoop of hair. Although bearing arms, Thomas did not fight now and was in constant pain. He had never married, and a succession of male stewards had always managed his household, whilst he supervised the mining and forestry when not about the Queen's business.

Alice said, looking at Walter, 'Whilst you've been away, I have had to berate our kitchen and field girls as they are sullen, gossip incessantly amongst themselves and are unwilling to learn our tongue.'

'I am sorry for this, mistress. You should know that I do have them beaten. I insist that they learn to repeat, in the English tongue, "I must make malt, I must sweep, I must scrub, and I must spread rushes"....'

'They expect to be punished for wrong-doing,' interrupted Alice, selecting a sweetmeat and looking hard at Walter, 'although it is as well not to be too harsh.'

'Recently, Redmond has been much slower in paying dues to the Crown.' Thomas mused. 'Even some of the loyal earls' kin are allies of those men of the mountains who are always equivocal about the Dublin regime... but I have some sympathy with their attitude after the Crown's harsh reprisals following the last rebellion. I witnessed many hangings, and saw long dirt roads lined and staked with the lifeless heads of nobles and their captains. Many were killed who did not bear weapons. The howling of grief-struck and starving women still disturbs my sleep on occasion.'

'I appreciate that the Queen's justice was severe, but I was told that the cruelty went both ways and that they were but savages, deserving such a fate,' Alice answered sharply. 'The Sheriff, who graciously welcomed me in Dublin, told me, as you often do, that cattle theft and fighting are the only inclination of the people. His wife also told me that many of the women are probably witches, judging from their potions, their songs and their superstitions, and those who are not witches seemingly still have nothing but praise for their menfolk's unholy deeds.'

'You have not had many dealings with the higher-born Irish, sister. Do not judge them without thought. The women are religious, albeit in a misguided faith. Many of their men are courageous and intelligent with skill-at-arms. The septs and clans have a fine tradition of music and the God-given Arts. But most do not speak our tongue and have no desire to learn it.' Thomas paused. He recalled meeting and being impressed by the young Hugh O'Neill who had been in fosterage in England and who had been given an Earldom by his Queen, access to her Court, and audiences with her royal person. 'Not so long ago, Alice, the Earl of Tyrone was admired as strong and loyal. Indeed, he fought for the Crown in Munster some years ago when the Popish old English rose up. All this makes her very angry at his treachery now.

But he should know the strength of her mind and temper when she is suspicious and crossed. Pride and self-interest will be his fall, as will his recent alliance with the Earl of Tyrconnell.'

'Will the MacFeaghs and their Overlord not remember the Earl Tyrone turning his coat? Surely they will not trust him? We need to know we can rely on loyalty from our nearest neighbour!'

'We can't be sure, Alice. Loyalty to an Overlord is everything. Even now they must accept *their* authority, rather than ours. But in the last rebellion, the Overlords disputed amongst themselves, leading to bloodshed and changing sides, contributing to their defeat.'

'Then and now it seems impossible to truly keep track of their goings-on, although the Crown requires this. Sometimes I wonder that you have lived here so long, Thomas!'

'All I can say is that at the moment, we settlers serve our Queen and keep strong garrisons. At present, Redmond and his people negotiate with me. It is vital that their women and churls be let alone so that they can work the fields and forests in safety, weave the frieze for export and transport timber.'

Walter interjected, 'Indeed, we also need them to make ale, butter and cheese and serve in the manors and Great Houses.'

'I would think that there are many riches to be earned by all who dwell in this fair isle- even more than that which my husband acquired in the cloth trade.'

Thomas nodded in assent and smoothed the delicate line of his moustache. 'It is ever my duty to civilise this country and help it prosper, as has our England under good rule.' He winced as he raised himself again from the chair, preparing to leave. A servant had quietly entered and whispered to Walter that a fast messenger had arrived from Dublin. 'We must summon Niko and hear what he has to say about the shipwreck. The Constable will want a full report. The deaths of foreigners will be questioned. Walter- you must send messengers. Niko MacFeagh is to attend us immediately.'

Alice's breath came somewhat faster. She quivered deliciously at the thought of Niko's strong bearing, and knowing seductive smiles. He was not a man easily forgotten. Then she was struck by a fearful thought.

'What if Redmond comes instead, Thomas?'

He smiled, saying as they left, 'You fled last time when you saw his long fringed hair, goatskin cloak, and enormous mastiffs! But Niko is always Redmond's envoy. Do not be deceived by those elegant looks! He is as slippery and suave as your dancing masters of yesteryear! All right. I must leave you and see to matters.'

She put out her hands to be kissed, then picking up her embroidery, she called to Walter to send for her maidservant to bring more wool threads and wax candles, and seated herself in the large carved oak chair.

CHAPTER TWO

I must seek air to breathe… to live… my limbs do now push away these heavy rolls of water… I am turned to face upward, the rolls still drench me even though I raise my head… cloths and stuffs and fogs and strange slimes approach me through the fog, swirling, coiling like a shroud… will they be my shroud?… I must push, I must lunge upward protect me, Lord Jesus…… dwell not on that vision of the sloping deck that slid you into the wave, my father, and took you, I heard your screams as the cold engulfed you… Or were they mine? Or theirs, all theirs, on that benighted ship, your staring eyes follow me… I ache, I tremble, and I freeze, where is the light of day? Is this water the anteroom of Hell?… something catches in my throat, my breath comes but hard… I am in your hands now, Lord. I am doomed, my young life will unfold no further… kick through grey and violet. I am so cold and I hurt. I gag with the taste of salt and vomitus in my mouth… I am so cold, so cold… dripping cold, gushing cold, trembling cold, deep cold… mists will be my shroud… a weak sun appears or is it our Lord come to rescue me from these slow pulsing seas. My feet are cracked and jarred against coarse sand and small rocks… now this plank to which I am tied resists the sucking of the surf… the light of the sun burns me… credo in deum patrem ominpototem creatorum caeli et terrae… such pain …

A distant glinting had drawn Redmond to this part of the shore-line, no-one else having yet ventured so far. The rest were seeking the remains of the ship, wrecked near the headland. It was thought English at first, but its pennants and passengers seemed otherwise, from the detritus so far recovered. Shielding his eyes against the sun, now emerged from the heavy fogs of the night, he squinted at a glowing phantasm in the glare hitting the cliff. Looking harder, he made out a barely clothed body tied to a spar leaning out of the rocks, facing down with its head just out of the water. The rocks all around it were spiked and slippery, and the sea still ran over its legs on the outgoing tide. He could not reach it without toppling himself into the surf. He considered whether it was alive or dead, and decided dead was the more likely.

He continued foraging further on the shore, on and around sea-weed hummocks. He divested corpses of sodden clothing, belts and purses and their contents, and collected weapons and barrels from between the more accessible rocks nearby. He put an engraved silver dagger on a fine leather belt round his waist. As he expected, from tales of the Armada galleons wrecked on the western shores of Eire ten years previously, two of the heavier doublets had gold coins sewn into their linings that, he thought, would have drowned them even faster. He glanced further up the beach. The noonday sun burnished the growing pile he had left there.

He returned later as the tide had nearly fully retreated. He drew nearer to the figure on the spar, leaping from rock to rock. He stopped at a ledge above. It seemed to be a young female form. He looked around him. A group of black and white oystercatchers were digging delicately at their feast of cockles beneath the sands at the water's edge. Mules headed towards him in the distance. He hopped nimbly towards the girl. She was fastened with thick woven belts to a wide plank with jagged crosspieces above. This, stuck fast between two rocks, had the appearance of a crucifix. Her over-garments must have been discarded as she was almost naked. The lower belts had loosened as she hung down, so that her buttocks and sex were obscenely displayed. He noted a wide gold ring and jewelled cross on a gold chain hanging from her neck. Straggles of blonde hair, luminous in the morning sun and braided with seaweeds, were strewn round her head and shoulders. She was beautiful.

As he regarded her, to his surprise, she raised her head, gasped and vomited several times. He considered the likelihood of a ransom or a grateful parent and that she must have been precious to someone, as she could not have tied herself to a sturdy beam.

He said, 'This being Sunday, the Lord has clearly meant you to survive.'

A scene of blind, wild despair during the fog-bound night, the seas and shore were clear in the noonday sun, which was drying the corpses and highlighting the cargo, strewn between pebbles, heaps of bladderwrack, kelp, rocks and sand. Balanced on the jumble of rocks within which she was trapped, he briefly contemplated her body. Her arms were thin but strong. Her hands had short, now blue, fingernails, matching the bruising on her long shapely legs. Caked salt on her eyebrows and closed eyelids and lashes enhanced her ghostly but attractive pallor. Her almost bare body briefly aroused him, although it was streaked with blood and wounds and reddened from the sun, until he remembered coming upon another bruised and stripped female form. His heavily fringed brow contracted in pain and hate. His mother, Eithne, who had resisted his return to unhappy fosterage in Dublin, had been as desecrated and broken as the Irish shrines in the time of old King Henry. He knew that his revered great-aunt, the Lady Medb, pleaded to continue the peace, thinking this would bring resolution for past crimes. He, though, considered that she lived in a world of old-fashioned fancies, and that revenge was resolution. He was only grateful to the English occupiers for teaching him how to fight.

The beach was rapidly drying. He reached her, using a makeshift staff from some flotsam to help him balance on the bearded rocks striped with limpets and barnacle encrusted mussels. Cutting the belts around her with his dagger and lifting her free, he then laid her face-down on a nearby curved rock, at which she vomited again and again, exhausted and semi-conscious. She felt cold in spite of the burning morning sun. After a while, he turned her, put his mouth to hers and breathed into her, then hawking in disgust. Carefully placing his staff, he slung her dead weight over his shoulder. Looking around to see if he was observed, he tee-tered nimbly back to a sandy area of the shore where, putting her down with her back against a rock, he tried to remove the ring and the gold chain. She woke and her renewed vomiting and groans together with mutterings in Latin made him desist. Shoul-dering her once again, he continued to make his way, loping fast some distance westward along the beach, over sand and rocky outcrops, and then scrambling up a fallen cliff edge to a cave.

Although this was on the rocky shoreline, it could not be seen from the sea or beach, being covered with a vast overhanging tree root. The cave was high but not deep. He had discovered it when, during a raid and separated from his companions, he had fallen down the cliff edge into the tree. Climbing beneath it so as not to be seen, then and subsequently, he had often found seclusion, succour and silence in its depths. It was his own place, where he could not be betrayed, either from malice, or the torture of kin.

The cave had been protected from the worst of the wind and spray by the tree and its roots. There he kept some weapons, dry straw and bracken wrapped in goat's hair frieze for bedding, a thick sleeping cloak, a hat made from the thick fungus on horses' feet, some light and fibrous peat for a fire, one barrel of smug-gled brandowine and another of good beer infused with laurel. In a small metal bound chest, he kept bags of oats, hazelnuts, and sometimes a pot of salmon smoked back at the village. He made up a bed for the girl at the back of the cave, on a wide platform shaped from the rock. He laid his woollen cloak over her and forced some milk from his flask mixed with some brandowine from the barrel into her mouth. This revived her momentarily and her eyelids moved but with difficulty as they were almost stuck together with salt. He rubbed them gently and forced them apart. She then started gabbling in a foreign tongue, loudly and hoarsely, with strange twitching movements.

Going under, coming up, red, bleeding, blood swirling. Stinks, stinks, like the mordant used to dye our cloth, in my hair, trailing, slimy near my face, slimy like the serpent, who has come to take me. I am in-nocent – do not take me, do not touch me, go forth serpent, go forth – you have swallowed enough in the night… credo in Deum Patrem omnipotente, creatorem caeli et terrae et in Iesum Christum, Filium Eius unicum, Dominum nostrum, qui conceptus est de Sprito Sancto… credo in Spiritum Sanctum…

'You shriek like a banshee on a winter's night,' he said, and, not knowing quite what to do, took a wooden cupful of brandowine and continued 'God, the Father, God the Son have mercy upon you! Dominus vobiscum. I wonder what Lady Medb will think of you?' He paused. 'I will call you Gile – the maiden from our myths whose father and brother were tragically killed.'

Hearing him speak some Church Latin she became silent. He then said, in Gaelic and English, 'I will return.'

Her breathing slowed, she relaxed and seemed to sleep. He left some milk and oats by her side and leapt speedily down the cliff to load his pile of booty on a mule hobbled further down the beach.

By late afternoon, the foragers had finished picking the shore and all the mules were laden. The atmosphere was one of delight and cheer. They greeted one another with slaps on the back and joking respect. Some drank from one of the barrels. Halfway up the cliff path above them, balancing on a rocky step, Redmond's foster-brother Niko was whirling a finely wrought rapier that he had found on a corpse. Thickset with a prominent nose, deep black eyes, tawny complexion, and neatly trimmed beard, he was waiting impatiently to depart. His hair was short, except for a single curling lock, pushed back behind his ear, on which danced a jaunty gold ring.

Niko revelled in wearing 'civilised' hose, flat lace ruffs and doublets with jewelled clips in the English style. Slung over his shoulders was a fine, if damp, dark red brocaded short collared cloak with a matching braided hat that he had garnered. He wore a wide leather buckler which held a flat Irish sword and small dagger. He knew that his exotic looks, his dress and tall muscular build were attractive to many - women in particular of which, he hoped, Alice Plymmiswoode was one. He was aware that his looks and his fluent knowledge of the English and Gaelic tongues all helped in his dealings with the English and Scottish Settlers.

Although Redmond was as reddish-blonde as the old Gods, the Tuatha De Danaan, he was not tall and blue-eyed as they were reputed to be, but short, wiry and brown-green-eyed. Redmond always wore tight trews, cloaks and full-sleeved jerkins, woven in shades of ochre, brown, blue and viridian, melting into the landscapes around him.

His lanky squire Ronan greeted him with relief, somewhat shamefaced.

'I lost you, my chief, in garnering these.' Tied around his neck were some dripping thigh length leather boots.

'No matter Ronan. I too have found handsome pickings. This good wine will help our people suffer the labour of the ironworks and the felling of timber – or endure the coughs and burns from the charcoal mounds. Ho, brother popinjay,' he called to his foster brother with a brief smile, then turning away.

'Hurry Redmond!' Niko called back. 'The Crown's Searchers will be here soon. The path has widened with our passage, but now some of it slips. It will be harder going up, although, when the sun came out, I set the men to strengthen it with rocks. We found many full barrels!'

He admired Redmond's gifts of leadership and was gratified by his brotherly love. Their years apart had accentuated their differences, but their regard for each other was deep. But he felt occasional irritation and resentment towards Redmond. At times he wished that he, like his foster-brother, was an Irish baron, whose parents were kin to earls, and whose father and uncles had been martyred in the last rebellion. He, Niko, was a true vassal. He was the bastard of his mother, gently-born Lady Orlaith McMurtagh. He always tried to shake such thoughts away. Until he, as a youth, was sent away by the Crown to soldier in foreign wars, he and Redmond had been inseparable; hunting, raiding, feasting, both cared for by the Lady Medb and Lady Orlaith. He had never doubted that he belonged to the sept, and that Redmond was his chief to whom he was lieutenant, helpmeet and ally.

Redmond had been a mere stripling when, following the executions and his ailing uncle's death, he was chosen by his people to be the head of the sept MacFeagh, after which he had been unwillingly sent as hostage to some minor gentry in The Pale around Dublin. Here it was intended that he should learn the ways of the English and secure his people's acceptance of the Crown and its Law. But the opposite occurred. On his return, he had raged about how he was forced to abjure his Catholic faith, in public at least; about the condescension of his foster family; and the bullying from his peers. He had become aware of bribery and the sale of official appointments. He had concluded the English were self-serving and arrogant.

The men and women, many carrying barrels of brandy and butter, urged the laden donkeys up an overgrown path on the cliff face. They conversed desultorily, their voices having an inimitable lilt, the cadences like the murmuring of the surf dancing in an on-shore breeze. The evening swallows twisted and skimmed the air for flies above them, whilst a lonely curlew pecked amongst the stones. Redmond moved to his horse and checked its girth and panniers. Satisfied, he made his way toward the line of mules, turning and shouting to his foster-brother,

'I'll go and scout in front, if you keep the rear.' He smiled a wide smile at those he passed.

Following the train, and the jingling of bridles, Niko, holding a large barrel, climbed easily through crumbling stone, tough grasses and buckthorn until they reached those at the top waiting with ponies and carts, together with an escort of gallowglass, fully accoutred with halberds and light open helms. When all was ready, the whole cavalcade, lighting torches as darkness and mists fell, then travelled many miles inland. They went through rain and returning deep fog towards the cleft in the mountain where, straight ahead, lay the green road, the Standing Stones, the Place of the Cross, and then Castle MacFeagh.

They stopped to drink at the Holy Well. There they prayed for the souls of the drowned foreigners at a shrine with a wide worn stone kneeler with massed wax candles placed at its front.

Nearby, an ancient granite Cross, the roundel in its centre having Christ with outspread arms carved within it, fronted the skeletal ruins of a small monastery or chapel. This was now inhabited by a tracery of tall trees, barely in bud, and dotted with the nests of rooks, whose alarm calls heralded their approach. After this brief halt, the clansfolk journeyed on, even as night fell, through massed spikes of purple willow herb and clumps of golden ragwort, furze and waymarked bogs towards a rough stone bridge, where the streams had become a waterfall. This formed the last part of the approach road to the settlement around the castle. A tall round abutment to the bridge, night and day, held guards, provisions, braziers and arms. Its purpose was to warn against enemies and to deter wolves and the occasional curious bear.

Their stronghold, surrounded by clachans, high in a fold of the hills, was finally reached. During the entire journey, Redmond had not mentioned finding the fair young woman he had named Gile.

CHAPTER THREE

Lady Medb MacFeagh's father had been descended from the ancient Kings of Ireland and she was the widow of Lord Padraig, also of ancient lineage, but summarily executed in the last rebellion. She sat slouched on wool cushions in a sheltered spot under a large oiled canopy by a wide guttering open fire. Some children, swathed in thick blankets, were huddled, sleeping, by her side. Medb could not read the annals of their ancestors. The laws, old tales and lays had been suspended in her head since childhood, when the lineage of the Gaels had ever been regaled and celebrated in the Halls. She sighed, wearying of old age with its stiff bowels, blurring eyes, forgetfulness, muffled hearing and swollen joints. This last bitter winter had been hard. Around her, the sky was dark-grey and quilted, brushing the edges of the hills to the West, which were soon to be covered again by thick mists. The previous night, whilst all was silent and still and surrounded in the fogs, she had heard the owls crying, sent by those from the 'Land Under The Wave', grasping souls with their talons and depositing them in the deeps. She slowly drifted into a restless sleep.

At dawn, hearing the riders approach, she lifted herself on to her heels, crouched and began rocking, trying to ease from her mind the demons and spirits who lurked in the shadows of her life. The children around her began to stir into life and Medb crooned, pretending this crooning was penance, rapidly fingering her beads near the glowing ashes.

'You sin, mother, when you speak of the wrath of the Old Ones being visited upon your people,' the friars constantly adjured her. 'You must only fear God, as must your people. You must do penance for the heresies you have committed.'

'Those foreign devils – and yes, our friars – scorned me for a heathen Druid,' she muttered to herself. She had discovered it was wise to mumble agreement, so that she could be left alone to care for her soul as she wished. Words could not console her as she found them empty, in a life from which most peace, joy or stability had been drained.

'My sin was to fire our warriors to great deeds. We wanted revenge when King Henry tore down our altars. I wanted my sons to follow the dictates of honour and conscience. I encouraged them to rage and fight for the Pope and drive the Devil Protestants hence. But my sons were driven instead, to the very fate of our religious houses and worse.' She moaned and hugged herself. 'The indignation and fear amongst my kinsfolk at the violence to their Faith!'

She sniffed and hawked. She knew in her heart that whatever she had done, or said, her people would have risen against the Crown and the English Law. After long years of grief and famine, she had counselled against further plotting. 'I told them, I told them… each time a rebellion fails, so much disease, so many deaths…' She moaned again muttering, 'I told them that our people have wept too much. So many executions of the well-born, hardships for the churls and our manors, forests and best pastures granted to favoured adventurers, like that young English settler, Thomas Hurst.'

She snorted loudly, drawing the attention of the waking children, who looked at her with a mixture of alarm and amusement.

'We were forced under the yoke of the proud English Queen if we wished to retain even some of our lands. And then we are not given the productive parts!' Noticing the children's attention, she said more distinctly, 'I have always cleaved to my kin whatever they were, and are, minded to do.'

In exchange for meat, milk, roots and cresses because she was too old to work, Lady Medb had become a storyteller, amusing the children and keeping her people's heritage alive in their hearts. From time to time, she, a servant and a pannier of oats and distilled spirit were hoisted on a pony. Then they visited those deserted, ruined raths where the stripling bards gathered to learn poetry and songs. Once there, she told them of sorrows arising from Ireland's mythical and current invasions, of the old Gods, the Tuatha De Danaan, of the arrival of the Gaels, of battles fought over beauteous maidens, of Cuchulainn and the Knights of the Red Branch, and of Tir-na-n-Og, the Land of the Forever Young.

Niko and Redmond had their doubts about the ancient traditions and beliefs. Redmond was more inclined to acknowledge these. Niko's view was that the innocent suffered before, during and after conflict, often for no reason other than man's rapaciousness, and that God, Spirits or 'Old Ones' did not intervene.

The cavalcade arrived overflowing with leather and wooden goods, barrels of butter and wine and sodden cloaks, cloth and blankets. Discovered weapons were quickly secreted away. Medb heaved herself to her feet and hobbled to greet Redmond, holding on to his bridle.

'You look pale, Medb, you could not sleep?'

'Did any live?' she asked. 'I heard all the souls descend, but there was a faint voice in the winds that I did not know. A soul has returned. We should rejoice.'

Redmond shivered. 'Go, Medb! Sit in the castle and rest.'

She nodded and smiled, with a glistening thread dangling from her blueish nose and said, departing, 'There's nothing wrong with me that the Spring sun will not ease.'

Cloaked in a heavy dark shawl, and supported with a silver topped cane, she slowly made her way to the castle on the way observing the fine goods being removed from the pack animals. She found herself remembering again, remembering the golden time when her children were growing, and her elder kin had sagely made peace with the loyal Irish Earls. Although many of these were of English descent, she knew that they both valued and absorbed the way of the Gaels. The Crown called him and those nobles like him 'degenerate' and distrusted them. They were tolerated only because of the numbers of their vassals and their influence. She stood and watched, thinking of that time of peace, when she and her people had stuffs and clothing like those on the mules, new half-timbered cabins and stone chapels and towers. She had rented fertile fields to their churls from the surpluses, had golden rings and clasps fashioned for her delight, and duels fought over any slight to her honour. But the Earls quarrelled, and for many other reasons too, the thunderclouds of rebellion gathered and then burst into a fearsome and lengthy storm. Shaking her head, she silently relived the indiscriminate reprisals and the attacks from mercenary soldiery.

'I told them... they must seek peace,' she muttered. 'I told them... it began again, after that that brutal English devil De Wilton's victory at the battle at Smerwick.'

On a rocky mound in the village, deep trenched on three sides with pigs rooting amongst the detritus, and with a fourth side overlooking the loch, there was a tall armour-coloured four-square castle. Ivy-clad walls softened and partly disguised its martial intention. It had a small sally port door, garderobes on the turreted wall facing the loch below, and a drawbridge to its front, the chains now disused, leading to a large covered arched gateway. There was an iron bell pull, sconces, and hooks for cloaks and weapons. A substantial studded timber door led to oaken stairs to the upper chambers. Alcoves, with small wooden doors for smoking fish and meat, were built into the chimney wall into which a small fireplace had been set. The only windows were plunging arrow slits. The courtyard leading from the porch held posts to tether horses and a twisty stone stair led to projecting rooftop platforms on which were placed vast rusting cannon. There was a walkway alongside the tiled roof and ornate chimneys. Sentries could see across the valley and the loch to their fields and their grazing herds, and even further to the mist-covered hills. Folk and livestock shared some thatched longhouses added to its extensive courtyard.

Below the castle were other dwellings made of wood and stone, or even woven willow with turves on the roofs, around which scratched hens and hounds. There were some windowless lime-washed circular bothies without chimneys but with a hole in the rushes for the smoke from the fire to escape. Cattle, dogs and hobbled horses were grouped down the gully to the loch shore, where boats were also moored to a long wooden jetty. Offshore there was a 'crannog', or island, with thatched structures upon it, homes in ancient days, but now used to store goods and barrels. In the early mornings, vapours swirled thickly around the lower village, leading in damp weather to shivering agues, brought, as Medb believed, by concealed and offended devilish sprites.

Lady Orlaith, square-faced and stately, was sitting by a hearth in an upper chamber with the children, who had run ahead of Medb into the castle. Orlaith, captured as a young woman in a raid by corsairs on Irish coastal waters, had been subsequently sold into a harem, then bearing a child, named Nikola from her master, Mustafa Reis. After some years, and constant petitions to the Pope, her release was negotiated by the Holy Roman Emperor Charles's priests. She and Niko were brought back to Ireland. Soon after, Orlaith's marriage to Medb's ailing youngest son Fergus, Redmond's uncle, was arranged; a union from which there had been no children.

Long, high-backed wooden benches lined many of the chambers, cunningly made so that they could be used for sleeping. Linen, robes and cloaks were kept in scavenged carved Spanish Armada chests, a prayer stool was in a prominent position and large bright tapestries and heraldic flags were draped everywhere to absorb the chill. Alongside Orlaith sat fat and witty Oonagh, the wife of Lord Fintan. He had been severely injured as a youth during the earlier rebellion, but somehow managing to survive and still remain a warrior in the sept. Whilst eating a breakfast of goat's milk and bread, the two women desultorily discussed whether the latest truce in the war in Ulster would last. A large dog lay nearby. Oonagh, eating fast, said, 'So many truces have been made and broken since it all began a few years ago.'

'Medb counsels us to try and live in peace with the Occupiers,' said Orlaith. ' She says that the traditions of Honour justified her support of the Desmond Rebellion, but that these traditions should be abandoned as they cause too much death and hardship. It's good that the English plant fragrant flowers…'

'And good vegetables, fruits and grains,' added Oonagh.

'And they have, in their parks, wonderful great trees like those I saw in the courtyard of the Mahommedans. But they disregard our Gaelic Law and bring cruel and swaggering militiamen to harry us…'

'And they expect our fighting men – our gallowglass and kerns – to labour in the forests hewing timber and smelting copper – and they take most of the profit!' Oonagh said then wiping her mouth. 'So we raid and skirmish when we can. Why not?'

'Because it irritates them. Remember they give our freemen and churls employment, so they do not starve like they did in the past.'

Oonagh stood up to leave. One of the children held up her arms to be carried.

'We are gentry, but have few servants. We have pasture, but few cattle. We have guards but few muskets. We have forests but must pick up their chips for our fires. We are a nation but have their laws. Why do they even bother to call us to their Councils?'

'Because they are fools. I fear they will never understand us. Niko says that it is true they do not wish to listen to us. They blindly follow the Old Queen and think she and her nobles are touched with divinity, no matter that they have abjured the Pope and are steeped in bloodshed.'

They both started for the stair at the bustle of sounds below.

'Father Ignatius sent word of the deep fogs on the coast. It was still foolhardy to travel to the shore. But now, God Be Thanked, it seems they are back…..'

Medb arrived at the castle gateway soon after, was greeted and helped to the upper chamber by Niko. Medb sniffed the lavender-scented rushes that Orlaith insisted were changed daily.

'I know our churls, men and women, and even our kerns, must labour on the plantations and serve as their guards and in their manors, but our lives would have been worse, if some of our lands had not been re-granted,' Medb said suddenly to Niko. He helped her into a cushioned alcove by the fire and bade her rest.

She smiled and nodded. When he left the room, she muttered on to herself,

'The English like Niko, and call him "civilised". But they do not know him; no more than the Irish; half his mind comes from the Mahommedan and he looks both ways.'

CHAPTER FOUR

The fogs returned that evening, ghostly against a purpling sky. Those back from working the forests, mines and fields gathered by the castle. A deer carcass was spit roasting over the charcoal-filled pit. Bread, made from beans, peas and acorns, was rolled and flattened ready for placing on the hot stones around it.

Medb loved these impromptu feasts. Her kinsman, ageing Conor, his eyes bright and mischievous in his square grooved face, carried her into the centre of the group and encouraged her to regale ancient tales in her carrying, if creaky, voice.

'Did you hear tell of the mighty Michael, the ancient hero with hams the size of a wild pig, who could bend an iron bar into a milkmaid's yoke? He, and he alone, would survive in the most terrible storms that the angry creatures of the Otherworld would send!'

As she intoned, noses twitched at the smell of roasting meat. Donal, the harpist, identified as such by a badge with a design of a singing bird embroidered upon it, supplemented her stories with liquid chords. After the feast, with brandowine warming their bodies, insistent piping and the festive mood set feet tapping. There was dancing and clapping and singing echoed across the lake.

Redmond, slight, muscular, followed by his mastiffs, and as alert as once was the roasting deer, checked the guard posts throughout the evening and half of the night. On one of his rounds, he stood with the crowd near the fire-pit, listening to his aunt sing a pure, moaning refrain to the ballad of Deirdre of the Sorrows, a woman unable to escape her fate.

Orlaith, still slim, hair streaked with grey, was wearing his gift, a fine fur-lined hooded and collared velvet cope edged with gold embroidery with a matching tasselled girdle. She smiled with pleasure and embraced him.

'You cannot settle, Redmond.' Her brow creased. 'You think the Queen's men could be making their way to the wreck and, alerted by noise and maybe the smell of the meat, they will make their presence known?'

'Perhaps, but, even with our fires, we are shrouded here. I doubt they will travel at night along this way. They know the fogs lurk in the uplands and they are not familiar with this territory. They know the spring rains can turn the streams to full spates and render the forest ways impassable. They prefer to inhabit the valleys and ride on the easier road to the west which passes near Hurst Place.'

Orlaith said, 'It is best if all is disguised or hidden by tomorrow.'

Redmond continued to move in and out of the surrounding pine, oak and sycamore, feeding ponies and observing, followed by his stealthy youthful squire, Ronan, never far away, honour bound to protect his Chief. Half-obscured by a swirling mist, they stopped and listened to a group lounging in a glade. Some, replete, picked their teeth with sharp twigs. Niko was polishing his new rapier with the gilded hilt until it shone in the firelight. They spoke of wet summers and plagues in the English cities, now reaching Dublin, of the cruelty and suspicion of the Old Queen, the ambitions of the Earl of Tyrone, and the ubiquitous presence of English spies, even amongst the clans.

Fintan, a senior member of the sept, kin to Redmond, warned, 'We can trust no-one, maybe not even the friars. When captured, they are but fodder to the torturers. Look how that devil Topcliffe treated the Jesuit Southwell! They imprisoned and destroyed him, slowly, piece by piece. His crime was to write, with good sense, that Catholics would be loyal, could they but worship freely. That is what we demand of the occupiers and that, they will not grant.'

Ronan emerged from the trees and asked Niko keenly about weaponry he had seen used in battle. This was always a popular subject. Niko told of cavalrymen and captains with petronels or pistols that were fired rank by rank into enemy horses.

'Also, they possess not old Spanish cannon retrieved by us from the wrecks, but a great deal of powder and new mortars, a species of cannon which cause great damage at close range, even though slow and tedious to fire.'

After a short silence, Fintan, whose lower legs were missing and who sat in a small carved and wheeled cart, said, 'Only the Devil employs such inventions, because he wants to make us kill one another.'

To which Niko quickly replied, 'I have heard it said that once the Devil invents, can God then uninvent?'

'He will find a way to protect us from the Devil's works,' said Ronan, moving into the circle, repelled by this heresy. 'So the friars tell us, and they are near to God.'

'We can be protected best by not facing them in the open. Such weapons cannot be brought easily into our furze and bogs.'

'True indeed,' said Redmond, moving out from the shadows. 'Choosing our ground with care, ambushing in narrow valleys or leading their soldiery into sucking bogs will bring victory.'

'But we do have many unwalled towns, unprotected clachans, and open fields. We cannot always fight them in our fastnesses,' said Niko.

Redmond shrugged, finding uncertainty hard to tolerate. He and Ronan then left the group to check the sentries on the bridge and elsewhere.

When the weather cleared, the summons from Thomas Hurst arrived. Redmond sent Fintan, Niko and his sharp-eyed squire Dermot, whose fringed shoulder-length hair shone like bladderwrack after the tide, and two other riders. They had set out as soon as the sky reached a pale washed blue and the mist was draped like muslin over the flood plain below them. Some way behind, two laden mules followed by hounds were led by long-haired churls with worn green caps and short swords in their belts, stopping, through air pungent with peat smoke, to distribute packs to the homesteads along or not far from their route.

The armed men guided their small hardy ponies steadily through paths and forests high in the brooding hills on a route mostly familiar only to the folk of the mountains. Fintan, with his bulldog neck and shoulders, thighs like small hillocks and thick brows almost meeting in the middle, rode in front as scout. The occasional passer-by made way for them, as they looked raw and dangerous in their battered half-helms and prominent flat swords, buckled across their short yellow woollen tunics. Their cloaks displayed Celtic badges in what passed for livery. White Irish blankets were rolled at their backs. Only Niko looked the gentleman with a starched collar over a velvet doublet and a beaver hat decorated rakishly with an eagle's feather. A vivid silk officer's sash with a gold jewelled clasp was tied across his chest and waist. A heavy pistolle was tucked within it, half-hidden by his fur-lined dark cloak. Niko found himself hoping that Thomas's winsome widowed sister would commend his choice of garments and smile upon him, in spite of all.

It took a forenoon to travel the high route to Thomas's desmesne. Along the way, bothies, ancient round towers and monastic buildings, old raths and ruined castles were glimpsed or passed. Eventually descending from the stony screes, the men followed the edge of a broad river, gilded by the sun. Climbing above the river, they proceeded along the new military road and finally halted on the wide stone bridge where stood the castellated guard post half-a-league from Hurst Place. Away above it was the crag, where the extensive ruins of their Overlord's hereditary L-shaped castle, destroyed in the last rebellion, were silhouetted against the noon sky.

They were challenged by gallowglass guards badged with Thomas's livery, searched and requested to hand in their weapons until they rode out again. Afterwards they drank ale and exchanged banter. On the arrival of the mules, barrels were taken from the panniers and given to the guards, one of whom rode swiftly to the Manor house to tell of their arrival. The visitors were then escorted along a curving avenue lined with pine trees and thick undergrowth, disturbing a host of screeching crows.

The large new building had three-storeys, a tall castellated gateway, gables and towering chimneys. Long thick-glassed windows overlooked a large square courtyard. Leaving the others in the stable yard, Niko stalked up wide stone steps into a lobby, his nailed boots echoing on the flagged floor, like a summons to malign spirits. He was met by Nuala, a squat-framed middle-aged house servant, with red curls and good teeth, a long apron and her head swathed and twisted in folds of white linen. She curtsied and he moved up to her, holding out his cloak and gauntlets. A silver ring fell into her waiting reticule as she took them from him, and a small parchment was slipped into his sash. He thought ruefully that it was a pity that she could read as she did not know the significance of what she acquired. He wondered if she also informed elsewhere or whether Thomas Hurst knew of the message-passing and used it to mislead him. Medb had told him in the past to keep his distance from Nuala's father Seamus O'Byrne. She called him bitter and unreliable with a history of family violence, greed and malice. He had heard that, now much increased in years, with sparse hair and pustules on his face, Seamus was nearly blind, and, as unmarried, Nuala would soon be recalled to nurse him. Niko thought he would not wish her life from then on. She breathed quickly before she was pushed aside by Walter, who bowed Niko into a raftered hall, then remaining.

'They hunt my uncle, Feagh O'Byrne, fearing he will overrun The Pale.'

The waiting English couple, both attired in discreetly brocaded fine dark worsted, stood as their visitor entered. Niko was not aware of Alice's approval of his clear dun-coloured face and embroidered green doublet, slit with black satin. She could not see a mark on his clean collar and admired his fashionable gold earring. His courtly bow pleased her even more. She was reminded of their last meeting in which he showed a liberal spirit, eschewing fanaticism. He had been dignified in his responses to their inevitable challenges, unlike the discourse of those Irish gentry she had met so far who could speak of nothing but monumental lack; lack of respect, of power, of fine gardens, of fat bacon and good cheese, of more pastures. Yet she had seen, and indeed, both Thomas and Walter had confirmed for her, that there was so much beauty and provender all around on land and sea.

Niko looked up at her from his low bow. She held out her soft fingers, heavy with silver rings, then suddenly felt lost in his gleaming eyes, and pinned in his gaze. She felt a murmur in her sex, and was confused by dangerous imaginings. For his part, he was disappointed at her stiff and unyielding manner and thought that this concealed dislike. He turned and also bowed low to Thomas who did not respond in like manner but snapped, his eyes hard and seething,

'So, Niko! Redmond has done well out of the heavy fogs, unusual it seems this time of year. I have had a search made, and you are fortunate that nothing has been found in the clachans in your town lands. Would Redmond set the south provinces alight with his actions? You know that all wreck salvage belongs to the Crown. Which is particularly interested in arms, powder and cannon shot.'

'The fogs were dense in our stronghold for a day and a night. It would have been foolish to venture to the coast.'

'Harrumph! The wreck was laden and the seas not great. The ship could not have moved far once it had struck the rocks. My informants also tell me there was a window in the fog when the sun rose.' Thomas paused. 'I am told the vessel carried an Ambassador- a speaker of foreign tongues- some craftsmen and preachers and a cloth merchant. Did any survive?'

'How would I know this?' Niko gave a thin smile. 'I will tell you what I know. It was a merchant ship that broke its back. Some local folk did go down to the shore during the hours when the weather cleared, to see what could be found for the Crown. It seems the way was perilous even for a mule. I am told that they only found dead horses and corpses, sodden clothing along with broken timbers, a few barrels and valueless detritus, some of which they recovered for their own use.'

'If looters went to the shore, why, when the customs men searched your clachans, did they find nothing? Did it vanish into the furze?'

'There were a few barrels of butter, brandowine and one of Malmsey, which the churls left for our stronghold, and I have brought them here. The butter may be rancid and I fear the brandowine barrel was breached in transit and its contents halved.'

Looking at Thomas's face, Alice was unable to suppress a small smile. Niko kept his eyes blank and his expression immobile, adding, 'Did your men search the Old English fortresses? It is possible that if there were any pipes of wine, barrels or bales, that they would have found their way into Earl Ormonde's cellars. I must protest, sir! A mule fell from the cliff in seeking salvage for the Crown and Redmond has asked that the churl be compensated!'

Thomas tapped his staff against his thigh thinking gloomily that Niko was only too aware that, even if his men were ever able to find or get into the MacFeagh stronghold, there was no way it could be searched, nor indeed the loyal Earl of Ormonde's ancient castles, without escalating violence. At Alice's questioning, he had once described the powerful Earl as haughty, dissembling, with cruel eyes. Recent meetings had given him no reason to change his opinion. Thomas did not want to give the southern Irish gentry any excuse to plot with the Earl of Tyrone.

'You are an insolent knave to ask for compensation. The Queen's justice and our Lord's justice are but the same. All venality will get its deserts at Hell's gate. This you know.'

'I suggest your men search the rocky bays further along the coast, as the cargo may have shifted in the currents,' said Niko ignoring what he deemed a spurious threat of eternal damnation. Thomas looked thinner and greyer since he had seen him last, the lines on his face more pronounced.

'The inaccessible bays?'

'We had the friars bless all the lost souls,' said Niko, crossing himself. 'God give them rest.'

'Your sept, as nearest to that shore, most certainly will be charged with Christian burial of the dead. I will send Protestant clergy to see that this is done,' said Alice hastily, becoming concerned at Thomas's increasingly puce features. 'Thomas, Niko has travelled many miles in the mountains to your summons – will you not offer refreshment?'

'No doubt he has been well fortified with brandowine and Malmsey! No! Tell Redmond I am seriously displeased and if any of the listed goods are found amongst your people, the Constable will be informed and they will be punished. You may go.' Thomas turned away and walked stiffly to the fireplace.

'Theft from the Crown is not the way to get peace,' said Alice, speaking directly to Niko and spreading her hands, 'and I am sure that is what all in this corner of Ireland desire, and goodly trading likewise. Does Chief Redmond not think that there is enough profit in this rich land, with hard work and negotiation, for all to benefit? After all, the Good Book tells us that the Lord will provide for all who trust in Him.'

Niko inclined his head. He glanced at the huge new ornamental stone fireplace and the bright new tapestry of figures, water and rocks above it. Nearby, a richly carved court cupboard had been topped with an oriental bowl filled with leaves entwined with yellow wild flowers. Frowning, he seized her soft unproffered hand in farewell. He recalled the knobbly, work-hardened hands of his well-born mother.

'At present, the benefit seems mainly in one direction, mistress. The Good Book also says that the greedy and rapacious will be weighed in the balance and found wanting.'

Alice snatched back her hand and turned away. Niko, gradually retreated in a low bow before being shown out by Walter.

One blustery day later that Spring, Orlaith dozed on the cushioned stone seating at the side of a huge fireplace in the castle. She jerked awake, as her dreaming had swirled into disturbing images from her youth; of her violent capture by corsairs from the Barbary Coast, the humiliation of the slave market and the fierce dogs that guarded them; the dreadful journey in chains in suffocating heat. At first, purchased for the harem of an Ottoman Captain, she had been cooped up like a pigeon to be fattened, in a dry panelled chamber with windows intricately latticed with dark wood. She had spent long hours counting the dusty beams of bright sunlight that pierced the gloom, or peering with one eye through the carved shutters to the private courtyards below. In the women's quarters, known as the Beit, she grieved for her people, longing to walk beneath wide skies with soft mosses and heathers beneath her bare feet, sweet-smelling after rain. At times she had wondered, confused by the powerful teas served to her, whether the world outside even existed. Orlaith shivered. She quietened a young child teasing a puppy nearby. Nikola, now called Niko, was born, healthy and strong. God forgive her, she thought guiltily, relieved at being sheltered, fed, and clothed, she stopped resisting and had accepted, and even enjoyed the petting of her master, Mustafa Reis, with his bright eyes, fleshy mouth and soft hands, recalling that he had ensured that she and her son were surrounded by comfort and delight.

She had wondered at the crowd of womenfolk and the few strange men that were around her. Some were of yellowish hue, others tawny or the deep grey-black of charcoal. Some had high foreheads and wide eyes that were round and staring. Others were low-browed and hirsute. Eyes could be crystal blue, or thin and slanting with eyebrows plucked bare. Noses were all lengths and shapes. Hair could be short, black and crinkled, or straight and gleaming white, reaching to the floor or held up with huge combs or wrapped around with scarves. Some of the men were ear-ringed or without an ear, long- bearded, or heavily moustachioed or smooth as a piglet. She saw one whose head was completely shaven, with one lock only kept, and this reaching to the shoulder. Niko affected this style, although his scalp was not shaven and the rest of his hair was short-clipped. Many were not of moderate stature. Some were short, fat or gross, others tall, thin and straight. Some were lumpen and misshapen. There were men who acted like women and women who acted like men.

She had decided to learn from her captors. She learned much more than she could have ever imagined. She learned about the treatment of illness, picking herbs, roots and flowers from the gardens at their behest. She was shown which of the plants made cures and tisanes and which healed wounds and fevers, and had shown them some of Medb's poultices in return. After this, their physicians had let her observe procedures such as how babies could be turned in the womb if the mother laboured in vain. She saw how the perfume of flowers and the bathing of the body and the dwelling helped to deter biting and itching insects, as well as the plague. On her return to Ireland, her folk were shocked that she bathed herself, and any who would go with her, in the glittering loch or sea in all but the most severe of weathers. But Lady Medb had been encouraging, having noted that insistence on cleanliness of the body had led to less disease and infection. Medb had told her that such practices were mentioned in the annals of their ancient forbears.

Redmond came in and advanced towards the fire. The puppies around Orlaith yelped. He removed the white blanket which covered his doublet, squatted down, and deposited a small girl. He had just toured the camp and been asked by Oonagh to remove her daughter, blue-eyed Fionnuala. Oonagh and some other women had been trying to skim curds with outstretched fingers in a large wooden vat whilst children were under their feet. As the biggest woman in the village, Oonagh, sturdy and strong-boned with a round face, was used to being the butt of many jokes. She had been wearing a fine embroidered and trimmed cap gleaned from the shipwreck, which was falling over her eyes. Redmond had taken this off and had put it on Fionnula's head, laughingly saying that the curds would taste better without it.

'How many baskets would it take to weigh you now Oonagh?' Redmond had asked, standing back and surveying her.

'That is a very easy question,' she had replied. 'Only one basket if it was big enough! I nearly burst with the sufficiency of venison last night, Redmond. I wonder how and where you managed to bring it down, as you are not noted for your skill with the musket?'

'Well,' he had smiled, 'when it saw me on Thomas's demesne with my crossbow, it knew it was beaten and gave itself up!'

Oonagh was much-loved as the wife of Fintan, 'the Legless' as some called him. Fintan took this in good part. He doted on his wife and enjoyed rolling with his children like a puppy on the floor of their cabin. He could have led the sept, rather than Redmond, but had cheerfully rejected the nomination.

Sitting in the fireside inglenook, watching the children, Redmond and Orlaith exchanged pleasantries. Then he stood up, began to pace and, abruptly, chin jutting, told her about the girl he had discovered alive on the shore. Orlaith's square face creased with displeasure.

'This could bring trouble.'

'She is young and was hung on a plank like the Christ. I think she is French or maybe Dutch or Fleming, but she does not comprehend my words. I have named her Gile. She speaks little, only babbling Latin mutterings to our Lord. She was, and is, in God's hands, there is no doubt of that. Perhaps she has been sent to me – a portent of what He intends for us- that we should perhaps combine with the French or Spanish to defeat the English! Her skin is white, like pearl. She does not seem of low rank. She wears a jewelled cross and ring and could well be ransomed.'

After a moment's silence Orlaith said slowly, picking up an importunate Fionnuala and stroking her hair, 'That someone should survive such a wreck! Why do you want this maid? Perhaps as she wears jewels, she will be of enough importance to cause us difficulty. The English, needless to say, will only be concerned about a Frenchwoman if she is noble or wealthy! They will find out about her eventually and will harry us. '

Smiling crookedly Redmond said, 'She is still not recovered and may yet not survive. If Thomas the Settler does find out we have her, he can do little – we are many in Leinster and they are few – he will need a very good reason, rather than desiring a small ransom, to seek her out and prise her from us. I will send word across the waters. *We* should benefit from any compensation, rather than the English Crown. '

'If you think that she is a portent, can you imagine what her appearance on the shore will mean to Medb? Many here listen to her, even though the friars rail at her talk of myths and magic.'

He continued as if he had not spoken.

'Anyway, I could not leave her to die, almost destroyed though she was. She reminded me of someone precious.'

Orlaith knew he was thinking of his mother Eithne, but continued to frown. First shrugging, he then said, stonily, 'I will bring her here when she can travel. Who succoured you when you were freed from the Ottomans with a child, and returned to our coasts?'

Her lips thinned. Her stomach clenched with guilt and anger. It was wrong of Redmond to remind her of her duty to her husband's kin and of her enslavement. There was a silence before she said without looking at him,

'You should go to Father Ignatius – to his chapel on the cliff. You must ask him to say more Masses for those foreign dead, and absolution for those on the shore who had killed out of mercy. He should bless your stranger too – or a Religious should, if she is of the Protestant faith. She will need sustenance and clothing and will be on your charge.'

He nodded.

'You must replace the hooded cloak, clogs, chemise and drugget skirt you take from my Spanish chest.' She picked up the little girl, whilst Redmond tucked the puppy under his arm.

'I'll put him with the other hounds,' he said.

Orlaith then called after Redmond who was striding out without a backward glance,'Does Niko know of this?'

He left without replying.

CHAPTER FIVE

hose fat blue fingers, that arm floating beside me, brushing my face, blocking my gaze... aah... last night, was it night? Now warmth and light is upon my head and chest – my eyelids burn and I cannot now look. The moonshine burst on a staring eye, but then there was a blessed rain on my tongue... where are the others? My father, my maidservant and nurse. They must have perished, unless the Lord also saved them. Oh Lord, forgive me if I have sinned. Who was he? His voice was soft. He spoke the language of the Church. Was he angel or devil? I am still cold, so cold, cold from the memory of those fogs, that creaking, that crashing, those screams... were they mine? I sleep, but do not sleep. Am I forsaken?

Painfully raising herself to standing, Gile found and greedily ate the bowl of oats, curds and wrinkled apples left on a rocky shelf. Gagging, she blearily scraped moisture from the walls around her and licked her palms, then collapsing back on to her pallet.

Where is the light of day? It is ahead of me. I must find it. Am I alone? My stomach is sour and there are insects and sands amongst the branches on which I lie...

After a while, making her way towards the mouth of the cave and looking down, she saw waves crashing against the dark and lumpy cliff. Birds, white and slate grey, skimmed the surface of the water. She retched, gasped and leaned back against the rocky walls.

I was so cold, so cold. God the Father, God the Son, have mercy upon me. Am I in hell, my body aches and I can barely move… where are the devils? My voice rasps and chokes… I cannot speak aloud. My breath was taken as I was ducked without mercy into the deeps. There was blood… whose blood? Blood – blood swirling like wine, coiling through the seawater, trickling down beneath my shift and my belly and thighs. Am I in hell? I cannot see the devils. Where are you?

Some days later, clambering in, Redmond saw that she was alive, half-awake, restless, without coverings, muttering and groaning.

Who comes? Is it devils? Who comes? Is it rats that creep towards me? I cannot breathe. It is he…

He noticed that she had moved about the cave, eaten, and had drunk from a flask near the breached barrel of brandowine. Her pale face was less blue. He set about lighting a small fire to make hot porridge and a herbal draught. She screamed hysterically when she became aware of him and moved to cover her breasts, the cloak he had left with her having fallen away from her naked body. He proffered the women's clothes he had brought with him. She did not move to put them on, but glared like a wild cornered creature. She did not respond to his grin and questioning in Gaelic, English and Latin.

'Dress, drink,' he said, using gestures to show his meaning.

Some time elapsed but she ignored him and his requests. He became bored and angry at her silence, and quickly ate and drank for himself, watching her carefully. After sitting back for a while, he went up to her, putting one hand over her mouth and exploring her body with the other. He waited, but she did not resist, although her stare was unblinking throughout.

Is he angel or devil come to hurt me, to punish me yet more? I dare not resist. My trials of faith are not yet done… Aaah, aaah… what is he doing… he turns me… what else awaits me, Lord? I fear him. He hurts me! Will he desist if I cry… aah, aah… this is pain inside me but less than all the other pain. He gasps and grunts so… now I am released. He looks away, moves away. I am ashamed. I know what he has done. I have been treated like a beast in the field. He is devil indeed. The old man Christian Calvet, to whom I am handfasted was promised my virtue before God. How great are my sins and miseries… may I be delivered from them…

Satisfied he sat back. It seemed she had been a virgin. She curled into a ball, sobbing, when he released her. He shook her and turned her towards him, pointing at the food and drink. After a while, with a fearful glance, she nibbled at the bread, drank from the goblet and shakily tried to dress in the clothes provided. He watched her every move. When she began to fall, he helped her finish dressing, stroking her round buttocks and small breasts. She was rigid, and would not meet his eyes.

Later, he spoon-fed her with curds and some brandowine. She did not look at him and soon lapsed into sleep. Then he climbed down the cliff, quartering the shore with his hounds, previously left tethered to a rock below. Redmond saw some swollen remains floating at the water's edge, otherwise only timber and detritus was left on the sands. He covered these with rocks and stones and said a prayer for each. Most corpses had been removed and, at a new austere stone chapel some distance away, under the gaze of a pastor and some armed guards, were being buried by Ronan and his churls. Climbing back to the cave, he gave Gile the skin of spring water, and the bag of shelled hazelnuts he had left near the dogs. She was drowsy, but awake, barely aware of him it seemed.

'I will return,' he said. 'You will see Friar Ignatius. Pray for the souls of your companions and give thanks for your rescue.'

My head is heavy, and I ache in all places, known and secret. What said he before he went? He spoke some Church Latin and perhaps English. I knew the word 'friar', but he must be a devil and I am in Hell. He has left me food, but has taken my body in exchange. Young men have the nature of dog. He has allowed me to live, and does not seem to want to kill me. What can I do? I only know that I must honour, love and fear God, whatever He intends for me even though He has taken all away from me, but some say I am one of The Chosen… I must take what He has left me but for my soul to be saved, I must work, I must work, I will be saved by my faith and good conduct, I must be still, and keep faith… I must work… I must eat…

The next time he came she seemed much stronger and all the provender he had left before was gone. She was subdued and spoke little except to repeat Latin and Spanish words he did not seem to understand, and to make strange waving movements with her hands.

'Opus. Labor. Work, I must work.'

Supping eagerly from a wooden cup of brandowine he drew from the barrel, she then ate the fresh oats he had brought. She did not seem to care what he did, but prayed afterwards, at which he glared and frowned.

My head reels and warms. He seems to get pleasure from me although I avoid his lips. He smells of some strange smoky substance, his brown-green eyes glitter and stare. I am not strong enough to escape from here... Lord, forgive my sin......

On each subsequent visit, he brought oats, smoked fish and curds, and sometimes a woven basket filled with mussels and oysters. After eating, he made her climb some way down the cliff to a ledge, then carried her back up again, encouraging her to climb as far as she could herself. Then he always enjoyed her body, at first often taking her face in his hands and searching it curiously. Sometimes he sat and looked at her, playing jaunty tunes on a tin whistle or rummaged through the barrels he kept at the back for something to put in his pack.

His apparel is savage. He is savage. He probes my face with penetrating eyes, looking for my hates, my thoughts, my submission. His posture is arrogant, the curls on his head and brow excessive, his doublet is strange ..goat's hair with gold ornament! and it is too short... his trews wool I think, but fine wool. His boots are soft leather. He thinks my name is Gile, although I tell him often that I am called Susannah...

Once, she tried to leave the cave on her own, but halfway down, her strength and bruised and bleeding feet failed her. Hours passed before she could haul herself back into its shelter. When Redmond came next, he observed the wounds on her feet but said nothing.

Each day, my head is thick and sore. I think he means to let me leave here one day. I must leave. The gulls call me to the land. My soul is not that of a hermit whose inner space does not need the world... I cannot be at peace here. I cannot gainsay him. I pray and pray but I am submerged in my dreams... going under, coming up, red, bleeding, blood swirling. Stinks, stinks, like the mordant used to dye our cloth, in my hair, trailing, slimy near my face, slimy like the serpent, who has come to take me. I am innocent – do not take me, do not touch me, go forth serpent, go forth – you have murdered enough in the night... I must leave... I must...

One day, under his watchful eye, she was able to climb down the cliff and back up without assistance, although she had to be hoisted up at the very top, as her feet had again suffered grievously. On his next visit, soon after dawn, he brought her some salve and some newly stitched rawhide slippers and some strange long footless pantaloons, tied her skirt over her shoulders like a shawl and encouraged her down the cliff. Although protesting, in the end she was glad of the stockings that protected her legs from the scratches of the gorse and furze. She felt a warm sun on her head, smelt the salt wind and heard the distant crashing of the surf as they made their way along the shore. He led her up an incline to a beaten cliff path where his dogs, a barrel and a satchel lay and where a small pony and a mule were hobbled. Lifting her on to one, tying her hands and blindfolding her, he mounted up and led the mule on a rein as they made their way inland. He took a barely visible track above a marshy area with deep trenches where peat cuttings were taken for fires. He stopped on a headland hours later.

I must cling to this mule. He travels with such speed and ignores my shouts to stop, my thighs, my soft places... all aches... I see the sun even through the kerchief. He seems unheeding of the need for rest... or my fears. Thank God, he lifts me down, and takes off the blindfold, but my legs fail me and I have to grasp him. He nuzzles me like a dog. The sun blinds me... I pull away...

Gile, stumbling at first, began to run inland. She heard him laughing as he whistled to his dogs who quickly surrounded her, snarling and barking. Redmond then walked slowly towards her, picked her up and put her back on the mule.

Now we are still on a high cliff, but what is that that I make out not far down… I am dreaming… surely I am dreaming. It must be a small chapel with its ancient flints and stones gleaming in the daylight. Its windows are all arched except for one round hole above the oaken door. We are stopping. He lifts me and unties my hands… I must run to the chapel… to my God… the dogs! But he calls them back and follows me…

There was a distant rumbling from the waves below. He left her prostrate by the simple altar, as he looked for Father Ignatius, who he knew would be thereabouts either cutting peat or in his straw-topped cabin. The robed priest was sleeping amongst clumps of lichens and grasses with his back against a tomb, a silver chalice of ale by his side, and a pikestaff under his hand.

'Ho there, Father,' said Redmond, shaking him. A gull called overhead. 'You'd do well to stay alert. Since the fogs and the wreck, there'll be militias coming this way!'

Friar Ignatius started awake and gripped his staff, and then relaxed, saying, 'You should not creep around a fellow so! And Englishmen have been already-the Searchers found nothing. Ronan was here but, not knowing where you were, has now returned with the others to the stronghold.'

He smiled as Redmond tethered the animals, put down the barrel he had brought on the back of the mule, and then handed him two rabbits, caught by his hounds, hanging negligently from his fingers. Friar Ignatius had a thin face with deep creases between cheek and nose, a pitted skin and flaring nostrils. He was slightly built and with a thick grey tonsure, but his brown belted and hooded robe was cut at the knee, showing gartered woollen trews and leather boots beneath.

'I thank you… brandowine, is it?' Redmond nodded and crouched beside him.

Ignatius then asked, 'Is Medb much troubled by aches and agues, my son? Does she still prophesy and cleave to the Druidic ways?'

'Medb is well enough for her age and says her beads, though with what conviction I do not know.'

'I thought of her during those deep long fogs, where even the chapel was fully obscured. I tolled the chapel tower's bell in warning-'

'Folk near here heard it and, having seen the ship earlier, ghostly in mists on the horizon, quickly sent a messenger before all was enveloped,' interrupted Redmond.

'- And I prayed that the large vessel would have avoided disaster,' continued Ignatius without listening. 'But the winter's strong winds had moved the channel marked for such ships and deposited tons of shingle and rock below us. The pilot should have known that. He must have been French, not an Irishman from this coast. I heard it crash on to the rocks, sinking very quickly. The screams of the drowning were muffled and soon ceased. We said many masses for those poor wretches, as your message asked.'

There was a pause before Redmond said, 'I've brought another with me. She is in the chapel. She needs your comfort, although I do not know her Faith. I found her almost dead on small rocks near the water's edge. I must ask you to hear my confession, as I have sinned against her.'

'A girl – surviving that wreck?'

'She speaks little – and not our tongue. She just repeats some sort of catechism. She is almost recovered now – leastways in her body; I am not sure about her mind.'

'Is she a nun?'

'No, she did not have those garments, but I think she is of at least middle rank.'

'She probably had kin on that ship,' said Father Ignatius, rising to go to the Chapel, where Gile lay prone in the nave. Once there, he took Redmond's confession. Redmond then said, 'We will speak more when I wake,' and went to the Ignatius's cabin, drank from the barrel of brandowine and curled up outside it, sleeping alongside his hounds.

The friar remained with Gile. He understood when she spoke a few words of church Latin and French, but he did not understand her mother tongue. At first sight, he had felt a stab of amazement and alarm. She had the pale and clear look of an angel, but the cold and distant eyes of a demon. He asked himself how she could have survived that fearful shipwreck with so little damage to her person and without some sort of divine or devilish intervention. She rejected the rituals of the Mass, but at his gentle urgings, prayed with him and accepted his blessing.

'I hope she does not hate you,' he said thoughtfully later, when Redmond had awoken and lit the cooking fire. 'There is something of an angel about her, although also a strangeness. Her hair is as pale as her face. Do you know if her body is of normal form with no devilish marks?'

'There is nothing like that. Her flesh, apart from fading bruising, is perfect.'

'She is very beautiful. If she does not speak, you do not know her mind or the state of her soul. She could be the devil's work. Remember, "the viper glides amongst the flowers and is not seen before he strikes," said Ignatius, shaking his head.

Annoyed, Redmond replied, 'Gile is neither viper nor sprite – she is more like an angel come to earth, sent to make me understand that I must nurture and also to give me comfort.'

Redmond looked down and said, 'When I found her, she hung, albeit upside down, like Christ on the Cross and barely alive. You are right – she is beautiful, in spite of the action of the storm upon her body and her mind. I have dishonoured her and am sorry for it.'

Moved by his own words, Red found he longed to touch the young woman's fragile heart. There was a silence.

Ignatius considered and then said, 'She seems devout enough but not of the Roman Faith. Come, I have heard your confession. Your penance will be to wed this poor girl – our sacraments will erase any devilment.'

Redmond blenched and was silent. He went to his hounds and fondled them. Returning, he said, 'I suppose I must now wed her. French, Dutch or Flemish is better than English! You are hard, Ignatius. It takes more than the courage of battle to err and then publicly confess it!'

'You do not need to tell all you dishonoured her! To wed her is enough.'

Whilst Ignatius prepared the rabbits for the pot, Redmond said, 'I think her given name is Susannah, but I will call her Gile. She is half-mad, but she is appealing. I have done wrong and must make recompense. I am being pressed by the Crown to forge an alliance with a settler's daughter, but I could no more marry an Englishwoman than sleep with a sow.'

He had accepted Ignatius's punishment for many reasons other than penance. If he married one from another clan or sept, there would always be rivalries and difficulties from past quarrels. Also none had much dowry to bring him. In the end, no-one would argue over a marriage to a woman from France or the Netherlands, as many of them were Catholic. If not, he would encourage her to convert. Also, from her demeanour and the jewels around her neck, she could have wealthy guardians who could be of use.

Leaving the fire, the two men went back to the chapel and Gile.

What are these words the priest says? I tell him my given name… now he offers the Host which I will reject! I thought he was blessing my survival but now he makes me join hands… a marriage, surely not… I am already handfasted before God! I try to explain but they continue. I point to the ring on the chain around my neck, my handfasting ring, but wait…aaagh… Redmond pulls it towards him and makes me bow my head so the Friar can bless it. I am so shocked I cannot even cry. They take my cries and prayers for consent. I suppose he thinks that to wed me, he retains some vestiges of honour! I find this marriage is no marriage and I will not accept it.

After the ceremony, Gile ran from the Chapel to the cliff's edge.

Oh blessed God you have sent ships for me. I can see them from this headland…but he stops me... he stops me from being found, the savage! Dear Lord, keeper of my soul… What of my soul? Am I saved to live in God's Grace or damned as hardened in sin?'

'They will not see you waving,' said Redmond, pushing down her arms and holding his own around her. He had loped towards her with the same speed and stride as his hunting dogs. He nuzzled her neck but she stiffened.

'You are too far away. Cease wailing, woman! You have just married into a Barony… your rank is now higher,' he said, caressing her.

'I must eat,' she said sullenly in Latin, trying to pull away from him. Nevertheless, he wrapped her close to his body and carried her back to the firepit.

I cannot resist. The monk has food in his cauldron… all I can think of is the taste of fragrant meat and fish. We have eaten little all day… I have need also of a cup of that strong liquor. The friar is kneeling for Grace before we eat and gestures that we should do likewise…

She waited impatiently by the cauldron until Father Ignatius served them tender rabbit, oat bread and baked fish on pewter church platters.

'This is the best I can do for a wedding feast,' said Ignatius.

'Indeed, it is good,' replied Redmond, sitting back, savouring his mouthfuls.

'You know of course,' said the friar, 'that they have attacked Ballinacor, the Rath of the clan O'Byrne and that Feagh was slain by the Lord Deputy's men.'

'That is bad news for the O'Neill and his rebellion,' said Redmond slowly. 'Feagh O'Byrne has long been his ally, whether the English knew it or not. He has always slipped out from their net or talked his way out of difficulty. I hear they sent his head to the old Queen.'

'Our people rage and curse but it is futile. You know how I wish the invaders and their persecution gone, but,' Ignatius shook his head, 'they are so strong and will not give up until we are all made to be of their mind. Perhaps God wills that the clans should again bend their heads to the yoke, and preserve what they can. Slippery Tyrone fights them one day and sues for pardon the next. Perhaps he will betray your trust.'

'You counsel cowardice, Father. We have heard that Spain will send another fleet. We can still recover our pastures and remaining townlands with planning, good weapons and bravery, I am sure of it.'

'At what cost, Redmond? At what cost? Their fleet turned back last year and may well do so again. Do you, or the O'Byrnes, the O'Tooles, the O'Moores, the MacMurtaghs, have a right to continue with a conflict where many will die in agony and needlessly?'

'I know that, as chief of the sept, I should follow our traditions of Honour, Father. I know that the English will cause deaths and may take all of our wealth. But we cannot let them insult us and scorn our faith, our language and our customs.'

Honour was the common theme of the ancient Lays and Irish myths. Honour in these Lays was achieved by legitimate conflict, finally resolved through sacrifice of the innocent.

'You must think well on this. The Honour conflicts in the Lays are of our past - not our future, Redmond. Our future is in the hands of God, the Holy Father and the Lords of his Empire. Eat, boy, eat. The girl is ravenous – see how she gobbles the meat and swallows the brandowine.' Father Ignatius looked at Gile more carefully. 'See, Redmond – she tries to tear off her neck chain with the ring and cross – stop her – she needs His Grace. I fear the devil tries to grab her.'

Redmond put his hands over Gile's own, and glared at her. She was frantically pulling at the gold chain around her neck. She glared back at him, but finally subsided again into sobs. Ignatius filled her bowl with more meat and fish. She took a fistful, cramming the food into her mouth. Afterwards she sat back, twined her arms around herself and moaned quietly.

How can I eat so greedily when my duty is to repent or join with the departed Chosen ones. My father was shouting as he bound me and pulled off my outer garments so I should float, his shouting muffled in the fogs... false something he said... what were his words? Was he telling me to abjure false Gods? I paddled so as not to be engulfed... the seas rolled but were not high. Perhaps Our God has sent me strength with this food. His purposes are not clear to me. I must honour, love and fear our Lord even though He has taken all away from me... perhaps I am receiving His Justice. Perhaps He was displeased at my good life, my pride in my fine clothes and skills. I loved good meat, dance and company. They stop me from ridding myself of my neck adornment- which has been falsely blessed... now I must repent...

Redmond wrapped her close in his blankets that night, and, having eaten much and drunk a cup of brandowine, she did not resist his caresses, more tender than usual.

The following day, as Redmond and Gile entered the MacFeagh

stronghold, the sun, disappearing over the loch, gleamed like a huge new ducat against a velvet sky. The wind came unexpectedly, accompanied by large raindrops. At that moment, Redmond appeared between the cabins surrounding the castle, leading a drooping woman on his horse. He walked slowly followed by some kerns, churls, barking hounds and children. All stopped their activity, staring and muttering amongst themselves, some making the sign against the evil eye. Although she wore the Irish high-necked chemise and a fraying gathered skirt, she looked unlike them. Her face with its pointed nose was almost translucent, her eyes grey as the winter sky, whilst her long braided hair, white-blonde, twisted around her in a violent gust of wind. She half-closed her eyes against the blast, and hunched her long frame whose limbs, encased in wrinkled hose, hung idly each side of the unsaddled pony. The wind grew more insistent.

Medb knew it for a 'fairy wind' as soon as she saw the girl.

'She is fey, sent by the lemures,' she thought, 'from whose influence man cannot withdraw. She and the lemures, the harbingers of evil, must be placated.'

When Redmond took Gile from the horse, Medb, her long grey hair blowing beneath her wide-brimmed hat, came forward as quickly as she could and grasped her tightly round the shoulders, protectively. Gile pulled away in shock and dismay. Her eyes were wide and wild. She began gabbling and sobbing by turns.

Who is this crone, this witch? I am to be given to devils. Lord, Lord, forgive me if I have sinned…

Redmond, occupied in settling the startled pony, saw in alarm that Medb had turned and was addressing the company. He hurried to where Medb faced the gathering crowd. She had stretched her arms wide, and was declaiming,'… and she is one of the Old Ones, a soul re-born from a death at sea and must be cherished. I name her Murna.'

She then crouched before Gile, stroked her legs and grasped her knees. At this some of the folk genuflected, crossed themselves and murmured prayers. Others just stared curiously, or muttered loudly, agog to know from whence she had come. Redmond came forward and gently tried to pull the old woman away.

'Medb is so old now,' he thought as she clung on tightly.

'Thou must slay me before thee slay her.'

'I'm not going to slay anyone, Medb. She is my wife.'

Medb turned and fixed him with an iron gaze.

'What have you done?'

'The friars are not going to like your words, Medb. You must be silent. She is *not* one of the Old Ones. Father Ignatius has wed us and she is now Lady Gile Mac Feagh.'

The wind dropped, but the rain fell suddenly and heavily. Orlaith hurried forward, soothed Medb, whose drenched hat brim had overflowed onto her clothes, and helped Redmond to turn her and disengage her.

Then Orlaith took the shaking Gile by the hand and murmured, 'Dominus vobiscum.'

Half pulling, half leading, she took her into a stone cabin where she washed and dried her hands and face and gave her brandowine to drink.

Medb, her eyes alight, ululating an ancient chant, allowed Redmond to take her through the crowd to Oonagh who took her into the castle. Looking sadly after her, he considered that his old Great-Aunt's trials had bitten deeper into her mind than she knew. He had heard her rehearse Earl Desmond's final defeat and execution so many times, heard how her remaining kerns and their families had had to leave their dead unshrived, how they had lurked in poor shelters and desolate poverty in the forests, biding with the wolves and dying from the bone-chilling damp.

Turning back to the crowd, Redmond then formally announced his marriage, saying that the marriage could bring gold from the Flemings or the French. Soon after the villagers, gossiping, began to disperse as the rain continued to fall heavily.

Niko, standing at the side, had been deeply shocked at Redmond's secret marriage and Gile's unearthly appearance, although he had tried to keep his face expressionless. He wondered how Medb knew the girl had been acquired from the sea. He looked sharply at his mother and Gile as they passed him. Orlaith's face, which had a loving quality when she smiled, now betrayed only a melancholy dignity. Niko then sighed. He had travelled afar, and had spent enough time amongst the Ottomans to hold within him the seductiveness and gentility of beautiful women kept for pleasure. He knew too that many abused their sexual power and were cruel and cunning. He felt for the gold medallion with Arabic characters and an engraved scimitar which hung against his breast, given him by a harem favourite all those years ago.

The rain soon cleared again, and left a freshness all around. To celebrate the marriage, a hog was prepared and barrels of ale broken open. After the meat and bread, festivities began and continued for many hours. Gile, now passive and sleepy, had been festooned with flowers around her neck and in her hair. She would not get up to dance with Redmond and he soon took her to his chamber in the castle, soon coming back to join his aunt.

'I thought you would have stayed longer with your new wife!'

He gave her a quick smile.

'Our place is strange to her, and she has a taste for brandowine to stop her mind straying often to the night of the fogs. I've calmed her and she sleeps.'

Later, he and his hounds moved in and out of the trees as usual.

'You are never one to sit when you could be moving,' called Oonagh. 'Your fleas must be nobler and more troublesome than ours!'

Wherever he stopped, Redmond was besieged for information about his wife. Some, like Medb. believed her to be otherwordly and also named her Murna, a shape-shifting being.

'Gile is the name I have given her. She is a person not a substance! I assure you she is woman in all her parts!' he said to raucous laughter and grins.

He was questioned as to why he had said nothing before.

'I wanted to be sure she would survive before bringing her to the village,' he replied, his chin elevating when he looked at Niko, who commented,

'Well the maid is beautiful – irresistible, in fact. But girls are trouble – especially foreign girls.'

Niko's single lock of hair under his left ear was a nod to the Irish long-haired style. He had also seen it on northern warriors. It tumbled merrily as he told a ribald story Redmond had heard before about his travels in the Low Countries when he had fought there as a youth. His foster-brother gave a cold smile, vaguely irritated at Niko's frequent reminders of his early adventuring and war experience whilst he, Redmond, was quietly chafing amongst the bullies and beatings from the pastors in the place of his fosterage. He changed the subject to an arquebus salvaged from the wreck that Niko was weighing in his hands. He took it from him.

'Have you seen these fired in battle, Niko?' Redmond held the weapon in the firing position. 'This seems too fine for the violent discharge of gunpowder.'

'Indeed – Fleming, I think and finely worked. They can mean victory in some situations – if, but only if, the kerns and gallowglass are skilled in pitched battle – and have the powder – which most often they do not! I don't think they are much use to us. You said yourself that we fight best when lightly armed and able to harry and ambush. You know what must also be carried by the arquebusiers – cartridges! Heavy cartridges as well as halberds and other accoutrements – the weaker kerns could fall without a shot being fired at them!'

Fintan frowned, 'Those who use these are not valiant true soldiers fighting face-to-face. Arquebusiers are cowards who kill from a distance.'

Redmond raised his eyebrows. 'But we too use cannon!'

'Yes – and they wound more of us than the enemy!' replied Fintan, at which Redmond shrugged helplessly.

Redmond replied, lowering the gun, 'If we are forced into pitched battle… can you train our people in their use?'

'Some, maybe,' replied Niko, 'but we will waste a lot of powder. Tyrone holds on to his supplies, and those barrels we salvaged from the sea may not dry or be unstable. And our troops could concentrate so much on firing the gun that they will not see where other danger lies. A pity we can't sell it to Thomas Settler! I hear the English want more arms and powder for their gallowglass but the Crown will not meet the cost.'

Redmond returned the arquebus to Niko saying, 'The Earl of Tyrone might buy this fine weapon and the others we gleaned from the shore. Or we could sell it to our Overlord in lieu of some tithes. Ronan – send messengers, but be sure they are not intercepted.'

'We should keep out of the war at present, Redmond. You will play too dangerous a game. You know that the Lord Deputy has lost patience and hunted and killed Feagh O'Byrne, Hugh O'Neill's ally, suspecting he encouraged the southern clans to rise against the Crown, as indeed he did.'

'Consider, Niko,' argued Redmond, 'we will be harried whether we join The O'Neill or not! They do not, have not, respected us, our faith or our traditions. They think their queen is touched by God – the devil is more like. She hungers for our lands. We must defend our families. The O'Neill knows the mind of the English. He is for us now, not against us! If anyone can help us drive them back, or reach an honourable agreement, he can!'

Fintan opined, 'Perhaps The O'Neill will not make terms because he wants to govern the whole of Ireland and not just hold Ulster.'

Niko said gravely, 'Are we destined to repeat the horrors of the past? You may know what beasts war makes of men, but you have never been part of it. You don't know how atrocities can burn slow in the heart, until you become a beast too. Remember the aftermath of Earl Desmond's rebellion when all of Medb's sons, except her youngest, Fergus, and her brothers, including your father, were killed, as well as Lord Padraig, and many more of our close kin. My mother Lady Orlaith, whilst she suffered at the hands of corsairs, did not have to experience those bloody reprisals. She was lucky to be released from the Ottoman Beit, for which we have Medb's persistent advocacy and the Catholic Alliance to thank. I could have been made eunuch!'

Redmond had been tapping his foot impatiently, but then he slapped him on the back and laughed ironically.

'And even more luckily, I have you as a foster-brother, have I not, Niko?'

'Redmond! Listen! I fear Tyrone and Tyrconnell and what they may lead us into. Whatever they may say, some warriors in the clans, out of need or godlessness, will traitorously fight on the side of the English. You know that this happened in times past, and that vengeance and quarrels have interfered with our cause. We have some of our townlands back now and some peace and prosperity – as well as many opportunities for undiscovered raiding.'

Redmond grunted, frowned and looked away. He was tired of this discussion, which had taken place in many forms in recent weeks. He was aware that Niko now wanted a life of comfort, instead of battlefields and camps, and knew that he agreed with the Crown's emphasis on 'civility' and security in Ireland. In this, he had been supported by Lady Medb who was vociferous in counselling against committing to Earl Tyrone and his allies' insurgency. Redmond usually acquiesced without much comment, but then, at times, he became fired by the undisguised disdain of the English and Scots occupiers. He changed the subject.

'I will send messages about Gile- her given name is Susannah and I think Baydel or some such- to the harbour pilots here and in France and wait to hear if there is a response.'

Ronan intervened hurriedly,'But I doubt if we can do this without the English knowing.'

'Ha! The English know everything. It is rightly said that they have more spies than oats in a porridge pot… but now we are married, they cannot take her from me and get any compensation for themselves. And I am entitled to a marriage portion or gift from her kin! I will ask Orlaith to question her and find her value.'

Fintan said, 'At present, they will still be smarting from finding no cargo from the wreck. I counsel against sending any messages for a while.'

'Very well,' said Redmond, after a pause. 'The women can find her some suitable work, although she must fully recover herself first.'

'You are not usually so tender with your women, brother! This does not surprise me– she is quite startlingly white and beautiful.'

Redmond frowned and Niko added hastily, bowing 'but my congratulations on your good fortune. Now we can stop Thomas talking about a Crown dispensation so you can marry a Scottish or Englishwoman!'

Redmond smiled and walked away, as those around all nodded sagely.

Niko slept badly, troubled by the thought that, although he loved his kinsmen here, perhaps in time this land, its romantic view of warfare and its long-held resentments were not for him. He wondered when Redmond would tire of the delicate ethereal beauty he had rescued, and share her with him, as he had often done with others. He decided he would refuse.

Redmond's mother is less savage than most and has some vestige of womanly kindness. She shoos away the hag they call a Lady! Orlaith finds food that I can eat. She calls that tan, dark one, Niko, to tell her of my wishes. Although he knows my tongue, he looks haughty and speaks in a dialect with foul words…

Orlaith could speak little french. Gile knew only a little English, so Niko, familiar mainly with sailors' and soldiers' slang and some Dutch and Flemish dialects, was an occasional interpreter. Soon after she arrived, Redmond said he wanted Gile to know about his life and lineage. With Niko's help, Orlaith told of Medb's ancestral relationship to the noble Irish and Old English families of Leinster and Munster.

'More than twenty years ago here, upwards of thirty thousand souls from all nations perished from war, execution, imprisonment, starvation or pestilence, including Redmond's father, Lord Lorcan, the old Lady's nephew. Lord Fergus, Lady Medb's youngest son, was ever sickly and had been cared for by monks in Italy during this war. When he returned afterwards, he alone of Medb's warrior kin was allowed to live and be named Baron MacFeagh .'

Orlaith stopped and took a mouthful of food. Redmond then looked up from his bowl and said harshly, 'A sept baron is entitled to sixteen townland settlements, each of which include at the least, three hundred kine, pastures, arable land and forest, but, after the war the Crown took all, later re-granting the least productive townlands with few cattle, and uncleared forest.'

Orlaith then added, 'Lady Medb arranged my marriage to the MacFeagh sept chief Lord Fergus. When he died, Redmond, his nephew, was elected Chief. Then my son Niko and I were ransomed and freed from enslavement…'

She paused as Gile had started and stared.

Niko said, stonily regarding Gile, 'Lady Orlaith too was forced by circumstances away from her kin. In recent years, we have put in place some agreements with an English settler who was granted our lands – one Thomas Hurst. This has improved the circumstances of our people.'

Gile picked at her food and looked bored and as though she wasn't listening.

… The dark one they call Niko is a bastard! The crude tongues and dialect that he speaks must have been learned from ports or soldiers' camps or sailors' brigs. He tells of outlandish names and ever about earls and ancestry and lands and the English Crown. The woman Orlaith looks kindly on the two men. Niko has a harsh expression. He regards me with dislike and I do not respect him. Many here seem to fear him, the warriors love him, the hag avoids him…

Orlaith's head was still down as she finished her platter of fish and greens. She was thinking that, already scarred by finding his mother's mutilated body, Redmond then had to suffer routine humiliation at the hands of the English family where he was fostered. And then her Fergus could not help nourishing the bitterness in his heart with the remains of the feast of his own disappointments and privations. She did not clearly know her son's mind but feared the revenge that burned slowly in him.

Later Niko walked to the shore of the loch, sat on a rock and smoked a long clay pipe. He was remembering happy boyhood years, both in the sunny courtyards of the harem, and also with Redmond after his mother's return to Leinster province, where they were taught something of the use of weapons, and to ride, snare, fish and hunt. Their Overlord, loyal to the Crown but guilty at the ferocity of the reprisals, had protected the remaining MacFeaghs, but they were all subject both to the Earl's arrogance and to many small humiliations. He sent Redmond into fosterage and he, Niko, when grown into a youth, to fight with the English army that had been sent to the wars between Protestant and Catholic factions in the Holy Roman Empire. Niko recalled his despair at being parted for so many years from his loved ones, and the boredom and terror of the soldier's life. In time he found out that Redmond had come home after Lord Fergus's death and that their scattered and depleted people were burdened with taxes, penury and fears of harassment. To his joy, his return to Leinster was agreed following petitions from Lady Medb and Redmond. After a year, he, Niko, was granted permission to travel from Tralee on a Dutch ship to Eastern shores, to try and repair the fortunes of Redmond's people.

Niko smiled as he recalled the wonders he had seen on his voyages, his success at trading, and the gold and silver he had been able to seize at sea. He had bought a half-share in a three-masted ship with another adventurer, Spanish-born Alfonso da Cuellar. One night on a quiet shore, they delivered to Redmond and Medb, gold for gifts and bribes. More of the sept's ancestral lands were re-assigned, repairs to the stronghold were made, and cattle and some sheep purchased. Profit-sharing agreements and employment on Thomas Hurst's demesne and manor quickly followed. He had then returned as a mercenary to standing foreign armies for a while, but had now come back, settling again with Redmond and Orlaith, taking control of the trading, sometimes ferried by Alfonso, and enjoying the welcome and relative prosperity of their people.

Niko's remained confused about his immortal soul. Whilst a boy, taught by the mullahs, he was told that Allah rewarded with a blessed afterlife warriors of Islam who killed those of other Faiths. As a youth in Leinster, the friars said that God punished those who killed, and consigned them to the fires of Hell, but there were dispensations for the taking of human life in defence of the Catholic faith. As a fighting man, he found Lutheran sects obsessed with disputes about the language of the Bible on the outward forms of their worship. Some pastors told him with breathtaking arrogance that only the Chosen from their sect could dwell with God in Heaven. To be Chosen, he must reject the Catholic rituals and religious iconography and listen constantly to their preachings.

He reflected that it seemed all faiths administered assassination, or torture and death for those they named heretics. As a mature soldier who had killed and fought on all sides, he decided that, in the eyes of God, he was probably forever damned.

CHAPTER SIX

ospitality to travellers had long been within the traditions of the Irish people. Fresh food and rest soon enabled Gile to recover her physical strength. She spoke occasionally when prompted in Church Latin or broken English, but over the following weeks said little to anyone. If she acquired Gaelic words, she made no sign of it, ignoring all overtures of friendship or sympathy.

In my dreams whose staring eyes do I see? Whose fingers brush my face, my body? My eyelids burn. Oh Lord, take my sins and miseries from me… dead, all dead. Corpses fill my dreams. My soul is in pain. I have nothing to say to these savages; they are heretics whilst I am of the Chosen and will sit by my God…

The men were often away from the stronghold, herding, trading or hunting, and in any case Gile shunned them. Orlaith was forgiving, having been no stranger to horror, massacre, and disorientation. She defended what was seen as discourtesy. One morning at the castle, Orlaith cut woollen fabric from a bale and fitted it on Gile who had asked for a better skirt and matching hooded cloak. Orlaith noted that the silver and jewelled cross and large ring attached to the gold chain, had not yet been removed by Redmond.

Then, Gile suddenly launched into a torrent of words, none of which Orlaith understood, but she was shaken by the girl's sudden intense garrulity. She pushed a bone needle and some thread into Gile's hands, wondering if this is what she wanted.

'Orlaith! Come quickly – Oonagh asks for you!' called a voice at the door.

Shrugging, Orlaith left. Gile sat, then sobbing quietly.

She cannot understand how the great mist-shrouded seas had taken my breath, ducked me without mercy into the deeps, roared in echo of my pain, and, when the waves subsided, how they whispered of my nakedness and my bruises. My soul aches. Sometimes I see him, my father at the prow, as the vessel began to tip heavenwards, then turning on its side. I was hurled into the sea so they slipped into the fog. I see him in my dreams, weaker, no, frailer, with watery eyes and weeds in his hair. 'Pray, child, pray,' he said. 'Pray for your salvation from these lower ones, who till fields, tan hides and expect you to use those skilled hands, which have woven and broidered colours for the finest of France, to root the devil's tubers from the black earth and, with freezing fingers to crudely gather their bitter cresses' Lord, I have known my duty. I thought You ordained that I work for those above us, for the betterment of first my father, then in time my husband and then my children. What have I done to offend thee Lord, that I now lie amongst these creatures? I should have perished with the rest. I must work to redeem my sins … I can work with my needle..

Gile got up suddenly and ranged around the tower chamber, rummaging through the chests and baskets until she found threads of gold, indigo and green. Then she hung the cloth and used the coloured silks to work on complex floral patterns and knots. On returning some time later, Orlaith was impressed.

In a few days, when some of the men had returned from hunting, Gile appeared at the castle in the finished clothes. Niko particularly nodded in satisfaction, appreciating her skill of hand. Redmond was non-committal.

'Orlaith should have told you to work the whorls and twists of my badge and the crest of our Overlord.'

She did not understand him, but she sensed his dismissal of her work and lifted her chin, then blenched as Medb hobbled up, fingered the fabric and peered at the embroidery. Medb glanced up at Redmond with a sly look as Gile removed the old woman's fingers, turned, and walked to a seat nearby. Redmond frowned and left the room.

Medb watched him go, fearful and muttering, 'Is she harmony or hate? Will she heal or tear his heart?'

Preening in her new garments, and clogs of alder and fine leather made for her by Fintan, Gile often strolled around the village, watching others work. The young people stared or laughed at her or tried to pull her hair, then running away. Some women adjured the children to keep away from her and made the sign of the evil eye in her presence. They feared that, if not lemures, she was one of the amoral 'Sidhe' who existed in a shady realm between real life and magical life and who might steal the young ones away. Gile often followed Orlaith around like a new-born calf.

'Like a wraith' Orlaith said, exasperatedly to Niko. 'And this haunting does not diminish over time… and it offends me that she handles and eats our food as if it would poison her.'

Orlaith could not help but notice that Redmond's wife continued to be irritated by or fearful of Medb's approach, moving away and crossing herself in agitation. On one day when this happened Orlaith held Gile by the shoulders and looked deep into her eyes, laughing a little.

'What? Do you fear a sad old woman, child? Why, she is probably your best friend in Erin did you but know it!'

One day, Gile presented Orlaith with a purse sewn from scraps of wool, ornamented in the colours and shapes of a waterlogged Irish landscape, with steely hills in the background. Looking directly at Orlaith's delighted expression, the girl's eyes glowed, although she did not smile. Her good feelings did not, however, extend to Redmond with whom she was consistently cold. She lay unresponsive in his sleeping pallet, and resented the probings of his hand and the intrusion of his member into her private parts, an activity which became increasingly rapid and ungentle as her time in the stronghold passed.

'Twas our Dear Lord who saved me, who urged this animal to rescue me. 'Twas not the fullness of his heart for my plight – he was but the agent of the devil's will. I am his creature, but I refuse to take pleasure in his gropings, but he does not smite me when I pray after he moves off me.

Perhaps his eyes go to my soul and see my lament. He promised he would get word to my kin. He wants weapons and he dreams of victory over the English. The men, who smell of the stable, the peat and the dogs, now, as the Summer is here, swim in the loch with much shouting and rough play. Sometimes Mistress Orlaith takes me with the women to a strand by the loch, but I resist immersion as I then recall those other waters. Also that hag watches me so keenly as if I will disappear before her eyes into the water. Would that I could disappear through the waters back to my home…

Redmond had soon realised that her moans were not those of passion, but the odour of her body and her barely concealed distaste, her praying, tossing and jabbering, had lessened his desire. He began therefore to banish her from his blankets, sending her to sleep with the unmarried women who sniggered knowingly.

…he says I stink and must bathe, but he, and this place are full of stinks… putrid vats of mordant, manure from horses, ordure from hounds, stink of peat fires…

Gile's attitude irritated others in the stronghold. She was asked to join those who foraged for firewood, or collected mushrooms, greens, sorrels and garlicks from clearings in the woodland above the lochside, but she refused more often than not. Sometimes she agreed to help Orlaith with the spinning and carding, and went about this task with competent hands, but with a sullen or abstracted countenance.

Usually, Redmond and Orlaith simply countered complaints with a demand that all be kinder towards her, but Redmond intervened one hot day, after speaking with amiable Oonagh and the generally unruffled Niko. Oonagh had seen Gile ostentatiously holding her nose in front of all, because of the smell of the wetted wools and leathers from the urine-filled tanning pits was brought upstream by the wind. Niko was annoyed because he heard Gile ignoring or refusing requests to help with either the brewing or the grinding of cereals or the churning of butter. This day, Redmond confronted his wife sternly in the English tongue.

'To live, wife,' he said, 'we must share the labour. Someone must pummel the fleeces in wood ash soap and cure the leather, or you would have no mantle or pattens to keep out the rain and cold.

Someone must fetch water and grind corn or we would have no ale to drink or bread to eat. You should praise them for their industry, not show them your haughty face!'

She lifted her chin in the air and looked away. He called Niko to tell her of his reprimand in her own tongue and then, leaving, asked him to take Gile to where the village folk worked. Gile stood, frowning, whilst Niko pointed to the tasks in which they were engaged. She tossed her head.

There was ironical laughter, and one of the bent old weavers, standing by an ancient rudimentary wooden loom outside the cabins, derided loudly, 'You'll be lucky, Niko, to get some women's work out of her. She will do only that which she thinks befits her rank, like embroidery or giving orders! If I did not know otherwise, I would say she was an Englishwoman.'

Then Gile, flushing at their laughter, moved over to the weaver and pushed him aside. He had just finished his repair of the old loom with its shuttles cut from coppiced wood, and was about to set it for a new piece of work. Curious, Niko held him back as she adjusted the loom and set a measurement for a plain weave of twenty-four threads to the inch. The weft threads, she told Niko, to his raised eyebrows, would be beaten down to thirteen threads. She then sorted through the skeins and hanks of yarn from the baskets, chose some, tied them and announced that the work would contain indigo stripes. After her preparations, she positioned herself on the stool and began to relax into the rhythm of the loom. Eyes fixed in concentration, she seemed scarcely aware of those around her, and hummed happily. Those nearby watched for a while, amazed at the dexterity and speed of her fingers moving like fluttering birds, knotting and beating the lines of threaded yarn.

Hearing of this, Redmond asked that her finished work be brought to him. He, Orlaith and Niko agreed that the cloth was elegant, finely beaten, and that embroidered or trimmed, it would command a good price. After this, Redmond made it clear she must work with the weavers whenever she wished and was gratified to see a small smile on her pale face. Over the following months, her accomplished weaving and unusual designs sold well, when with other bales of cloths and thick white blankets, they were carefully parcelled up and taken away on packhorses accompanying the cattle drovers heading to the coast or inland.

I am soothed that I can use my craft to bring order to the tangle of my mind. Lord deliver me from sloth and worldliness. The way they manufacture their homespun twills and plaids is of some interest to me, although they are but brute unsophisticated churls. Perhaps I will help to form the woad, dandelions and other plants into balls, to be dried for dyes, although when I have examined and plucked some small woad plants from the fields, they have nothing of the quality we find from France, but I will help as more woad will deepen the dyes... linen does not take colour easily. But I will not work on the Sabbath... I will just sit, whether they curse me or no...

At first light one cold morning, Gile was briefly roused and wooden bowls of oats, warm milk and an infusion of mint leaves were thrust into her hands. The murmur of activity grew as the light advanced. Around the castle and the cabins, people everywhere were binding packs onto mules or into carts and filling satchels. The last of the night fires were doused. It was time for the MacFeagh sept to move with their beasts, carts, litters and baggage down to those sheltered parts of the southern coasts where there was winter grazing and where wild ponies could be gathered. They would slowly make their way not only on the valley roads, but also through the old routes, some thickly hedged and others just stone-strewn tracks. Redmond would set armed guards to remain and protect the tower, whilst he, Niko and Fintan would go and visit neighbouring clans and hunt. They would also raid cattle from the plantations and the Crown estates in places such as church lands, where harsh reprisals were unlikely.

Some of the folk were bound for snug, low built accommodations within lively, populous towns. At this time, winter feasts were celebrated, and alliances, including marriages, were made. Many spent time in what remained of the great schools, where, some remembered, there was every sort of learning for all the young and old who wished to listen. These schools, dominated by the friars, used to be run by lawgivers and schoolmasters, but were now based in churches and what remained of former monasteries.

Yet other folk would go to bothies in little-known, sheltered creeks not far from the wide beach where Gile had been washed ashore. When the westerlies were blowing hard on the surrounding rocks, all manner of goods would come ashore, as if, Friar Ignatius would remark, they were 'Sent by the Good Lord to succour us, as, to be sure, the old Queen is rich enough without getting what comes floating in from the sea!'

On calm days, the men would put out in their small light corraghs to fish or barter along the coast to augment their winter rations, and to, from time to time, pass messages. Redmond and Niko were masters of this trade; their network, aligned to the key Irish nobles, rivaling that of the Crown.

Medb encouraged this. She said once to Niko and Redmond, 'I have seen all sides changing just as the winds turn according to the season. Information is more valuable than the trade of salt and wines for salmon and wool frieze.'

Ronan, Redmond's squire, who charmed all with his playing of the tin whistle, was also a fleet and trusted messenger, able to run over mountains. He was urged always to carefully check all sources, being told, before setting out on each journey, 'Our information must be reliable, even if this commands a high price.'

Why are they binding together their goods and placing so much on their carts, pack horses and mules? Redmond motions me to lift and carry my personal satchels and does not tell me where we are going. Most of the menfolk left this stronghold Wednesday last with the drovers, carrying some trade goods, including no doubt some of the booty from our poor sunken ship, the freebooters… What do they plan now? As I turn my back on Redmond, that foolish, fawning old woman ever follows me, even though bent almost double with the size of the pack she shoulders. Now she tries to hold my sleeve and tell me something – something to do with the whips. I do not wish to hear her. Aagh, she stinks of peat and the tanners' pits. Laisse-moi, sorciere! I cannot understand her barbarous tongue. Orlaith casts me black looks and ignores me. Why should I assist them – I was not born to such labour…

Medb said, hobbling away from Gile, 'If she knows – which, as she paces so agitated, she must - she cares not. She cares not about the ghostly whistling in the air and the ghostly cracking of a whip, presaging a death either of her or around her. I warned her, I said "Spirit of the Sea, you must catch that whip and strike back with it." Last night I sat by the loch, watching the last rays of the setting sun being submerged into the mist, and I saw the reed swamps glow red like blood and I thought I glimpsed Tir-na-Nog, the land of the ever young. But tch! As she is not concerned at these omens, I should not be either. My eyes and ears are those of an old woman and often fail me. How could these old eyes glimpse far-off lands across the loch? These old ears, that heard Orlaith calling from her enslavement, already muffle speech, and may now be hearing sounds that are not there. On this, I must now keep silent. But what is agitating her, what is changing?' She stopped suddenly and turned round. 'She is growing a child in her belly. I know it and soon she must know it.'

I look back and the old crone has dropped her pack. She stares hard at me and looks strangely at my person, as if into my body and soul. Perhaps she'll give me agues to add to the sickness I feel when I wake in the morning. They are now cracking the whips to set the carts rolling. Now Orlaith approaches with great frowns, thrusts satchels into my arms and gestures sternly that I walk with the other women who have started to follow the carts. I look back now at Redmond who, his dogs at his heels, also frowning, nods and points, and mounts his wild pony. He does not bow or bid me farewell, but watches me. Orlaith goes to Medb and shoulders her pack as well as her own. That woman looks like a greyhound, but is as strong as an ox. I must go with them, perforce I must... I will follow Orlaith. That heathen bastard Niko, who often stands so still in the shadows, and, when he ever observes me, gives me black looks, has not yet mounted. He comes towards me. He stands tall and regards me coldly with his hawking eye, the violence in him smoulders. Sometimes he has spoken to me in a crude dialect but I have ignored his words...

Niko briskly approached Gile noticing how she hurried after Orlaith, trying to avoid him. He clasped her by the arm and made her face him. He felt her tremble and pull away.

He said in the Flemish tongue, 'I am commanded by your husband to travel across the seas and find your family in Leiden. He asks if you wish to return to them if they can be found and if so, he requires them to compensate him for losing you.'

A light flared in her eyes.

'I wish to return to my family. My father's name was Hendrick Breydel. You know that I have told Redmond this many times before. My uncle Andreas De Hem lives and works both in Leiden and Amsterdam. My mother is his sister-in-law. They will all be known in those towns. We are successful cloth finishers and mercers with many artisans and they will be seeking me. They will find and punish you if I am not kept safe. My kin owe Redmond nothing. I was handfasted to one Christian Calvet, a London cloth finisher and should be wed to him, not Redmond who,' she then spoke loudly in English, staring fiercely at Redmond, mounted nearby and watching them, ' I do not call husband.'

..At last I am given hope that I can be with my own ones.In this place my spirits have been wasted with grief and travail…

Niko went over to Redmond and spoke briefly to him.

Returning to Gile, he said, 'You will have your wish. Lord Redmond will send you back to your family.' He paused. 'If I can find them and if they will have you. Lord Redmond asks that you give me some proof of your survival – that ring,' he pointed to the one on the chain around her neck next to the jewelled cross,' will suffice. I would also remind you that you are no longer handfasted. Whether you are with him or not, or wish it or not, you are wife in the eyes of God to Redmond, chief of a Barony in Leinster and as such he has honoured you, and requires to be compensated by your family for his loss.'

Redmond insults me to so summarily dismiss me, to ask for a gift when I have been forced into a form of marriage. God forgive me for the curse that came to mind. I do not trust that one, that Niko of dark hue, to deal fairly. He struts like a courtier in what he thinks is civilised garb, but his cloak is Irish weave, his boots are too heavy, and his slashed doublets are too large and marked with water stains… that lock of hair by his ear marks him for a Fool… he must not take my precious ring from me, this gold and crystal ring, which, when fully opened, has engrave, that 'what God has joined together, must no man put asunder'…

Furious, clutching the chain and the ring, Gile looked again at Redmond, still silently watching. She spat defiantly in a mixture of

French and English, 'That was no marriage – you – you heathens…
I will not let you take my betrothal ring and indeed it cannot be
removed from the chain. The clasp has rusted and fused…'

Niko drew his finely worked rapier from his buckler and delicately picked up the girl's chain from around her neck with its tip.
Gile screamed in alarm, and Niko put down his sword.

'Kneel by that mossy stone, and place your chain upon it. Put
your head to one side! Now!'

Trembling, she knelt and placed the chain, hanging from
which was a ring and a cross, on the stone in front of her.

'Heathens? You know nothing of heathens,' said Niko, his
eyes narrowing. 'If you had been captured by the Moor, then lady,
you would have been quickly repudiated once used, and sold to
lower ones.'

He suddenly swung the sword and severed the chain. Gile
gasped with terror and shock as the blade whistled past her face.

'Hand me the ring. You may keep the cross. Someone will knot
your chain.' She gave it to him, sobbing with shock.

Niko turned and left saying, 'And now thank your God my
hand did not slip, and for your timely rescue from the fogs.'

She looked angrily at Redmond, but he, followed closely by
Ronan, had already turned his horse away towards the hills. His
thin lips were slightly curved into a small malicious smile.

During the movement of the septs, Alice Plymmiswoode was
heading north from the southern coast. She was lying flat, enveloped in furs, in the heavy wooden carriage, travelling back from
a Churching to another Leinster Settler family, the Nethertons,
originally hailing from northern Britain.

'Well, they are now blessed with a strong son to join their pretty little daughter,' Alice mused, 'but whether God would approve
their great oak-beamed manor even more stacked with new brick
chimneys and turrets than Thomas's own, I am not sure.'

Drowsily, Alice then reflected on the suitors, and overtures to
her person – indeed even before Abraham's death. She crossed herself guiltily. God had decreed that her two pregnancies bled away, to
the relief of Abraham's sons from his first marriage. She thought she
herself was unlikely to ever bear children, even if she married again.

As their father, and indeed her own, had wished, Alice worked alongside her stepsons when requested. They trusted her with their ledgers. They knew she was competent, interested and familiar with their trade. She did not often see them, as they had married advantageously with foreign wives from the merchant class and travelled much. Alice recalled Cecilia's trials. Obsessive piety, she thought, had not prevented Cecilia's many stillbirths, or allowed their children to survive infancy. She hoped that the woman had found solace in becoming chatelaine of the re-built Somerset Abbey.

Now she tried to ignore the jolting from the cart ruts, and the draughts that whistled through the flaps of the thick curtains when they lifted in the wind. Rising and peering outside before attempting to secure one more firmly, she saw a loch beneath her on her left, dark under a heavy sky. Then she noticed a large line of other travellers, on foot or on laden mules, coming over the bridge at the head of the loch in their direction. The air was damp and smelt of drying seaweed. She called to the sergeant of her escort.

'You do not need to fear, mistress, they always journey to the coasts for winter trade and feasting,' he said, but she noticed that he carefully scrutinised the densely packed firs, clothed with lichen, covering the ridges above and ahead of them. 'They will be women, children and old men. Just in case stay behind the curtains, and do not let them see you.'

They doggedly rolled onwards, avoiding potholes that Thomas used to say could have sheltered an ambush, and were now, she thought gloomily, likely to fill with rain from the threatened downpour.

She had asked Thomas why Ireland's highways were in such poor condition, often passable only on foot.

'I'm disappointed that Her Gracious Majesty refuses to finance roads and bridges although frequently requested to do so by successive Crown Secretaries,' had been his answer.

She had remonstrated, 'Surely such investment could only assist the process of civilising the Irish people, give them work other than raiding cattle, and more prosperity!'

Prosperity, in her view, invariably diminished thoughts of rebellion.

Her brother had replied, 'The Irish are not a meek people, as God commands of us. I doubt if they will ever accept conquerors, no matter how prosperous they become.'

Thomas had banged his staff on the floor telling her that their priests and friars fomented trouble and spoke against the settlers. They were protected by some of the nobles, and also travelled widely across the country, so were hard to locate. He said that it did not help that many of the missionary Protestant preachers that came from the Low Countries did not even speak English, let alone Gaelic.

'The folk here need good missionaries to show them the errors in their faith,' she had answered. 'Nowhere in our Isles are there enough educated preachers. Even in England, they have been of poor quality. There is too much talk of hell-fire and not enough argument on the meaning of the Scriptures.'

Her carriage now jolted suddenly, sharply throwing her so its curtain flaps lifted. She held on to the armrest bars to keep steady. Glimpsing the terrain, her thoughts turned to the landscape of Ireland, its wild coasts and hazy mountains, its many lochs, peat bogs and fir-clothed slopes. She sighed.

'What savage beauty is in this Isle! No wonder there is wildness in its people.'

Eventually, the procession of Redmond's people, with its barking dogs, laden mule-carts, many carrying children in baskets, emerged round a wide bend in the road which had become much narrower alongside the loch. In the press of laden, slow moving people and animals, the carriage was forced to stop. Her guards stayed on horseback front and rear, whilst the two following foot guards stationed themselves alongside the carriage, slanting their short pikes so as to keep a distance between it and the curious, murmuring crowd, which was forced into two or three abreast as they passed. The travellers were ungainly. Their packs, long cloaks and heads were covered against the soft rain now falling,

'….like a flock of black crows on a field,' thought the Sergeant leading the escort. Dark cloaks then lifted in a suddenly arrived wind presaging a storm. The bulk of the travellers having passed, he moved ahead of the carriage to scout the state of the road beyond the bend.

When all at Castle MacFeagh except the guards had departed, Niko and two men took a horseway route to the coast, travelling separately from the main body of the clan. They wanted to avoid militias so rode along riverbanks or stony screes, passing moorland, wood and bog. In the distance, waterfalls trailed like ivy down the mountainsides, and wavelets glittered on the surface of the lochs. Eventually, the wide misty marshes of the estuary were below them. At the harbour, Niko met his friend Captain Alfonso, on whose sea-faring skill, opinions and guidance he had so often relied. Their ship was named 'Green Isle' and, after courtesies, all helped in supervising the loading of a cargo of MacFeagh trade goods, arrived lately and guarded on the harbour, to be carried to Le Havre.

Once underway, Niko stood, feet apart, in a covered area of the deck, his sea boots covering his thighs and his earring swaying under a tall-crowned hat, wet from spray. He briefly regarded his two companions sitting cloaked on the deck, up against a bulkhead. Conor, his frame broad as a bothy and clothed in thick beige fur, was barely distinguishable from the accompanying hounds. He began twitching his bulbous nose against raindrops and snored, earning a curse from his sleepy compatriot, Dermot. Niko and his squire had much in common, both born out of wedlock, and skilled in parleying and in juggling their daggers. Young Dermot, pale with highly arched brows and dark eyes had been assigned to him the previous year. He invariably dressed in the Irish fashion.

Niko reflected that Redmond had at first wanted to win the damaged heart and mind of Gile. He had seen how his foster-brother's face was filled with longing when he stared at her pearl-pale hair and wax complexion, her long fingers and legs, and her eyes like a loch in summer. For himself, he was impatient at Gile's contempt for his people, and was pleased that now Redmond wanted rid of her. One of the more reserved men in the stronghold, Niko admired the levity of many of the women there, their energy, their skill at throwing knives, their love of talk and dance, their stoicism in times of trouble. Elsewhere he had too often met coquettes or hard-eyed matrons with an eye on his purse, or respectable women who were dull, stiff and lacking in grace. His thoughts then went to Alice Plymmiswoode, wealthy, intelligent and handsome. He was aware of more than a spark of interest and wondered if she felt it too.

In Le Havre, Niko sought out his usual trading agents, setting his companions to seek harbour pilots informing them that a woman, Susannah, was the only survivor of the shipwreck off southern Ireland earlier in the year and asking if they knew of cloth merchants, Andreas De Hem or Hendrik Breydel. They all also frequented the ale-houses in St. Francois, spending time with some of the corsairs trading out of St. Malo and La Rochelle. These were fiercely independent men, vassals to no Overlord. Alfonso and Niko liked to game with them, and dine on collars of brawn and flagons of rich red wine. As well as listening to their views on defeats and victories in the religious wars in the Holy Roman Empire, Niko heard that the Spanish fleet bound for Ireland had turned back again. He enquired if they thought that King Phillip would continue to support the rebellion in the north. Some opined that the Spanish nobles did not trust the Earl of Tyrone to keep faith with them. They reminded him of Irish treachery and brutality to the survivors of the Spanish Armada shipwrecked some twenty years before.

'The Ulster Earls are greedy and take the wherewithal of their people to pay for a luxurious life in the English style,' said one.

'I'm told that their growing army of mercenaries is hired from dues they exact from their clans, leaving them to endure hardship,' said another.

'You have no doubt heard this from one of the English spies.' Niko was nettled, but knew that there was truth in their comments.

'Your nobles walk a tightrope,' said Captain Alfonso, grizzled and often sardonic, 'a tightrope, not only above the Protestant immigrants and officials of the English Crown, but also amongst themselves. You know yourself that long-standing blood feuds regularly erupt between them!'

'I know there is no love lost between the Earls of Desmond and Omonde, but indeed the Crown should fear us,' said Niko. 'They have done much to deserve our hate.'

'Stay clear of this, Niko, for your people and your honour's sake,' said Alfonso. 'The English and the Irish nobles – and even the French - fight in the name of dynasty and ambition rather than in the name of freedom or civilisation – as they all trumpet! And the English Queen is determined to crush Ireland once and for all. You know she fears a lasting Irish alliance with the Pope and Spain.'

Niko could not but agree with them and his stomach tightened.

CHAPTER
SEVEN

lice arrived in Dublin from Hurst Place, and, soon after, was summoned in front of the huge oaken table behind which sat Sir Rowland Porter, the Constable of the largest castle in The Pale. She had previously sent Gile to him, with a brief letter, explaining that Mistress Susannah Breydel was in urgent need his protection and that she herself would follow as soon as possible.

'Although I am given to understand that she is the daughter of a drowned cloth producer,' he said, his voice querulous, 'I have been told that she is named Lady Gile MacFeagh ! And when she arrived she was dressed as an Irishwoman. Serious disturbances in the south-east have been reported as a result of an incident on the road. Give me a full account!'

'It all happened so quickly,' she said, bowing her velvet-capped head. 'It had been raining on and off since I left Munster, where I had been invited to a Churching. It was very overcast and black clouds were threatening from across the loch with the wind becoming quite strong. A large number of Irish people, heavily covered against the weather, were passing slowly and in groups alongside us. The road was narrow bordering the loch and only just above the level of it, so my escort stopped the carriage. I was curious and raised my curtain to observe them. The woman Susannah and her companions were towards the end of the line of horses, carts and folk. They were all carrying packs and straggling.

The others were quite far ahead. The people did not look at me...'

'They knew it would be presumptuous,' interrupted Sir Rowland. 'You were a foolish woman to make yourself known.'

Alice flushed. She had met him before with Thomas who had said the man was brave, but arrogant. She continued, 'Then I opened my carriage drapes, and called out loudly to my Flemish guard. I thought they were pointing their halberds too near the people – now that,' she emphasised, 'would have been provocative!'

The Constable sniffed dismissively.

'The line of folk was much thinned. It was raining hard. I can't remember exactly what I said to the guard, but I think it was "stand back". She was walking slowly alongside two women and heard me speaking in the French tongue. Without warning, Susannah stopped, dropped her pack and stepped quickly forward towards my carriage. She was then grasped by one footguard and forced to her knees, whilst an armed guard on horseback confronted her companions who had stopped. There was another small group slowly coming towards us from further back. The girl looked up and beseeched me, loudly and prettily, in French, to be allowed to serve me. She also spoke to a guard, Jan Rijten, mounted on a large sturdy mare, in the Flemish tongue. It was unfortunate that one of my dressers had been taken ill after the Churching and was to follow on later, so when she said she had many skills with sewing and weaving and would earn her keep... although her dress was uncivilised, I could tell her quality from her accent, her pale comely face and hair and huge blue eyes... then she pleaded to be rescued from, she said, her kidnappers. Anyway, I agreed to take her with me for a few weeks and was going to allow the girl into the carriage but for her stink...'

'You were *what*! What if she had attacked you? Why in God's name did you listen to her? Did you lose your wits?' exploded Sir Rowland.

Alice lowered her head and addressed her hands. 'Well, I did wonder whether she was friend or foe, but she clearly had no weapon and seemed so desperate.' Then she defiantly raised her chin. 'Our Lord himself showed mercy and expects us to do likewise.'

'Do not tell me the scriptures, Mistress. You were naïve in the extreme. Where was the Sergeant?'

'He had ridden on ahead beyond a large bend, past the end of the line. He told me afterwards it was to check the highway and how many remained on the road,' she replied. 'The light was low, it was still raining and a mist had risen from the loch, obscuring our way ahead.'

Rowland said impatiently, 'Continue!'

'I told the guard Jan Rijten, mounted behind my carriage, to put her up behind him, which he did.' Alice had spoken slowly but her speech gathered pace as she re-lived the events. 'Then the old witchwoman, Medb – I did not know then who she was – I had never met her or heard of her – or that she was regarded by them as a noble if not a Queen – moved right up to Jan Rijten and Susannah. A huge mastiff stood beside the old woman, barking. A footguard threatened them with his pike, telling her to move away. He was another Fleming. The old woman looked appalling, her hat blown off in the wind and her long grey hair loose and wild, her face stretched over the bone and her skinny arms raised as she screamed I don't know what. Susannah cowered on the horse, screamed back in Flemish and I shouted at all to stay calm. The skies suddenly seemed to get much darker. Lightning began flashing high above us illuminating the Irish people standing like statues. Then thunder started crashing and rolling, and someone else started swaying, screaming and keening, and the group behind began to move quickly towards us.'

Alice took a deep breath as she remembered.

'The rain became heavier, and I closed my drapes. I heard chanting and sobbing, the horses were neighing and pacing and trying to bolt. I thought my litter would overturn. I shouted at the guards to move on. More dogs began barking. I heard screaming, the woman Medb bellowing and making a shouted incantation. Then, I was told, – *Lady* Medb, is it? – the old woman – with her arms still held high, and a barking dog by her side, walked right in front of the already disturbed carriage horses, and continued her chants and wails. Everything seemed to happen at once. It seems that one of the guards nudged his horse forward, but it retreated from the old woman's mastiff, causing my vehicle to lurch alarmingly. Badly jolted, I fell back against my cushions, so I did not see that, not on my order, exasperated and afraid, Jan Rijten-Susannah may even have shouted for him to intervene – killed the dog and also speared the woman Medb through the heart. Through the pelting rain, I heard a great rumbling, sounding like "geis, geis". Then my carriage and the mounted guards moved off quickly. I gather the pikemen held the people off before rapidly retreating under cover of the escort Sergeant who had come galloping back.'

'The "geis", Mistress,' said Sir Rowland heavily, 'I am informed was a terrible lifelong curse which will follow the whole life of the cursed one, and bring shame and distress if not death. Do you know who the old witch – savage though she seemed, she was one of their noblewomen – was pointing at when it was said? You must pray to God it was not you! Here they say that she was a Prophetess.'

'No, I didn't see. I had already started on my way. The guards said that they could not have passed without trampling her. It is possible that one or two other folk who moved forward were injured, as I felt the carriage hit something. I looked out and back once we had gained some speed, as I noticed, did Susannah, seated behind Jan Rijten and following closely behind us. Through the gloom, figures and misshapen lumps were slumped, almost submerged on the road. I heard the Sergeant riding back. I heard musket fire. He later said that two or three had come running after us rending their clothes and screaming, so he had fired at these cloaked stragglers…'

'At women, children and old men!' interrupted the Constable.

'He told me later that those around the old woman's corpse had set up a savage barbarous growling and wailing. He said some were wounded but only Lady Medb MacFeagh was killed.' Alice caught her breath and wrung her hands.

'That's not what the Irish people say,' said Sir Rowland.

'My Lord, I must tell you.' Alice implored him. 'The woman Medb had no tokens of nobility about her – her mighty voice and the storm unsteadied everyone, and the mercenary Fleming Jan Rijten who did the deed – who has now fled, we don't know where – slew her, thinking her a demon, deliberately through the heart. I had no intention of killing anyone! The Sergeant told me that had he realised that she was an important woman, he would have tried to seize her as a hostage against possible rebellion. He is most rueful about the events.'

'He has failed in his duty and will be punished,' said Sir Rowland, who had got up and was pacing the room. He looked at Alice, finally saying, 'what have you been able to find out about the Hollander woman? She was sickly on arrival, and we have kept her apart. My servants say she has half lost her wits – or is fey or a witch herself. One of the Gaelic-speaking loyal women here says that she was named Gile after a mythical sea-nymph with magical powers. She has kept to her bed, taken herbal draughts, ate and said little. Is she a witch, a French spy, or suborned by Redmond MacFeagh and sent to discover our plans?'

'I do not know, Sir Rowland. I only know that before leaving Hurst Place, she told me she had been kidnapped by the MacFeaghs and held to ransom. Her distress and desire to escape was genuine, I am sure. Her actions caught everyone by surprise. I sent her to you I reached Thomas's manor in case of pursuit and murder. I spoke to her only briefly before sending her immediately to your castle. We were both tired and distressed. As to her background, she said her mother lives in Leiden in Holland. She thought she was the only survivor washed up on a shore in those deep fogs in spring. Her vessel had made a disastrous detour from Bordeaux to Cork, I think, or perhaps Waterford en route to London. Baron Redmond MacFeagh found her and took her in. It seems they treated her kindly, although she had to endure their savage way of life. She said they thought her Redmond MacFeagh's wife, but she did not consider herself so. This confused me.'

'The Irish people here initially described her as Lady Gile so, if this is true, she may well be wed to a MacFeagh chief,' said the Constable. He tapped the shiny pink lip protruding through his beard. 'I know that in the Queen's Law, we English cannot marry with the Irish, but I am not certain about the laws of the Empire or the Dutch, especially as they have many there with Catholic sympathies. Hmm. Niko MacFeagh led us to believe that Redmond would agree to marry a settler's daughter of good family and would consider converting to our Faith.'

'Susannah may be of use to us,' said Alice, hopefully.' She calls them savage and could not wait to flee from them. She is bitter. Having lived amongst the clan for some months, she may have information of use to us.'

'I remember that spring rain and the wreck in the fogs very well,' said the Constable, rising from his table. 'An Ambassador- a Speaker of Foreign Tongues, and some preachers lost their lives there, as well as a reputable cloth merchant and his train. I suppose that man could well have been her father.' He was silent for a while. 'So there *was* at least one survivor. There were rumours from the waystations. Your brother asked me to send Searchers but they found little, needless to say.' He frowned. 'The Irish people seek any sort of material gain.'

Unwisely Alice said, 'Not just these people, I think, my Lord.'

His eyes narrowed. 'Are you referring to your brother, mistress? Did he take a share of the salvage?'

'Of course not! Thomas always suspected the local septs found a great deal more than they admitted to. But he had no evidence. If Redmond managed to find and keep the girl alive – for his own ends no doubt – it follows that they must have taken advantage of that brief respite between the fog and the rain to pick the shore clean – and murder those still alive who could report on them. Everyone he questioned about the wreck shrank like worms down a hole, denying finding anything but a few barrels high on the shoreline…'

'Shipwrecked goods belong to the Crown and the Crown only. Thomas should have used torture. I shall follow this evidence of their guilt with a few hangings,' announced Sir Rowland. 'That should also calm things down.'

Alice's voice sharpened.

'I would counsel you to let any hangings wait – I doubt if they would be any deterrent and may inflame the situation. The MacFeaghs may well deny anything Susannah says. Listen to me Sir Rowland!' She leaned forward saying 'you may not know that I had to confront a furious Baron Redmond. And was lucky not to have been killed there and then and Hurst Place attacked. I have been discomfited… just for doing my Christian duty.'

'Mistress Plymmiswoode, I'm afraid that even more discomfort is likely to come your way! Lady Medb was an Irishwoman of noble descent. Many years ago, she was in the household of a favourite Earl of our great Queen. This knowledge has, to some extent, protected the MacFeaghs. Susannah Breydel was indeed fortunate that the Lord in his wisdom saved her. But I have no doubt that at some point there will be unpleasant consequences for your brother.' He paused. 'Although Thomas has forces at his demesne, it would be hard to resist a concerted attack. The same goes for other plantations in this region. You must know that here we are vastly outnumbered by people from a different culture with a different faith, particularly in this region. This gives them much power. But, in view of your pleadings, I shall take no immediate action. We try to rely on diplomacy in our dealings with the Irish although this is a view with which I often do not agree. I shall have to request some reinforcements from the north, even though they are needed there.'

Alice knew that when she journeyed in England, there were always vagabonds, and desperate men without employment. She usually took no notice of the myriad warnings that swarmed about her when she prepared to travel, although it was always sensible to have a small escort. Now she wrung her hands and bitterly regretted that Thomas had not taken the mercenaries with him on his diplomatising journeys to the Irish Earls' Great Houses, where he had gone to try and discourage the rebellion from spreading from the north. Thomas had told her before she went to the Churching, that for many years, ex-soldiers roamed everywhere in Ireland, all looking for easy gains, and that she must go to Munster with men-at-arms. She reflected sourly that she would probably not be in this situation had he sent her with men like Walter who knew this land and its people, rather than mercenary Flemings. Alice regarded Sir Rowland, lifting her chin.

'I am sorry at the old Lady Medb's death. You should know that… but I have already confronted Redmond's anger and desire for vengeance and he did not attack. You surely know, my Lord, that the MacFeaghs, Thomas and the Crown all profit from the trade they undertake together and indeed peace, however uneasy, brings profit to the people more than does war… which only seems to bring profit to the mighty.'

Sir Rowland Porter looked at her sharply, thinking that, although some would think her courageous, Thomas's sister did not sufficiently know her place in his life, in the life of Ireland and the world. To her credit, she was known for almsgiving and the generous way she honoured God's ordinances and sacred feasts. He had heard that her father and her husband had allowed her unbecoming freedom of speech and overly involved her in his business affairs.

'You speak bitterly, Mistress Alice, and I would spend time disputing with you, but now I need to know how we can turn the arrival of this foreign woman – this Stranger – to our advantage rather than bringing the wrath of the populace upon our heads. You were foolish in confronting that chief of the MacFeagh sept –'

'I had no choice…' she spluttered.

'He could have let his anger override his common sense. We need him to stay loyal. At present we await the Queen's response to the breaking of yet another truce and the Earl of Tyrone's plotting with the Spanish.'

'Susannah is most probably the daughter or related to the drowned cloth maker. She seems to be of that class. They may have means and homes in Holland or France. Their gratitude for her safe return may be worthwhile…'

Sir Rowland sniffed disparagingly, then saying 'I will have enquiries made as to her kin. There is a small community in The Pale from Flanders and France, refugees from the religious wars. Our Queen wants the Protestant Dutch as allies.'

'I have heard of the horrific massacres there, perpetrated by both sides of the religious divide. I pray each day that Ireland will not descend into such Godlessness,' she replied.

'And we all hope that those massacres will prove a deterrent to all here in the south wishing to join the Earl of Tyrone. One thing is sure – rebels will never be able to overcome the might of the English Crown.' He paused. 'Are you sure you believe the woman? About the wreck, her rescue and the marriage?'

'Her story is so strange it could well be true! I will speak further with her, although she said she knew nothing of plots. She was lucid with me, and, of course I speak some of the French tongue, although her northern accent is strong. I am given to understand that many of the Irish folk hold marriage loosely. Do you know anything of this?'

Sir Rowland leaned back in his chair.

'Marriage *and* parenthood. It is astonishing that the former Baron Fergus MacFeagh's wife Lady Orlaith, returned from concubinage with the Ottomans and with a bastard son, was given to him in marriage, and not sent to a nunnery to make her peace with God! She was lucky to be ransomed. At that time the Dukes, Regents and crowned heads of the Holy Roman Empire finally had enough of the corsairs' coastal raids and depredations on the treasure ships and sent a fleet to attack their strongholds on the Barbary Coast. The MacFeaghs would have had to pay some sort of compensation to the Bishops. Our Lord only knows how they raised the money – cattle thieving, probably.'

'Ah yes, Niko Mac Feagh,' said Alice, a sudden image of his eyes delving into hers as he rose from his courtly bow. 'So his bastardy and his mother's concubinage did not affect their position amongst the Irish nobles and their people?'

'It seems not. They are spoken of with respect. He may call himself Niko MacFeagh, but my spies say his correct title smacks of the heathen – I am told he is also called Nikola bin Mustafa Reis, and he speaks the Ottoman tongue – which is useful for trading of course. His father was a warrior of some sort.'

'But this Niko is not ungodly- indeed he is more civilised than many of the natives here', said Alice. 'I am told he has fought with the English armies. Thomas has hopes that he will influence those in the south to continue to accept and bow to the Queen and her laws. But, pray, who was Baron Redmond's mother?'

'I am told her name was Lady Eithne Kavanagh. She died young in tragic circumstances I believe. We, of course, were blamed.'

'Thomas told me that the Kavanaghs dwell in high mountain fastnesses and have never been subdued'.

Sir Rowland grunted. He noticed, when her face was caught in a shaft of autumn sunlight, that Alice Plymmiswoode possessed fewer wrinkles than many women of her years, and a large fine bosom. He was aware that her recent bereavements had enabled her to become wealthy. Then, suddenly irritated at the trouble she had caused, he spoke sternly.

'You must now stay here and take good care of Mistress Susannah and have her watched. I do agree she could become useful. I say again that you were lucky that the travellers on the road were mainly women and children. I repeat, you should not have lifted your drapes, you should have ignored her pleading, and moved on without incident. The killing of Lady Medb MacFeagh has a resonance beyond your understanding and the tale is not finished yet. Pray for your soul and hers. A noblewoman has died through your intervention. The loyalty of many clans and their vassals within and without The Pale is in doubt, and we fear plots and recruitment to the northern Earls' cause. Treachery must be punished or the degenerate English born here – and some Welsh and Scottish nobles – for their gain, although they will say it is for their Faith ! - will open this door to invasion of our England by popish France and Spain!'

Alice bent her head, curtseyed and left the room. Returning to her quarters in the castle, Alice lay down to rest. She considered what she had been told of Redmond's background, and reflected on that fearful twilight when she had confronted Lord Redmond.

After the incident on the road, she, Susannah and their escort had travelled many hours to Hurst Place without stopping. She had left the litter to follow on and ridden fast on horseback, as did Jan Rijten and Susannah. Whilst the daylight was still with them, they were only too aware of figures seen in the bush, bog and wood that they passed, and, as the half moon rose, of what looked like shadows looming amongst the swirls of mist and rain. They arrived deep into the night amid the flare of their torches in large iron sconces in the stable yard.

Damp, cold, stiff and hungry, Alice had sent for sustenance and for Walter, originally from a loyal Irish family in Dublin, to be roused from his bed. She remembered Thomas saying that Walter often helped to resolve local disputes. The panelled vestibule was still warm from a fire guttering under the exuberant carved overmantel. A dry fur cloak, some cheese and small ale had arrived with a tousled Walter. His sculpted face had become grave as he heard what happened on their journey, not least because Thomas was not due to return for some time. His manner was unusually direct.

'The woman who was killed – was her name Lady Medb? A 'geis'? An Irish terrible, lasting, curse? Did she direct it at you or another?'

'I did not see her cursing. I know nothing about the old woman. I didn't understand her curse or spell or whatever it was – but it was delivered in a wild and violent manner. It was a great pity that the guard panicked, but the mad old crone would not get out of the way and her shrieking was causing chaos.'

Walter had not been able to suppress a groan.

'If it was the Lady Medb, she is or was a person of consequence, mistress, and much valued by her remaining kin. She is of noble lineage and rank and is cherished as a martyr to the Irish cause. There are rumours that she is heretic and follows the Old Ones, and also that she has something of the gift of prophecy. But her kin had always resisted Old King Henry's Reformation of the Church and subjecting her people to the Queen's Law. They thought he wished to be King of Ireland. Since the executions of her husband and sons, Lady Medb has counselled her great-nephew Redmond to be loyal to the Crown.'

'Good riddance to the witch,' she had said, crossing herself, but Walter had not done likewise.

Increasingly realising the situation was very serious, her supper had become dry in her mouth when Walter had said, 'Although the MacFeagh people have descended into a semi-nomadic outlaw state, selling their labour to survive, they are very proud. I am sorry, mistress, but Lord Redmond will be almost certain to come here, in a rage and seeking revenge. Master Thomas is far away.'

'Will he take gold with an apology instead? I am given to understand that the clans will do anything for gold. Niko MacFeagh knows us well here. He is altogether more civilised – I hope he will accompany Redmond and restrain him.'

'Not necessarily – and in any case, he is likely to be trading abroad at this time of year – and Redmond acts impulsively. Do not offer gold to Lord Redmond, Mistress Alice, or he may well kill you regardless of the consequences.'

'Then what do you suggest we do? Surely he would not dare attack us!'

Walter had remained silent.

'Well! What am I to do?'

'You must meet him if he comes and use your wits. Mistress-I know how it is here. I have often spoken with Master Thomas about how to keep the peace. I help him to negotiate. He will want me to speak their tongue and interpret for you, so his men will know what is said. Remember Lord Redmond was in foster-age and speaks English. You must not show fear. They expect the English to be arrogant, and they value courage.'

Then she had penned a brief explanatory letter commending Susannah to the Constable's protection, saying she herself would follow as soon as possible with further details.

'The gatehouse guards have reported no arrivals in our absence. See that a fresh escort takes the foreign woman on horseback at first light to Sir Rowland Porter, the Constable in Dublin. They are not to stop.'

Messengers were also sent immediately to Thomas asking him to return with all speed and more soldiery, but they knew it could be many weeks before he received the message. And then they had waited.

Alice's heart thumped as she recalled the noon when Redmond and his escort arrived. They were allowed through the gatehouse with their weapons, which she deemed just as well, as she was later told they were only too prepared to fight their way in. She had greeted them on the highest step in front of the main entrance to the manor, Walter standing slightly behind her. He had posted a small number of guards in livery and carrying long pikestaffs on each side of them. As the mounted men slowly approached, she had fearfully observed Redmond's hand on the pommel of his great sword, his long, curled, fringed hair, the long mantle fastened with a glittering jewel, his lean frame, the gold torque around his neck, his leather thigh-length boots, and a barking mastiff each side of their small muscular horses. She had schooled her face when they came to a halt, too near for comfort, barely controlling their horses which had sensed their tension. Redmond had commanded Walter to speak in Gaelic, and their tongues became active under the plethora of syllables.

'Where is Thomas?' Redmond had sneered. 'Does he hide behind his sister's skirts?'

'He is with your Overlord, sir, telling him of the Queen's army which is being assembled and will soon be bound for Ireland,' she had said, which had produced a silence.

'You know only too well why I am here, mistress. A life for a life.. although no life can properly replace that of the Lady Medb.'

Bowing her head, immobile with fear, she had breathed deeply, and then fixed her gaze upon him.

'Sir, it was not my intention that your noble relative should die. A foreign guard panicked, afraid of her curses and none of us knew who she was. I am sorry – I am truly sorry.'

Walter repeated this twice with more words than she thought she had said. Redmond had then leaned forward and his horse had become suddenly restive. He almost spat at her,

'You had no right to take up the Stranger who is my wife, Lady Gile MacFeagh, and under my protection.'

'She told me she wished to return to her family and had been kidnapped. What would you have had me do, if one of your women had stopped you and said such a thing? I'm surprised you married one so unwilling and homesick.'

'Who I marry is not your concern, woman! You Settlers offered me a marriage, but only to an idle Scottish woman from a class of impoverished low-born adventurers. Lady Gile is young and has foolish imaginings. She was probably tired of the journey to the coast. You should not have concerned yourself.'

There had been further silence broken only by the snorting horses, until he had snarled, with his hand on his great sword, 'Now give me Lady Gile! We will also have Lady Medb's murderer.'

She had noticed that his eyes searched the upper casements for movement, and his escort were alertly observing the courtyard and beyond. Deciding to be more conciliatory, she had told him calmly that Susannah was not at Hurst Place, neither was the Fleming who had panicked at the curses and that Susannah was now with Sir Rowland Porter for safe-keeping.

'I can understand you wishing to wed her as the Dutch woman is beautiful and has the looks and speech of quality.' She then challenged, 'Is it true she was kidnapped? I do wonder, and Thomas will wonder too, how she came to be with you – please enlighten me. If you wish to kill or kidnap a defenceless woman, then do so with me – but at your peril of reprisal.'

'Why should I believe that neither Lady Gile nor the Fleming are here?'

Walter had then said that 'your spy in this house' would say truly, and went to fetch Nuala who came out nervously and confirmed that neither Gile nor the Fleming were inside.

Alice had then said, in as confident a voice as she could muster.

'The guard has fled, both from our punishment and yours. He was a hired soldier anyway- not one of Thomas's garrison. If you can find him – you can have him and do what you will. His name is Jan Rijten. He is probably trying to get to the coast.'

She had nodded assent when Walter said 'You, sir, and your men must have travelled for a long time with few stops and must be both hungry and thirsty.'

There had been a long tense silence.

'Let Nuala bring your cakes and ale, mistress,' Redmond then spoke in lilting English, 'but out here. I will not enter this murdering house.'

Nuala and another servant had fearfully brought out round large trays of pastries, bread, cheese and jugs of ale.

Redmond had then said to Walter, 'Send Nuala back to her father.'

The Irishmen had not dismounted and Redmond had rudely requested that she and Walter to try each of the flagons and dishes first. The men then ate and drank in silence. Alice frowned as she remembered the implication of poisoning, and the way they, replete, threw her vessels on to the ground and any remaining food at the dogs. At the time she had not commented but had tried to look composed, wishing heartily that they would soon depart. She had lied firmly and convincingly, hoping he would not know Thomas's whereabouts exactly.

'Thomas is now travelling home with a large contingent of mercenaries as troops are being mobilised across the country because of the Spanish fleet said to be approaching. They have no compunction, as you now know, and will be paid on his return. If harm befalls his demesne, Hurst Place or any person here, I have no doubt there will be hangings and severe reprisals. Let us all hope he arrives safely and finds us all well.'

Glaring at her, Redmond had then wheeled his horse around and signalled to his escort,saying fiercely in English,

'Know, mistress, that the Lady Medb had powers beyond your understanding, such as the gift of prophecy. Her geis will stand. One day Thomas and all that he owns will be destroyed.'

Alice had countered loudly to their rapidly disappearing backs, 'A hard winter is looming. If trade and food supplies are disrupted by rebellion, there will be famine.'

Pushing away these disturbing memories, Alice fell into a restless sleep.

*

In the driving rain and semi-darkness, Orlaith knelt in the blood around Medb and gently closed her eyes and kissed those cheeks, whose once sharp planes were weathered by age. She ululated and wept at the waste of life, at all the losses in the past and likely in the future. In time, kind hands lifted her and half-carried her with Medb's body to a forest glade, where a bier was contrived. The next day, they slowly made their way through their town lands, gathering mourners as they went. Redmond and Fintan had hurried to join them, Father Ignatius intoning Masses all the way up a high hill. On this stood three standing stones, one propped on the others as a roof, and the ruins of an old religious house, which contained the bones of many of their folk. Such strange happenings had been known to take place here over time that even armed English soldiers in victory had left it alone. One by one, each mourner put a stone they had picked from the slope, on the bier until the Lady Medb was completely covered.

Orlaith wept and remembered. She stood, head bowed, counting the ways in which Medb had supported her. First, Medb had badgered those of her kin who had fought with the Crown, and were later struck with guilt at the decimation of the Irish gentry, to pay compensation to the Emperor's bishops for her release. Then, she had encouraged her not to feel shame when she came back with Niko. Then, she had arranged her marriage to her son Fergus. Orlaith grieved again for Fergus who had loved her. She was grateful that he had never reproached her and had been kind to Niko. She remembered how her husband had re-lived his anguish many times at Lord Grey De Wilton's decision to execute all his male kin but not him. Lord Grey had told Medb harshly that her youngest son would soon be dead from his wasting illness and he would not spare his suffering. She remembered Medb telling her that Eithne's murder had destroyed a part of Redmond's heart.

Orlaith's people finally slowly led her, haltingly, away from the place of the ancestors.

Oonagh said to her quietly in the castle later, 'Some are asking why our Medb had made such a great 'geis', rarely uttered. I told them that the Lady's mind had been slowly failing for some time, and she lived much in the past, but Orlaith, there is more that can be said perhaps?'

'Remind our folk that Medb thought that Gile had the body of a woman, but the mind of a spirit that could cause good or evil, and therefore needed constantly to be placated. When Gile fled to that small guarded English convoy, she thought that Gile had decided to turn a malign influence against us. The only way she knew to try to prevent this was to summon the Morrigu – a greater power but sadly unpredictable in its manifestation.'

In the days after Medb's death, the rain stopped, but a heavy grey ash fell over the land, covering her cairn on the high ancient abbey ruins and its dolmen. Other wonders were reported. Hailstones as big as pebbles battered the cabins and a strange pale green mist bathed her grave for many days. News of the Irish noblewoman's casual murder spread like a foul wind through the country, as did her great curse. A formal protest was sent to the Lord Deputy from the discontented southern Earls, whilst the rebels in the north were gleeful at this fuel on the fire of their rebellion.

After the burial, whilst Redmond and others went to Hurst Place, those of the clan, including Orlaith, who had not continued to the coast, rode back to the stronghold. Strong westerly winds whipped their faces whilst flurries of heavy rain soaked their heavy cloaks. Everyone grieved, numb and angry by turns, not least at Gile's betrayal of Redmond and their hospitality. They passed the friars, kneeling at the Place of the Cross, Ignatius with his crucifix held high towards the mountains, praying for Medb's soul as he had done each day since she was killed.

He had comforted Redmond and Orlaith, 'Although she believed in the Old Ones, I pray continually that our Lord will hold her in his bosom now.'

Discipline in the sept had never been maintained by the lash. Living always at close quarters, the folk and the fighting men's actions were never unobserved, so that behaviours of all kinds could be commented upon or dealt with. Redmond's men remonstrated with their leader as soon as they had put some leagues between them and the Hurst desmesne. They denounced Alice as full of guile, grumbling that all of them should have taken firmer action. Redmond was aware that he had been uncertain how to handle this Englishwoman.

After hearing their views, Redmond had spoken, bowing his head sadly.

'You must know the shame I feel since hearing that my wife deserted our people travelling the south road -and my shame at the killing of our noble Lady. We said Masses but you have all seen her in trances, and know that she belonged to our past. She can never be erased or forgotten, whatever the friars will do or say, either now, or in a future of which we have no knowledge. We sometimes looked with amusement at what we called her "antics". Her actions will now shape our lives. You know that she summoned the Morrigu – the Morrigu, the powerful primordial triple goddess from our myths. You saw the violence of the storm at her dying and the ashes our ancestors strewed on the land. The Morrigu now hovers over us.'

'She urges war,' said Ronan. 'As loyal vassals, we must all, even the churls, leave our kin and go to war if our Overlord hears her call.'

There was some whooping at his words, but another asked, 'Does she also hover over the Spanish or the Catholic French so that they will help us?'

'You know that Spain has no great love for the English,' said Redmond, 'and The O'Neill woos them, and the Holy Father too, in the battle against heretics.'

'Father Ignatius says that if we go to war, our immortal souls remain safe as we fight heresy as well as men,' said Ronan.

'We are doubly blessed by the Holy Mother Church and by the old Gods. Remember the words of our Lady Medb who believed that we are merely on a ceaseless journey, that our deaths are just a change of place to another world and that we will join our loved ones again in the land of Tir-Na-Nog,' replied Redmond, his eyes distant.

'The season is stormy. The Spanish may yet turn back their fleet, if they have not already done so. And Niko says Earl Tyrone cares more for his herds and his hunting than he does his God!' muttered Fintan who was always irritated when Redmond became somewhat visionary.

Redmond turned to Ronan, saying, 'When Niko has made contact with Gile's kin, he was going south for the winter, from Le Havre towards Portugal to trade. He will send me cyphered messages at the way stations. You may be too late to find Niko and his men. If you can, make sure they know of the Lady Medb's killing. Tell him the southern barons will be gathering after the snows, and that Fintan will accompany me. Tell him to stay south until the Spring and await further news. When you return, go straight to Phelim – our contact at the Constable Porter's castle – find our what you can about Lady Gile and also try to intercept and send on any plots, messages or letters which tell of English troop transports or Spanish fleets arriving. Then go to Dublin for the rest of the winter and seek our people with skills in sabotage. Should it come to it, we will be ready to give invading ships a welcome they will not forget. Speak to the Jewish traders – they know everything and suffer under the Old Queen's yoke too.'

As they prepared to ride on, Redmond looked at his uncle Fintan, proud that he always rode fearlessly, his neck and shoulders thick and strong, jumping and galloping more skillfully and bravely than all the others.

'It is good that I accompany you to the Gathering,' said Fintan, nodding.

Redmond grinned and then raised his voice.

'Be damned to the arrogant English. A time will come when Medb will indeed be avenged.'

At the stronghold, not wanting to be alone, Orlaith went to Fintan's cabin, sat by the hearth and shared their bread and beef. Eating rapidly, her mouth stuffed, Oonagh nodded, then put her platter down with finality. Orlaith ate little.

'In spite of this and Feagh O'Byrne's killing, I doubt if the south will join the northern Earls,' said Oonagh.

'Nothing is certain as yet. We may know more after the Gathering of the southern sept barons after the snows.'

'What do you think now, Orlaith?' asked Oonagh.

'My mind churns after Medb's murder and my heart is full of anger. They think that because we quarrel with those that betray us or trespass on our lands, that we are like dogs that fight for supremacy.' She was silent for a while until the hound sitting beside her panted loudly for some petting, then laid its large head in her lap.

'Tyrone is powerful,' said Oonagh. 'He dresses like the English in velvet and gold lace.'

Orlaith replied, 'He tries to make terms. He can commandeer a large army. He has been training his men in English battle methods. He knows his enemy. He could bring them to their knees – or at least hold the north with the O'Donnell for Irish governance. Earl Ormonde here in the south is for the English Queen, although I hear that, to his embarrassment, some of his nephews are close to the rebels.'

'Earl Tyrone wants to be king of all Ireland rather than just Lord of Ulster! No doubt, Earl Ormonde would rather be the King!' said Oonagh.

'Earl Ormonde does well out of his loyalty to the English Crown. And he is on good terms with our Thomas Hurst,' replied Orlaith. 'That man Hurst will live to regret his sister's hasty action! I heard no ill of Alice Plymmiswoode until now. It seems she does not condescend, when our people visit with goods, or when they introduce new servants. She agrees that Thomas's catamite steward Walter should allow their servants and retainers to visit their families on Holy Days.'

Oonagh shook her head sadly.

'It was Redmond's strange wife, Gile, who Medb called Murna, that caused Medb's death rather than Mistress Alice, I am sure of it. Try as I might, I could not warm to her. Even Redmond eventually tired of her sulking ways. I'll wager that on that terrible day, Gile cast a spell on Mistress Alice. You know, of course, that many of our people who work at Hurst Place have left there?'

Orlaith got up to leave, followed by the hound, saying, 'We do not rightly know what happened. I agree that Gile – she is young – never settled well with us or accepted our ways. I doubt if she was aware of the consequences of her actions. Alice may have ordered the guard to spear Medb, we do not rightly know.'

'The Morrigu was summoned.' Oonagh called as Orlaith went out of the door. 'Some say that Lady Medb grew an ell or more whilst cursing. I'll tell the women to prepare stores and put them where they cannot be pillaged.'

CHAPTER EIGHT

The loss of their loved ones, their fine ship and their valuable cargo, hung like a pall over Susannah's kin and and those in their worksheds all that year. One day, early in that hard winter, Susannah's uncle-in-law and his factor Pieter Heyden met in a lofty town house along the canal in Amsterdam. Wrapped in furs, the two sat close to the fire. De Hem had a bony frame, a thin face with a pointed beard. His robe was brightened with several long gold chains. He pressed his seal, carved from a large emerald and attached to a gold fob, on a number of documents and handed over the pouch to his plainly dressed secretary.

'I understand M.Breydel kept much of his business in his head and mind, and which orders he had fulfilled and which not, is still coming to light,' said Pieter.

'Yes, the disentangling of Hendrik's affairs is slow and difficult,' said the older man. 'Our losses in the Irish seas were significant. We must be given time to pay any dues. Speak further with the creditors. We must also seek new markets.'

De Hem looked into the fire.

'I must tell you that it seems my niece is most likely alive. God be thanked. An English Official in Dublin has informed me that she, and she alone, was rescued on an Irish shore by a local baron and, also, that he has wed her before a priest! I do not know if their gentry have the rank of ours. Poor Susannah cannot easily follow our Faith now. It will be discovered by many that she is married to a Catholic. This might affect our trades.'

Too stunned to reply at first, Pieter eventually muttered, 'It is good that she is not dishonoured. I too thank the Lord that she lives. Her fate now is in His hands.'

The previous year, M. Christian Calvet, who had recently opened a cloth-finishing workshop in London, had visited the Breydels in Leiden. He saw and examined some of Susannah's weaving and her brocade designs, and had then asked for her hand in marriage, wishing to ally his business with that of her family. He said that everyone would gain because Susannah's talent and skills could be used to train his workers and that both firms would gain a wider market for their wares. Hendrik Breydel and Andreas De Hem finally agreed to a handfasting, but a delay to the wedding until Susannah had completed outstanding orders.

Pieter was a man not easily fired with emotion, but had felt a particular grief since the shipwreck. He had met Susannah Breydel many times in her short life, at preachings, Thanksgivings and Feastdays. He knew that her fair countenance and shy smile would be forever lodged in his heart. He had not dared asked for a betrothal, knowing the family would reject a husband of his rank and limited means. They may even have dismissed him for presumption.

He thought savagely, 'At least she is not now to wed that sly old Walloon widower who would never have made her happy. I did point out, but was ignored, that Calvet had been implicated in brutal assassinations of Catholics, which is probably why he went to England. I had also heard in Antwerp that his products had been of poor quality and he barely traded at a profit. Now my life's love is wed to a savage Irish Catholic.'

But he said to M. De Hem, 'She is a pious maid and it seems she has been chosen by God to stay in this world. I'm surprised that she agreed to marry the Irish baron, after the handfasting vows.'

'Well, as you know, that match can no longer be. Calvet, thinking her dead, has wed another. He and Susannah must answer for their decisions at Heaven's Gate.'

Pieter nodded agreement and then queried, 'You are aware that Calvet still pursues you for his betrothal expenses, even though his new wife has brought him valuable orders from her dead husband's London business, and even though M. Breydel is now by Our Lord's side ?'

'Yes! And I've heard that he has a stepson, Edward, who now works with him. I've refused to pay them anything, so waste no more time on correspondence. As well as Calvet's demands, that English Official requested - angel coins or our Dutch royals - for his Constable's safeguarding of Susannah. I do not understand this – why is she not living with the Lord who married her?'

Pieter raised his eyebrows, 'perhaps it was for her safety. The country is unsettled.'

After a pause, De Hem said, 'If the Ulster war spreads south, which my messenger says is very likely, could the Irish prevail, do you think?'

'I am told they are a warlike people, much given to raiding amongst themselves. Also, unlike a foreign army, they know their terrain.'

'I think that Queen Elizabeth will inevitably conquer, fired as she is by her desire to rid the island of Popery,' said De Hem. 'But it is not so long since the Spanish Armada was destroyed and Spain will want revenge.' He thought for a moment. 'As you know, Susannah is the only one of Hendrik's children left as her brothers were killed in the wars in France. My wife says that grief over her losses has made Susannah's mother care little for herself and, already ill, she pines and keeps to her bed. We need my niece returned to us – her designs are in demand and we have no comparable new styles. Already we are losing orders. The baron may let her go if offered enough- or at least allow her to return to see her mother.' He looked decisively at Pieter.' Now- I have word that an Irish envoy, one Niko MacFeagh, seeks Susannah's kin and is lodging in Le Havre at St.Francois. Seek him, and, if necessary, you may tell him that we will consider a handsome dowry- remember that we must not be compromised- and providing that Susannah is returned to us safe and well, even if only for a long visit. Also send a note to the English Official enquiring why she is not with her husband. In return for some trade introductions, we could consider honouring any debt their Crown think is due.'

He dismissed Pieter with a wave of his hand.

'We will take our time in giving out our gold. Much may change. We do not know everything there is to know.'

Pieter bowed and prepared to leave. M. De Hem called after him

'God be with you and aid your mission.'

It was a cold but fine and clear morning when Niko took his usual stroll along the harbour wall in Le Havre. He stopped to watch the mist rolling back from the sea. White-bellied gulls wheeled and wailed above the incoming boats and the noisy crowd on the shore further down. From the corner of his eye, he then noticed a tall man with sword and buckler across his chest, wearing a black hat of continental style, plain black doublet and polished leather boots, walking swiftly towards him. Niko turned warily and waited. Pieter Heyden, making a slight bow, introduced himself in French as an emissary from the Company Breydel, cloth finishers and fine weavers, now known as Company De Hem and owned by Susannah's uncle by marriage. Heyden then, unsmiling, gave tokens of his authenticity. Niko showed him Gile's betrothal ring, then suggesting that they breakfast at a nearby inn.

'We know Susannah now as Lady Gile MacFeagh. She was given this name as she was too ill to say her name at first.'

'We thought all had perished,' Pieter said heavily, as they walked along the harbour wall. The two men crossed themselves. 'When we learned she was alive, I was sent by her kin to find her. Is it true that she is now wed ? This surprises us as she knew she was already handfasted before God.'

'Which woman of sense would turn away a scion of an ancient Irish Barony? We had had no claim for her from any Betrothed, and until your message, no-one contacted us to ascertain her fate.'

'Well, her Betrothed believed her dead. He has quickly married another. It seems that his new wife, Margery, a widow, was already well-known and successful in London's cloth-working districts, which no doubt spurred him on.'

Niko called for ale. Pieter continued,

'The Company Breydel lost much when that ship went down

in those fatal fogs. We pray night and day that those Calvinist Chosen Ones will be by the Lord's side and for the departed souls of the other drowned Protestants.'

They made general conversation as they ate, after which Pieter wiped his mouth and hands ensuring no trace of food remained either on the thin line of his moustache or his clean linen cuffs. Dermot and Conor sat in a corner where the shafts of sunlight from the mullioned windows and the open door had not penetrated. At a nod from Niko, they departed quietly leaving a smell of peat in their wake. Pieter wrinkled his nose, looked sardonically at Niko, and returned to his meal. After a pause, he said,

'Is it true that her -' he blenched - 'Susannah's husband is a Papist?'

Niko looked up from his trencher, his eyebrows raised and nodded affirmatively.

'But you must know that her family are staunchly Protestant, and this distresses them. When she was not working, her only study was *le Divinite*. Her family are Lutheran , but she leans towards the Calvinist persuasion.'

'Indeed', replied Niko, impassively. 'Gile – Susannah – also prays constantly for the souls of those she has lost. So you know her personally?'

'I have had that honour and attended her at preachings on the Sabbath on many occasions. As you no doubt know, she is youthful and beauteous. In Holland, she is known as modest and skilled at the design of brocades and the weaving of damasks and satins. Her work was sought by nobles in the Low Countries and indeed France.'

Pieter frowned as Niko said, 'Lord Redmond has not insisted on the rituals of the Mass, and she worships in her own way. But we do not seek out preachers of her persuasion.'

'You could have done – to ease her mind. The English would have directed you to a pastor.' He sighed. 'There were several such drowned with Hendrik Breydel – transported at our charge at Queen Elizabeth's request to reinforce the most righteous path in Britain.'

Niko was irritated at this smug, dapper nobody who presumed that only those following the Protestant Faith were chosen to understand the fundamental mysteries of life and spirit.

He said, looking hard at Pieter, 'Gile was the only one who survived on our shores. Let me be frank. We both know that God, in his mercy, has seen fit to save <u>her</u>, but not the preachers. Perhaps it was God's Will that they perished. Such terrible fogs do not occur often in our land.'

Pieter banged down his tankard.

'It is surely God's Will that the pernicious rituals of the priests from Rome be abandoned!'

'The preachers that have been sent so far to Ireland are uncouth. They demand alms from those with nothing to give, and they, unlike our friars, leer at or waylay our women. The churls say they tell of damnation and not Grace. Few try to learn our tongue. It has been difficult to talk to Gile because she does not try to study Gaelic, the language of our people.'

Pieter's lips tightened, thinking that it was understandable she would not want to learn a savage tongue. He noticed that Niko had a strange charm or badge hung on his doublet and that, although saying he was brother to the Irish Lord, he was dun-coloured and Moorish in appearance.

'Well' said Niko smoothly. 'You must agree that interpretations of the Holy Book should be justly disputed by our learned men.'

Pieter breathed heavily, then saying, 'In much of the Empire and indeed Britannia, your words and even we here discussing the scriptures, could lead to accusations of heresy.'

Then, calming, he pushed his trencher away.

'However, it is right that the religious conflicts in the world, which cause and have caused so much suffering should be resolved.'

Niko said, 'Most Irish people in their hearts have not accepted Old King Henry's desecration of our Holy Mother Church. This is one of the roots of our continuing conflict with the Crown. However that may be, Lord Redmond, knowing our country is unsafe, would rather Gile – Susannah – be cared for amongst her kin until the war in the north of our country is settled. She also wishes to be once again with her mother and will no doubt return to the worship in which she was raised.'

The Dutchman was pleased at these words. He had decided that, from his manners, dress and forms of speech, this envoy was civilised and diplomatic. Although his attire was unusual, he carried a rapier and sash and was not the ill-educated Popish savage that he had expected. However he was unsure whether he could trust him to keep to any agreement.

He said, 'The insurrection is why *Susannah* – kindly use her given name – is not with her husband at present? I hear that she is in the household of the Crown's Constable in Dublin.'

Niko was confused at this piece of information. He wondered if Orlaith, or Redmond, had sent her away and became concerned that their winter lodgings may have been under attack.

But he said, 'Be reassured that Susannah has been tended and honoured since her rescue. It must be that her husband sent her to the Constable, fearing for her safety as the war is gathering pace.'

After further conversation, they discussed terms of a dowry or compensation for Redmond, Niko unsuccessfully trying to insist on an advance payment. Pieter was vague about at which point, as he said pointedly, a 'ransom' could be made.

'There are a multitude of spies in the pay of Queen Elizabeth who could find out we are paying out to one whose Overlord could rebel against her authority.'

They agreed to meet in Calais as soon as practicable, with Niko to escort Susannah.

Niko warned, 'The Crown, of course, may wish to keep Susannah as hostage to be assured of Lord Redmond's loyalty, so I cannot guarantee when I will be able to return with her. However, now, as a gift from her husband for her kin, I have brought salt, brandowine, and a bale of linen frieze for finishing.'

Pieter Heyden nodded his thanks, giving a small bow before they parted.

Later, Niko asked Dermot and Conor if they had heard of any attack on Castle MacFeagh or their people lodging at the coast.

'No – why so?'

'Well, Lady Gile is with Constable Porter for some reason. Dermot - investigate and also take this letter to Redmond and then return if you can'. Your journeys will not be easy as the winter promises much unrelenting hardship across Europe.'

To My Brother

I have been in contact with an emissary from Gile's kin, a Pieter Heyden. He is a factor or secretary to her uncle, a M. De Hem, a partner with Gile's father in the business of cloth design and finishing. You will be interested to know that the man to whom Gile says she is handfasted is now wed to another! Heyden received your gifts gracefully as a sign of your kinship now with them, but it seems that their Protestant Company does little trade with Spain, most with Northern France and within the Dutch Republic. He is wary of the conflict with the Crown in Ireland. Heyden says that the religious wars in his land have, until recently, created many trading problems. He said the shipwreck led to great losses. As Lutherans- even perhaps Calvinists- it is doubtful whether they would support us if the rebellion escalated. Heyden said that any marriage portion they might give – he would pay nothing now – may depend on you agreeing to have, in our midst, a missionary Protestant preacher! So – we may end up with little gold or benefit for our pains. I therefore wonder whether we should waste any more time on this venture, especially as he told me that Gile is now with Constable Porter for some reason. If you no longer want her, why not leave her with the Crown and let them have the expense of sending her home? I have heard that the storms in the Irish seas turned back the Spanish fleet. This may also delay Dermot. I shall now travel south for the rest of the winter. I will gauge further the commitment of Spain to the Earl of Tyrone should an army invade.

My respects to our dear mother.

Winter 1597 and Spring 1598

Dermot rolled Niko's letter in the hilt of his dagger and departed. He could not cross the sea until the storms abated and then, the rest of the year and the following months, turned out to be long and harsh. Lashing storms and freezing rain followed by snow-drifts and icy roads prevented most journeys. When he was able to travel, jaunty, lithe, long-limbed Dermot could not resist stealing a horse from another clan, running the gauntlet of mercenaries, and an English guardpost and seducing a maid he had met selling ale the summer past. From her he heard about the killing of the Lady Medb. Wandering troops then further impeded and delayed him. He was forced to shelter in hillside caverns, sleeping in the fleece of a dead sheep he had skinned, only emerging to trap food, break ice and let his horse forage where it could, until breaks in the weather allowed him to slowly continue. He arrived at the stronghold in early Spring. Once sighted, ill and almost falling from his horse, Dermot was escorted to the castle. On a pallet, placed by the hearth in the tower, he pushed away the broth Oonagh was trying to spoon into him.

'Orlaith, his eyes roll!' said Oonagh. 'Pray God he does not perish!'

'Dermot – listen to me!' said Orlaith urgently into his ear. 'Redmond has not yet come back here. Travel is difficult. We have had no word, but I believe he is talking with other vassal Chiefs. How is Niko? Is he well? What message did he give you?'

'Orlaith, he does not hear us!' said Oonagh, Dermot's sister, crossing herself and murmuring prayers. 'His head is as hot as the embers in our fire pits, and he looks like death itself warmed up to speak to us!'

Lifting himself, Dermot tried to reach for his dagger, but shook his head and fainted. By then, another fever, incubated in Ulster, was fanning rapidly outwards – that of war.

CHAPTER NINE

oon after her uncomfortable audience with Sir Rowland, Alice had asked for the Dutch girl to be summoned to her quarters. It was the first time she had seen her since arriving at the Constable's castle. Alice had been given chambers in a tower at the end of a long draughty gallery inhabited by lurking servants. Lurid murals depicting mystical and classical images decorated its walls.

Susannah had stood near the fireplace examining the naturalistic carvings on its surround, turning as Alice walked in. Alice sat and plucked at a tray of almond tarts and preserved fruits. A white starched cambric ruff and a string of well-matched pearls, smaller versions of which edged her headpiece, accented her black fine-wool dress. Susannah gazed at her. She did not curtsey. Her silver hair framed a decorous folded linen cap. She suddenly pulled her chain with its sparkling cross from underneath her bodice, and placed it deliberately on her breast.

She is not a noble lady, her dress is of the guild and merchant or middling rank. She seems passing wealthy – like my kin – as she wears good cloth and jewels…. whilst, I, at least of her rank, must be arrayed in an undyed linen skirt and jacket, as if I were but a rough countrywoman! At my remonstrances I was at least given a coarse indigo shawl. And then they swathed my pattens, Irish fashion, in frieze up to my ankles. They think me lowly but I am no peasant….

Alice regarded her also, thinking,' I wonder why Redmond rescued such a poor sickly thing. She does not look strong enough to work! He had not even known whether there would be any compensation for her rescue, and he has given her that jewel. I suppose he was attracted by her pale beauty, although this is not very evident today. She has some unsightly pimples on her nose and cheek- but I am told they are not plaguey.'

She pointed at the dish of sweetmeats. 'Take one of these, Susannah.'

The young woman moved forward suddenly and took two tarts, pushing them into her mouth with her fist. Alice stared at her until Susannah blushed hotly and then hung her head.

I thank my God that the retching in the mornings has abated. The water I was given could not have been from a Holy Well, such as that drawn for Redmond's castle. This sweet food heals me and warms my stomach. But she angers. The sin of pride in my beauty will be my undoing…

She said quickly and heatedly in French,

'God bless you Mistress for coming to my aid. I have been too long amongst those savages. They make no obeisance to each other, or to me, and nor do they show their leaders many outward forms of respect.'

Alice inclined her head.

'It is true that they do not acknowledge that nobles and kings are touched with the Divine.'

Susannah then continued, speaking so fast that Alice could barely follow her tirade about Redmond and his people.

'There is little Godly about Redmond or his lieutenants. They choose brutes for their leaders. How they could call a "Lady" one who had been concubine to a heathen Moor! And this Orlaith commands the churls! How could they countenance or trust and love the warrior Niko, spawn of her heathen paramour, who also commands. Yet another Commander has no legs and a hog of a wife.'

Alice inwardly smiled, thinking that she would never have thought of tall, intriguing Niko as 'spawn'. She thought of him more as a consummate diplomat and appreciated his skills. As a woman of business, she was cynically aware of the respect accorded to incompetent men and profligate women, who had been advanced in life purely by an accident of birth.

She looks like a magpie in her black and white and with her fat bosom and her glances that dart round and about. Her cap does not become her. But God was with us both when she let me travel with her that day. She smiles though. What does she want? What will she want? She is not shocked at my speech that bursts out like a dammed stream... I must not be intemperate... am I lost to a civilised life forever?

Alice gestured to Susannah to drink and eat more fruits and sweetmeats, and then sat, silently wishing she had been able to see Thomas before coming to Dublin. Currently he had been even further embroiled in civil administration, political negotiation and dealings with the Queen's spies.

She and Thomas were both, at times, sceptical about how the world should be ordered recognising the many sins, not least cupidity, corruption, envy and bigotry, which swirled around them as they carried out their duties.

She sighed. Thomas's political preoccupations meant that she had been taking on more supervision of his farms and contracts. Now, for the moment, she had to leave all these matters to Walter, and to trust him to be loyal and capable.

'Tell me about your sojourn with the Sept MacFeagh. I did hear that his kinsman Fintan MacFeagh has a better claim to be chief than Redmond. Did you know him? Were they close?'

'I know nothing of this. Redmond <u>was</u> close to his foster-brother Niko. He was the only one who spoke my tongue - but crudely.'

Alice nodded. 'I remember Niko MacFeagh from his visits to my brother's mansion. He wore civilised dress.' She was thinking, with a frisson of lust, 'I should not muse upon his tall frame, clear visage and fine leg.'

She may call it civilised but it was but a clashing motley of looted garments.. but, Mon Dieu, those peoples' clothes, those savage clothes of frieze and serge wool... shapeless for women and tied around the men in bundles as mere repositories for their many tools and weapons. I was fair frighted by such garments, and those great hounds that roamed the woods and courtyards. The hound belonging to the one with Redmond's scowling squire would race towards me and stop just before at a com-

mand from his master. Niko hated me too – I could tell from his stone face and the gravel in his voice. They were all jealous… jealous that I belonged to Redmond…

'I have spoken with Niko MacFeagh.' continued Alice, 'But I have rarely met Chief Redmond. I know that as a young man he spent time in Dublin as a hostage. Sir Rowland is afraid that he will rebel if his Overlord commands him. His Overlord is from one of the old Irish families who often flout the Queen's law. Tell me, do you know if Redmond had bitterness towards the Crown in his heart?'

Susannah shrugged.

'I know he had little love for the English. Fintan was an old lieutenant with a big pock-marked face. Although grievously injured, he followed Redmond and he and his horse were one. He was ever armed. Fintan's wife is a vast strong woman, to whom the children flock.'

'Do you think Redmond and Niko will rise against the Crown?'

'No-one talked to me of rebellion. But I moved amongst those savages but little. I would not trust them mistress. I had no wish to learn their barbarous tongue. Redmond knew English but I know little. I have no facility with foreign tongues. I was tricked into a blessing with Redmond, who then said we were wed.'

'You were wed in the eyes of God - by a priest? A Catholic Priest?' enquired Alice sharply.

I was in extremis after being trailed across the cliffs. I could not gainsay Redmond. The so-called Father wore a priestly robe but was shabby. His speech was Gaelic except for the Latin of the Service. I know he blessed me, blessed us both…surely I cannot be wed to that savage who took my maidenhood. I was already handfasted! I shall repudiate my marriage and continue my prayers for forgiveness…

'I did not accept the Host, but we were blessed in chapel by a man Redmond called "Father", but I am still betrothed before God to Monsieur Christian Calvet, a Walloon with a Company in the cloth trade in London.'

'Betrothed? I cannot hear you well,' said Alice, leaning forward. 'Speak up.'

'Aye. I was schooled as a craftswoman for my father's Company – Breydel and De Hem. They aspire to the merchant class in Leiden, Ghent and Amsterdam.' Gile's voice rose and became imperious. 'I was to have been of use in guiding the use of the damask and broidered brocades to help M. Calvet develop trade in Britain and gain entry to a weaving guild. It is my desire now to be returned to him in London or to my kin in Leiden.'

Having never heard of Christian Calvet, or Breydel and De Hem, but interested that Susannah was married to Redmond, the Lord of an Irish Barony, Alice stood up decidedly.

'It may be that if you are wed, you must return to your husband.'

Gile gasped and began to weep.

'You may well weep, but a woman has been killed because of you and your actions have given rise to much disturbance in this county. But, for the moment, we will seek your kin.'

She says I caused the death of that witch... the Lord was guiding me against the Devil. I can smell her savage smell now. Jan Rijten said there was no blood. Deliver me now Lord, against worldliness and from all evil. The Lord punished us in heading for Cork that day instead of the usual ports of call to London from Bordeaux. They all wanted to make profits by bartering salt and wines for frieze and timber. Those southern rocks proved fatal to their enterprise. Would that I had demurred... but I was like to be sick with the motion of the seas. The Lord had visited my father with success but his acceptance of the accoutrements of wealth brought him divine punishment...

After Susannah had recovered herself, Alice said, turning to the servant waiting by the door,

'You must now show me your skills to help me trust you and your strange story. You must embroider gloves and other accessories I will have sent to you. You may leave the maids' quarters during the day.'

'I am skilled with the loom also, mistress.'

'Well then, you may guide the setting of a loom in the solar chamber near to mine and choose some patterns and threads. You may alter the patterns if you wish. Now you may go and begin your labours.'

Susannah lowered her eyes, said nothing, but curtseyed and

left with the servant.

Over the next weeks, the Dutch woman became increasingly strange, seeming barely aware of her surroundings and having to be forced away from her loom, sewing or her prayer book. She only reluctantly conversed with anyone and began to eat and drink voraciously. The servants were convinced she was losing her wits or had been invaded by a incubus.[2] She kept asking for water from a Holy Well. Tension in the household increased.

I must rise from this hard stool. I have worked here since the morning brightened, and have spoken to no-one. I have a tray with rush lights, bread, soft cheese and small ale. The loom fills this narrow chamber, un-lined by wood panels, across the stairway from Mistress Alice's apart-ments... her tones can be harsh and haughty. There is some heat from the kitchens far below, and shafts of sunshine cross the walls but the cold entered my bones until I begged for my good Irish cloak. This chamber has sunlight from the opening in its walls but is sadly unlike the fine weaving room in my family's townhouse which had padded stools and tall windows full of southern light. Would that Niko MacFeagh or Mis-tress Alice soon find my people! I see the little birds swoop and dive or race from one perch to another... would that I could fly hence... I would be one of those little birds. I told Orlaith, speaking slowly but I doubt she understood, that I have been in the presence of many a Milord and Lady, and other well-born, when they have received our fine work. We lodged in a humble quarter of their chateaux or in the country mansions of the Milords' acquaintance. So many of the nobility and their Ladies will remember me and my work. I must recover my place in the world in which I was born, working for the betterment of my father, and in time, to work for the betterment of husband Calvet. They all wish to buy or commission from us, the Breydels, all the fine clothes and accessories. My father said some were arrogant in their Faith which would be their undoing... but it was him who was undone. He so loved to adorn... was that such a sin? Last night I dreamed he was beside me, weaker, frailer, but still there with the weeds around his face touching mine. Then I saw him hovering lightly above the rocks and vanishing into mist... he was calling to me. How Our Lord tests me...

Over much of the winter, the roads were not passable, but at last Alice did receive some letters from Thomas in Hurst Place and also from other friends and family in London. Just before Christmastide, she was granted an audience with Sir Rowland.

'Thomas writes that the Earl of Tyrone had broken agreements and treaties yet again and is preparing to continue campaigning against the Crown in the spring. He is still seeking the support of the southern Chiefs, who profess loyalty, but who are also entertaining Tyrone's envoys.'

'You have said nothing that I do not already know,' Sir Rowland had replied irritably, his table piled high with large documents. He rose and stood by a tall thickly glazed window. 'And it is a pity that the Hollander woman has little of interest regarding rebel plans to tell us. If and when Her Gracious Majesty allows the Earl of Essex to bring an army here, Tyrone will know who is master. As for Susannah – it is true that she is niece to the Dutch cloth trader and finisher called De Hem. He wants her sent back to the Netherlands, even if only for a visit. It would be best to obtain Chief Redmond's permission for this. So far he has not demanded her return. No doubt he remains angry at the death of Lady Medb MacFeagh and her death may be demanded. I have requested Thomas to summon him, ask about Susannah Breydel, and parley with his commanders. The Clans and their septs must not be provoked into further rebellion. And no - I cannot agree for you to travel to Leinster or give you an escort at present with the snows and desperate folk at the walls and on the ways.'

He was about to dismiss her when she produced a parcel wrapped in pale silk, from a large reticule attached to her girdle. Smoothing her elaborate dress and then making a deep curtsey, she moved across the room and held the parcel out to him, saying, 'Forgive me my unwise actions, Sir Rowland. I have a Christmastide gift for you by way of recompense. Susannah was schooled since her early years as a craftswoman in her uncle's business, and can embroider, weave silk damask and design brocade patterns. It is clear, from the work that I have seen, that she has remarkable 'broidering skills. I also marvelled at the careful design of the foliage and figures in my own tapestry and the unusual threads she chose.'

Sir Rowland raised his eyebrows, opened the parcel and found soft kid leather gauntlets exquisitely sewn with pearls and gold thread.

He examined them, then put them aside, saying, 'The ornamentation seems excessive.'

Alice frowned. 'Our monarch wears fine gauntlets.' She pointed at her neck. 'See also the taffety-broidered collar she has made for me – such as our Gracious Queen wears!'

Sir Rowland moved forward unexpectedly and fingered the stiffened collar, standing very near. His glance lingered over her ample bosom. Flushing, she quickly stepped back.

'Having rescued her,' he said, 'you must not work her too much, or you will cause her to flee in despair from us as well. Any hope of the gratitude of wealthy Hollanders will be lost!'

Alice bridled even more at this, although guiltily aware that, when she thought Susannah was weaving for too long over her loom, she had set her to enriching her best robes with glittering ropes of gold and silver spun threads.

'You misunderstand me. I showed mercy and pity towards her as you well know. Sometimes I have allowed her to sew in my rooms where the light is good, which gives her comfort, and enquire of her the mind of the MacFeaghs – in the French language even!'

'Are you aware that my servants complain of her strange conduct? They think her mind is lost or mutter witchcraft.'

'The woman is merely suffering from being in a foreign land with different customs. One 'stranger' woman in London told me that this caused in her a stripping out of who she was and from whence she had come. I believe that if she works hard, her mind may better settle.' Alice then continued smugly, 'She prays much and I have urged her to remember the Last Judgment.'

'As must you, Madam,' said Sir Rowland, turning to sit again at his carved oak table.

Alice crossed herself. Her voice became querulous as she could not resist continuing, 'She was thin as a needle – with a blank stare like its eye and a nose as pointed as its tip! Now at least she becomes rounder.'

'I congratulate you Mistress Alice. You have been excellent

at putting her to work for no reward other than her charge – for which, and for yours too, by the way, I expect re-imbursement from your estate.'

Sir Rowland then called a servant to escort Alice from the room.

The beams of this chamber are carved with strange beasts and foliage. There is one wider leaded glass above the arched embrasure but even in the light from the window now, I can barely see the effect of the colours. The sun is fading. I will humbly beg Mistress Alice to seek my cot. Tomorrow, I'll choose the violent red and brown wools to weave the Christ figure on this panel, Popish though it seems. The blue is expensive, so I am told to be sparing… but the Blessed Mary's cloak must be blue. The work satisfies my soul. She thought I was one of her spirits, the addled old crone. I must cleave to these English. They alone are responsible for my life and charge. Mistress Alice has given me a silver coin and some groats today. They have let me eat good day-old bread so I should not suffer heartburn.

As the Spring of 1598 approached, her maid told Alice that Susannah was missing her courses and that her belly was enlarging with child. Then, in one of the brief intervals between the coverings of deep ice and snow across the land, when the poor were congregating like wraiths in the shadow of the castle walls, Thomas managed to visit Alice at the Constable's castle.

Alice, in a green high-necked gown with blackwork trimmings and a large gold cross pinned to her bosom, had greeted him with relief, then saying

'I am longing to return to Hurst Place.'

They sat beside a large grate heaped with logs the length of a man, and sipped hot wine. She noticed that his neatly folded ruff did not adequately disguise the deep creases on his neck.

'Travelling through the country is increasingly unsafe, and there has been much desperation amongst the common folk this winter. The Ulster Earl of Tyrone is increasingly referred to as "King of Ireland", one who would free the country from the English yoke. He is rallying some support but we still have MacFeagh churls working on our estates when the weather permits. I have improved the defences of my demesne. Walter eventually heard from Chief Redmond after my summons about the Hollander. He said that there would be no objection at present to his wife's return to her kin.' He continued jubilantly, ' The daring Robert Devereux, Earl of Essex, who, with Lord Howard and Sir Walter Raleigh took Cadiz, forcing the Spanish to burn their fleet of 150 ships in the bay lest they be captured and used against them, will likely replace Sir William Russell and be appointed Lord-Deputy of Ireland.'

'I did hear of the Hero of Cadiz in London. It caused some controversy. They left it a smoking ruin when they could have secured even more ransoms and treasure. There was much slaughter and pillage.'

'However that they may be, Lord Essex vows to finally subdue Ulster and keep Ireland for the Crown. Although we are somewhat vulnerable as I have holdings marching alongside parts of The Pale, I am sure that his appointment will tip the balance for those wavering about allying with Tyrone, and that we will ultimately not be too much affected here in The Pale and the south.'

'In that case,' said Alice, 'I want to soon leave Susannah Breydel with Sir Rowland and return to Hurst Place. I wish to take no more responsibility for her. The Constable leers at me, the castle is cold and uncomfortable, with narrow stairs as twisted as eglantine, noisy pantry boys, an ignorant and superstitious staff, and many sweaty soldiers patrolling the public areas.'

'No, Alice, at present you must stay here. I would not have it on my conscience if you were attacked, and I cannot spare a full guard. I am being sent further west to get pledges of loyalty and I might then be sent further north. Even if his great army is permitted, it will take months for Devereux to muster and provision – let alone to travel across these winter seas.'

Alice sighed. 'In that case I'll go to London when the weather improves. I miss my friends, particularly dear Hope Polsted, who sent messages that she has been safely delivered of a daughter. I wish to visit her and also see whether our business needs my attention.'

She got up and produced a garment from a carved court cupboard.

'Susannah works constantly, even though I do not expect such obsessive industry. She enjoys working tapestry. Her weaving and embroidery are exceptional – see, I had her ornament your red doublet.'

Thomas put it on, limping to the window.

'This doublet is now somewhat large and perhaps over-embellished. I can wear it only at festive occasions.' He ran his fingers over the front and glanced at his sister. 'I usually don the plain darker shades so as not draw attention or provoke envy.'

'Wintering here, I could not obtain black cloth, brother. As you know, the dyes are very expensive.'

'I thank you for this gift Alice. Tell the Dutch woman I am happy with it.'

Alice said, 'I have a vexing problem with Susannah…' then giving him her news.

'So – the Hollander is breeding Redmond's child? I'm not sure if that is good or bad. Does Sir Rowland Porter know? He has asked to see us when I have rested.'

'I don't know. I thought we could discuss it with him at your audience later. I hardly see him and when I do so he is haughty and remains angry at the old woman's death.'

'The murder of the Lady Medb, you mean,' her brother said sternly. 'You deserved reprimand, Alice. You should have had had more sense than to listen to that foolish woman's pleadings. Indeed, she has imperilled her immortal soul. But Walter told me of your bravery.' He put a hand on her arm, continuing, 'It was a pity that I received your message when I was many days away. I wish that I had been there when Redmond arrived. But you handled it well.'

'The killing was not my fault! The guard acted without instruction – has he been found, do you know?'

Steadying himself on his staff, Thomas stretched an arm, away from his broad shoulders and wheeled it round so as to exercise the joint.

'There is no sign of him, and there won't be if the Irish clans discover him first. Apart from her belly, how is Susannah in her spirits? Does she show remorse for the killing?'

'She will not talk of it. She eats well but speaks little and then only to me. I am the only one who speaks French, although she rudely wrinkles her forehead in scorn at my phrasing and accent. She's a strange and difficult one. She is excessive in her weaving and needlework tasks and her devotions. It is as if she were a very pious nun! When I pointed out that she was with child she showed no joyful reaction. This is, I suppose, not surprising if she speaks truly when she says that Redmond took her maidenhood when she was ill and dazed, and then later forced her into a form of marriage given by a priest.'

She added,' That he wed her is to be admired to be sure, but some local servants suspect that she has been bewitched – or is a witch – or a substance to be feared or placated. They all call her Lady Gile MacFeagh, not Susannah Breydel.'

'Our churls at Hurst Place confirm that they believe she was wife to Chief Redmond.'

'She says it was merely a Blessing with her, Chief Redmond and a friar – she said his name was Ignatius - at a chapel on the cliffs.'

Thomas said, 'I know that man, Friar Ignatius. He is a scion of an Irish noble house, a joker and bard, but popular. He no doubt foments trouble whenever he can. He is elusive, and is believed to conduct their heretical devotions. He is ordained.'

'Indeed, the way she described it, the Blessing did sound like a marriage. But she still considers herself violated rather than wed, as she was handfasted to a cloth finisher who lives in London Spittle Fields. She does not accept Chief Redmond, although some may say she improves her rank.'

Thomas frowned. 'If truly wed before God, her child will then be legitimate and indeed Redmond's heir. A first-born heir to his Barony must be of interest to Redmond – and the Crown!'

At that moment, a servant entered and told them that the Constable would receive them in the rooms above. They slowly followed the servant up the wide stone stairs to a reception hall, Thomas leaning heavily on his cane and the carved banister.

Courtesies were exchanged, and Thomas nodded as Sir Rowland said,

'The rebellion, especially in the north, is spreading slowly but surely under Tyrone and O'Donnell, like the plague. The

Queen is highly displeased.'

The brother and sister bowed in agreement, Thomas adding 'All praise to our great Queen, our anointed monarch.'

The Constable continued, 'The traitor Tyrone thinks himself King of Ireland and has already had his acolytes spread this myth. We can only hope that their damnable, incomprehensible Gaelic laws of succession and dynasty lead yet again to many quarrels and wars amongst their nobles, and that the infection spreads no further.'

Sir Rowland moved to the bottle-glassed window overlooking the surrounding town and peered out at the swirling grey sky.

'More snow threatens. I know the great Lord Essex begs to be sent to put Tyrone down. If this is agreed, the insurgents will regret their actions. Do you have more information from beyond The Pale for me, Thomas?'

'This winter, labour and communication is, and has been, difficult. Sir, in the last months, some of our Irish servants have left suddenly, without payment, and other folk are not returning after wintering at the coast. My churls, and even some of my house servants, are sullen, and work slowly, blaming the weather. My steward, Walter, also tells me that from time to time, vicious fights break out with churls known to be from loyal clans. I have reinforced my garrison. I know many of the clans are arranging a Gathering.'

'The Earls Desmond and Ormonde, hereditary bitter enemies, say they will both swear allegiance to the Crown. Whether all their kin will do similarly is indeed a moot point.'

'The mountain septs' views are unclear but as you know, they are a law unto themselves. I do not know if Redmond MacFeagh will turn. The killing of Lady Medb, witch though she seemed to be, has inflamed many.'

Sir Rowland Porter glanced at Alice, who now did not look in the least repentant, and put up her chin as he glanced up and down her body.

'I wish I could meet up with Niko MacFeagh, who is their main trader, envoy and linguist and who exerts much influence,' continued Thomas, 'but I heard he has been wintering and trading in the warmer Mediterranean coasts – the fortunate one!'

'Yes – I have been told of him,' said Sir Rowland. 'His spy network rivals ours! They listen to him, and so do we. He is the most civilised of them all, despite his heathen blood, and has fought for the Crown in foreign wars. But is there a chance he could be mobilising mercenaries?'

Thomas shrugged. 'Who knows? The weather will have stopped his early return to Ireland, and there will be no campaigns before Spring. We have time to watch the plots.'

The Constable then said, 'My enquiries have confirmed that the Dutch woman is the only surviving child of a Protestant cloth trader and finisher, Hendrick Breydel and that her uncle, one M. De Hem, wants her back in Leiden or Amsterdam. You wrote Thomas, that, because of his fury at the noble Lady Medb's death, he would not object to his wife's return to her kin.'

'Indeed and I am told that he has sent someone to inform them that she is alive.' He looked briefly at Alice. ' But as regards the woman Susannah – sir, I am told that whilst she was married to Chief Redmond, she conceived his child. That may change his views. '

After a pause, Sir Rowland sat heavily in his large oaken chair and said smoothly, 'Something of this has already reached my ears. Are you sure, Mistress Alice, that it is his child?'

She nodded. 'She is a pious woman, truthful and quite naïve.'

'Many Hollanders, as well as crew, ambassadors and pastors, were drowned with Breydel. I do not know if this De Hem is one of those violent Calvinists who do the Protestant cause no good. If so, knowing that she has married a Catholic and is now carrying his child, they may not accept her back. So far, messages have been exchanged and all they know she is wintering safely here with Mistress Alice. Also that I require compensation for her board, charge and guarding. Whilst on the subject, I will require more loyal men to be sent from your demesne, Thomas. Mistress Alice, I also require further funds should the insurgency develop further and, indeed for your protection, bed and board. My clerk will prepare the details.'

Alice took a deep breath, irate, and would have spoken if it were not for a warning glance from her brother.

'Meanwhile,' continued the Constable, 'do not confirm to anyone, and let nothing be said, beyond current rumour, of Susannah Breydel's pregnancy, because a living heir may be useful to us as a hostage, and we do not want her seized.' He thought for a moment. 'As soon as the weather calms, Mistress Alice, I want you to take her to a safe place in England, and see that, if possible, she is birthed successfully. I will arrange an escort, but this will be at your expense. After this, the woman can return to her kin, but if the babe survives, he will be an heir and should be held by us to help maintain loyalty from the MacFeaghs.'

Alice then realised that Sir Rowland's plans would be a means of eventually getting out of his castle and to London.

'Thomas, go back and hold your land for the Crown. Talk to Niko when he returns and ensure continuing loyalty from Leinster. We must hope that the Lord Essex gathers his army, but it is unlikely, if so, that he can start campaigning before next, rather than this, season, so we must hold Tyrone in check until then. With luck, the prospect of invasion will draw him to seek a pardon yet again.'

He dismissed them and turned away.

As they descended the staircase, Alice said crossly, 'So – he wants the child, if safely delivered, and if proved to be legitimate, to be kept as hostage for Irish loyalty to the Crown and gives me – no relation, no politico or spy, a cloth wholesaler, not even of the higher merchant sort – responsibility for all this!'

'You have only yourself to blame, Alice,' he said. 'Send her to Cecilia in Somerset and then you can go on to London as you wish.'

Thomas and Alice's step-mother Mary's family had been Catholics. Her brother Richard Walford and his wife Cecilia had been known for their piety. Richard would have been imprisoned were it not for death claiming him first - and for Selwyn Hurst's bribes. Cecilia was then persuaded to recant, and accommodated within Selwyn's household before becoming chatelaine of Somerset Abbey.

The blood spreading in the drenching rain… the stare and grey face of that dying witch comes unbidden to my mind. Many in that place pretended to love our God but kept to their old Faith in case ours proved perfidious. I miss Orlaith's soft voice even if I knew not of what she spoke. The Irish speech is as restless as their lives, she would have been glad to find that I am with child. I feel I have Redmond growing inside me, restless and kicking… she was but an addled old crone…

CHAPTER TEN

I told the brutish sailor that I would not board. My desperate father last kissed me on such a ship. Such a ship marked the beginning of all that has befallen me. That night the sky was some time obscured by still and creeping fogs… now the tendrils of the same fogs finger my face and penetrate my cloak. Dear Lord, Alice's face is fierce as she tells me to cease my wailing and my discontents. I will not go. I will not. He slaps my face so that I will have a mark. Now there is a brief flare as a brilliant streak of light passes across the crescent moon. An omen… of what… of what? I am carried, struggling… I cannot prevail…

Having changed vessels in New Ross and crossed the cold calm sea under the cover of the next night, Alice and her escort travelled with only brief halts for rest at the way stations. They followed river valleys and a coastal path, journeying past villages, forests, rounded scrub-clothed hills and bald lofty moors.

Men showed no courtesies during the voyages from Dublin. On one vessel, I must needs to piss on deck in a pot and they jeered at my discomfiture. Thanks to Our Lady, the stinks of my vomit kept them at bay, except for one, sent by mistress Alice, who gave me a bowl in which to void. He spoke my mother tongue, and later gave me small ale and forced some bread between my teeth. And then I slept. Can it truly be my fate to be so near the shore again? I do not wish to be here in this silent landscape where I understand no voice. In the midst of my trials in Redmond's stronghold, there was laughter, prayer and singing and the courtesy of 'dominus vobiscum'. I was allowed much freedom both to go about and to sit and sew even though my husband is a Popish savage. Perhaps Our Lord has decreed that I have no right to pleasure or to comfort – or am I to be a repository for the malign purposes of the Devil? Will his child be an incubus in my womb? My thighs ache…I wish to sleep…. I must pray. I must yet pray…'

It was mid-afternoon when, having turned off on to an unsignposted track, they gradually climbed for at least three leagues up into a stony road, flanked by fields. For some time they had been aware of riders in the distance, clearing any bandits from their way, but no folk or foresters had been observed for some time. Finally they descended into heathland where horned sheep grazed. Above them stood a cluster of buildings above them on a promontory. The ancient former castle and then Augustinian Abbey was sprawled over an uneven summit, giving extensive views of the coast, the cliffs and fingers of rock reaching into the waves. To the east there was a village. Greeted by the screech of sea birds, they had reached their destination. Susannah, who had been travelling on a fat pony with its panniers full of gowns, gasped with fear and exhaustion as they approached and she caught glimpses of the grey surging sea beyond. She turned her face into her voluminous Irish cloak as the wind whipped all around.

Abraham Plymmiswoode had bought the ruined buildings, derelict farms, gardens and fields from the Crown soon after King Henry's Reformation. It had been attacked and looted but had good additional pasture for the Plymmiswoode flocks. A young neighbouring landowner, recently widowed, Lady Anne Templeton, had also sold him some adjacent fields. Abraham had later given Alice this monastic desmesne, wanting to distract her from her miscarriages. She had been pleased to busy herself arranging repairs to the square keep, the chapel, cloisters and adding outbuildings, not least as she had seen an opportunity to rid herself of her step-mother Mary's sister-in-law Cecilia.

She had never been close to this woman or her husband. She considered their Catholic piety to border on bigotry. Richard had been recusant and heavily fined prior to his demise from an apoplexy. Cecilia, having little means and sharing their household, had been irritating Alice, and worrying Abraham, with the constant use of her rosary and name-dropping of the Saints. Alice's early Catholic upbringing had not been strict. She and Thomas had accepted that their family had to pragmatically embrace Protestantism, and were only too aware that Richard and his wife Cecilia's resistance could have caused the family's ruin.

Cecilia had agreed to be chatelaine of the Abbey, make it more productive and ensure increased rents. Some former monks, joined by some dispossessed nuns, creeping back into the parts that were still roofed, had been eking out a living nearby and had later petitioned to be allowed to remain. This was agreed, along with some repairs, as long as they tended the house, operated at times as a staging post for drovers and maintained a hospice for the sick. The fields were used for extra grazing and shelter for the sheep and goats.

The travellers from Ireland entered through a stone-roofed porch, originally the ancient portcullis. From its pillars glared fierce gargoyles. The remaining part of the moat had been turned into fish pools. They jangled the stout bell pull and rumbled steeply upwards on a paved carriageway through arched gates into the flagged courtyard, where retainers were waiting. The courtyard led on to vegetable and fruit gardens surrounded by low hedges and walls and was partly bordered by old cloisters carved with much weathered forms of ancient knights in prayer. Servants led the carriage, ponies, pack animals and escort away through the postern gate to the stables, kitchens and the servants' quarters. Meanwhile, Alice, with Susannah lagging behind, entered a square hall, above which an overhanging upper storey had been added. Small mullioned windows, some ornamented with the Tudor rose, allowed some daylight to pierce a general gloom. The hall was lined with wooden benches and had no fire in the grate. Torches in wall sconces lit a gilded and carved figure of the Madonna and child, surrounded by carved Saints, placed in an alcove above the vast fireplace.

Bright-eyed Sister Benedicta, freckled with sparse eyebrows, dressed in a robe similar to a nun's habit, bustled forward smiling and saying warmly, 'Mistress Alice, it is good to see you once again. May God watch over you in the undertakings that bring you here.'

She curtseyed to Cecilia who had emerged from a corridor from the hall to the chapel.

Alice also gave a perfunctory curtsey, smiled and gestured for the pregnant girl to come forward.

'We arrive at last! This time, I have brought you a young woman from the Low Countries to birth later this Spring.'

Cecilia was wearing, Alice noticed, suspiciously abbess-like robes. Her normal halting gait was more pronounced.

Tall wax candles on a vast oaken table lit a wall where hung a tapestry, worked with strong red, gold and green threads, of Christ taken down from the Cross. Susannah had ignored Alice's gesture as she was kneeling in adoration before this, gazing upwards, her hands folded in prayer.

Pious hands have made these works, but it is sinful to so admire them. How can such beauty be thought to be idolatrous? I have the gift of artistry which my mother cherished in me. The Lord is here in this place and my soul rejoices... such skill of hand. But some of my people would chastise me for so glorying in these images, and would hurl them down and trample on them. I cannot be repelled by them, they speak to me of gentleness and resurrection... my drowned kin are now in His arms... I give thanks.

'So I see- she seems a pious soul! But I believe it is at least a twelve-month since you have visited us here, Alice.'

Alice raised her eyebrows.

'Ah, but you have received my messengers – sent each month?'

Cecilia nodded. 'Mostly a list of requirements and questions – as I recall.'

'As you know, my dear husband, before his death, God rest his soul, enjoined me to take proper care of this estate. Also the journey from Ireland is not to be undertaken lightly, Cecilia. Especially in the cold months as now.'

'And how does Thomas?' enquired Cecilia, after a pause.

'His injuries increasingly trouble him and he is anxious that the country is not quiet. He had, and indeed still has, much need of me. 'Tis a pity that I am ordered by the Crown to leave Ireland and bring this woman here to safety.'

'That land has never been quiet, even within The Pale! I'm surprised that you risk yourself in living amongst them.'

The way the folds and shadows in the virgin's robes are realised is exquisite. The pastors would surely see this talent as guided by God…

'Get up, girl,' commanded Alice crossly. 'Sister! Help her if you please! She is tired- as indeed are we all! Now Susannah, greet the chatelaine of this place – Dame Cecilia Walford. You will be glad to know, Cecilia, that this Dutch woman is a most devout Protestant and has prayed the whole way from Ireland. She answers to the name of Susannah Breydel. I am commanded by Sir Rowland Porter at Dublin Castle to have her birthed and kept safe. Thanks be to God, the babe has not been jolted into the world on the long journey here!'

The cold, sleeting drizzle had sometimes forced them both into a following carriage in which Susannah had been poor company, silent and morose. As they bounced from one pothole to another, Alice had felt some concern for her charge, and decided that drizzle or not, they would fare better on horseback.

Susannah curtseyed clumsily and bowed her head. Cecilia nodded and gave a thin smile with a formal welcome speech. She was taller than many, deeply wrinkled with watery blue eyes. Her hair and brow were completely covered with a large, complicated, old fashioned white headdress.

'Is she wife to someone of note, Alice?' Her graven features cracked into a frown.

'Of that I am not entirely certain. It is a long and strange story, and it is best if I do not give you details.'

'Well now, it would seem that this girl may need God's forgiveness. And our charity. Girl, we will give thanks for your safe arrival and that of the unborn babe and then we will all eat from the bounty that God has provided us with here, in this once consecrated place.'

Alice followed, cold, and somewhat unreasonably annoyed at Cecilia's tone and, being hungry and exhausted, that they were not to eat first, having only had only apples and some brown bread since daybreak. During the journey, aware that her stomacher had lately become tighter with the heavy pies and pastries that kept out the chill, she had asked her escort to pass the sweetmeats carried with them to Susannah.

'Recall it was a castle once Cecilia, made for war, rather than prayer. By the way, how you survive in such temperatures within this place, I do not know. Please have braziers put in our chambers – my husband always had good fires in all the rooms as you will remember!'

'See to it!' said Cecilia to an accompanying servant, then slowly leading the way back to the chapel, Susannah hung back, making strange sounds as if she was gabbling to herself. Cecilia then stopped and turned to look at her, saying to all present, 'Walk by my side to the chapel, girl. We will pray together.'

Susannah gave Cecilia a strange look and went beside her, head lowered.

Alice added, 'We will eat soon and then you can lie in your cot until night prayers.'

'You will be given some work tomorrow, girl, as idleness is a sin to be abhorred,' announced Cecilia as they moved on. Alice sighed, but then felt pangs of exquisite pathos for them all; Susannah for her labour to come, herself for her own miscarriages and the sorrow of widowhood, and Cecilia, for her babes died in infancy and the husband she revered taken by God.

In the chapel, Susannah was still and silent, her face immobile, although her lips worked. The service was lengthy with chanting and incense. On her knees, she did not appear to feel the numbness of the flagged floor, unlike Alice, who moved constantly in discomfort.

'I will tell them to make some kneelers,' Alice thought, glancing with irritation at Cecilia's taut frame and uplifted, rapt expression and Susannah's bent and shaking head. 'The wretched girl is mumbling and making rude snorts and gasps. Cecilia does not seem to notice. She has become more Popish since coming here, no doubt about it. She seems to have forgotten she could have so easily shared the fate of her arrogant husband who broadcast his Catholicism to all and sundry with no thought for the consequences for either himself or his family. Only my husband's money saved her supercilious skin. If she hadn't been kin, and well able to keep this useful secluded place in order and make it profitable, I'd report them all here as needing the influence of our Protestant pastors. As it is, it is better not to draw attention to this place.'

She sighed and resolved to warn Cecilia before leaving the Abbey. Then, she felt guilty at what she decided were unbecoming thoughts and began to pray herself.

'Welcome, child, and God's blessing upon you all,' this old abbess Cecilia said. Her headdress is tied and starched into white horns of which I have never seen the like. I choked back a peal of laughter, a laughter without humour. I detest the images on the altar. I fear this place is idolatrous, but must kneel and stay still. The gentlewomen take this as piety, and will praise me for it! I ache between my legs from the jarring of the journey, my baby stabbing and growling his discontent with this position and his need for bread. I can hear the old woman sing now, her voice cracked and harsh in the high register. I sneak a view of her face at my side. Oh this laughter overwhelms me! Her headdress wobbles above all, a bulge moves up and down in her turkey neck and her mouth is a wide cavern in her long face. I feel I am being swallowed in that cavern, at the brink of traversing a passage I will wander forever whilst I wait for the light of the Lord to shine once more upon me. I see more sisters and other girls, great with child, who must stand, not kneel… servants, children… I see hard faces on some and soft eyes on others. Alice, at the end of the row in front, did not sing. She frowns and moves in discomfort. When will I be allowed to eat? My son, I know it for a man, demands bloody meat, milk and creamy curds. My body too is all ache and soreness and my consciousness like the fleece of a sheep in winter…

At supper, Cecilia partook frugally of the plentiful meal of fresh wheaten bread, roasted fishes with sweet herbs and green vegetables, followed by jellies and pears and apples with a thick covering of buttery paste. The guests ate ravenously.

'You did not come across any vagabonds or bands of Egiptians,[3] or 'gypsies' as they are sometimes known, on your journey? That is good, as they can be violent and sometimes many are seen around our lands.'

'Really, Cecilia, you must remember that here you are most fortunate! The laws made by our Great Queen are enforced if you do but request it. Lady Templeton's steward cleared our way with his men-at-arms, when informed of our travels.' She sighed. 'In Ireland the myriad of self-proclaimed Chiefs see the travel licenses that must be procured before we journey and that are compulsory both here and there, as another ploy to divest the people of their lands and their traditional way of life. But these licenses are only there to ensure that the landowners know who is on their land and who, therefore, may be bent on mischief.'

'I do not encourage Lady Anne or her household to come near here, for many reasons which I do not propose to discuss,' said Cecilia.

Alice found herself wondering about these reasons. 'I thought Lady Anne made generous donations to your work here?'

'Yes, they are generous enough'.

There was a silence during which Cecilia took more mouthfuls of food. Alice drank heartily from her tankard.

'It is so different over the water in Ireland! All the Irish gentry seem to want is freedom to wander and raid cattle as they will. Other nationalities particularly brigandish Scots, take advantage of this and fetch up there, sometimes with their dependents, throwing themselves on our charity, sometimes robbing and raping where they can. We never know whose side they favour – I suspect it is their own.'

'I wonder again that you have stayed with Thomas in Ireland, Alice. The Templetons' men-at-arms do not stop those 'Egiptians,' or their women, from France – or further – to live off our lands without our Queen's permission or stop them from coming to beg at our doors! They ask us to birth them in the name of Our Lady and then beg us to keep their offspring, saying they cannot support them. So- if the babes survive, we then have to find them God-fearing homes. We send the women away- except one or two meek and pious ones as wetnurses and servants. We do not have the wherewithal to house hungry beggars or their offspring.'

She looked meaningfully at Susannah, who had finished one plate and filled another. Alice took Cecilia's comments as a warning of some hard negotiations ahead on the cost of Susannah's care.

'There are as many demands on our charity in Ireland as you have here. Not only do we have the depredations from brigands and freebooters, but the recent severe winters there have often brought famine in their wake. Thomas, who, since his grievous injuries it is my duty to assist, has made the Crown aware of the need to bring more land into cultivation, to ease the peoples' suffering.'

Alice then returned to her meal and after a while continued, 'So who finds homes for the infants and other children left here? And surely the mothers must be desperate to part with them?'

Cecilia answered vaguely.

'There is a man who visits each month. He takes them to the authorities in the nearest towns. We cannot spend all our time nursing infants. As you know, our main work here is the study of the Bible. The Lord will take care of the infants.'

Alice wondered if the Abbey demanded payment from the man who took the children away. If so, she thought grimly that the babes were most likely sold on to be abused or treated as slaves.

She said, 'I sincerely hope you check that this man speaks truly when he says he takes them to the Parish Board- and that you assure yourselves that they are lodged in God-fearing homes. Would it not be more Christian to keep the parents, at least until they have fully gathered their strength, so they can take care of their own - and others? I understand the Abbey demesne is show-ing a profit. I respectfully request that you take more care of the mothers, and that, wherever possible, you help them to diligently seek suitable foster-mothers for their children if they so wish – as is your duty before God.'

'The Egiptian women are not known for their trustworthi-ness, industry or reliability. And we do not have the means and time to arrange this!' exclaimed Cecilia.

Alice put down her fork. 'Well then, I would like to examine your ledgers while I am here and the daily duties of the Sisters.'

Cecilia looked at her, almost in tears.

'Of course. They will be made ready for you. But you will see in those books how our profits are spent on glorifying the Lord God, rather than throwing good money at ingrates.'

'I noticed the carved Madonna in the hall – and the tapestry

– and I suspected I saw the Host vessels on the altar. They were not there on my last visit. I cannot permit idolatry. Monies should not be, or have been, spent on such. This is a domestic residence now, and you – and indeed I, as owner of this place – could be accused of heresy. You, of all people, should know that there is much suspicion of those not fully committed to Protestantism. It is feared that they are traitors – that they seek to join with Spain to attack our islands yet again. Remember your recusant husband's exorbitant fine – which my husband paid, Cecilia. I will not pay yours if it comes to it.'

Cecilia poked angrily at her fish.

'The carving was recovered from the moat when it was cleared of weed. It was so beautiful that we decided to renovate it. We did it ourselves! I could not sanction such a beautiful object being burnt. And the tapestry, found wrapped in a hidden chest, is an image I understood to refer to a story of the Ancients.'

Alice was derisive. 'I think not! Have you asked Lady Anne's pastor for his opinion?'

'No I have not, and pray, do not talk of this in front of my household!' Cecilia, with heightened colour, looked down and continued with her meal. There had been a stirring from amongst the other women present.

That meat has soothed my belly and that of my son. I wish him to be stout with a broad frame like my dear father, not lean and sharp-featured like that devil Redmond. I must eat and eat more. The old woman Cecilia looks askance at me. I find I have longings for fat bacon and good cheese following that dread diet of thick oats in milk ever eaten at Redmond's tower. Mistress Alice indulged my longings, but will that be so here? The two women have red faces and seem to be exchanging harsh words. That tapestry with its image of our Lord's travails and his disciples around him is so pure and loving that my heart aches... oh Lord, save my immortal soul that I found it so compelling...

Cecilia looked up again from her plate as Alice tapped at the heavily carved oak table so as to get full attention, saying loudly, 'Hear me, Cecilia, the idolatry must be removed – and soon. Susannah will be kept at our charge not yours, but she must also work as much as she is able. She is a skilled needlewoman, and will be pleased to stitch for you. Plain work though – blackwork perhaps- on soft chapel kneelers and surplices for the choir – as you know, too much decoration is an affront to the teachings of our Church.'

Cecilia stared hard at Alice's stone-set rings, her brocaded cap and the jewelled cross on her rich velvet gown.

'Do not look so. I follow the style of our Queen, the greatest of women, as I have always done,' challenged Alice. In annoyance she tossed back her head, then taking another gulp of ale. All continued with the meal in silence.

In a few days, Alice prepared to leave for her London residence. She would meet her stepsons there, as she had heard, before leaving Dublin, that they had tasks for her in England. She warned Cecilia that Susannah's child was important to the Queen's cause in England and in Ireland and that there would be severe consequences for her if the baby were not given the best of care. She left two guards, 'spies' Cecilia called them bitterly, and continued to reinforce her position as owner of the Abbey. She made it clear that she wished to see a change in the febrile religious atmosphere there, which she felt was not suited to an ordinary household, and would merely inflame Susannah to even stranger conduct than that which at times she showed. She congratulated Cecilia on the high profits but said they were ungenerous to the retainers, that rents from the tenant farmers were too high and that the chapel walls must be lime-washed with no more gilding and decoration.

'Men will not labour hard in the fields or be loyal to you for no reward, ' she said, 'and when the Crown get to know of high profits and gilded shrines, they will demand even higher taxes – or even find a reason for you to lose your head. Your own needs as pious women are few. In future, you must report to me directly on all profits and keep a written tally, with receipts, on charitable disbursements from these profits. I expect these to be allocated according to the industry of the individual and their needs. There needs to be a balance maintained between those resident here and indigent mothers and babies at the door. I realise that Susannah will be an extra charge and will leave some silver to cover this.'

Mistress Alice leaves me now and my heart constricts in fear. Her voice to us all is stern. She tells me I must obey Mistress Cecilia in all things as she understands the pains and sorrows of birthing. I do not trust Mistress Alice's mind. She says she will see me again but I do not know if I believe her.. She has given me a fine wool shawl for the Churching and says that if it is a boy it should be named Matthew. I would wish to name him first 'Hendrick' for my dear father and 'Robert' for my brother, killed in the wars, but she says this cannot be. She says I must study the English tongue, and English prayers but my head is full of mists and I have no ear for strange speech, unlike Niko MacFeagh who spoke many tongues... sometimes he and his mother conversed in a harsh crackling way. I feared Niko above all others for his stern gaze. Why do I think now of those Irish people... I wonder that I do. I think Orlaith too knew great sadness. Here I may sew plain surplices for the choir which will soothe me...

Just before she left, Alice presented Cecilia with some cuffs that she had asked Susannah to design and embroider. Alice had meant to keep them but found the pattern, a single trim, worked in pale silver thread, was too plain for her taste. Cecilia thanked them for the gift but managed to indicate that she thought the cuffs overly decorated and unseemly.

That Spring continued cold and long. Hoar frost painted every branch, every remaining leaf, every spider's web. The vast tree trunks shone like silver damask studded with crystals under a washed winter sky. The state of Susannah's body, encased in flowing robes sewn together from a dead Nun's habit, was clear for all to see, but her mind appeared hostile and her thoughts remained a mystery. Although chastised when found, at times, eluding her guards when they warmed themselves in the Priory kitchens, she disappeared for some hours. She wandered around her surroundings but never even glanced at the sea. She did not study the English tongue or the local dialect, and seemed interested only in sewing or listening to Cecilia's Latin Bible readings.

I push my stick into this snow. It is half an ell deep. The ridges in this bark are rimed with frost. I think on my Isabelle, my maid-of-honour, perished in those fogs. Perhaps I will lose this child or we will die together. Will I remain in the first circle of hell? I cannot bear that – not to be one of the Elect, the Chosen – to be separated from my God who has allowed me the chance to pray and make full repentance of my sins – and those of others. This babe's father has used me, and sinned against me. He has saved my wretched life but he has sinned in so doing... would that I had died with my maid Isabelle and my kin, in innocence and Grace. These women feel my belly and nod and ply me with fresh bread, roasted meats, fish and greens. I thank the Lord that they give me no roots which my mother says the devil grows to penetrate my body...

Carters came to the Abbey regularly when the weather permitted, collecting salted fish and produce to deliver to the Plymmiswoode farmhouses further north, then going to their London residence. They imparted significant news. The death of the Queen's trusted Adviser Lord Burghley caused much consternation.

Cecilia had been told to send reports on Susannah's progress to her via these men. They, and many others, such as retainers, guards, and even visitors, found Susannah alluring. In spite of Cecilia's disapproval, she refused to cover her hair, as pale as her face, catching her tresses instead under an old-fashioned dark cap and snood she had been given by Alice and which she had embroidered. Her enlarging body was round and buxom.

Benedicta puts my clogs on my feet, binds them with thick wool and pushes me outside to walk. The walls are trimmed in white. My clogs sink deep and the boughs lie heavy with icy lace, no matter that the season is soon Spring. That guard who gazes on me with calf-like stare follows me and beckons me to go back in. They watch me always. If I were not so cumbersome and tired, I would prevail on him to take me hence... but not yet... I doubt that we would succeed and stay alive in this barren land with its uplands, snows and brigands. This babe growing inside me takes my strength. The sisters irritate me with their fussing and soundings of my belly. I can tell from his restlessness when I try to sleep that he thrives. I think that I will breed a healthy boy. There has been no word about my kin. Although sickly, my mother has a kind heart and will want me at home, babe or no... the sin was not of my making.

I wonder does Redmond know of my belly? In this place there are faint-hearted women waiting to deliver. I can make them tremble and retreat when they presume and when I speak sharply or put out my hand to slap them. In this place these sisters are not worldly women like the Beguines were in Flanders but they know birthing, and no woman has died whilst I have been here. They say they do not bleed us after childbirth but not to be fearful. They say they have learnt that the babes and mothers survive better when they are not bled and all the cloths are kept clean and changed often. I am one of the Chosen- in God's hands and, for the most part, they too are pious here…

Daylight was coming earlier. More folk scavenged the rocky beach below and more ships were seen on the horizon. Some horned cattle were released from the rough-stone byres, edged with stunted trees, and cropped the growing grass in the Priory's fields. Thick black smoky cloud bundles shaded into wide skies, blue as the paintings she had seen of the Madonna's robes. Blobs of grazing animals dotted the distant mountain ridges.

Susannah, alone, sat sewing on a chair placed in the cloister.

When I looked back, her strange brimmed hat had gone. This thread I am using was the colour of her blood spreading in the rain across her head and leaving the edges of her long white hair unsullied. Her bony fingers clutched at the earth, were clutched by the earth. Her old woman's green stare penetrates my mind's eye. In the loom sheds at Leiden there were up to 8000 warp threads and up to three wefts. We prepared plain weave, twill weave, taffety weave and satin weave… brocading was special, using only silver and gold, backed with silver threads, the weave limited to the contours of the design. Aaagh… I must catch my breath and my womb moves with a sharp wrenching pain. My mother bled and cried so in labouring my baby sister who God took soon after. What will become of my babe, the child of such parents as wild Redmond and I, who is lost? Aagh…. the pain again… my waters are loosed. I must stand… guard! Fetch Sister Benedicta… make haste! Will he have Orlaith's green eyes so that I am forever haunted? Lord, give me courage and protect me, but I need fear nothing for the worst has befallen me…Credo In Deum Patrem Omnipotentum. I will be subject to his irresistible Grace…

'Go in person and tell Mistress Alice at Plymmiswoode Hall.'

Cecilia looked keenly at the carters. 'The Dutch woman has borne a son. The birth was late in coming, then short, violent and bloody. The infant needed much wiping and was loud in the pulsing wails that filled his lungs with life. The girl also screamed so long and loud it could have reached the City of London! I had the headache for two days after. She was torn, but heals now quite quickly and after the birth, the bleeding did not come again. We put the child to the breast and she screamed again and tried to refuse, but we have few wet-nurses here and we hold him to her breast whenever he cries. She does not look at him, or want to nurse him, but suffers him to feed. He is not pretty. He is long and pale with little hair and eyes that are strangely coloured and very large, but babes change quickly in appearance. Go now and tell Mistress Alice everything that I have said.'

Today, although breathless, I am on my knees in the chapel with Mistress Cecilia and the company here to give long thanks to the Lord for my safe delivery. God stretched out his arms to me as I laboured, which was quick as He heard my cries but now anxiety hardens in my belly like a stone. I know not what will happen now. Will I be taken from here or have to stay suckling this greedy babe and guarded by this hard-faced woman? Or is it only my babe they wish to guard?

After the Churching, when the child was given the name of Matthew MacFeagh Breydel, as requested by Alice. This was pronounced Mathieu in the French fashion by his mother. Breaking their fast with cheese and new bread, Cecilia regarded Susannah, trying to suppress ungodly envy. Good food and motherhood had only increased this girl-woman's comeliness, giving her tall frame a pleasant softness and a bosom noticeably plump under her shapeless gown. Her white gold hair invariably escaped from her cap and shone like a silver chalice. She turned the heads of all she passed.

'Girl,' said Cecilia sharply to her one day, 'now you are recovered, except when you are feeding the babe, you may work with your hands, but not for any kind of adornment. We have need of many new sacks for the produce – you may sew those until I hear from Mistress Alice. You may also help with the brewing.

Yes I like to work to assuage my sin but that rough cloth will pun-
ish and roughen my hands, and filling the sacks with the malt will stain
my skin. She knows this but perhaps she is carrying out the will of the
Lord, though I doubt He means to be as cruel as she. Will Mistress Alice
take me back to Ireland? Pray that God forbid my return to that heathen
place. I have heard nothing from my kin. I cannot stay here. I must think
what to do… I must pray… I bow and go to the nursery where the babes
cry for food – that fat pock-marked servant Benedicta with the twist to
her mouth and no eye-brows makes me suckle Matthew and then slaps
me when I refuse to suckle others. I tell her I am not a cow for the milk-
ing, but I must obey. I think that Cecilia and many here are Papists – I
have seen some gaze at idols and pray with beads, but to whom can I
denounce them, and will they take me from here if I do? I must leave
here….I must find Christian Calvet…

Susannah tried to run away with the child but was quickly found.
Cecilia then sent retainers to ask Alice for further instructions.
She understood that the woman was trying to get to London.
Meanwhile, Thomas, after learning of Matthew's birth, had written to Alice requesting that the pair be sent to her for safe-keeping, as the Irish war was gathering pace. So Alice sent Cecilia's
retainers back asking her to arrange for Susannah to soon travel
to Plymmiswoode Hall in London with an escort, Sister Benedicta
as nurse, and mule-carts carrying more provisions. The cold season had been severe and there were shortages in London.

Just after arriving at Somerset Abbey and delivering Alice's message, a week of late Spring blizzards swept across the west of
England.

The cold Spring had arrived in Ireland too. In Dublin, a messenger from London, with letters for Thomas and others in Leinster,
had searched out a timbered harbourside ale-house where he
could recover from a rough crossing. Men, huddled by the log
fire at the end of the room, had filled all the benches. Alone in a
poorly lit booth near the door, Ronan, badged as a loyal Irishman
employed in the Hurst demesne, had hailed him and smilingly
offered him a seat. Garrulous, Ronan had joked about Walter,

Thomas's steward and played his tin whistle for the company. At first, the messenger was surly. Then, cold and hungry, aggressively displaying the knife in his boot and the sword in his belt, he had sat down, putting aside his suspicions. Ronan's guileless young face, lack of arms and familiarity with Thomas's household had reassured him. Ronan had ordered two jugs of ale from by a thin serving girl with rounded, defeated shoulders. Drinking quickly, the two men had talked of the appalling weather that year, expressed disgust at the treachery of the rebels, and the war which set neighbour against neighbour.

As the afternoon advanced, they had both drifted into sleep. When the messenger started snoring, Ronan, coming suddenly awake, had nodded to the girl. She had deftly slid a small hand into the man's damp doublet withdrawing parchments from a sealed leather wallet. Taking care not to be observed, Ronan carefully slid a small knife under the seal, whilst the girl had fetched an elderly man in Jewish robes. Producing a wax candle, he lit it from the rush lights on a small ale-house table, and quickly perused the parchments. He had then whispered to Ronan of the letters' contents. One was from Alice Plymmiswoode to her brother Thomas Hurst. She wrote that Susannah and Matthew were thriving with Cecilia, and that they would arrive in London for safe-keeping ere long. The old man had then carefully re-sealed the documents with a counterfeited seal ring and left the ale-house. The girl had dexterously returned the wallet to the messenger's doublet. An hour later, waking dozily, the messenger, alarmed, felt for his wallet and money pouch. Relieved that all was well, he had slapped the snoring Ronan, apparently insensible, on the back, and left the tavern to deliver his documents.

CHAPTER ELEVEN

After the worst of the snows, Redmond and Fintan MacFeagh and their retinue arrived at the appointed gathering place of the southern clans. This was a rath built on an earthen mound, ringed by a tight circle of high ancient beech trees, believed to be the boundary between the spirit world and the human world. It was said that there were magical stones in that place, deep beneath the bogs. The rath had four enclosures, one for stabling, guards and guests, one with fire pits and middens, a granary and stores, and one with a timbered, flagged hall and arched porch.

Spurs, cloaks, swords and bucklers were divested in the porch. Instructions were shouted to servants and escorts. The rath resounded with wind and rain, shouts to the ostlers, the neighing of dozens of horses, the barking of dogs, and the stamping of booted feet. Tankards of ale and arrack were brought around, amidst the roar of animated voices and greetings in the raftered hall. When the flood of arrivals dwindled, the young servant boys brought wooden trays with hunks of bread, portions of goat, fowls and rabbits which, after being gnawed, were thrown amongst the rushes on the floor for the accompanying hounds. The air was pungent from roasting meat, wood smoke, dogs and the steaming woollen cloaks drying nearby on makeshift racks near the stone hearth, which was piled and crackling with huge logs. Above this was a long overmantel, with carved panels on which were painted armorial symbols and livery badges. In huddles, alliances and betrothals were negotiated or cemented, news exchanged and trades agreed, but the main talk on all lips, was the progress of the war and whether it would ripple across their townlands.

The clans kept a close network of informants and spies, who could be sailors, harbour officials, household or body servants or minstrels to both the Irish and English gentry. Many there, whilst finding this useful on occasions, were wary of information gleaned in this way, aware that messages could be deliberately false, or withheld because of rivalries, the arrogance of nobles, or old scores unsettled. The older heads amongst the Gathering remembered how easy it had been for reports of concerted action to be exaggerated, and how allies had seemed to melt away, leaving their kin exposed in a mist of plots.

All fell silent as the huge brazen horn sounded long and loud. Its origins were lost in antiquity, and its resting place was in Navan. The Ritual of the Horn was a part of important assemblies, signifying respect for the heritage and old faith of the Gaels, even if this was now superseded by the Christian faith. The ancient Brehon Laws decreed that there should be no violence during the life of the Gathering, and that all who wished to speak should be heard. This decree was rarely disobeyed, as all either half or completely believed in a curse or 'geis' that would fall upon transgressors. The burly carrier of the Great Horn entered and moved slowly through the Hall, blowing with a steady booming beat as the crowd parted before him. After he left, the company began to stamp and chant, followed by a great shout as three Irish nobles entered. All present were vassals of one or other of these leaders. Some called them kings, as did many who called the Ulster Earl of Tyrone a king – when they were not in earshot of the English. The nobles wore a mixture of English and Irish dress. The youngest had, slung across his shoulders, a short Irish cloak ornamented with Celtic whorls. Another had a square ruddy face encircled by a stiff muslin ruff and a full goatee beard. He was wrapped in long thick Irish mantle, its collar embroidered with heraldic motifs. The last, senior and more grizzled than his fellows, had a stiff sleeved doublet embroidered in gold braid. He wore, high on his shoulder, a large gold enamelled clasp fashioned as a harp supported by fantastical creatures from whom hung crystal drops. The jewel glittered when caught in the light from the sconces.

A small crowd had surrounded Redmond and his uncle. They were well-known and respected as full-blooded from an ancient lineage. Redmond had a reputation for cunning, and opportunistic action. All were aware that in fosterage he had been treated to condescension and contempt and that he avoided direct dealings with the settlers and Crown officers as he was obliged to bend the knee. Fintan was known for his horsemanship and his valour in the occasional skirmish, in spite of his serious injuries.

'You are our vassals, but also freemen, kerns and gallowglass with skill at arms and hunting, choosing your leaders and true to the Faith,' roared the youngest of the nobles, answered by much stamping. He was stocky, with a long lugubrious face, fleshy lips and deep-set eyes.

'Those not at his Wake know that Feagh O'Byrne – our ally and ever a thorn in the side of the English – was slain last year by the Lord Deputy's men. Also his Lady – Rose - was tricked by Chief Governor Russell into turning her stepson, my cousin, over to him. She has vowed not to let the sun warm her face or the rain splash upon her, until she is avenged. She stays in her rath, and receives no-one.'

There was a humming and a hissing at this announcement. Redmond whispered to Fintan, 'Do you recall meeting that fair-skinned, chestnut-haired beauty? I don't blame her for hiding herself away. She probably doesn't want another old goat like Feagh come near her. There are too many like him around the south. Now – would that I could share her captivity!'

Fintan reminded Redmond that when Lord Feagh O'Byrne's pickled head was sent to the Queen Elizabeth, she was not pleased to receive, as a gift, one she regarded, not as a baron, but a common outlaw.

The Earl had continued sonorously, 'Our hereditary system of electing our chiefs and the granting of lands is not acceptable to the English – they scorn it as different from their own strict hierarchies. We call these tyranny. We can find no common ground. The English have laws which say if they but build a chimney, they can claim rights to the land around it! Also, they defied the Holy Father and give prominence to the Protestant heresy. But they fear us, being greater in number than they. Our northern cousins are in the ascendant. Now they want to march south and ask for our support.'

Fintan spoke up. 'After our defeat and the executions, yes – of our nobles, our uncles and our fathers – after many hardships, now we exist in relative comfort and tolerance - and can raid when we will!'

There was sporadic growling at his words.

'Hah! Comfort!' said the long- mantled Earl. 'Your people are sprawled along a remote miasmic lakeside with steep banks, and a little poor grazing land, and must labour in the forest for the settlers.'

Redmond blenched and answered angrily that not all their enemies in the last rebellion were the English. The murmuring grew. Another chieftain then spoke, emphasising that now the Gaels had a chance to achieve victory which may not come again.

'Our Irish skirmishing is hated by the English forces. We do not stand ground as they do, but lead their forces into the bogs and then spirit ourselves away along secret paths. They fear the manoeuverability our light armour gives us, and our hand-to hand-fighting. They will not fight at close quarters. We could prevail in battle. '

Fintan raised his burly arm again. The hall quietened. He valued Redmond's leadership qualities and commitment to his people, but whilst also angry at Medb's death, when he thought of his merry and irrepressible family, part of him hoped that the current, albeit uneasy, peace would remain in place.

'Niko says they have modern cannon and arquebuses which throw fire and death. Can we match this?'

A Chieftain of the O'Toole clan, still bitter at the decimation of his kin in the last rebellion against the Crown, spoke up.

'We can destroy them and their weapons before they destroy

us. I do not believe their weapons are so dangerous. They will be heavy and will soon sink or be discarded if we attack and lead them into our wild places.'

Then the grizzled Earl opined, 'I long to see the Crown reduced, but we do not have the engines to lay siege to towers and take castles. A great army with an experienced General at its head will have these. We must wait until we are equipped.'

He was asked, 'Is it true that the old Queen hesitates over sending the Earl of Essex?'

'Yes, she does hesitate - but it could well come to pass. Last year he was made Earl Marshal and Master of Ordnance. He has much forewardness in arms. It is said that he was the first in the engagement against the Spanish there to scale the walls of Cadiz and enter it.'

'She hesitates because she knows that Earl Tyrone is a shrewd and better General than Lord Essex, The Devereux, and could capture his artillery,' commented the youngest noble.' Essex failed against the Spanish in the Azores Islands campaign and works constantly for his own aggrandisement.'

A MacMorrow chieftain then said, 'The north has been warring for some years now. Lord Tyrone often sues for pardons when his kin are taken prisoner, but he gets few concessions. How do we know that he will support us once his own demands are met? He has the wit and stealth of a fox. He could turn his coat again.'

The debate ranged to and from all quarters of the Gathering for some time. Some flattered their earls, arguing that their knowledge and generalship would give the Irish forces an advantage and lead them all to victory. Others heaved sighs, weary of the raids and war against the Crown, and fearing devastation of their homesteads. Yet others warned of the torture of prisoners or the sufferings the people may have to endure in the aftermath of a possible defeat. Although some indicated they wished to fight from militant piety, Fintan and Redmond knew that many present would fight for the English if they were paid enough. Although dilatory, Redmond had not reneged on his tithes to his Overlord but was cynically aware that when his Overlord chose the side he would support, he would be dispassionate about the fate of vassals such as the MacFeaghs.

As darkness closed in, the horn was blown to signal the end of discussion. The crowd became vociferous. Some pledges were made to the nobles, but no concerted action was clearly decided. It appeared that not only were the earls not united, but that many Chiefs were holding back until the outcome was clearer. Only one of the powerful landowners was trying hard to persuade the assembly to war – the others, including the MacFeagh Overlord, seemed to be less open in their thoughts. Many present hoped that the English commanders would fear excessive reduction of their soldiery through ambushes and raids, and move to safer and less troublesome regions, discouraging new plantations of settlers, and even allowing the clans to take back more of their ancestral lands.

Fintan found the dreams of victory inspiring, as did Redmond who loved to rehearse the triumphs, glories and heroic bygone battles. But he reminded his nephew of the reality of the wholesale violence which would ensue.

After they returned to Castle MacFeagh, on one cold bright winter morning, Redmond looked down from the high pastures and watched the line of cattle, goats and sheep descending to the more sheltered valleys in the foothills. He could just spy, amongst a grove of tree-tops, the tall, ornamented chimneys on Hurst Place and the curling smoke from the charcoal platforms within the adjacent forests. He regarded the tower ruins of the clan's ancestral home, perched on a rocky precipice overlooking water. The timber causeway to the moorings on its banks had long since disappeared. An English merchant had made some repairs and leased it from the Crown after it was sacked in the rebellion twenty years previously. But he had rarely stayed there, saying that the ghosts of the rebels haunted it still. It had been allowed to decay.

Redmond gazed at the peaceful scene knowing that it would not last long, not least because ironworks being built near the coast would increase river traffic and settlements. Although the Spanish fleet had retreated the previous year because of late autumn storms, more troops were arriving from England, who increasingly feared invasion from Spain. He knew that if a huge English army invaded, it would traverse the valley routes, living off the land. His responsibilities weighed heavily upon him. He longed for the opportunity to call his lands and herds truly his own, but, rather to his surprise, his rage at Lady Medb's death had not festered. Indeed, she called to him in his dreams, urging peace. Except for some stealthy raiding, he had taken her advice to keep out of the war creeping down from Ulster, mindful of how much of his peoples' wealth, acquired with much risk and labour, would be needed for weaponry and clothing and indeed for any coming hardships.

He set to thinking about his kin; that Fintan was brave and loyal, but would always want to put Oonagh and their children out of harm's way. Orlaith lately appeared to him at times to look sick and vacant, as if her spirit was wandering in another world, whilst Niko's frequent references to the brutalities of war could mean that he would not to commit to another. He decided that he and his men-at arms would go to war, if it came to that, but that Niko must stay out of conflict with the Crown and protect the sept, if rebellion spread and then failed.

Spurring his light, piebald horse, bred from wild mares and called 'dainty' by the English and perfect for this terrain, he whistled to his churls and dogs and rode to marshal one of the herds of cattle onto a nearby plateau.

'Keep them at this higher meadow,' he called. 'And drive up some sheep! They will be better hidden from the militias and more difficult to reach.'

The higher meadow held some ancient roofed granite tombs, stone walls and shrubby mounds in which the beasts could shelter from inclement weather. He also decided that he would set the churls to further disguising the way to Castle MacFeagh with piles of timber, brushwood and dammed streams.

Orlaith too was in contemplative mood that day whilst carrying pails of goats' milk on the yoke across her shoulders and trudging to the cabin which served as a dairy. Overcome by a spasm of distress at Medb's horrific death, followed by a fit of breathlessness and coughing, she went into a patch of scrubby trees and rested on a fallen log. She drank from a wooden cup suspended from the pail and reflected on her eventful life.

The many eunuchs, women and children inhabiting the warren of chambers hidden behind perforated delicate wooden screens in the 'mashrabiya', had usually discussed or practiced the arts of music, dance and love, as most wanted to receive favour from their master by their skill. Even she herself had honed her voice. Here in Leinster, her twisting lilt would now carry across the Loch when she was minded to sing. Although never violent, her mustachioed Captain Mustafa had gradually seemed less terrifying, and she came to know who to avoid, and how to please his mother, the most powerful woman in the harem and with whom she spent many of her days for seven long years. She learnt the Arabic tongue, helped in some part by the daily marshalling of the women and children to listen to solemn readings of the tenets of their Holy Book. Understanding their speech enabled her to eventually adapt to the strange world in which she found herself. It had annoyed her that Gile had not done similarly. She wondered if she could find again the resilience she had when a slave amongst the Ottomans. Then she spoke aloud to herself.

'I know Fintan and Redmond fear the influence of the Occupiers on Niko, and Medb feared the influence of the Ottoman. But they do him wrong. When I was enslaved, I spoke, crooned and prayed in the Gaelic speech to Niko, and told him stories of our land, so teaching him loyalty and honour. My dearest Medb requested her youngest son Fergus to give me his hand and take in my bastard. My Lord never reproached us and gave Niko utmost respect and responsibility. He said that it was fate that had intervened in all our lives. I never lost my belief that Mary, Mother of God, would forgive my sins and return me to Ireland. Once home, I was pleased to confess, do penance and be received again into the Catholic faith. But I know that Medb believed we are governed by the Old Ones. Perhaps it was Oisin, moving on the surface of the foaming sea with his fairy Niamh, who led me into sorrow, and that perhaps their enchantment became fainter from Medb's incantations so I could be brought home.'

Then Orlaith bent her head and prayed silently. She often wondered about her son's immortal soul. She once noticed him, before leaving for foreign lands, put a small printed book in Arabic script from the small bundle of belongings in his bedspace. Although doubting if Niko would waver in his allegiance to Redmond and the sept, she knew that he now wanted peace, as he had confided to her that he had had enough of the constant talk of war in Ireland, and the killing for others, and was now working for a life of civility and security, placating the settlers and the sept by turns.

'Medb told me that, after the reprisals, life had been fraught with hunger, wandering, uncertainty and hard labour. All this,' she thought guiltily,' whilst Niko and I had been pampered in the harem. Redmond knows of the likely consequences, but, fired by his fears of the ambition of the settler adventurers, the disdain of the English, and being unheeding of the blessings of a comfortable life, he is unlikely to resist rebellion when his Overlord beckons.'

She could see no easy future resolution, either for herself and the pains that often overcame her, or for her people and what pains they would soon have to endure.

CHAPTER TWELVE

onan's travels, as well as Dermot's, had been delayed and beset by severe cold and blizzards. He had quickly returned to Redmond before the worst of the storms, so had not been able to find Niko and Conor and tell them of the death of Lady Medb, or deliver other news from Ireland. In fact, little information from Britannia had reached the two men over the winter months. They had travelled widely in the south and around the Mediterranean sea, sometimes trading cargoes with Captain Alfonso, and knew more about the Holy Roman Empire's wars than their own. They were relieved to hear from many quarters that treaties between warring France and Spain were on the verge of being signed. The Dutch fleet had come back after years of adventure exploring Eastern seas; hearing about which caused Niko a stab of envy.

They enquired about support for the Irish cause from seafarers, freebooters, priests and politicos everywhere in the south. The replies were not encouraging. It seemed that Spain had given thanks to God that their treasure ships had not been seized after the battle of Cadiz. Niko met with some sympathy, but was advised that the heavy waters around Britannia were a constant danger, that the re-built Spanish fleet would not be lightly risked, and would turn back if need be.

As he stood on the deck of a north-bound flyboat, Niko stared at the grey and choppy sea and thought about women. Hakim, a merchant he had visited on the warm Barbary Coast had loaned him a sensual 'houri' named Fatima. Niko did not agree that delight and passion outside marriage could be a sin and considered that perhaps priests and pastors mistook some of the scriptures. He decided he would not do penance for his pleasure with the houri, or for visiting the mosque with Hakim. But he had found beautiful Fatima a poor companion, in that she was unwilling to converse. The everyday humour, gossip and conversation in the stronghold always lightened his days and had helped him regain humanity after the brutality of battle.

Rolling with the motion of Alfonso's ship, he suddenly realised, rather to his consternation, that competent Alice Plymmiswoode, older and buxom, sharpened his wits as well as his desire. He understood she was wealthy, and knowing that Thomas's age and injuries would take their toll sooner rather than later, he pondered whether he should speak to Thomas about a marriage. Alice was not above his rank, and a cemented alliance with the sept could lead to peace and increasing prosperity for all.

Niko was relieved, after having had no word from his squire for some months, to hear from one of the pilots that Dermot was now on his way back to Le Havre with important news. They all met at a livery stable. Dermot passed on respects from their kin and then explained what had happened to him after he had left them the previous year.

Conor surveyed the squire, saying, 'Was ever a man so beset by trials! You have the shanks of a new-born foal, Dermot, and the thin face of a greyhound. Eat well or women will not listen to your wooing,' and then unfastening the door of a back stall, he led out a fine young Arab pony, then giving its reins into Dermot's hand. The squire was delighted at this gift, but, as he stood fondling the horse, he became increasingly nervous,

As Niko demanded,' What has happened in our land since we left.'

'This has been a hungry winter, for me and those in the stronghold, and also for a multitude in our country. Our supplies are much reduced. Folk are restless. And I have other sad news.'

With mounting anger and grief, they heard about the circumstances of Medb's death.

Conor, scowling, gripped his dagger asking fiercely, 'Was she avenged? Was there slaughter of Thomas's household? That our great Lady should die unshrived!'

'Oh brave, if otherworldly Medb, our lifelong support and friend!' said Niko, pacing and trying to master himself.

He recalled how Medb had always recognised the Ottoman part of him, even if suspicious of it. Once she had told him that he should cherish his father and his dual heritage as there was honour and valiant history in both. He knew of no other who ever expressed such sentiments.

Dermot spoke sadly, 'After the burial at the place of the ancestors, Redmond and a band rode to Hurst Place. Thomas was away and the woman Alice, his sister, had sent Lady Gile to Constable Porter in Dublin for protection – of that we were sure, as it was confirmed by Nuala O'Byrne. Lord Redmond was like to kill Thomas's sister, but then became fearful of reprisal, as new troops were known to be in Ireland. He left reminding the woman of the geis and instead sought and killed the Fleming murderer.'

'Alice Plymmiswoode, the Englishwoman- how did she receive Redmond? Was she arrogant and haughty ?'

'Seemingly, the Englishwoman was ashamed, denied that she had ordered the murder and prettily begged forgiveness. Later we heard that over the winter, she and Lady Gile remained with the Constable in Dublin.'

Conor said, ' But what she allowed to happen was unforgiveable. Niko, the occupiers and Lord Redmond's traitorous wife should fear the revenge of the Old Ones.'

'There were portents,' added Dermot excitedly, 'a heavy falling of grey ash, early snows and other wonders. A glowing phantasm was seen in the sea, shining in the glare of the sun. Redmond's wrath and sorrow knew no bounds. He has vowed that one day, his revenge on them all will be swift and sure. The settlers will pay dearly for the death of Lady Medb. Her 'geis' demands it.'

Niko was fiercely disappointed with Alice and Thomas. He had considered them more pragmatic and understanding than they had now shown themselves to be. He wondered whether he would have allowed her to live after such insult and atrocity, but acknowledged her courage as the band would have been many and armed.

He sighed, saying, 'Our lands are likely to be plunged again into warfare and hardship.'

'There is more news, Niko.' Dermot paused dramatically before announcing the contents of the letter, intercepted in Dublin, that Lady Gile had been delivered in England of Redmond's son at an unknown place, and that mother and child had been sent to Alice Plymmiswoode's London dwelling for safe-keeping.

'You should have seen Lord Redmond's joy,' said Dermot.' He has named the boy Rory after one of our ancient heroes, but the letter said he was given the name of Matthew.'

Conor sniffed. 'He will likely have been churched already in this English name!'

Niko was shaken that Gile had successfully carried and birthed. He had thought her too thin and frail to breed a healthy child.

Redmond had indeed been in high glee at the news of Susannah's safe delivery.

'I thought her rumoured pregnancy was but a tale,' he had said to Orlaith. 'A feast must be prepared, with bardic songs and music – we will also celebrate Medb's love of our heritage. Friar Ignatius must lead prayers for the well-being of the child and give him my Irish naming.'

'Redmond, you are too hasty. A new babe may not survive.'

'Medb prophesied that I should and would bear only sons. I see no reason why Thomas's sister should not keep her well-fed. I see no reason why the English would have starved Gile. I think they will want to ensure that my heir survives. They place importance on God-given heirs – Earl Tyrone follows their example in his ambitions for his sons… in which case so will I! We want future control over our ancestral town lands and demesne. I want the boy, my son, my heir. I have a rightful claim to him. Orlaith, I care not for Gile – or even her marriage gift - the English, Dutch or the Flemish weavers can have her. Constable Porter will no doubt send her back to her kin if I show no interest in her person. But I will not let them keep the infant.'

Dermot now faithfully repeated Redmond's words and dynastic ambitions to his companions.

"Orlaith," Redmond said aloud to all within earshot, "Rory must not become a hostage for loyalty to the Crown. I must have my son, my true heir, so that when we and our Overlord, steeped in common purpose and believing in our Cause, eventually treat with the Crown and prevent more English governance, we can give him our lands." Our sons must have their birthright as there are so few of our noble line left.'

Niko considered, then spoke.

'I wonder what Pieter Heyden knows of all this. He is expecting us in Calais later this month. With Lady Gile. Redmond has need of Gile's marriage portion.' He sighed. 'This will not be easy to resolve. It is unlikely that the English Officials are fully aware of the significance of Medb's murder. Many will now listen to Tyrone's call to join him in rebellion.'

'When I left Leinster, the newly arrived Crown militias were not marauding,' answered Dermot. 'But it was clear that more soldiery is about. Some make easy targets to ambush, but Lord Redmond tells us to hold back as we have had no call to arms.'

'Conor!' ordered Niko. 'Find out quickly the latest sailings to our shores! We must go home. Pieter Heyden can wait.'

Still brimming with fury, Conor quickly left, too late for Dermot, quietening the hound which was disturbing his new pony, to stop him. He sat heavily on a nearby bale of hay and spoke hesitantly as he had commands that he knew Niko would not like.

'Redmond has heard that the Earl of Essex, a mighty warlord, victorious in '95 against the Spanish, has now been granted leave to raise a huge army. Up until now, only stragglers and stray militias come near our stronghold and are easily dealt with should they threaten, but such a horde could seek and find us. Not having been ordered to leave their labours and muster their arms, most of our churls still work and are loyal to the Settler Thomas. When I left, Redmond was reinforcing the stronghold against siege. He was called to a Gathering of southern nobles and their vassals.'

'I should have been there.' Niko clenched his fists.

'Fintan accompanied him. They did not find out the mind of our Overlord but he could well go to war when he judges the time right. We have heard that some earls have already declared for the Crown and will sail to greet Essex and his army if and when it comes.'

'Lord Essex will try to recruit the corsairs and captains here in this place and St. Malo to transport or join him. Also the Dutch mercenaries that William The Silent had organised into a better fighting force, may well, for pieces of eight, ally themselves with the Crown,' said Niko. 'We must hope that the rest of his army will contain many untried troops and youths from the towns and cities who have not lived in bogs, forests and mountains like ours.'

Dermot's eyes were hard slits and his eyebrows fully arched.

'Tell the mercenaries that Ronan says there will be an unpleasant surprise for the Earl of Essex should he come to Dublin Bay. Tell them not to lease their ships and to stay away if they value their lives. I will say no more.'

'You heard this from Ronan?'

Dermot nodded. 'Conor will soon find us a passage to Ireland. These are important times, and I can help my brother.'

'No, Niko.' Dermot looked down miserably. 'Redmond says that his way cannot now be your way. Being a vassal chief, he will likely be away with the armies if called. Conor may return to the stronghold but Redmond says we are to travel to England soon to Alice Plymmiswoode's London house. He asks that you and I find Lady Gile and his son. You may watch them there or escort them to her kin if she wishes, but you must guard his heir, ensure he thrives and is safe, and bring him to us in Ireland, best without his cursed mother, when the time is right. Also before we leave here, you must try to obtain the marriage portion from his wife's kin so we can pay mercenaries to fight for us.'

Dermot handed over the pouch of gold that Redmond had given him.

'What! How can I accomplish this?' cried Niko with a mixture of hurt and fury.' I cannot believe I am commanded away from Redmond! Mistress Plymmiswoode could have us arrested and do we even know where her lodging is in London?'

There was a long silence. Dermot shrugged.

'He said that you must be near his son Rory, whom the English call Matthew. It seems the Plymmiswoodes are well-known fleece and wool traders and wholesalers in a cloth guild and her residence should be easy to find. You know this.' He continued hurriedly. 'He, Redmond's, words were, "this is the most important task I have ever set Niko." He said you must not fail. He and Orlaith decreed, and our Council concurred, that you must not fight the Crown. If and when our Overlord calls us to arms, if this is not so already, you are to go to England or remain on foreign soils and find us information and supplies to help us. At the same time, you must try to ensure you are seen as loyal. Orlaith said that should the rebellion not succeed, someone must protect our people – it must be known that you were not involved. He said, "Tell him remember how Fergus's absence during the last Rising was able to help us when we were "in extremis".'

Niko was for once speechless as Dermot said, 'I am also unhappy that I cannot return with Conor. I pleaded to fight when the time came, but I was commanded otherwise – as are you.'

Abruptly Niko turned away bidding Dermot depart.

Later, he sat thinking whilst he smoked a calming pipe. He remembered Medb's proud, fine-boned face before she aged, her trials and her fierce loyalty to her people.

He murmured, 'What have you done, Lady Medb, to summon the Morrigu? Why such a powerful spirit?'

Conor departed soon after for Ireland. Dermot and Niko made their way to Calais to where Pieter Heyden was waiting. After exchanging bows, the Dutchman said abruptly, his voice nasal and resonant with suspicion,

'Our rendezvous is later than I would have wished, but snows and frosts have overwhelmed the Provinces, affecting our travel and transports. I see you do not bring Susannah. Why does she not live with her husband? It seems that she stayed most of this last winter in the English Constable's household and then went to England. Why? If she does not want to return to the Irish Lord, why has she not been sent here with you? Nothing has been explained to her uncle's satisfaction. The English Crown demands many royals for her board and charge, which he will not pay until she is received at home.'

'I have not been able to return to Ireland this severe winter and have had no word, other than to also hear recently that she had been sent to England. Lord Redmond may have sent her on her way to me but perhaps she sought shelter with the Constable, the storms being so harsh. I only know for certain that Lord Redmond does not insist on her return to the sept.'

'Has she then been kidnapped by the Crown? Is she perhaps a hostage in return for her husband's loyalty? If so, this is outrageous.'

Niko shrugged. For whatever reason, so far it seemed Pieter Heyden was not aware of the circumstances of Susannah's sojourn in Dublin or her baby boy. He decided not to be the one to enlighten him, not least because this could complicate his mission.

Pieter lifted a fine cambric handkerchief to a dripping nose.

'She may well not want to stay with her husband. I have heard that the savage Irish are quick in temper and that many in Ireland live like beasts in the forest.'

Niko frowned, but realised that Pieter was determined to provoke him, and with difficulty kept calm.

Pieter continued, 'Susannah is a pious, willing, modest and obedient maid. I know her disposition from her childhood. I suspect she was unable to tolerate your brother's Faith and style of life and may have been given asylum by the Protestant English in Dublin.'

Niko thought that he would have used 'sullen', rather than modest, for Gile's demeanour, but he said, 'I agree that the Irish way of life in a stronghold must have seemed very different to Gile – Susannah – and no doubt she has been much affected by her losses and is missing her kin and her Faith. I do know that a Mistress Alice Plymmiswoode has been her chaperone in the Constable's castle so Susannah may well be lodging with her in London. We know this family – they are respectable and worthy Protestants. Mistress Alice is the widowed sister of Thomas Hurst, an English settler in the Leinster March.'

'Whatever the case,' replied Pieter, 'at present, in view of the war, Mistress Susannah will be more safe in the bosom of her family than anywhere else - even London where there are ever alarums about Spanish invasion. That is the request of her uncle and mother.'

'I doubt if Lord Redmond will argue with that. If he wishes, he can send for her when our country becomes quiet again,' answered Niko. Then he offered to visit Mistress Alice in London and ask her to let Susannah return to Leiden, and to escort her there, if his expenses were paid. He then again pressed hard for a marriage portion or compensation for Redmond to be given in advance.

'Her marriage may well not be legal in our land! So you, as well as the English Crown, want our gold royals! You know that we lost many goods as well as our people in those treacherous fogs- and we are highly taxed to pay for the large standing armies to keep the Spanish at bay. Susannah's husband could soon be in traitorous rebellion. Do you think us fools? How can M. De Hem pay both sides and keep his honour?'

'He may have to, if he wishes Gile's safe return. Some say even honour has a price.'

'Do you not think of the maid – whose name is not Gile but Susannah – in this, bartered like goods to a Moorish corsair?' said Pieter, his hand creeping towards his dagger.

'She is a maid no longer,' said Niko breathing heavily. 'She is Lady Gile MacFeagh, and her life was saved by my brother. Perhaps she longs to be in Leiden, and her kin long for her return, but she is Lord Redmond's wife and he wishes to be compensated if he is forced to live without her. Sir Rowland Porter, and Mistress Alice could have returned her immediately to her husband, but did not. But, in spite of your insults, in return for your gold pieces, I repeat that I will contrive to get her back to her home if that is her wish. I intend to travel to London anyway to assure the Court of our loyalty.'

Pieter relaxed slightly, saying, 'Very well, you may try and, if all comes to pass, you may be compensated. Her uncle and mother's request is clear to you and you must make it clear to Susannah. It is possible that M. De Hem will also send me to London soon. If I see Mistress Alice or Susannah before you, much will depend on what she tells me. I will leave the address of my lodgings at the Church of the Austin Friars.'

Pieter made a sketchy bow and took his leave.

Pieter's journey to M. De Hem at his chambers in Amsterdam was uneventful. The season had become warmer and pleasant, and sneezes had subsided. There was jubilation that the Edict of Nantes had been recently signed allowing limited tolerance of the Protestants in French territories. He had felt safer as he discharged other duties in Paris before travelling north.

As he disembarked from the canal boat, the gaily- painted bridges were vibrant against a pale spring sky. There were shouts and thumps from goods being hauled up from the adjacent canal barges to storage chambers on the first level of the tall gabled, town house, then being passed through to carts on the other side. He made his way to a narrow chamber and stood before his employer, who was seated in a fur-lined cope, beside a long window. M. De Hem put down his quill and looked up, his brows creased. After perfunctory courtesies Pieter described his meeting with Niko MacFeagh.

'I have paid nothing as yet, other than for information from independent sources. No trade introductions have yet come from Dublin in return for any compensation, as you suggested. I am not sure we are hearing truths.'

De Hem pursed his lips, plump and glistening above his beard. He said, 'I do not trust her husband's envoy. You need to find and talk to Susannah.'

'Should I seek her in London, or visit the Constable in Dublin?'

'Ireland is a dangerous place for you to delve in at present.' De Hem paused. 'The Dutch States Council is allowing merchants some secondary loans to help finance our defence and exploration to other markets in the East. I have applied for one to expand our business and recoup our losses. I mentioned before that we could well transact some cloth finishing business at the London Exchange now that the winter has passed. I have messages that our work is much better than our rivals in England and that the samples we sent have been authenticated with seals of quality.

We must also be sure that Susannah is well and unharmed. So – as well as the bastard Irishman, go to London to this Mistress Alice Plymmiswoode who before her marriage, may have been born a Hurst, and find my niece. I seem to remember a cloth dealer named Hurst, from some time back. They supplied us with some washed and combed fleeces and some spun spools. I have heard nothing against them. Send messengers when you find Susannah. Requests for her fine work have had to be denied. Also she does not know her mother, my wife's sister, died two weeks since and is now with God.'

Pieter was open-mouthed. 'Susannah's woes increase. I should have been at the burial.'

'No matter. Pray for her. But you, not I, will have to inform my niece. Go now.'

Pieter bowed and turned to leave, feeling upset at this task and discontented, not only wishing his skills in negotiation could be more recognised by M. De Hem, but also wishing that he was not so often set unwelcome tasks. There was a family portrait on wall facing him centred in which was Susannah's perfect countenance. Her face and shy smile danced before Pieter's eyes. He blinked as full sunlight from the window blinded him suddenly. Then a dark grey shadow moved across the room, falling across his face.

CHAPTER THIRTEEN

ot long after Susannah's son was born, travellers arrived at the Somerset Abbey.

I hear voices and bridles echoing in the still air, though no cart has come through here for many a day. I look through the arch. It begins to thaw. The icy rain is heavy. There are men leading horses and pulling carriages, men scurrying. Sister Benedicta greets the visitors as if she knows them. But one of the travellers is a stooped woman holding tight on to a portly man. Both are wrapped in cloaks and furs. They look like gentlefolk. The man speaks quite slowly in an English tongue.... what says he? I know some words...'we journey to London' 'highways' 'shelter'...... Abbey'...

Benedicta curtseyed and fussed, leading the drenched young man and older woman to the fire in a room lined with heavy arras fabric. She then left. The servant who had helped the couple remove their cloaks, shoes and the man's tall brimmed hat followed her out. Watching from an alcove, holding her baby, Susannah then pushed her full cap far back on to her head and walked into their line of sight. She made a deep obeisance. They stared at her. She spoke slowly to them, trying to use a Parisian accent.

'Oh what a deluge the heavens have sent! I too have been a traveller. My husband in Ireland sent me to England for safety but I came into my labour early and they birthed me here, but oh how I long for him to see his son!'

'Indeed!' replied the older lady, but somewhat bemused. She moved to a large wooden chair near the hearth, and leaned back exhausted against a cushion. Another servant came in with a tray of warm drinks, threw more huge logs on to the open fire, and then backed out. The man warmed his hands and stared at Gile. His expression was lively.

'You were fortunate,' he replied. 'As are we, to be stranded so near this place. My mother was carried here by a strong young servant, but I nearly had to swim my horse on the flooded road! Snowdrifts halted our carriage a distance away and then such a sudden thaw!'

There had been long pauses in his speech whilst he sought the correct phrasing.

The older woman added, more fluently, 'Such a weather is unusual for this season. This long hard winter still has a sting in its tail! I am told that many have starved or frozen to death, God rest their souls, and some now will be drowned or have to flee their homes. I am Lady Anne Templeton.' She held out her hand to be kissed. 'And this is my son Edmund. We have lands further west. Our felicitations on the birth of your son. You are from France?'

The man, brushing down his thick doublet dusted with raindrops, continued staring at Susannah. The infant stared back, but she modestly dropped her eyes.

'Susannah Breydel, my Lord, my Lady. I am Protestant, hailing from Leiden in the Dutch Republic.'

The man, bulky, with a round face and trimmed curly hair, made a brief bow. In the distance, Susannah heard Cecilia's heavy step in the corridor, followed by a servant.

'My babe grows heavy.' She smiled. 'I will go now that Mistress Cecilia comes to welcome you.'

They watched as Susannah walked gracefully away.

Cecilia greeted her neighbours somewhat anxiously. She generally kept her distance from the Templetons, as she feared they might suspect her of following the old Faith. They had been generous two years back with monies for the indigent mothers. Cecilia had diverted these funds for repair of the chapel altar and roof.

After courtesies, Edmund requested shelter for his party until the floods subsided.

'But for as little time as possible, as we are expected in London. Who, pray, is the lady who greeted us? She looks like an angel, sent to rescue us from these treacherous lanes.'

'Dutch it seems – not usual in these parts. She speaks prettily. She chafes to leave after her birthing,' added Lady Templeton.

Cecilia acquiesced with a tight smile, annoyed that Susannah had greeted them before herself. She had been relieved to get Alice's instructions, before the late snows, to send Susannah and the babe Matthew to her London residence. She thanked God that now it had begun to thaw. She knew it was a sin, but, aware of unspoken contempt, she had come to dislike the woman, even though Susannah was forever on her knees praying. She had often thought, savagely, that Susannah was in some way possessed, appearing to float silently and sullenly from unexpected corners, even in pregnant bulk. She rarely heard her make a happy remark and never a grateful one. This latest appearance confirmed her view that Susannah was devilishly wayward. She also feared that at any time, some 'wild Irishman' and his cohorts could arrive and demand her, committing who knows what violence and sacrilege in the process.

'She was not here long before you came in,' answered Edmund.' She said her husband in Ireland had sent her to England and that you had birthed her here. May she join us later? Some conversation may cheer her and will help me improve my knowledge of that tongue. I take it she is not one of your indigent women?'

'No, no, she is of the middling sort. She is named Susannah Breydel. She is a protégé of Mistress Alice Plymmiswoode – Abraham's widow- kin to me as you know.' Lady Templeton nodded, and Cecilia continued, 'Susannah married in Ireland, which is most unsafe just now. I think it inadvisable that she spends much time in talk, as she must make ready for travel to Plymmiswoode Hall in London when the roads are passable. Also she is still weak after the birth.'

'Susannah? A musical name! But she had a healthy glow and a quick step when we saw her!'

'Ah, Mistress Alice,' said Edmund's mother ignoring his interjection. 'I had some hopes she would consider an alliance with him,' she gestured towards Edmund, 'through which she would have bettered her rank and us our fortunes! But, on broaching the matter, she said she could not consider re-marriage whilst her brother in Ireland ailed from old wounds and needed her.'

Her son gave a short laugh.

'She would not have me or knew that our farms were so prone to flooding! I was quite relieved. She is years older than me, and unlikely to bear children, but I'll allow she is very rich, and I could do worse.'

His mother rounded on him. 'If you did not eat and drink like one of those huge beasts they display in the Tower of London, she may have been more partial. However, you could still press your suit when we return to London.'

Cecilia intervened hastily, saying 'As Susannah pleases you, I shall ask her to join us after Evensong at our supper, but I doubt whether she will have much conversation. She is pious and prays much. I would humbly ask that you converse with her in the English tongue. She knows little of this and must improve. I fear it will be a long time before she can join her husband. Mistress Alice will care for them well.'

She thought that they would condemn her if Susannah was kept in her room, but also that she could not control what she might say if allowed to converse freely in French of which she understood little. Then she had an idea.

Cecilia sought out Susannah later and told her that she should never have accosted the couple, and must do penance. Also she said, in no uncertain terms, that Susannah was to speak little and then not in the French tongue.

What penance could be worse than living here and not with mine own kin? I thank you Lord for sending these people to me. Old Cecilia's voice crackles and bruises. The soft tones of Orlaith, although I understood them not, calmed my jumping heart. I want to be in London. There may be messages there from my family or from Christian Calvet. I shall insist that Mistress Alice releases me to him as he is my betrothed.. But perhaps she will not do this… the English Constable wants me and my son guarded as a hostage for Redmond's good faith. I did hear this from the sailors on a ship that carried me here… they spoke my tongue…

Susannah remained quiet and demure throughout the evening supper, smiling uncomprehendingly at Edmund's overtures made in English. Desultorily, the company discussed the Irish situation.

'If the Queen agrees that the Great Lord, the Earl of Essex, can raise an army to suppress the Earl of Tyrone's revolt, it will soon be resolved,' said Lady Anne. 'I will send some men from our demesne if it comes to pass.'

Cecilia eventually broached the subject that had been occupying her all evening. She asked if Susannah could travel with them to London, saying with bravado that Alice would reimburse the monies for their guards and fresh horses and refreshment – no matter how many stops along the way.

'After all,' she thought, 'why should this be at my charge? Alice can scarcely refuse to pay this and can well afford it.'

Edmund and Lady Anne looked at each other. Edmund then said, as his mother opened her mouth, 'Of course she may travel with us. It will be safer than whatever you ladies can provide – no doubt yokels only as escorts!' He tapped the hilt of his fine rapier and his dagger in its velvet scabbard. 'And we have men-at-arms with us.'

It was then agreed that Benedicta and the infant Matthew would accompany them in a following covered cart whilst Susannah would ride on Cecilia's own pony, Dapple. Cecilia rode rarely these days and thought with satisfaction that her neighbours would send him back well-fed and exercised.

They all set out when the floods and rains had subsided, stopping overnight several times en route. Those on horseback made more speed on the wider and better maintained highways. Not far from the main carriageway to London, they halted for a change of horses, resting and breakfasting at the Lion Inn. Around this were clustered cottages, shops, pedestrians and bothies. The Inn was spread over a large area, its back part shaded by an enormous holly tree which obscured a view of the river beyond, whilst its front was alive with dismounting passengers and servants in various states of distraction. The braying of laden pack animals and snorting, steaming horses mingled with the shouts of the ostlers, the jingle of bridles and the clatter of hooves and wagon wheels on cobbles. Later that day, Lady Anne's carriage and the mule cart carrying Benedicta and a fractious Matthew eventually joined them.

As they prepared to continue, Lady Anne requested Susannah and her infant to join her in her coach for the final part of the journey, so that Cecilia's horse and mules could be rested and returned to the Abbey.

That endless damp ride is now behind me. That goggling full-cheeked wet-lipped Englishman was forever moving to hold my bridle in order to touch my breast. The hat, too small, on which he now displays a large medallion and a feather, does not become him, but he did converse a little about the silk weavers and cloth finishers from the Low Countries. In Leiden Christian Calvet told me that his domicile was beyond Aldgate on the City Wall, in the area of Spitle Fields. Sir Edmund told me that the Foundation and church of St Mary Spitle was seemingly, before the break with Rome, of very great extent, reaching from Shoreditch to its north and Berward's Lane to its south. He said it is now much built upon, and is known for its market, but also that the great Cross in the uncovered part of the churchyard has been made good and Preachings are held there, especially when crowds gather at Eastertide.

'Sit still, mistress!' complained Lady Anne. 'What agitates you so? The jolting of this vehicle is bad enough without you getting up and down to peer through its slits at the road. Your child whimpers at your restlessness! There, there little one... let me hold you quietly, so you can sleep.'

We go slowly. This way is clogged with carts, and loud with shouts and curses. I can already hear the bells; so many bells... the spires and towers of the city lie before me and beckon me. I feel as intensely as when my father and I rode towards Paris. The old Lady Anne does not know my mind. She would have me whipped if she knew my intention. I would that I could have her tawny velvet gown trimmed with fur...'

Lady Anne continued to talk, partly in English and partly in French.

'Aagh – I always know we have arrived near the London Bridge because of the stench which seeps into the coach. When will the Privy Council, Mayors and Aldermen address this? Some parts of the city are so filthy that men must wear thigh boots to enter them. I often regret coming to this plaguey City, but the goods I can purchase here cannot be found elsewhere. Also it is best if Edmund pursues his legal studies and fashionable pastimes near the Court so they can know us and his name. He enjoys this hive of a town and its amusements… more of that I do not wish to know. See how this little man's blue-green eyes begin to close… his mouth is thin and wide, his hair reddish and he looks a little sprite rather than an angel like you his mother…'

She looked up but Susannah was not listening, but still peering through the top slits of the old-fashioned equipage.

Here I can spy the celebrated London Bridge, which runs between the north and south banks of a wide river they call Thames…. there are tall tenements and a throng upon it. Sir Edmund told me there are many fine houses along this river belonging both to the gentry and to those who do business at the Royal Exchange. Alice told me she keeps a large household in the City within sight of its Tower and near to a Gate on its Wall. She has a warehouse, yards, chambers, offices and gardens reached through a winding lane. She said it is a brisk and active place where all are occupied both day and night. To what Babel have I come? The shouts, ringing and alarms of this place… the stinks! I think on that stronghold village and Redmond's sharp odour, the odour of blood. The old witch woman too had a savage smell… even now, I can feel her claws pulling at my skirt whilst I was seated behind the guard and beseeching my attention… that strange old flat-brimmed hat fallen from her head. Oh, how she screamed like the devil she was… why did the Irish people hold her in such honour? Now the afternoon draws in…

Susannah turned politely to Lady Anne and asked about the specific location of those Protestant cloth traders and weavers from France and elsewhere.

'I believe that many who are here from France, Flanders and Holland live outside the walls and in the east of the City, or by the Tower of London in the ward of St Katharine. I fear there has been unrest because London had too many incomers from foreign parts… you are called, in English, "'Strangers'". Might you know any of these folk? '

'Non, Madame, although my father had acquaintances here.'
'Did? Is he dead?'

'Oui, madame. It saddens me to talk of it.' She crossed herself and then pleaded tiredness and dozed. Lady Anne suspected she was pretending. It had begun to worry the older woman that everyone was most unforthcoming about Susannah's family, and that Edmund was clearly besotted with her.

'The girl does not respond much to me in spite of the assistance we are giving her,' thought Lady Anne crossly. 'But I am damned if I will speak much more in the French tongue and see her smile behind her hand.'

She decided she would not encourage the relationship further once she had delivered the girl and babe safely to Alice Plymmiswoode.

Mistress Alice said that folk from all the regions of Britain, and many on the continent, have flocked to this London which grows bigger by the year. She said that the crowdings pollute the air and give rise to much sickness. She said she was fortunately away when, some four years ago, thousands died of plagues many near the BishopsGate in St Botolph. I recall her saying that she had been pleased, after her husband's death, to be invited to her brother in cleanly Leinster. She scolded me, saying she must bide in the castle with all the discomfort of the port and garrison because of me... but she must have known that war would have forced her to a garrison town. She did never have to live with savages... her arrogance would have led to a whipping there...

The sounds of the City intensified and Susannah opened her eyes.

This Lady Anne mutters on... I can hear little of what she says.. Matthew is sleepy on her lap but I wish him awake so that he will sleep later...

'Very well, you may take him and have him awake and show him the town, but I think he would sleep and will be fretful,' said Lady Anne subsiding into a frowning silence, whilst the infant wriggled and squawked at his mother's determined poking.

The Good Lord holds me in His Hands. In Redmond's stronghold, that Irish Friar Ignatius said that the Saints had interceded for me but my pastors would say his words are heresy. Mistress Alice was away from her goodly dwelling. Her steward greeted us. During our welcome, I had hung back modestly near the stabling, saying I would wait for Benedicta who was following in the cart, so as to allow Sir Edmund and his mother to gain entrance and refreshment first. All the servants were hurrying forward to help with the arrivals. I was capped, cloaked and keeping my reticule beneath. I had a small number of coins-some silver- from Mistress Alice for my work whilst in the castle. These I had, with difficulty, kept hidden at the Abbey. The daylight was fading as I, with Matthew, wandered around outside and behind Alice's fine residence with its windowed upper floors. The sky was glowing soft pink. At first I could no way to escape but then I spied an open arch and long gravelled path to a private courtyard with small beds of plants and a walled tree-lined garden with a guarded door to the outside. The door porter had gone, maybe to help the ostlers in the stables. On a hook by the side of the door was a vast key.

Matthew was already fractious with tiredness and hunger so I went back to where all were settling and greeting and pinched him hard so he should scream...so that he would not annoy all. I then told those about that I wished to nurse the baby outside in a sheltered place and they quickly agreed. I caught my breath as one woman seemed doubtful, saying it was near evening, not good to be outside when unknown spirits may lurk and that I should go in and she would calm my child, but I insisted. While all were busy, I went back into the garden and put Matthew to the breast... then I... now... my tears overcome me... then I finished feeding my son and kissed him. I quickly left my son, well-wrapped and sleepy,... I left the babe, God forgive me, but I knew the porter would find him and that Alice would care for him... by a love seat in the garden. I quietly let myself out, locked the door and threw the key into a midden by the City Gate which I hurriedly slipped through amidst the crowd leaving before the evening curfew. I am sorry for the whippings all will receive and will do penance for them. M. Calvet will help me to claim him back and intercede with my mother and my uncle. I could not risk him on the streets of London. I went eastwards to where Sir Edmund said many "Strangers" lived, and came into more crowded streets. I blended with the folk in the failing light and, although her retainers must have tried to seek me, they did not succeed, thank the Lord, as they would not have been able to leave the City after the curfew. I prayed and sheltered at an almshouse where the pious folk there spoke my tongue. For some groats, they gave me pottage and found me a place for a night with other wayfarers in the chapel buildings. My bosom still *aches with milk but I hope soon it will pass. I did feed some thin babes of the poor Flemish girls there… that was my gift. Before leaving, they told me that I must walk boldly as those here can be suspicious of pedestrians. They said that it was the parishes even further to the east where stood weavers' attics and sheds and that I must go near to a spacious ground where the men of the Queen's artillery fire their muskets. From thence I have to make my way to the hamlet where lay the former Priory of St. Mary Spitle with its newly built pulpit, surrounding mansions and a particular handsome new house to its south. They said I will walk for some time on hummocky roads and must not go too far from the Great Ditch….I walk quickly through fields and open spaces…*

Arriving back the next day, Alice was nervously told of Susannah's flight and abandonment of her baby. Her steward said that Lady Anne and Edmund had quickly departed on hearing that she was not at home when they arrived, and wishing to avoid the curfew. Before they left, Edmund had enquired after Susannah, but was told she was feeding the infant, and Lady Anne had peremptorily asked the steward to make their farewells. Shocked and angry, Alice ordered her retainers to continue their search for Susannah and bring her back and punishment for the door porter who had left his post.

Now it grows late and thrice I have lost my way following a stinking paved way, Hogge Lane, where meats are sold, and have now walked for many hours, through other lanes and courts. All around me are noisome gullies and alleys where all kinds of filthiness has been cast, sometime disguised by the mud. I pass many folk and stalls and great carts and stop to wonder at the colours of the markets. I know that I must only enquire my way from Dutch or Flemings or a Church. Now it rains and my skirts flap coldly against my limbs… would that I had my close woven oiled Irish jerkin. Oh noise of this place… the rumblings, the endless tolling of bells, and the shoutings of this great City. Here and there are starving bootless and frozen beggars. I would not be one of these! Lord, help me.I pray constantly that you will help me, my Lord God. Now I hear the musket fire from the Artillery Ground and now I see the Tenter Ground where great dyed cloths are dried, and here, without a churchyard, I come to a quadrant and many with the dress of Flanders or the Low Countries. Their faces are blank, or strained, or if they glance at me curiously, they stare. To the side of this lane, I pass a grove of teazels used for carding, I have been sent a sign… further on are some men building something in a field. Now I come upon some goodly almshouses and a fair two-storey house which must contain some Burgess and his kin. Two women are walking towards me with baskets of linen. Their headresses are in the French fashion so I will speak. They direct me to a street some way further on with a stretch of tall dwellings with attics and large windows facing south. They said that there is one in a narrow lane reached through a causey[4] which may be that of Calvet. It is being repaired. They swiftly walk on with their heavy baskets. There is a carcass by a patch of common land to my right. I see a large sleek raven alight upon it… its cries are like the croak of that old Irish witch. Dear God, it is a bloated sheep, swarming with flies… what stinks… the hooded bird glances at me and opens its wings… keening, she would spread her long black cloak with its ancient fraying gilded tassels around her to guard against the winds. I shudder as that old woman cursing comes into my mind.. I will walk faster…this here may be the workshop of Calvet. Men on a framework of poles beside the building see to the water spilling from a broken gutter. Two passers-by look at me sharply and are curious about my business when I say I seek one Christian Calvet. I smile and just say that I have come to bring Calvet good fortune. One wished me God's Grace. She said that many who found work there did not stay long. Calvet will not tolerate poor work, of that I am sure. I will tell him about Matthew and that we can rear him in our Faith so he too can sit with the Lord's Chosen. Please God, now, exhausted and hungry, I have come to the dwelling of a Christian man who will harbour and succour me…

Summer to Winter 1598

As the year wore on, all enquiries and leads as to Susannah's whereabouts came to nothing. Most thought it likely that Susannah had perished somehow on the streets. For Alice however, doubt remained. She remembered the girl's initiative in waylaying her in Ireland. She determined that the girl would have a thrashing when found, for so deserting her child.

Alice and Sister Benedicta cared for the happy babe, of whom they were becoming increasingly fond. Alice received no further instructions from Thomas about Susannah or the infant. She knew that her brother would be caught up in the English response to the spreading rebellion against the Crown.

Niko and Dermot had eventually arrived at the imposing pillared gateway of Plymmiswoode Hall, requesting, on behalf of Lord Redmond, information on the welfare of his wife. At first they had been denied entrance, as Alice's steward arranged for burly unemployed apprentices to watch out for unauthorised visitors. Hands were on daggers and swords. Alice was suspicious at first, but hearing that they had come, not only to see Susannah, but also to show loyalty to the Crown, had ordered her steward to let them in. They were shocked at Susannah's actions, but relieved that she had not left with Matthew. Niko told Alice of his meeting with her uncle's envoy Pieter Heyden, and both Redmond and her mother's wish that she should return to Leiden. Alice was finally persuaded to let the men help in the search for the missing woman. Niko had wondered silently if Susannah, when found, would prefer to return to her uncle without her son, and would agree for the child to be sent to Redmond.

In the bowels of the overcrowded and stinking city, their heads jangling from the sounding of innumerable bells, the two men hunted for Susannah, sleeping at ale-houses or Inns with their weapons to hand, and riding through the thoroughfares with their hands on their daggers or the hilts of large flat Irish swords. It was as though they were prey to be hunted down. The populace was antagonistic to foreign folk, not only concerned about competition for their livelihoods but also fearing a threatened Spanish invasion because of the rebel Irish Earls' plots with the Pope. As they meandered and questioned, Dermot hummed mournful songs about the myth of the Children of Lir, who had brought tragedy upon themselves, bringing a wry smile to Niko's lips. The two men were grim as they observed the numbers of diseased prostitutes, rogues and vagabonds brooding sullenly in the stinking alleys. The threat of plague was ever present. They talked of their longing to see Redmond, Fintan, and other kinsmen, not least induced by the surly manners of all they encountered. They recalled their rural and coastal life, hunting boar, deer and sometimes even wolf, when the packs ventured too near. Niko wanted to watch Conor, a falconry master with a golden eagle on his fist, finding food, when all thought there was none to be had. Conor had helped him train a goshawk. He wanted to drive horned black cattle to the loch beaches and again swim race there with Redmond. He wanted to test himself careering on a board in the wild sea surf. He wanted to hear the soft lilting tones of his mother and hear her wise words. His realistic self knew though, that the country, at least in the north, was alight. They followed the news from Ireland as closely as they could, ferreting out gossip and rumour as well as fact. But they trusted no-one, suspecting that the Crown's spies and agents may be watching them, even though their first act on arrival was to visit the English Court and protest their loyalty to Queen Elizabeth.

They also visited Plymmiswoode Hall at intervals to ask if she had returned there or been found. It was a relief to spend some days at the great oak-beamed town house, with its projecting storeys, offices below, its decorated, plastered hall and many chambers. Outside there was a substantial courtyard and stabling and its back windows overlooked the fragrant gardens of nearby great mansions.

The question of what should happen to Matthew if his mother could not be found remained unspoken then.

On one of the summer afternoons, Alice had sat in her panelled parlour, scented with herbs, and sent for Matthew.

'So, little one,' she cooed, stroking his face, and taking him from Benedicta, who she dismissed. The child wriggled to get free, and she put him on the polished planks of the floor of the panelled room. He sat down, fell forward and then tried to move underneath a large carved chair although his baby skirts impeded him. She thought about his mother. She reflected grimly that seemingly small events and opportunities, if seized at certain times, often impulsively, could cause harm, have unintended consequences and even change the course of history.

'Our Lord God's purpose is unknoweable,' she thought, and wondered what future awaited Matthew. She pushed away regrets at her childlessness, allying herself with Queen Elizabeth.

'This child will be my favourite like our Queen who also has favourites. Indeed the Earl of Essex is known to be one and may well be granted the great army for which he pleads.'

Matthew gurgled as if in response, and clung to her hand as she carried him across the room to a tray of sweetmeats. Sitting on her knee while she stuffed a squashed morsel of peach into his mouth, she was struck by how little he resembled his mother. His build was strong and wiry and his length not great. His soft hair was still gingery and his eyes startling in their brightness. She carried him to the window where she pointed at a trio of pigeons waddling across some hummocks of grass, peering for their lunch. Vocalising, he climbed all over her, impatient to see the world.

Niko had then entered the room, ahead of the servant who had come to announce him. Half-irritated at this, but pleased to see him, she noted his merry eyes, dancing earring and sturdy form, and realised yet again why she bothered with him.

'I was not expecting you, Niko,' she said, 'but I am glad you are here. So like me – you have no news. See how the infant loves you!'

Matthew crowed as Niko scooped him up and they went into play involving much turning upside down and gurgles of delight. Niko remembered his foster-brother and his people in this happy child.

At their first meetings, Alice had asked for guards at the door. Then, attracted once more by his civilised manners and charm, she put her suspicions to one side. It was helpful that he too was looking for Susannah. Slowly, they had begun to find out more about each other.

'What is your exact station in this world of ours, Niko?' she had once asked him.

'I am of half Irish noble blood, and half base-born Ottoman – although Orlaith tells me my father was of the warrior class in his land. My squire Dermot who accompanies me is but a kern, but a valued one. No-one draws a knife faster or beds a pretty woman quicker! Tell your women to look out for their virtue! Now what do I know about you? Just that you are a woman of inherited fortune, have given alms to many, and offer us Irish savages excellent food and refreshment at your table.'

'Have you *no* fortune, being of half Irish noble blood?'

'The Crown's taxes take, and have taken, our peoples' fortune as you well know. And any of my own would lie in the Barbary Coast amongst the Ottomans. But my wealth is in the respect of our sept, the worldly goods that we share and the grandeur and plenty in our lands where we trap and hunt to feed our people.'

In his mind's eye had loomed the square tower of the stronghold, silhouetted against an ash grey sky, shining in the soft rain as if it was covered in a filmy pall. In his ears were the melodious lays of the harps, and the wind that whined across the boggy streams and heaths, whilst his nose had recalled the peat fires and the sharp salt air.

'Cattle that you rustle you mean!' she had snorted. 'How come you and Redmond wear gold, have fine swords and chased breastplates, unless they have been thieved?'

'I have been a soldier.' He refused to take offence. 'What I have gained in the Crown's foreign wars is mine to keep or share.'

With Matthew quiet on his arm, he had gazed at Alice and she at him, Niko finding himself confused by Alice Plymmiswoode. He had always thought her stiff and haughty, but on closer acquaintance, he saw that she had all the attributes of the English middling class – a mixture of brash and unthinking patriotism, spontaneous kindness, piety and progressiveness. She admired his clear skin, neat beard, hawkish nose and generous mouth. The sun was a golden disc speared by an arrow of light. She had wondered when he would stop playing the gentleman. As if divining his thoughts, she moved close to him to take Matthew. Having loosened her bodice as the day was warm, when she lifted the child from his arms, her breasts were almost exposed, as if aware that she had all the physical charms he most desired. She glanced sideways at him provocatively. He had watched her, silent and immobile as a hunting lion. Moving away, feeling embarassed at her daring, quite pleased that he had not insolently presumed to touch her, even though invited.

'I am privileged to see such beauty, Madam,' he said, bowing. 'Your husband was fortunate indeed.'

She had turned away, and speaking over her shoulder, had said, 'My husband was kindly, generous but old. Thomas said you have had no wife? Death ends so many marriages in these plague-stricken times.'

'Not yet affirmed by God.' He paused. 'I am, and have been, a soldier and a trader who must travel where the armies are and where the markets are. These are not places for respectable women.'

Still not looking at him, Alice said 'I have heard this week from Thomas. The insurrection proceeds apace, although Redmond is not yet in arms. If he rebels,' she turned back to watch his face, 'will you return and fight with them?'

'I cannot say whether Redmond will join Earl Tyrone, whom we call The O'Neill. As far as I know he has not yet done this. But you must know that my foster-brother is a Vassal Chief. All of us, including you, are governed by the actions of our Great Temporal Lords. Choice and conscience are luxuries only for the Bishops! The southern Earls are divided in their loyalties. I am not a Vassal Chief. I have been charged by my brother – Lord Redmond – to come to England with messages of loyalty to your Queen.'

He had then changed the subject, deciding to challenge her.

'I know your brother, and some merchant notables, hearken to your advice, and yet you act most foolishly at times.'

'Whatever do you mean?'

'You should not have listened to that woman we both seek, I for Redmond, and you for Matthew.'

'She was pale as bone and so urgent in her pleading.' Alice had looked down. Her sleep was often disturbed by visions of that fatal afternoon.

Autumn approached, enveloping the City with unseasonable warmth. On one of Niko's visits,ostensibly to see if Alice had received any further news of Susannah, she told him that Susannah's uncle , one M. De Hem, had sent an envoy, Pieter Heyden who was seeking a meeting. He seemed to think that she was accommodating Susannah Breydel.

'I think you have already made his acquaintance?' Alice queried.

'Ah yes! May I be present? What happens if and when we find Susannah? I am uncertain if Pieter Heyden or her uncle know about Matthew's birth.'

She reflected that, although appearing to be quite straightforward, he was also politic and devious.

'I will send a messenger explaining all. If and when we find Susannah, she will not agree to return to Redmond. She hates him, and indeed, all of you, and I will not force her, or Matthew, back there, not least because of the Ulster Earl's war and the wishes of my brother Thomas.'

'What if, in time, her husband, Lord Redmond, decides that he wants his wife and son back in Ireland?'

'Believe me when I say she will not have him- at any time.'

'If she is found safe, Redmond wants a marriage gift or compensation, rather than her person.'

'Gold and silver probably – to support the rebels! If anyone should have compensation, it surely should be me!'

'He also wants his kin to see his son.'

'He cannot wish his son to be returned in the middle of a war. No, Matthew stays here until she is found or unless the Crown commands otherwise.' She added, aware that the breath of honesty had passed between them that day. 'You may come to my meeting with M. De Hem's envoy. I have said he should come here in two days' time at noon.'

Niko nodded and prepared to leave.

Hearing of the many successes of the rebels in Ireland, and escalation of the war, he had become convinced that Matthew should remain in Alice's safe hands until, in the ensuing parleys, the return of Redmond's heir could be demanded, and he could take the Irish name of Rory MacFeagh, as his father wished.

'Although the last cold winter has held back the plague, it is now becoming rampant in parts of London. This is not good for Matthew.'

'I know. The town empties. I am planning to travel soon with Matthew and Benedicta.'

'Where will you go?'

'I will see my kinswoman Cecilia, who lives outside Bristol in a remote part.' She added rather diffidently, 'Benedicta misses the Sisters there. But what about yourself – when will you go?'

Niko was reassured. He knew that Redmond's son would be safer out of London, as it sickened, but also that he could not watch him in the less populated lands without being discovered. He would not follow her. He trusted Alice to return before midwinter. He said,

'We will soon travel to Canterbury and the coastal counties

around London. We will trade and search for Susannah in the ale-houses and alleys frequented by our people, as well as the gathering places of Moorish traders and those from the Low Countries. Even though I have been in many plaguey places, God has, so far, spared me.' He went up to her and tipped her face towards his. 'So you care what happens to me?'

She flushed, but did not move away until the cries of the child moved them apart.

I have been betrayed by Calvet. He married another! God will punish him. I could hardly speak at his wickedness. His new wife Margery said they will not send me back to Mistress Alice because it is better if I am with those from my country who know my kin and speak my tongue and that she would send word to her and M.De Hem that I am here. I must stay with them until my uncle Andreas fetches me and then takes Matthew from Mistress Alice. Margery said she cannot also take in Matthew. I pray that he still lives. Mistress Alice will not harm him, indeed she has no babes of her own, and has never had, she will treasure him, I feel it. The weeks pass but slowly. When I ask if they have heard from Uncle De Hem or my mother, Dame Margery says that they have not. Please God they hear soon. Does she lie? Calvet is harsh. He says I must work hard for him to redeem my sin with the Catholic Irishman. My back is sore, my wrists give me pain and the food is meagre. Our Lord must have willed this too. Calvet is eager to take up and sell my work. He took my purse of coins, including my silver halfpennies, for safe-keeping he said, and she took my chain with the jewelled cross which I foolishly showed them. He promised me more silver for my work but has given me nothing yet. I feared my uncle, but am sure that he will send someone…..perhaps Pieter Heyden…. to take me home…why does he so delay? I know he is a hard man. My mother said once that De Hem's only study was gold and jewels, the filthy lucre condemned in our Holy Book, but without which we will live like peasants in sod houses. My father confided that skill and artistry was to his brother-in law worth only what someone would pay. It was Uncle Andreas who persuaded my father to the handfasting with Calvet, saying that my nimble hands would bring them both the commissions he was seeking from the Court of England. My mind dwells on my uncle's secretary, a neat and pious young man, unmarried. He gave me burning looks. Indeed my heart would jump when he did this, foolish maid that I am. What now? How long must I stay here?....

CHAPTER
FOURTEEN

t the Sign of the Crown on Cheapside in London, Pieter wiped his forehead and lips on a coarse cloth, then discarded it. He looked around, wishing he had taken better lodgings. These ones had been recommended by the crew of the eelboat which had brought him into the port from the Zuider Zee. The alehouse was large and centrally located with some rooms for travellers, but the potboys were surly, the benches were hard and dingy with fraying cushions and there were fleas in the mattress. Accommodations in Hull and Norwich he had used when previously in England had been cleaner and his people were more tolerated. He idly looked out of the dirty thick-glassed windows, and fingered the amulet he had bought to protect himself from illness. He heartily wished he had not come to this city of London with its heat, stinks, unruly apprentices and streets clogged with livestock, market stalls, carts, drays and thundering, shouting wagoners. He had to constantly keep his wits sharp and his sword by his side. His initial euphoria at the pace and vibrancy of the town had now ceased to appeal.

As well as searching for Susannah, now that the Edict of Nantes had been signed and his land was at peace with Spain, he had brought a cargo of good quality finished cloth to sell. He shook his head with annoyance at the time he had spent at the Exchange, haggling over exorbitant demands for taxes, porterage and other impenetrable dues which did not seem to be charged to English merchants to the same extent. He also gloomily realised that his attempts to find Susannah on his own had ended in failure. Believing that, having somewhat mysteriously left the Irish clan, the girl was safe in London, Pieter had been disagreeably surprised when he heard from Mistress Alice Plymmiswoode's messengers about Susannah's birthing, abandonment of her child, and disappearance into the London streets. He had not thought the girl callous or thoughtless. He supposed they should have guessed she would get with child, and was uncertain what M. De Hem would say about her infant. Pieter fell to wondering when she was found, if the Irish marriage could be annulled, if his suit for her hand may be agreed. But he was sure that her uncle would do everything possible to get Susannah back, child or not, as he had to resolve and manage her inheritance, and wanted her skills in design and luxury embellishment.

His thoughts then turned again to the bribery, which was rife, and the port, clogged with English shipping. Even after receiving a large purse of gold royals, the harbourmaster had made the captain of De Hem's chartered cargo vessel when it arrived from Amsterdam moor, so far off the dock, that even more ferry and carriage costs for his cargo to be unloaded had to be paid. The wholesalers also took an unreasonable percentage, as indeed it turned out, did the retailers.

Angrily tapping the rough ale-house table, he recalled examining the coarse and badly dyed English broadcloth at the Exchange and muttered to himself, 'It was far inferior to that produced by our workshops.' He knew that courtiers, with their extravagant tastes, would pay well for the one hundred bales that were sent, but realised that M. De Hem was unlikely to have much profit from it. The only redeeming feature of his journey was the time spent with certain Merchant Adventurers with whom it seemed likely that M. De Hem could make some advantageous investment.

As I am released from my handfasting vows, Margery now talks of my marriage to her lascivious son, who at first tried to handle me and wanted to give me a private chamber until I told them I would only work if I could stay on a pallet in the chamber with the other female weavers…a young woman's only protection is the support and sympathy of other young women… or brothers… would that my strong brothers were not killed in wars before I reached adulthood. I did not tell Margery that I will repudiate Redmond if I can, only that I was already wed to Irish gentry. They laughed and sneered saying only if I wed Edward would I preserve my reputation and that there was no response from my family, but if I wished I could leave after I designed some new damasks, but I did this and they have not let me leave, and now have me ever watched. I am placed once again in jeopardy. That English scold Margery, bedecked in silks and satins orders the whip should their tasks not be completed in the time she allots, and now I have to scream and shout to get good bread and meat. Today I refused to work unless they stopped Edward from touching my body. Redmond merely smiled when I refused him, and took to caressing and calming me as he did his horse, which Lord Help Me, I sometimes endured with sinful pleasure…. but, when I am alone, this one grasps and forces and then backs away and looks around to see who may have heard me shriek…

Pieter had visited Calvet, as it seemed had Niko MacFeagh, but she had not been there. He snapped his drooping eyes open, irritated at his sleep being disturbed by the late noise from the street and inside the tavern.

Calling for a pot of ale, he recalled his recent visit to the man to whom Susannah had been handfasted, reflecting that he had seemed as pompous and greedy as when he had first met him at the betrothal.

'Before God, surely they could not have hidden her!' he thought, clenching his fist.

Christian Calvet and his wife had greeted him effusively on his arrival. It seemed that they had heard of his approach. Pieter had found them unkempt and obsequious. He had noted that Calvet's ear was bandaged and that he had long thinning hair and a straggly beard, low eyebrows and a small mouth. He recalled the man's foul breath. He thought that the wife could not be pious as she was bedecked in heavy figured silks and wore gaudy jewels. Her long face was framed by a black brocaded headpiece. They had all sat in a panelled parlour, stuffy in the summer heat.

'Please tell M. De Hem that I was devastated at the loss of his ships and his family,' Calvet had said. 'Poor, beautiful Susannah has been the victim of a sad fate.'

Dame Margery had sniffed sadly at Susannah's misfortunes, said little and had soon left them to supervise the work in the weaving room and sheds at the back of the property.

He had then asked why Calvet did not wait for Susannah's death to be confirmed before marrying, and Calvet had looked slightly ashamed. He insisted that they had only wed each other because they were sure that Susannah had drowned.

'My dear M. Heyden', he had said. 'A year ago, my business was failing. I began to suffer greatly from an infected ear, exacerbated by the noise of the looms, so I could not weave for long. It still pains me. I could not pay my debts. My livelihood would shortly have been lost. God forgive me, this was why I requested Hendrik and Susannah to come rather earlier than first envisaged. Hendrik was sympathetic and, as he had arranged to effect some business in Bordeaux, said he would travel to London from there, bringing his daughter, a preacher and members from his Church. His wife was ailing and could not travel. The fogs were their undoing.'

Remembering this exchange with Calvet, he wondered if he should have pressed harder. He had challenged him saying,

'It seems that you are now a competitor for supplying stuffs to the high-born English.' To which he had replied.

'My now Goodwife Margery and her youth Edward inherited from her first husband, who was well-known amongst the purveyors at Court. Knowing of my experience in the trade, it suited us both for her to accept my offer of marriage. There were some good workers in his sheds, including a talented designer of brocades whose work has pleased the courtiers.'

'You say Susannah has not been here even though she could well have sought you after arriving in London. You will, I am sure, speak honestly, Monsieur, before God, and as the Good Book teaches us.'

Calvet had stepped back, a slight sheen on his forehead.

'Believe me when I say that here in London, there are many weavers who can weave satins and damasks. Many impoverished young immigrant girls come to us and look for work, some indeed called Susannah – a popular name. My steward sends them away unless I say I am seeking more workers. She must have perished or have found shelter in a religious house, having lost her mind. But I will ask my apprentices to ask those who live hereabouts about her on your behalf. You are not the first to enquire about Susannah. Earlier this summer, I had a visit from two Irishman, one wild and savage, one more civilised, calling himself Niko MacFeagh, seemingly the brother of a man he said was Susannah's husband, demanding her person. I did not know them. They became menacing when I denied knowledge of her and then refused to let them search. The dark one threatened me with a large strange sword and dagger, and my quick-thinking wife called our apprentices, who quickly sent for their friends, and we were finally able to make them depart. He left saying I would see more of him, which I hope I do not.'

Dame Margery had then returned and asked, 'Was Susannah married to an Irish Catholic?'

He had told them that this was probably so, and of her baby son. Neither of them had looked surprised.

The woman had shaken her head in disapproval, but then enquired, 'If you find her and her marriage is not legal, perhaps M. De Hem would allow her to marry Edward?'

Calvet had added, 'So that we can be partners in our enterprises as we planned. I doubt if anyone else would have her and we could take in the child, if it still lives, to learn our trade.'

Pieter made a frisson of disgust recalling this request. He had then asked to view the workshops to assure himself of their good faith. In the raftered weaving shed, sunlight had slanted across the many looms, dust motes sparkling along their length, Calvet had stood beside him the whole time. One young woman had been working at some intricate samples which could easily have been Susannah's, although he had not been able to see them in detail. For some reason, her loom and table seemed cast into a grey shadow although the room was full of bright sunlight from the unshuttered window spaces. The girl's speech was drowned in the vast clacking din of the worksheds, and she had shaken her head negatively at Pieter's shouted questions.

That is Pieter – surely that is Pieter Heyden who is leaving this house. I know him. I see him as he departs. Margery ordered me to do some work at the topmost attic loom and stood by the window, watching me for a while. Then she hastened out of the room and locked the door. Now I look out and see Pieter… he looks down-hearted… I can see it in his reluctant gait. He mounts and rides quickly off… I cannot reach him… he cannot hear me. That woman is heartless. I know him, I know Pieter from his neat black apparel, his calm mien, his graceful gait. I always admired his politesse, his punctiliousness. I knew in my young girl's heart that he admired me… he has come for me, but now he leaves. He leaves! Those monsters have imprisoned me, Pieter Heyden! Can you hear the cries that I send to you. He hesitates and looks back, but Calvet had followed him, bowing and waving farewell…

Pieter was not aware that, after he disconsolately left, Dame Margery had asked, 'What are we going to do, husband? They will discover one day that she has been here, especially if she is to marry Edward.'

'We will deny that we have hidden her. I shall say, that after Pieter's visit, our apprentices found her confused and almost dead on the streets. We gave her work and sustenance and Edward as husband to save her honour. Edward, once married, can refuse to return her to Holland. If she gives another story, I will say that her mind has gone because of her sufferings. If her marriage to the Irishman is legal, we can petition the Crown that she should not be forced back to live with savages.'

I tried to leave them and demanded my purse but they said I should not leave as the plague was becoming rife and that I must not go amongst other people if I wish to stay alive. Oh my Lord – why do you punish me so? I shall refuse to work for them… I shall tell them, no amount of beatings will prevail. But if only that were true…

Pieter finished his ale and sighed.

'I know I examined every female face the length of that shed, and every corner, but I did not see Susannah.'

He murmured a prayer and hoped that the meeting with Mistress Alice, graciously granted that afternoon, may be productive.

Pieter arrived at the Plymmiswoode mansion, neat in a broad-brimmed hat and clean ruff, barely concealing his shock at observing Niko, who was back in London, sporting a fine lace collar over a short silver-threaded jerkin, holding a smiling infant and sprawled comfortably on a cushioned window seat.

'I was not aware, mistress, of your acquaintance with this gentleman,' he said stiffly, frowning as he came up from an elegant bow. Shafts of sunlight glanced across the turkey carpet in the chamber, highlighting the figures on the bright tapestries which he immediately recognised as made in his homeland. The room was fragrant with large dishes of dried lavender and rose petals. Alice was richly attired in green Italian silk, her only ornament a small velvet cap brocaded in silver on which was pinned a jewelled crucifix.

'Well yes,' said Alice. 'The MacFeaghs' townlands march alongside my brother Thomas's desmesne in Leinster, and Master Niko often visited there to discuss matters of common interest. He also seeks Susannah on behalf of her husband. This little man,' she indicated, 'is named Matthew.' She looked hard at Pieter. ' My messenger's missive would have informed you that he is the son of M. De Hem's young kinswoman Susannah, who left him here by a garden shrine then tricking our concierge and fleeing. Have you any information which may help us find her?'

'Indeed I was desolated at this news Mistress, but also surprised not to have heard this from you' said Pieter, glancing coolly at Niko and then examining the infant with interest. 'She would be pleased to see her child is thriving. He has been churched in our Faith?' Alice nodded. 'He has the hair and complexion of the Celt. It was wrong to leave him but Susannah's mind, assuredly, must have been in some turmoil. Consider her many terrors and losses. I have searched in vain for her, and understand that you have done so too. Perhaps now we can further combine our efforts. I thought she may have sought shelter with her former betrothed, M. Christian Calvet. I discovered that she spent some nights at a Dutch church. They informed me that, if she was Susannah – she did not give them that name, she said she was named Gile – she talked of seeking one Christian Calvet, to whom she was handfasted. She told them she had a misadventure on the way to London which had left her homeless and her child lost.

The pastor offered to find Calvet and send messages to him of her situation, but she refused, insisting she would go herself. It seems she had some coins with her, wanted no alms and indeed purchased a large French headdress from them to cover her hair, which, she said attracted too much attention. But when I visited the Calvets, as I know you did, M. MacFeagh, she was not there. I am still suspicious of Calvet, but cannot do much more. You must know that her uncle wishes me to bring Susannah home, if she can be found. Her father's affairs are still unsettled, and,' he murmured a prayer, 'her mother died a month back.'

Alice said, 'God Rest Her Soul,' as they all bowed their heads. 'I also suggested that Niko should seek her at Calvet's workshop. I wish I had told her that it was believed Calvet had married another. Susannah was acting increasingly strangely in Sir Rowland Porter's castle in Dublin. So it did not seem necessary and would have caused her more distress. How did he receive you? I know that Niko was treated with great rudeness.'

'Calvet did not courteously offer me refreshment. Although his linen was clean, he looked ill. There was a grimness about his new wife. He told me, Niko, that you had brandished weapons and threatened him. He denied he had seen Susannah. He said that many immigrant girls come to his house seeking work with tall tales to elicit sympathy, but no-one had talked of shipwreck or betrothal – but his eyes slipped away from my gaze.'

Niko nodded in agreement.

'I did not trust him either. His contempt of us was barely disguised and his apprentices threatened us. He denied all knowledge, refused to let me see the work sheds. It is now in my mind to watch for his absence and try to question his servants.'

'Calvet did allow me into the weaving shed. The din was unsupportable – but I did not see Susannah or any like her. I asked a couple of the girls about new arrivals, but they shook their heads.'

Pieter also told them that the samples of a girl called Annette were intricate enough to have been designed by Susannah, and that the work would translate into many orders.

He added, 'My agents tell me that Calvet's profits have recently increased – which adds to my suspicions of him. Susannah's work is superlative and would be in great demand. Calvet seemed convinced that Susannah had died. Should she be found, he wants her to marry his son.'

'She is already married to my brother! She had no reason to flee from her husband,' said Niko, who had risen and bowed perfunctorily, still holding Matthew. 'She was indeed fortunate that Mistress Alice arranged for her to be birthed successfully after her incontinent desertion of Lord Redmond and his kin. They not only rescued her from death on the seashore, but also treated her with respect and kindness. Susannah is married in the eyes of God, blessed by an ordained priest. I also know nothing of her present whereabouts, Monsieur. It does not help that she wore that voluminous headdress common to those from her land. As well as visiting Calvet, we have searched many likely places since coming here. I suppose she may have succumbed to the pestilence if she stayed in the city.'

'We need to be sure if she has died,' Pieter said.

'Would M. De Hem accept the child without his mother?' asked Alice.

Niko answered, frowning.

'This is a matter for Matthew's father, not M. De Hem. Susannah is married, as I have just said, to my foster-brother, the Lord of a branch of an Irish clan. The child is his heir and, when this war is settled, he will want him. But, angry at the murder of his Great-Aunt in which Susannah was implicated, Lord Redmond has no wish for his wife to return at present, and I believe she does not want this either.'

Alice gestured to the servants standing by with cooled small ale and sugared fruits. She nodded at them, and they withdrew, having been handed the wriggling baby. They all drank silently, but no-one ate.

Pieter paced around and then said with finality, 'Surely it is better, due to the war in Ireland, if and when she is found, that I take Susannah and Matthew back to her family! Also M. De Hem will pay for Mistress's Alice and the Crown's expenses in looking after Susannah, and compensation to the MacFeagh clan for her rescue.'

Niko was thinking that it may be easier to get the child away in Holland as Alice and the Crown had too much of an eagle eye. For some reason, he found himself uneasy at this thought.

Alice remained worried about letting Matthew go because of Sir Rowland's interest in him, and the lack of further advice from Thomas. She said, 'I am not sure that the infant can leave England.'

'The Crown have no rights over Susannah,' commented Pieter.

'And the Crown also have no rights over Lord Redmond's wife and son!' interjected Niko. To further emphasise Matthew's paternity, he said belligerently, ' Lord Redmond wishes the child to be called Rory, not Matthew. He also calls Susannah "Lady Gile" – the name of a sprite from the sea.'

Pieter ignored him and turned to Alice. 'M. De Hem will, if necessary, make representations to the Crown if this causes difficulty for you, mistress.'

Niko was still angry and resentful at Medb's killing and irritated by Pieter's concern for the charmless, wayward Susannah. He insisted on detailing to Pieter, in case he had not been told the full circumstances of Susannah's flight from his people, which had led to the murder of an Irish noble lady. He ended saying, 'This killing has caused great grief and may have encouraged the clans in the south of the country to rise against the Crown.'

Alice's lips then tightened.

'That country is always considering rebellion, Niko,' she said. 'You and I have discussed this. It is good that you are still loyal to our Queen. We can only hope that Lord Redmond stays so too.'

Taking a deep breath, Pieter said, 'Forgive me, but it all sounds like an unfortunate and unforeseen sequence of events. Susannah could not have known what would transpire and she is still young, but I can understand, in the circumstances, why Lord Redmond does not object to her return to her kin.' There was a silence after which he continued, 'It seems that accurate information on the ferment across the Irish Sea is hard to come by, but, as it is so unsettled, it would be wise for the child to remain here at present, and for me, to return to Amsterdam to report the duties I have had in London and to discuss his future with M. De Hem. I have, in any event, been in London too long and must sail to Holland before the September storms commence in earnest. If you get further information, messages passed through the Royal

Exchange will be most discreet.'

Niko said,' Should the Earl of Tyrone shortly make terms with the Crown's Irish Council, it would also be wise and help to keep the peace, if Rory – Matthew – went to his father's people, who will be grateful to you and the Crown.'

Alice then said firmly, 'The unrest in Ireland is hardly resolved! Our Queen, like her father old King Henry, will require any rebels, whether north or south, to completely submit, and will undoubtedly send more troops. I would like Matthew to stay in safety with me, at least until the situation becomes clearer.'

Niko became silent and frowning. Events in Ireland were a cause of tension between him and Alice. It was a subject which both tried to avoid.

'I hear that the current Lord Deputy in Ireland will be recalled and his place taken by Lord Essex who will likely conquer,' Pieter said, pacing the room, then turning to face them. 'He is a great General with many victories to his name. Afterwards, that land will need good governance if it is ever to settle. But our priority is to find Susannah.'

Alice then said that she had other callers and asked both men to leave. Niko bowed, deeply kissed Alice's hand and quickly departed.

Pieter waited in the courtyard for his horse to be brought. He was intrigued at Mistress Plymmiswoode's seeming softness for the Irishman and wondered if Niko felt similarly. He decided that Ireland would come between them like an impassable hedge.

Later, Alice reflected on the conflict in Ireland, her brother's situation there, and her attraction to Niko. She trembled, also knowing that war and Faith were barriers they may well not overcome. Once in jocular mood, Niko had told her that he had many choices of liturgies and prayers from the Mahommedans, the Protestants in the English Army and Catholics from his mother's clan, so, if he insulted none of them, he may yet have a place in Heaven.

Annette told me she wanted to tell Pieter Heyden about me, but a grey mist came before her eyes choking her so she could not speak for terror and a cold blast filled her mouth. Calvet tells me that Pieter came to tell him that Uncle Andreas thinks I am dead and that, although Master Heyden searches for me now, he will soon give up, so I should stay and make my life with him, Edward and Margery. I am so alone... I pray that someone will come to my aid. Surely my uncle must prove my demise to gain any wealth that I may have. I begged Calvet to return my cross with its small jewel to ward off the Evil Eye... even Redmond did not take this. Perhaps I could find some stratagem to flee from here but I do not have but one groat to my name... on coming here, I passed starving wraiths, scrofulous heads, bootless children in this Babel London. I know that the soul is worthier than the body but I would not be such a wretch... They try to force me to wed Edward and threaten that I will be whipped until I agree. I tell him I will break my hands rather than accept... maybe my life too will be forfeit... I do not cling to it. Pieter, return for me... can you hear my cry? My kin will one day find me... I know it...

The Irish army's victory at the Battle of the Yellow Ford at the end of August that year became widely known. Thousands of troops were dead, including English commanders such as Sir Henry Harrington and the Constable Sir Rowland Porter. All the English ordnance was lost. There was talk of maleficium- witchcraft summoned by a heathen populace. Queen Elizabeth, increasingly angry at her 'over-mighty' subject, the Earl of Tyrone, was minded to give in to the Earl of Essex's pleas and appoint him Lord Deputy in Lord Russell's stead and to give him greater powers to deal with the unrest there.

Their spies told the MacFeaghs that the Crown's overwhelming defeat had caused much alarm at Court, of the new Lord Deputy of Ireland, and the plans to bring over an army in the Spring. All realised that their Overlord would be forced into declaring his position when the great army arrived and campaigning began. Amongst the folk, there was a mixture of joy and perturbation as the possibility of war in the south became increasingly real. Churls were ordered to cut swathes of timber for the fashioning of new pikes. Provisions against future need were collected and hidden. Weapons were honed and helms and leather doublets repaired and strengthened. Some of those men and woman working in Thomas's manor either returned to their clachans, or sought shelter in the stronghold, rather than being conscripted into a loyal militia. Many, including some settlers in the town lands, fled to those castles which held large garrisons. Large numbers of soldiers arrived at the Irish coasts, often at night lit by flares and sconces. There was much trade in supplies. The blood and stare and grey face of the dying Medb had come unbidden and was shadowing Orlaith's mind. All the ancient battles Medb described so powerfully were about honour or loot. She feared it was still so, as in the old tales, those who should know better gave in to every vice.

As the cold months approached, most of the women and children in the stronghold departed again for the coast, this time with armed kerns to guard them. The leaders and some churls stayed behind to improve and supervise the defences. Others rode into the mountains to herd livestock.

Although much time had passed, Orlaith's clothing was still rent from grieving and the marks of tears were often on her face, which had lately become more white and pinched.

'We've received few cyphers or messages from Niko or Dermot since they went to England,' said Redmond to her one day before she left. 'But it is difficult. They must fear the Crown's informers. The Spanish ships turn back for fear of fierce storms. A re-built Armada will not be lightly risked. This will make Tyrone's enterprise more difficult. Many in the south will hesitate.'

Orlaith said with a sidelong glance, 'I know you need Niko to talk to the Spanish captains and also Gile's kin and also to watch little Rory in London. Gile's people, of the trading class, will no doubt be pleased that she has raised her rank. But you need Niko's counsel now. Why not send Fintan to replace him? Perhaps the Hollanders will prefer to negotiate with one of Fintan's lineage, rather than one half- Ottoman.'

Redmond frowned.' You speak rashly, Orlaith. My brother's looks will not weigh with traders or merchants. You should not feel ashamed. You know this.'

Orlaith looked down, muttering an apology. Redmond, then

feeling guilty at his reprimand, explained.

'Niko has no doubt already found out who in Spain and Portugal will support us, who in Gile's family has wealth, and if they will keep their promises. He can sniff out truth from lies like a hound seeks a hare. Fintan's face is as open as the skies above us.' He looked directly at his mother. 'I know you would have Niko by our side now as he has, and will, protect me, and dispose of our enemies without compunction. But I have thought hard on this, and if there is war, as you yourself have said, it is better if he is not seen to join us.'

'It is just that he is one to consider all possibilities first, whilst you are like quicksilver in body and mind. But I am blessed to have had the rearing of you both, with your different ways,' she said regarding fondly the bright damp hair falling to his shoulders and his hardy frame, seemingly inured to every toil and hardship.

Redmond smiled – a rare thing for most to see.

'And we were doubly blessed to have one such as you to rear us.'

'Just make sure that you are both not lost to me,' she replied, lowering her eyes. A sudden coughing fit exhausted her. She put down her bread and turned, gasping, away from Redmond.

'What is it, Orlaith? Are you still sick?' He studied her closely.

'I swallowed my bread foolishly,' she replied at last.

After a pause he said, 'A war cannot succeed without much more silver. Quicksilver in abundance will not answer!'

Then his eyes went cold and he raised his chin, saying, 'Gile and the Hursts will pay for the death of Medb, if not by my hand, then another's.'

'She has injured us, probably beyond her knowing, but would you kill your own wife? That is indeed in the old tales!' Orlaith looked hard at him.

'She must fear the old Gods as well as our dear Lord,' said Redmond. 'That woman is now scoured from my mind and heart.'

'The geis will take its course,' said Orlaith, shaking her head. 'Maybe you should let it be – or you may bring her geis upon yourself.'

Redmond had been furious when word eventually reached

him that Susannah had left his son and seemingly disappeared. He gave a verbal message to a churl who had gone with a guarded consignment of salt and staves from Thomas to Alice, reiterating that Niko should stay in England and guard his son Rory. He said that following the Earl of Tyrone's victory, under the terms of a peace, Thomas Hurst could be forced to send the child to the MacFeaghs.

My dear Lord, I have prayed and prayed to confirm my Faith. You have saved me from the fogs and protected me until now. That Irish Franciscan had a lying tongue. He said that I was married to that savage but I am not. I did not consent when those holy words were said on the cliff… I was near dead from exhaustion… and their prayers were but a ruse, so that Redmond did not have to confess to the besmirching of my honour. Amongst Redmond's people, I could barely hide my scorn at the dismal shades of their dyeings, as misty as the mountains around… and one weave only! My God, harbour and succour me again! As I am one of the Chosen, I do not fear our dear Lord gathering me in His arms away from this world of sin and cruelty… but it is hard here…now that the light fails the sheds fill with the stink and vapour of tallow candles worse than the stink of peat. Orlaith would use only the dry turves cut from mountain overhangs and they did not smoke….

CHAPTER FIFTEEN
Anno Domini 1599

ack in London after Christmastide, still having no word of Gile's whereabouts, Niko and Dermot picked their way through noise and clatter and the ubiquitous markets clogging the alleys. When travelling to buy and sell goods, Niko departed from places when they had begun to pall. Now he was forced to remain. Over the months, the secretive, oppressive power of the English Crown, and the attitude of the people towards his adopted land, pushed him into more and more sympathy with the rebels. Chafing to be near events in Leinster, he longed more than he ever had done to lend his sword to the rebellion. But he knew his duty was to ensure that the Queen's Spymaster knew he was in England and not fighting her enemies in Ireland.

Dermot also wanted to go home, but his impatience was leavened by his love of intrigue and the willing kitchen maids who appreciated his arresting looks. He found it useful to learn more of the English tongue through dalliance. Women were always part of Dermot's thoughts and dreams. He knew what havoc love and desire could make in the mind of a man.

'It was a woman after all, that had caused old King Henry to disregard the Pope and dissolve the monasteries,' he had slyly remarked Niko one day, fearing the influence of Alice on his master.

Spring was the time when military campaigning began in earnest. Paradoxically, Redmond, his revenge on the cusp of being granted, was becoming disturbed about the prospect of war throughout the land.

Fintan was also conflicted, saying to his wife Oonagh, 'If Tyrone proves victorious, he may prove to be an avaricious overlord. If the Crown triumphs, the reprisals will be onerous and shocking. And whoever wins out, many warriors will be killed in battle. Also there is no plan as to governance once peace is achieved. All must agree – this is not easy – our land of Erin has too many kings who have too many sons, many of whom are jealous of each other.'

Alice received a letter from Thomas, gleeful that the Earl of Essex would soon be setting sail. He thought that hearing of his army, the groundswell of rebellion in the south of the country would dissipate. Seemingly the Gaelic chiefs were still divided.

Alice, and her friend Hope Polsted, stood with others at an open casement on the upper floor of Hope's mansion. The pair could see the procession from the Tower of London from this vantage point. Petite, bright-eyed Hope, garrulous and bold, was Alice's long-time friend and confidante. Both their fathers and husbands had been in cloth trades and Alice had spent time in Hope's household after, first her mother, and then her step-mother had died. Silently each woman wished she was more like the other.

They waited expectantly for the approach of the long and noisy procession of Lord Essex's army, winding its slow way through the streets, which had been cleared to give them passage. There were shouts and cheers for the Hero of Cadiz, flags were waved, pipes whistled and even more bells than usual tolled. They asked servants to bring their young children to see the soldiers and hear the drums and the heralds' trumpets. Hope leaned forward, gesticulating at one of the mounted men leading the phalanx of bristling pikes in the parade below them

'See Alice! See the great nobles! There is one with splendidly engraved armour! He is of comely proportions. I do believe it is the Earl of Essex, the Man of Action. He looks up at me!

She gasped, waving violently, smiling and cheering.

'I don't think he can hear you and he looks at everyone watching from balconies,' said Alice. She too had pressed forward inquisitively to view the line of helmeted officers, two abreast and badged with well-known liveries, prancing on their warhorses which were caparisoned with embroidered cloths, their plumes fluttering in the spring breeze.

'Look, Matthew, at the warrior with the blued breastplate. He will certainly catch our Queen's eye.'

Much of the morning, they watched excitedly, exclaiming from time to time when they recognised a courtier.

Later that day, alone, Alice stood again at a window, this time in a chamber overlooking her garden, where the buds of the pear trees were beginning to burst forth. She popped a sweetmeat into her mouth and watched the evening light gild her orchard. Behind a clear violet sky, she saw enormous storm clouds towering in the west. Her steward, bringing her ledgers, ink and some wax candles, commented that he hoped the impending rainstorm was not an omen.

Alice sat at a table, but found it hard to concentrate, and reached for the Gascony wine put by her side. She mused on Niko's taut face, his easy strength and the pride in his bearing, whether on foot or horseback. Exasperated, she felt as moonstruck as the maid she had been told was pursued by Niko's squire Dermot. But she remained suspicious of these men. She had noticed that Niko deftly deflected questions about his brother and the rebellion. There had been awkward conversations. One time, his eyes had hardened and his soft tones had been clipped.

'I say again, mistress,' he had said, 'Lady Medb should not have died that way. You should have controlled your guards.'

She had flushed and bowed her head at his stern gaze. A sudden draught had crossed the room and she had reached to take her fur cloak from a chair.

'You must know that I regret everything. In the mist, in the rainstorm, confused at the approach of this desperate girl- all was pandemonium.'

Niko had bowed and said he must leave. As the door opened, in spite of a lance of light from the window, another rush of cold air had swept across the room, causing him to shiver. He walked out, followed by what had seemed to be a small glowing ball of light. Bewildered, and hoping that this had been a reflection from the sun on his rapier, she had then knelt for some time at her 'Prie-dieu'.

Niko and Dermot, on horseback, had also watched the morning procession, but at the edge of the crowds. They were grim and silent. Dermot, now much fattened, his shoulder-length hair now tied back, silently worried about the coming onslaught on his homeland. Niko was thinking about the past cold winter which, like the previous year, had meant fewer deaths from the plague, but had caused hardship everywhere and would have continued to weaken his countrymen. He counted the heavy ordnance being pulled past and was concerned, thinking that the rebel commanders must stop this army holding a position above one of their fortified towns. Dermot observed that, although wearing Essex's badges, many of the troops appeared to have little protection from either the weather or concerted attacks, at this point in their journey only carrying staves, broken pikes and utility daggers, which they brandished proudly at the crowd. He grinned, knowing that their churls would use similar weapons, but would have an advantage as they often raided together and knew how to work as a team to pick off a superior enemy. Then he, lifting his brows almost into his Irish fringe, whispered during a lull in the roaring crowd,

'Essex seems to have pressed all the surly vagabonds and vagrants he could find into soldiery – and there are many in this land that prey on the people!'

'It seems true that this army has, as proclaimed, more than 16,000 foot, 300 horse, plus officers and ordnance – all to sail to Ireland, but I agree these men seem in poor condition,' replied Niko. 'As they travel through England and Wales, they will no doubt gather more conscripts as they go. But I would think many have never even seen a mountain, let alone fought a war or crossed bog and mountain with cannon, whereas the Earl of Tyrone has trained many of his men in the English way of war and many possess English firearms that we have supplied.'

'We can ambush and harry them unmercifully when they arrive in our terrain,' said Dermot, looking balefully at the column slowly marching past them.

As they watched, Niko reflected on what had ignited the desultory conflicts of the past years into hot flames across the land. He knew from attending past Gatherings that there had been many winter truces, when Tyrone or Feagh O'Byrne had sued for a fair pardon. But then the Crown learned of their overtures to the Pope and the Catholic Holy League. As a result, its officials set draconian and humiliating pardon terms that were beyond all acceptance. Then there was the greed of the English settlers and sheriffs, who wanted to create more 'plantations' such as the one granted to Thomas Hurst – and then, added to this, there was the status that the Irish gave to being warriors.

'Well,' he said to himself, 'peace is now impossible, and my allegiance must be with Redmond, Alice Plymmiswoode or no Alice Plymmiswoode.'

Hearing his master's deep intake of breath, Dermot felt disloyal. He had said no more to Niko about the secret plot planned for when Earl Essex arrived with his troopships in Dublin Bay. He remained concerned about his master's seeming attachment to Alice. He thought that her suspicions would be roused if Niko had said something of it in an angry or unguarded moment.

'Mistress Alice is too sharp not to question him further. The Queen's spies must not learn of this,' he thought guiltily.

Once he had challenged Niko.

'You spend much time with the Englishwoman Alice– does she steal your heart? I heard her urge you not to go to Ireland and to war. She said that her brother Thomas Hurst wrote that some of our churls have already left his desmesne and that, when Lord Essex's army arrives, any rebels from our sept who are captured will be hanged.'

Niko was unable to resist a sigh.

'You know that Redmond has ordered us not to go to war. Did you also hear her tell me that that Essex's army has been ordered to first go north to subdue Ulster? This means that the southern counties will be unlikely to take up arms immediately, if at all.'

The threatened storm arrived later that evening and they heard that a heavily overcast sky, fogs and heavy rain had dogged the army almost as soon as it had left London, and stayed with it for its entire journey.

The clacking of this loom soothes me and my fingers fly over the shuttles, but I still see, unbidden in my mind's eye, that witch gasping and dying, pinned to the road by the thrust of the halberd. The Lord decided that she should die. They all pretended they loved Him. Her sin found her out… which is why she stared at me and screamed. I was just His vehicle – His chosen vehicle – this is why I alone was brought out of the mists. Why does this not comfort me? Our yarns and brocading threads were better than this. We used only silver and gold threads not this white metal. Here the weave is limited to the contours of the design. Oh the sin of pride, my gold weave backed with silver brocading was in high demand and now Calvet demands it… he knows how my skill of hand is admired. He still says he will give me silver coins but does not do so.. and will not….

Soon after the Great Army's departure, closely wrapped in a cloak against a chill unseasonal wind and rain, Alice and little Matthew visited Hope Polsted in her tall house near the River Thames. She was always a source of interesting gossip, as her husband supplied fustians and linsey-woolsey blankets to the Court, and her brother was one of the many stewards. Matthew and a maid went to join Hope's children who were playing in a gallery over the gatehouse adjoining the cosy parlour in which the two women were esconced. They had left the door open, so the children could, and frequently did, crawl and totter in to see them. Hearing gurgles and shrieks of laughter, they smiled fondly.

'You have been very close-mouthed about this child, Alice,' said Hope, sipping spiced and warmed wine. She had noted quizzically that Susannah's little boy's bright hair was the colour of the monarchs of the Tudor house. 'But can you now tell me more? I have to say he looks nothing like you or your family!'

Alice gave a forced smile.

'I'm sure you are not the only one to have suspicions, but I can assure you, they have no basis. As I told you, he was born of Irish gentry on his father's side, but deserted by his mother. I have been given responsibility for him as we have not yet been able to trace her. Although this responsibility is somewhat annoying, I have to say that I am becoming increasingly attached to the little fellow, and he of me.'

'Did the Irish Council here direct you to look after him?'

'No. I do not know if they know about him. I don't think Thomas ever told the Council about his birth or that he was here and Constable Porter was killed in battle. It is best that I say no more, and that you do not speak of this to anyone.'

'So let's talk about this handsome tawny-faced man with the Irish accent. I am told you dote on him.'

'Who told you that?' said Alice shortly.

'Come Alice, our servants and retainers gossip!'

'Niko is indeed handsome. He is well-known to Thomas and other Crown Officials, and is an Irish envoy of his foster-brother who is an Irish Baron. He is here to demonstrate loyalty to our Queen.' - Alice continued as Hope smiled knowingly - 'and I fear that, although he himself is loyal, his kin may be traitorous. He stays in my household from time to time. He helps with the searches for Matthew's mother. '

Alice tucked some stray glossy hair under her bonnet, pulled it further over her ears and asked, ' Do you have any tidbits from the Court, as you are in the mood for gossip?'

'Our beloved Queen is raging at the Earl of Tyrone's betrayal – he is named an "Arch Traitor " and she expects Lord Essex's army to soon prevail.'

'Coming here today, the streets were not quiet. Folk are anxious that Spain will invade again. As he has the Pope's support, London must be King Philip's next target now he has almost a new fleet.' Alice added, 'There are many unruly people in Ireland, including those arriving there from the continent and Scotland. Some do follow our Faith but do not accept the Queen's Law. In his years in Ireland, Thomas has done much to accomplish the 'civilisation' of those in Leinster. Many now have proper livelihoods and prosper.'

Hope then replied, 'You know what it is like here in the City. There are always alarums and rumour. My brother says most of those he sees at the Court are not yet unduly worried. We must just pray for the Earl of Essex's speedy victory. But I must tell you! The strangest tale is going about. The Court Purveyors have, in the last year, found a new supplier of fine arras, damasks and bed brocades which have been much admired by the courtiers. The cloth finisher is a Walloon – from Northern France. His stuffs are cleverly designed and unusual, and as good as, but cheaper, than the ones previously commissioned from abroad. Well – this Walloon has died in the most bizarre circumstances.'

Alice frowned and leaned forward.

'Go on.'

'It must have been a punishment from God. He was walking past the ruined Priory of St John the Baptist and went inside to ease himself against a wall supporting a broken tower. Still sacrilege to do that, even if it is no longer a place of worship! God knows there are many places of easement alongside the river. Some of these "Strangers" are too arrogant in their faith. I was told that many are governed spiritually not by bishops but by elders of equal rank.'

'Many are pious and hardworking, Hope,' Alice said only too aware that Susannah had been forever at her needle, loom or prayers. 'But, please continue. I only know this Priory by name.'

'Well, it seems that many beggars, men and women, pass the night within the ruins. Some old ones are the old ex-nuns who survived after the rapes and sacking, and who refused to leave the place where most of their community perished, and now live on alms. They say the Priory is haunted by the screams of the Sisters. No-one has wanted to lease it from the Crown, because of the work that is needed to put it right. Also evicting those sheltering there would mean confronting the curses of the ex-nuns; no doubt, the Crown will sort it all out, but…'

'Hope,' interrupted Alice. 'Tell me, what happened to the Walloon?'

'Well, there was a tremendous gust of wind presaging a rainstorm, such as is happening frequently this year. This, or perhaps a malign devil, caused a coping stone to crash down, bringing with it a statue of the Madonna and Child – somewhat defaced– which was high up but obviously was loose in its niche in the wall. The stone and then the statue knocked him to the ground. He lost his senses and soon died, God Rest His Soul.'

Alice crossed herself, gasped a little and then looked thought-ful.

'What was his name? We may have supplied him with fleec-es for trimming.'

'I can't immediately recall his name. He dealt mainly in silks, brocades and embroidered cloths, and did no carding and spin-ning like your people. There were not many at the burial held in Tabernacle Alley, which my brother attended. I gather he was an unpopular man, a hard task-master who was slow in paying his debts and dues.'

'Did he have a wife?'

'I was told that he was wed quite recently to a widow with an adult son. She was not liked either. Her previous husband – God also Rest His soul – also had Court connections. You seem very interested in this, Alice – why so?'

At that moment, there was a commotion in the gallery as Matthew had slipped on the polished floor, was wailing for Alice, and they took their leave.

Later, wondering privately whether the dead man could possibly be Susannah's betrothed, she made further enquiries, and even-tually learned that he was indeed Christian Calvet. She had been informed that the widow's first husband had bought fleeces and skins from her father. She decided that she would contact Mis-tress Calvet. She sent a messenger expressing condolences using the name of Alice Hurst, and asking if she could visit urgently to discuss an order for finished cloth. She received no reply.

Taking a wagon, lurching from side to side behind them, and two armed mounted men, Alice, also on horseback, picked her way slowly through rain-filled potholes and grey hummocks on rut-ted roads. Their route took them through Tower St into Mincheon

Lane[5], then passing through streets lined with stalls of beans, cabbages, fish and oysters. They then found their way eastwards through quadrants, causeys and winding lanes into the French and Walloon hamlets of Spitle Fields and Petty France. There were many people on the streets. Some were cloaked groups of women sitting with their bobbins making lace; others, followed by their dogs, carried heavy loads of cloth on their heads. Yet others pushed covered barrows. The alleys were lined with small terraced hovels and tall blank-windowed timber-framed weaving sheds and storehouses. There were areas of scrub grass with grazing goats and tethered horses, and shallow stone ruins, and the vast area in which stood many frames of drying fabrics. Alice drew the attention of her retinue to a recently repaired ancient pulpit where preachers, for generations, harangued the populace on the Sabbath.

'I know the Crown keeps a close watch on these Protestant sects,' said Nat Gibson, a Plymmiswoode retained sergeant and head of her guard. 'From time to time, they put down riots from the masterless and tradeless apprentices who say their jobs are taken, their prices undercut, and that the 'Strangers' give work only to their own people, and do not train ours. Why does Her Majesty so tolerate this number of French and Walloons in our great London, if they only enrich themselves and take the livelihood of established city folk?'

Alice smiled cynically, replying, 'The "Strangers" are expected, if not forced, to pay taxes to fund our Queen Elizabeth's military campaigns, and the fleets she sends to apprehend corsairs and Spanish treasure ships. Their taxes are far higher than our dues, and the loans they give are expected to be given at low interest!' Thinking she had been unwisely frank, she quickly remarked to her companions as her horse stumbled on the cobbles, 'The people in these streets are indeed strangely dressed! Those enormous headdresses must take forever to tie. And these patches of muddy ordure are insupportable.'

'The stinks of the streets are not as bad as they will be near the dyeing vats and the Great Ditch,' Nat Gibson replied.

They continued to travel eastward for some time, avoiding the narrowest alleys. Then they came upon smart new mansions, almshouses, and a large field containing teazels and brickworks where, Nat said, many ancient Roman potshards and artifacts had been found. Eventually they stopped at a townhouse with large sheds at the rear. The door had been draped in black cloth.

She said to Nat, 'If I am allowed in, you, the horses and the wagon must remain on the street, even though you will be blocking the passage of other vehicles. Move the carriage into the yard if I buy some cloth, but I want my horse here at the front in case we have to leave quickly.'

A steward answered. He said that his mistress was in mourning and refusing all except the pastor. Alice had been told that the lady of the house was a scold, although, she thought to herself, this was often said about a woman with drive and ambition.

'Please tell your mistress that I too have buried a loved one - my father who was in our trade, but know that the wheels of commerce must continue to turn. I have an urgent order for silks or embroidered velvets.'

The steward hesitated, but then allowed her in. As she entered, the smell of tallow and wax candles hung heavily throughout. After a lengthy wait, Dame Margery received Alice and her guard in a chamber which was covered in fashionable brightly painted story plaques. She was dressed in black, in deep mourning - except for Susannah's chain and jewelled cross which sparkled on her bosom.

'I am sorry your husband no longer lives. God be with him,' said Dame Margery. Alice crossed herself.

'And I am sorry for your second husband's untimely death. Shall we pray together for the safe harbouring of their souls?' said Alice somewhat coldly.

'Thank you, but I have just come from my prayer stool and would return to it alone. My steward said you had an urgent request for silks?' Her eyes opened wide when she heard the size of the order Alice said she was considering, and she added, 'My weavers of silk damask are very skilled, Mistress Hurst. I am sure we have cloths that will be of interest to you.'

Alice arranged herself in the heavily carved chair, opening her mantle, exposing and chinking a leather bag, whilst Dame Margery sent for Edward to bring some examples of their finest work.

'I hope that you have what I need in stock. I am buying because my usual supplier has not been able to complete an order which I promised would be delivered this week. I will take the bales now if they are suitable.'

They then discussed colours and certain gold threaded velvets, when Edward arrived, bowing and presenting a carton of samples. One look told Alice that some of these designs were most likely created by Susannah.

'This design of mythical beasts couched in gold thread is most unusual and artistic,' she said to Edward, the embroidered satin weave soft beneath her fingers. 'May I congratulate the man responsible.'

'This is not a man's work. We have a very proficient designer and weaver, a young lady, whom I am seeking to wed.'

She looked up at scrawny Edward, standing too near her chair for comfort. He looked lost in his black padded doublet and hose. His lace collar was clean but she blenched at his heavy body smell, pouchy eyes and untrimmed moustache on which were stuck remnants of food. She thought how different he was to Niko whose manly natural odour she found pleasant.

'I would have thought that wedding you would be greatly to her advantage! When will we hear the marriage bells?'

Alice noticed Dame Margery looking warningly at her son.

'She is a shy maiden and, you will appreciate we are still in mourning.'

Alice gasped a little. 'Of course, of course. Do forgive this lapse. I hate my mind to dwell on unhappiness and am sure that this is so for you too, Edward, isn't it?'

'Yes, yes,' he looked nervously at his mother.

'But I should love to meet this talented young woman and indeed visit your work sheds. A professional interest only, you understand.' She held one large sample against her and then turned it over. She thought it most likely to be available as the weave was loose and it had been dyed a sickly shade of light green. 'How much stock do you hold of this colour and design? It looks similar on both sides. This will appeal more to those customers who do not want the expense of a lining. It is one of your cheaper lines, is it not? What price did you have in mind per bale?'

Although this cloth had been stored for some time, had faults and was worth little, Margery asked a large sum for the number of bales requested. Rather to her surprise, Alice did not unduly demur or bargain. Edward quickly departed to arrange the loading and also to deal with a certain clamour from the street.

He came back shortly afterwards and reproved.

'I have ordered your wagon and servants to drive into our yard. They are causing some obstruction. You surely know, mistress, that only your horse and one guard should wait outside a house in a narrow thoroughfare.'

Apologising, Alice stood up quickly so that the bag of coins on her girdle chinked, Alice counted out a large number of these into a wooden bowl on a nearby table.

She then asked, 'Would you allow me to see the sheds whilst I wait for the bales to be loaded? I may wish to purchase some of your finer work.'

Margery, smirking, had watched the counting with concentration and was now weighing the bowl of silver in her hands.

'You must be proud of your fine business,' Alice said. 'At the very least I can congratulate your clever weavers! They will be pleased to know they are admired and will do more good work for you.'

Edward suddenly addressed Alice roughly.

'Do you know one Pieter Heyden? He works for M. De Hem in Amsterdam, an enterprise which used to be Breydel and De Hem.'

Alice raised her thick eyebrows haughtily.

Dame Margery tutted at her son.

'Edward – go now and prepare some more samples of the brocades for this lady!' She turned to Alice. 'You may observe them working but do not distract them unduly.'

Edward added as he left, 'Say nothing to any of the weaving girls about my marriage, if you please.'

'Of course I will not. It would indeed be a discourtesy at the present time.'

The two women walked in silence through the flagged hall. Crossing the yard where the bales were being brought out for loading, a vast black cloud suddenly moved across the otherwise brilliant sky. Its golden rim formed an outline of a hunched figure leaning on a staff. Thunder rumbled in the distance.

'Why, look at that!' said Dame Margery, craning her long neck. They both crossed themselves. Alice shivered involuntarily and, as her wagon entered the yard gates and they made their way into the weaving sheds, said decidedly,

'It threatens heavy rain which will make the potholes worse and turn all to mud. We must quickly load the bales and soon be gone.'

Dame Margery approaches and sternly tells us to bend to our shuttles and wefts. She and Edward did not cause our labours to cease even though newly bereaved…God be praised that Calvet is gone, no doubt to the hell he deserves. Surely that is Mistress Alice with her? I stare to be sure that it is Mistress Alice that I see… now I am on my knees with beseeching speech for her to rescue me once again. She and Margery have sharp words. Mistress Alice tells me that she has been searching for me for many months, gestures to the yard and tells me to quickly get into her wagon…I run out and her servant lifts me in. I sit amongst some bales of cloth and she gives orders that we quickly leave. O joy of joys, we rumble out of this prison. Mistress Alice is twice my saviour…

Edward, who, bewildered, had come into the shed, stood, arms by his sides, opening and closing his fists, as his mother and Alice argued fiercely. Dame Margery finally handed over Susannah's gold chain and cross.

'Go now, lest my son does not contain his fury. Others will hear of your deception. That woman was married to a savage and learned his ways. I have friends at the Court. They will be told of your favour to one who was close to Irish rebels.'

Alice said sternly, as she turned to leave, 'Remember you have just been paid well for her board and charge! You know well that this inferior cloth is not worth the price you asked. I want no more bales than have already been loaded. As it is, I will have to give it away. I too have friends at Court. You may be sure others will hear rumours of your kidnap of a well-known Dutch merchant's niece. In your place, I would stay close-mouthed if you do not wish to see your son on the gallows. May God forgive you for your sins.'

She swept out back through the yard and hall, pushing aside the steward, who was jumping from foot to foot in agitation, at the main entrance. She mounted and bid Nat Gibson to leave the narrow alleys and be distant as quickly as possible.

I thank God that Alice did not have me whipped for leaving Matthew as she first threatened. I told her I was held against my will, that I would have been forced into another so-called marriage. When she heard of my sufferings she relented. I told her that I could not leave there, that I was ever watched and guarded. I told her that Our Lord must know that their house is not a pious house, whatever they professed. Christian Calvet received just wrath for his sins. Dame Margery said I had forfeited my place amongst the Chosen to sit by our Lord's side by lying with Redmond, but surely they have forfeited theirs… the Lord took and crushed Calvet, but has rescued me again… this is proof that I am Chosen…

Niko praised Alice for her initiative, and acknowledged her acumen and courage, but added, 'You should have taken me with you and Nat Gibson.'

'Your looks would have betrayed you! And your man Dermot looks like a bandit Chief.'

'We could have hidden somewhere behind, but been near enough if you had needed us.'

'I am well able to protect myself- do not fear.'

Her independence reminded him of his clanswomen and he smiled.

He had mixed feelings at Susannah's reappearance. He had become convinced of her death. She did not seem pleased to see him. He had greeted her, bowing, 'Why are you still bitter towards our people, in spite of your life being saved – and your honour – through marriage to Lord Redmond?'

Lifting her chin rudely, she had turned and left the room.

Pieter Heyden hurried across the seas to London, as soon as word was received from the Exchange that M. De Hem's niece had been found. After bowing low, he held Susannah's hands for longer than Alice thought necessary. Susannah's beauty had matured and given her a spiritual quality. Dressed in borrowed finery, she looked even more becoming. Her pallor, wide eyes and modest demeanour was enhanced by the overlarge dark velvet gown with a starched muslin collar and cuffs. The jewelled cross lay on her breast. The fair hair under a neat, if old-fashioned, cap of Alice's was smooth and shining, corralled like a halo around her face. After exchanging courtesies, Pieter told her of her mother's death. She shrieked and became voluble in her mother tongue, and was soon prostrate on the floor. Servants were called and she was taken to her chamber. On leaving, Pieter asked Alice to keep Susannah until he was able to complete the tasks he had been given in London for De Hem.

'Delaying her departure to Holland will allow her to spend time with Matthew and recover from her grief. Consider, Mistress Alice! She has been defiled, forced to abandon her child and enslaved. She sees herself as sinful with a ruined future and her immortal soul threatened. She must pray and do penance. I will take her to our Church where they will ease her mind.'

Alice had felt obliged to agree to this request, but added, 'Let her embroider and create designs too. It seems to give her comfort.'

Pieter called at Plymmiswoode Hall whenever his time allowed. He escorted Susannah to acquaintances in the "Strangers" neighbourhoods. They went frequently to the principal Dutch Church. Privately, Pieter told her that he had decided that the English merchants' hold on overseas trade was such that M. De Hem should seek business partners elsewhere, and he may well visit London rarely in future. Susannah said fervently that, once home, she had no wish to ever come back to Britain or Ireland again.

'Those two have a fondness,' Alice commented to Niko. His smile had not reached his eyes.

'She may be cursed. And she is already married to Redmond. No good will come of it.'

Susannah spent her time brocading and embroidering, ornamenting caps and gloves for Alice and her stepchildren, and embellishing, with religious symbols, warm robes for the Protestant pastors who preached in the open air. Pieter had brought her a letter from her uncle, granting that Matthew could come back with her. This had not seemed to cheer her.

Pieter's mien is calm and measured. He often looks at me and then away. Does he wonder if I am fond? Is he fond towards me? Our Lord will tell me this if I pray enough. It is good to speak my tongue. Here there are many good folk of great skill in silversmithing and printing as well as silk weaving. The Elders know of my spiritual descent but do not yet judge me... they say our God is a righteous God. They watch over me and send messengers to take me to where they preach. They are truly pious and love God. Also, like my father, they believe that their daughters should have skills, be literate and know the Bible. I have been taken with Pieter to their new fine hospital named 'La Providence' for our sick and indigent. Pieter's brow furrows when I talk of Calvet that he names a weak and greedy knave, or when I am with Matthew. The child is ever peevish with me, but crows with Alice. He even crows when that base-born Niko flings him into the air. I cry that he will kill the child. I long to be once more with my own people, but I fear crossing the seas. These colours will suit Mistress Alice's strong features and upright bearing....

It was noticed that Susannah was not unkind to her son, but sometimes careless, and that she left him with Alice, Niko or the servants whenever she could.

... Matthew keeps removing the little cap I made him... he is wilful, wants to move constantly and wriggles from my arms... I see Redmond's gaze in his green/blue eyes...

'Do you not wish that she spent as much time with her son as she did with Pieter Heyden – or on the embroidering tasks you give her?' said Niko to Alice when visiting one afternoon. 'Do not force her to keep Rory. Request her to give him to me to take to his kin in Leinster. They will welcome him.'

'So you keep saying,' Alice answered tartly. 'And I will keep saying that he is safer here away from the war! Safer even than in Holland. The peace between France and Spain that has been signed may not last, and the Dutch will be at war with them again. And his name is Matthew!'

As the season advanced into a wet summer, the talk in the household, and indeed throughout London, was of the dreadful drownings in the bay when the Earl of Essex's flotilla was entering the port of Dublin. Many ships with loyal 'Old English' lords on board had come out to welcome the English army and had capsized in heavy seas. Amongst those drowned, together with eighteen other noblemen and gentlemen, was the southern Earl of Kildare, from the noble House of Fitzgerald. None had survived, and mangled bodies washed ashore some weeks afterwards. Explosions had been heard, apparently from the gunpowder on board. When they were alone, Dermot was joyful. Niko had smiled at Dermot's capering, but had made no comment.

'Sabotage cannot be proved but the Queen is enraged,' Hope Polsted informed Alice. 'It is said that she has told Lord Essex to be swift in putting down the rebellion.'

As an experienced soldier, Niko believed that the men of Leinster would be vulnerable if the Great Army progressed through their county. He had been relieved that the Queen had ordered that the first objective was to subdue the north. The two MacFeagh churls who regularly brought goods to Plymmiswoode Hall from the Hurst demesne, found an opportunity to speak with Niko and Dermot. They said that, as well as incessant rain all the way to the crossing in Wales, on the higher ground at Penmaenmawr the inundation had been even worse. The English army's wagons, gun carriages and horses were stuck in mud. Already ill-fed men had been cold, drenched with incessant rain and many were fever-ridden and weak.

'Niko- the land in that part of Wales holds few folk, and little sustenance. The corn and other vittles the army carried had become damp in the ships and was sour or inedible. I have heard from Court gossips that Lord Essex himself was debilitated, having fallen sick with agues.' They all crossed themselves as a churl continued, 'And many said that, in the worst of the relentless rain storms, the clouds were shaped into a cloaked old woman and the frowning, long-bearded face of a towering God. Now I must give you Redmond's exact words as told to me. "Tyrone has not accepted the terms of the latest pardon. The O'Neill urges us to war with him, and this is also the mind of our Overlord now. After the killing of Medb, my heart has followed. We go today to defend the fortress of Cahir. I am leaving Fintan here with Orlaith and the women to prepare for resistance, skirmish where they can and protect the homesteads from pillaging deserters. Go now to Le Havre and encourage our Spanish contacts to support us and bring their troops by sea. But be careful who you trust and do not come here and join us! You must be seen to be loyal. Send Gile to her kin. It seems my son will be safe with Alice Plymmiswoode for now. When this is over, we will claim him."

Niko told the churls that their kerns should ambush, bearing down from the heights, hurling stones from the screes and then melting into the forests.

'Redmond must not get trapped in a siege in Cahir,' he said anxiously. 'Its walls may not survive the English siege engines, and he must live to lead.'

He was gratified that Redmond's decision to go to war echoed his own growing resentment towards the unfriendly or antagonistic English populace. He sent gifts back to Leinster with the informers, having found out that Orlaith sickened. His desire to go with the men and divert to the stronghold, or indeed fight with the clan, was almost unbearable. Dermot and the churls stopped him.

'Not yet, Niko. Redmond commands otherwise. You will be of more use here. Fintan and Oonagh are taking good care of Orlaith. They will send her to safety, perhaps to join you in Le Havre.'

Listening out near the Court for news, they rejoiced when they heard talk on the street confirming the disease and desertion which was continuing to reduce Lord Essex's battalions. But then Niko became uneasy. Instead of turning the bulk of his army north to Ulster, it seemed that it had headed south, much to Her Majesty's annoyance at the countermanding of her orders. Niko had heard that the Earl of Essex was given to impulse and now knew that this was the proof of it. He feared the power of the English ordnance, which, once set in place, could well be directed at Cahir. This was a bustling garrisoned townland, one of the chiefs' main strongholds, commanding important passes.

He repeated his worries to Dermot, saying,' Please God that when Essex traverses our lands, the kerns and gallowglass will use our ways of fighting – and will not confront the English troops, which should be led them into our sucking bogs so they lose their weapons, if not their lives.'

Later they heard that Leinster had not been completely subdued by the Great Army. The O'Byrne clan for instance had defeated the Seneschal in engagements in the Wicklow Hills. They also heard that southern clans had been reported as massing with some of those of the more northerly earls on the borders of Munster. Niko hoped that Redmond had gone to join these fighting men as he knew that the Crown had never, in the past, kept many troops and munitions in that County.

Around this time, Alice asked Niko if her brother's desmesne would be vulnerable, situated as it was on the marches of The Pale, also telling him that Thomas had helped to supply the Earl of Essex's troops. In reply, Niko said sombrely that he believed that Thomas would be wise to protect his holdings, and not reduce his garrison. At her anxious response, he had reassured her with an explanation of the defences of Hurst Place. Alice was disconcerted that he knew about its deep cellars with stores of weapons and passages to confuse marauders, its several plunging arrow loops built under the parapets, and the placements of his sentries of tough mercenaries.

'Why Niko,' she then asked carefully, 'do you still visit me, now that Susannah had been found, and that it has been agreed that she would return to her home?'

He smiled.

'We would like to accompany Nat Gibson in guarding and escorting Pieter Heyden, Susannah and Matthew to Harwich. Our knowledge of suitable fast vessels will be useful and I like to spend time with the boy. But we will soon be leaving for France.'

Annoyed with herself for being disappointed with his answer, she reluctantly agreed, part of her fearing that he would make off with Matthew. She knew however that the plague had reached Ireland and that Niko would not put Matthew in harm's way. Sometimes she wished she could find it in her heart to deny him entrance to her house and heart, but mostly she found she could not suppress a longing for his visits. But on the occasions when there was jubilant news of the Crown's victories, she noticed that he did not come.

CHAPTER SIXTEEN

aving finished his commissions in London, Pieter was ready to take Susannah home.

His brows met when I told him do not wish my son to accompany us to Harwich and that I fear what may befall us on the treacherous seas. I still hear the screams of the drowning. Pieter said the infant will grow much and will not know me. That Niko is angry. He tells me that Matthew should be with his father. I will never allow him to be reared by savages, savages now at war. Mistress Alice promises, thank the Lord, that she will keep Matthew by her until he is old enough to journey to me by himself…

Pieter gracefully accepted a gift from Alice who had asked Susannah to ornament a pair of fine leather gauntlets, which she did, spending long hours covering the cuffs with a subdued and delicate floral pattern. Not in Niko's presence, Pieter compensated Alice for Matthew and Susannah's board and charge. She asked him to recommend the Plymmiswoode wools and fleeces to M. De Hem for use as linings and trimmings. Some of their highway being dangerous, Pieter had no objection to Niko and Nat Gibson also going to the port of Harwich and indeed offered them some Dutch royals for doing so. Dermot was obliged to stay near Matthew, although fearing the disease and hostility of the City. Alice privately warned Nat Gibson to watch that Niko did not go anywhere alone with the boy. They started out at dawn but even at that hour there was a clamour from the crowds leaving London to escape from the plague and an insistent tolling of bells. They stopped as little as possible on the way. Pieter was withdrawn and frowning as they rode through the outskirts of the port. At the harbour, Niko found a passage in a sea-worthy vessel, less smelly, as it transported a cargo other than herring. It would dock at Flushing, from whence onward transport could easily be arranged.

Whilst we wait to depart from this stinking harbor, my Pieter regards me with concern. I sit still and tense. He has stroked my shoulder and I know he would hold me. Now he confers with that sly one, that Niko who I am sure cozens my mistress... her eyes go like pools when she sees him...

At the dockside receiving payment for his escort duties, Niko again harangued Pieter about Redmond's marriage portion. Pieter refused, saying irritably,

'It will seem as if M. De Hem was supporting the rebels. We do not yet know who will triumph in your land. Also, she has chosen to leave her husband and, indeed, it was Mistress Alice who rescued her from Calvet, not you.'

Niko was icy.

'Kindly recall that it was my brother that saved her life and then honoured her with marriage.'

Now away from Alice's earshot, Niko then confidently stated that the Irish Earls would be victorious and that Susannah and Matthew's status would be great. Even if she did not return herself, he promised many orders for M. De Hem's fine stuffs for the Irish nobles. Pieter demurred.

'I doubt if we could afford to trade there profitably, even with new Governors. Bribes and corruption are rife amongst purveyors of all types of transport of goods to and throughout Britannia! In the Low Countries, we are taxed heavily to pay for standing armies and, if and when conflict finally ceases, we must pay for the re-building of ruined towns.'

The Dutchman was anxious to get away to fresh sea breezes

and ease his head, which had begun to ache from the close and humid air and Niko's harangues.

'This man can talk for England – or perhaps I should say Ireland!' he thought. 'Britannia's avarice knows no bounds. Although bringing more gold than on my last visit, I have used much of it already on London City's insufferable levies and bribes. Once home, I can find some excuse to delay further.'

'The war has now spread throughout Ireland. I have no doubt that the Earl of Tyrone will prevail,' Niko insisted.

'You say that, but I have heard that the Crown has many recent successes – Cahir, for example, has been taken and garrisoned, and there have been some victories at Limerick and on the borders of The Pale. Your Queen's anger grows. She will see that the rebels are overcome.'

'Minor successes only. The northern earls have trained men in Ulster and now have support in the south. The Lord Devereux's troops are decimated by sickness and ambush,' Niko retorted, prepared for further argument, when Susannah suddenly announced that she would not board the ship, whose gangplank she had seen being lowered. She rocked on her heels and fussed loudly. Niko and Pieter frowned. Pieter said hurriedly to Niko,

'See me in Calais when you next travel to France. I will do what I can.'

Then he knelt and held Susannah's hands in his, and an impassioned and lengthy dialogue between them followed, whereupon Niko said 'Bah!' and turned away.

'You must be brave again,' said Pieter quietly. 'Where do we turn when life delivers its heaviest blows? Our Holy Book will aid you.'

He is perplexed and questions me but I smell the sea… that sea… I told him how my tears flowed as I boarded those ships with Alice, knowing I was not bound for my home, and that I had a babe in my belly that felt like an incubus. I told him how Alice scolded me for my shrieking and bid her retainers slap my face if I did not halt my wailing… perforce I snivelled for fear of their violence. I told him how I puked… I was in torment for my many sins… this dear man quotes much from the Bible, but I still weep. Now when he asks me to fix my eyes not on what is seen, but what is unseen as St Paul adjures, the trailing hair and dead gaze of my father, young sailors, my maid, appear between the mists and float by me. The sailors come to take our chests and Pieter turns to speak to them and looks red in the face… but now Niko approaches me and fixes his cold eyes upon me. He stands between me and Pieter, he tells me harshly that if I do not board the vessel, he will return me to my rightful husband… his hand is on his frightful broad-bladed sword. I must walk up the plank with Pieter to hold me… we do not look back… I tell him I fear Niko. He says he will ask my uncle's lawyers if my so-called marriage can be annulled. Pieter tells me this is a good new ship… now I will go below as I am like to be sick, which makes me quiet…

Returning from Harwich, Niko visited Alice and came upon her, with Matthew in her arms, circling the room in a stately dance.

'She's gone! She's gone! The sullen wench has gone!'

He smiled and said, 'We must all be gone soon as plaguey London sickens. Redmond's wife is now settled and on her way to her home. I have word that our townlands' stores of salt and linens have been sent to France to be traded. I must go there and get the best prices for my peoples' goods.'

She became silent and crestfallen. She knew that it would be some time before she saw his black eyes, or heard the soft tones of his accented speech.

Trading was only one of the reasons why the two Irishmen wanted to leave. Anger in London against their people had become insupportable. Dermot, fraternising with apprentices, watchers and spies, had been feeling increasingly threatened. Although they intended to journey to Le Havre, he told everyone that he and Niko were shortly to leave London for La Rochelle. This was known to be a staunchly Protestant city. Aware that they would be away from Matthew, Niko did not doubt that the child was well cared-for, guarded and that he would be safer with Alice away from the present heat of war. He also wanted to find Captain Alfonso, and those corsairs he knew, and obtain information about the course of the fighting from sources other than street rumour and the Court, as well as to continue to pursue Pieter for compensation.

He said, 'Are you also leaving London?'

'My steward is preparing to shut the house. I will visit my Aunt Cecilia again. I want her to see how Matthew thrives – and also to consult with the tenants of our sheep pastures. It seems that neither the Crown nor Thomas has shown further interest in Matthew. No doubt they have more weighty matters to attend to. I will be back here before the winter becomes too hard and hope that your country will be settled under the Crown once again then. Next Spring I may be able to go back to Thomas, but his last letter said that in no circumstances am I to return to his demesne at present. The usual seasonal produce, and messages from Hurst Place have not arrived this time. The war must have made transports problematical.' She paused. 'I know that feeling against Irishmen runs high. Will you return to London before winter? I suppose you have no reason to. Redmond must have heard by now from the Hurst Desmesne retainers that his wife is found, will be returning to the Low Countries and that, for the moment, his son is safe and thriving in my care.'

'Reliable communication with Ireland is difficult at present, but Redmond may well have heard this.' Niko was silent for a while. His eyes burned into her until she almost gasped. Then he continued, 'Dermot and I will escort you some of the way west towards your farms and the Abbey. We can then travel on to France from the nearest port.' He had not been able to resist adding, 'If I return, you will be my reason, mistress.' He was uncomfortably aware of heartache at the thought of being away from her.

Pieter has given me a bowl in which to void and seems not to feel the motion of the deck or the stinks of my vomitus. Later he came and forced dry bread and spirit through my lips. He comes again now, saying it becomes dark and he would sleep. I doze ... he has told me he wishes to marry me if my uncle will permit it. I have said I will think and pray on this. I trust only in God now... if marriage to Pieter is not permitted, perhaps I will dedicate myself to Him rather than any suitor...

The bells tolled mournfully as Alice and her retinue including Benedicta joined the long queue of wagons, horses, carts and people on foot leaving the plague-ridden city. Inland, they found cooler air on the heights where they travelled on rocky tracks winding through high moors. Descending into valleys they lost the breeze, and stifling air enveloped the small column. The cavalcade slowed and their energy dissipated. Matthew became fractious in the carriage. This was jolting so much over the dried-out cart ruts that Alice took to her horse, also unhappy in the heat. Flies buzzed around them both.

On the way westward, Niko's earring danced as he cantered back and forth, guarding their small column. Dermot scouted. Alice signalled to a servant walking behind, who eventually produced a skin flask of warm vinegary water for her to both drink and splash on her face. She envied Niko his short hair and open shirt. She grimaced at him, as, followed by his panting hound, he came up alongside. She had removed her thick cloak, her starched ruff and velvet jerkin. The fine linen shirt over her laced waistcoat stuck to her wide bosom. Her cap protected her to some extent from the sun, but her face was still uncomfortably red, enhanced when she noticed him looking at her. She adjusted her attire, glancing sideways at him, then looking away. Then she raised her arms to push stray hair back into her cap, watching him slyly. He smiled, his teeth glistening. She fixed pins in her cap. Then she became acutely aware that he was removing his damp cambric shirt to reveal a sculpted chest, and broad shoulders. One of his cordlike upper arms was adorned with a wide embroidered leather strap, on which were entwined in gold thread, circular motifs and what looked like a clan badge. He winked as he saw her watching him, then slathered water from his flask on his head and neck and stretched luxuriously. Alice wished she did not feel so lustful, and murmured a prayer. To dampen her excitement, she brought to her mind the memory of gold-torqued Redmond glaring at her, savagely turning his mount and galloping from Thomas's mansion. Quickly, she commanded her horse to trot as the skies began to darken until there was merely a fringe of sunlight in the distance. Rolling thunder and a flash of lightening then led to pandemonium amongst the horses, dogs and mules. All were forced to stop. Niko went to quieten her mount first. As his strong hands gripped her bridle, she smelled the sweat on him, and caught her breath at the thought that he and his horse were as one, both sleek and muscled, one controlling the other in harmony.

They rode on swiftly, seeking shelter from the bursts of torrential rain, through a wide forest bridle path with streams and high banks each side, towards a wooded valley. This sloped upwards into a large mossy glade not far from some broken falls of waters and their pools. The party stopped to allow the deluge to pass, and Alice sank thankfully into a cushion provided for her under the boughs on a mossy bank. Benedicta took Matthew to eat and cool his little legs in a shallow pool. Food was distributed, but Niko took only fruit and then went off with Dermot, to pray at a small ancient shrine to St Christopher at a spring by a rocky outcrop.

'This will be disturbing to my entourage,' she thought. Later, she called as he passed, 'Sit by me, Niko.'

He perched alongside on a rock outcrop and sent Dermot to be with the guards.

'I wonder that you are so obvious in asking the Saint for a blessing,' she said loudly. 'You are in Protestant England. In our belief, we pray only with living priests. We do not kneel before statues of the dead. The dead already have their place with their Maker.' Then she said more quietly, 'You must be careful at these shrines. Extremists abhor the worship in front of idols. Many will inform on you for a groat or two. Be mindful where you are.'

'We pray for peace and safety in our land, wherever there is a chance that God may listen.' He munched on his apples.

Alice had asked him once about the religious wars in which he had fought, for both sides at times, and which lasted so long, and led to much atrocity and hardship. He had answered that he had come to realise the pride and the power of those Rulers who considered themselves as ordained by God. He had learned that when these Rulers questioned each other's Faith, they were questioning each other's piety and power, challenging what was the structure and source of their governance. The legitimacy of their rightful noble lords, commanders, princes, archbishops, Imams, and emirs were thus also being questioned, which naturally could not be tolerated. Battles for supremacy, he had said, were, and would remain, inevitable.

'I did hear that you and your mother lived among Mahommedans, until you were ransomed. Did you and your mother have to conform to that religion? If so, your soul could be in peril.'

His mind turned to the gentle bearded Imam who had taught him much.

'We had little choice. We did not wish to be martyred.' His face shuttered. 'I was a young child and remember little from those years. My mother has done much penance. God will forgive her actions.'

Alice realised that there was much about him that she would never know. This intrigued and repelled her at the same time.

'I daresay I would have submitted too, although I would close my ears against arguments that oppose my Faith. But I have made compromises that I hope Our Lord understands.' She laughed shortly. 'In commerce, I meet with many men and women of different Faiths. It is as if we all profess one belief when we do business together. That is, the worship of mutual advantage!'

Niko laughed and thought this turn of the conversation echoed much of his own experience.

She asked suddenly, intensely, watching his eyes, 'Now that the Earl of Tyrone has managed to ignite much of Ireland, will Redmond join the rebels? And when you leave me, will you join him?'

'Do not ask me this again. I repeat that Redmond is a vassal chief and there – and here in England – all have to follow their nobles and Overlords. I am a vassal to Lord Redmond, the great-nephew of the noble Lady Medb. He sent me here to show his support for the Crown.'

'Rebellion is a matter of conscience, not just loyalty,' she opined.

'As I've told you before, conscience and choice are luxuries only for the monarchs and the bishops.'

'That is how God has ordained the world,' she said, thinking that wealthy merchants also had a part to play in the guidance of the powerful in such matters, and that perhaps God had also ordained that fact.

He stood up as everyone was preparing to move on. Trying to lessen what he knew was her growing love for him, and him for her, he said roughly, 'Your actions led to the noble Lady Medb's murder.'

'Please do not speak of this again! The actions were not mine but Susannah's.'

'It is a pity that you were new to our land and its beliefs, mistress. Gile also did not understand the Old Ones and the protection of the Lady Medb. She, and many others, perhaps you too, will suffer for this.'

He bowed and walked away to his horse.

She called after him, her voice mellow and distant, 'I thought you too worldly for savage superstition, Niko!'

He did not turn.

Although irritated at his bickering, Alice soon became glad of the Irishmens' escort as people, carts and bands of vagabonds had increased vastly in number since she had last made this journey.

....we must surely dock soon, the vessel rolls less. We must be in a sheltered bay. I will sit up, arrange myself and climb to the deck. A warm breeze fills my lungs. The sea captain now comes to me frowning. He looks at me closely in the dawn light and asks if I am sick. I pull away as he touches my face. I fear him. I am well now I say. I tell him I always puke from the sea's motion and it is now passing. I ask him to rouse Pieter and he goes away. I hear cries. I will doze again until we begin to dock... Pieter...

Niko and Dermot took their leave of Alice's party before they reached the wide paths and horse ways of the English earls' lands and rode off through the forest. Having obtained licenses from the many liveried retainers, Alice and her retinue passed through villages, hamlets and farmsteads without hindrance. Alice distributed small alms to the poorest cottages and the most ragged children that they came across. She also stopped at wayside chapels. On some nights they had stayed over at sparse and flea-ridden inns, so Alice was pleased, after her long journey, to settle into her great curtained bed at the Abbey, whilst Matthew waddled around and stared at the walls, brightly painted with artful designs.

'There was an unruly side to the Dutch woman, shown particularly to our servants, a devil – which I shall pray to Our Lord to expunge,' said Cecilia whilst they conversed over a supper of roasted fowls that evening. 'What is now intended for her son? I vow you have come to love him, in spite of his devilish looks - his long limbs and straight red hair! He often vocalises in a strange tongue.'

Whilst speaking, Cecilia had glanced sideways at Alice.

'He has a sweet expression and clear voice designed for song, Cecilia,' said Alice, nettled, and also annoyed that Niko had not stopped teaching him the Gaelic tongue as she had asked. 'I will arrange a tutor for Matthew when he is more grown. It is a pity he resembles his savage father more and more, which is no doubt why his mother's interest in him is variable. She has caused me much expense and difficulty, but now I hope that the woman finds the peace of God's love in her own land. It was clear there was fondness between her and her uncle's secretary, Pieter Heyden. But to answer your question, the situation in Ireland must settle before any firm decisions can be made. It is quite likely that many of his clan have gone to war and they may all be proscribed or killed, so it would be hard for them to claim the boy. Susannah may send for him – or the Crown may want him as a formal hostage. You are right that I am fond of Matthew and wish to keep him by my side for as long as I legally can.'

'I hear the Lord Deputy's campaign in Ireland falters,' said Cecilia.

'Lord Essex's enemies at court are finding fault,' replied Alice. 'He is accused of incompetence. But I have also heard that there has been corruption in the way his army has been supplied, and so it is short of weapons, clothing and food. His commanders have complained about the tactics of the rebels and the constant rain. But such a great army surely cannot fail, although I do not underestimate the valour of the Irishmen. Walter and Thomas have told me that their fighting men are hardy and brave, and know the country and how to find their way through forest and marsh. Also many of Lord Essex's troops are new conscripts, and may not stand in the face of battle. But I know that Thomas will give all the aid he can.'

'Well, our news here, as we are situated nearer the Irish shores, is sometimes fresher than yours in London,' said Cecilia, forking a dainty mouthful. 'There are tales of the manors of some

English settlers in Munster and elsewhere, being attacked and looted, as the rebels have become confident and jubilant. Many English refugees have fled to the garrisoned towns for succour, and are begging and in extremity.'

'Do you know if this is so in Leinster?' asked Alice anxiously.

'No, I do not know, but we have been praying for the safety of Thomas and his household. Come – join me after supper in the Chapel. Our choristers have been rehearsing a new psalmody. The child learns how to worship our Lord.'

After sultry London and the humid ride, Alice would have preferred to take an evening walk with the child amongst the higher of the Abbey's gardens and pleaded God's forgiveness for the irritation that Cecilia inspired in her.

In the coming weeks, more news of the war came to the Abbey. Lady Templeton sent messengers informing them that the Irish forces were far from defeat. The Earl of Essex had seemingly negotiated with the enemy and returned to Court; all without permission from the Queen. He was now deemed to have failed in his task and duty to subdue the rebellion. Shocked, Alice and Cecilia journeyed to Templetons for more news, learning that the Lord Essex had been captured riding with an armed band as if to attack the Palace and the Queen's person. As a result, he had been accused of harmful intent and treason and had been committed to the custody of the Lord Keeper at York House. A new Lord Deputy of Ireland and new officials had been appointed, and were journeying there as they spoke.

CHAPTER SEVENTEEN

It was noon and a November morning mist had cleared, but Alice, having returned as quickly as possible to London, did not notice. She was watching Thomas, anxiously surveying his gaunt face and frame. A gold cross was suspended over her dark wool travelling gown. He sat, propped by pillows, under the canopy of the great wooden bed, whilst Benedicta slowly and gently spooned broth into his mouth. He had arrived that morning by carriage to her London home, together with a letter from the Crown office in Dublin, which told of the violent attack on Hurst Place, which was all but destroyed. In an addendum, there was a request for pay for his transports and physicians.

Thomas pushed the spoon away as, in a distant dream, he heard the urgent shouts, the horses' whinnying and the smell of burning all around. He croaked his memories in fits and starts.

Walter had lain with him that night and had become aware of the fire sooner than he, shouting of the red glow from outside the window which first flickered and then flooded their chamber followed by tendrils of swirling smoke. They grabbed some of their garments and he, his sturdy cane. They groped their way along the line of rooms, some open and smoke-filled, crying out 'Fire! Fire!' until they came to the small wooden door leading to a first floor vestibule and a servants' spiral staircase built of flagstone. He, coughing and limping, holding on to the rope rail as its treads were barely visible through the murk, followed Walter down these and to a trapdoor. They heaved this open, shutting it behind them. They descended many more stone steps to a brick floor, and cellarage that held weapons and chests and the kitchen well. The smoke was less dense here, but by now he was sweating and exhausted. Walter swiftly threw some standing buckets of water at the steps, and they stopped for a few moments, pulling on their clothes. A sloping winding corridor took them to a deeper cellar with a heap of barrels, a massive log pile at the far end and a low vaulted brick roof. Walter half-dragged him up to a narrow opening in the roof above the log pile that was covered with a wooden slab. With difficulty, Walter unbolted this and threw it back. Smoky air rushed in. Desperately, pushed up by Walter, he levered himself outside. He heard beams crashing, explosions, screams and riders shouting and galloping. Looking back, he saw the fire glowing demonically behind the bulk of the house. Thomas muttered and wept.

'Of what terrors are you dreaming?' Alice asked gently, leaning over him.

'Walter, my beloved, could not get his vast shoulders through. I pulled at the bricks with my hands but he was too burly. Walter cried that I was near the lake and the fishponds, that I should go and save myself, that the two of us should not perish and that he would find another way out. I saw his bright mane disappearing back down the opening. I think I crawled to the ponds but the blaze had set the reeds alight. I submerged into the steaming waters when men or horses approached. Those running towards the ponds were speared and killed. I watched my manor and my terrified servants destroyed.'

'Brother, do not cry out so piteously. You are here and saved, thanks be to God. Dear Walter, such loyalty and service.'

'I am ruined, Alice.'

'Aiyee, and in mind and body too,' were Alice's screaming thoughts, but she said, 'You have survived the journey from Ireland, and are now safe here with me.'

Thomas's carriage and escort had taken many weeks to reach London, and had included a halt at a Hospice in Bromichem where he had been nursed through a fever. Messengers had finally reached her at the Abbey in Somerset, warning of Thomas's injuries, the extent of which was not known. Watching him, suppressed anger and shock now rose in Alice setting another fire in her mind. Thomas could no longer walk. Scarlet burns and purple bruises covered his limbs.

'Did you see any of them, Thomas? Did you recognise anyone?'

In spite of himself, he began to weep again, his chest heaving.

'The sawmills will be idle. They were but demons cloaked in a fiery mist, wheeling on horseback.'

'Try to remember before the Lord dims those images.'

'I think I heard one huzzah to Redmond and the Lady Medb,' he said brokenly, 'but I saw no man's face.'

'They will be brought to justice,' announced Alice quietly but with conviction. Unbidden, a wraith-like Medb, wildly shrieking her curse under the lowering sky, forced itself into her consciousness. She crossed herself, and prayed.

Whilst in France, Niko and Dermot had heard about Lord Deputy Essex's return to Queen Elizabeth's Court. He was also finding, rather to his chagrin, that he missed Alice's ironic smile and her wit. Leaving Dermot to wait for Pieter Heyden in Calais, he took a boat to the Port of London to visit Alice and obtain more recent news. If peace terms were being settled, he was tempted to ask again if he would be allowed to take Matthew, and perhaps even Alice, back to Leinster. He was uneasy that so much depended on the whether the Crown would pursue the war.

To Alice's consternation, unexpectedly, Niko arrived one cold late November morning. Taking a deep breath, she ordered the servant to take him to where Thomas was lying, gaunt, immobile and confused. The chamber, shuttered and warmed by a large fire, smelled of sickness and medicaments.

Alice, in a workday cap and apron, then joined them, frowning and stiff.

She ordered the nurses and servants out.

'Gaze on the wreck that is my brother Thomas. Your kin have

fired Hurst Place and killed all the folk living there. I could vomit in disgust at you and at myself for being cozened.' She went up close to Niko. Her voice swelled and ebbed as she continued to rage, 'We, as well as our Queen and country, must be of little account to you.'

Niko just stared at them, appalled.

'Look at him! Look at him!' she demanded, forcing his face to turn towards the figure in the bed and away from her. Thank the Lord he has escaped, but he may yet not live.'

He turned his face back to hers. 'It was not the MacFeaghs that did this. It could not be. Some of our people worked at Hurst Place…'

'Thomas loved Leinster and spent much of his life there. He was a righteous man, wanting prosperity for all and delighting in the song and dance of your people! I was thinking of giving you my hand and my heart, Niko.' She briefly stroked his swarthy face and gazed into his dark grey eyes. 'You could have lived in abiding love and luxury.' She then turned abruptly away, managing to stop her voice from breaking. 'But I cannot join with you in treason and violence and dissembling. You must go. I have torn you from my being and my respect. Why did my heart tell me that you desired me? I am not in the full flush of youth and I become stout. It must be my fortune and personal gain that drew you. I do not want to think that of you, but I must.'

'I did not know of this and if I had, I would never have condoned it. But I cannot control events in my country.'

He turned her towards him, kneeling, supplicant.

'Susannah's flight from Lord Redmond did much damage - other clans revered Lady Medb and would have sought revenge.'

Alice put her hands over her ears.

'I will not hear your excuses. One old woman's unforeseen death cannot be enough to explain their ferocity to Thomas and his demesne. Niko, Niko, how can you men plan horrifying acts, and yet be courteous and clever? How can you subordinate decency for the power of the flaming torch and the blood-soaked sword? How can you gather riches only to strew them away in war and bribery like dried grasses in the wind? You were Redmond's emissary to us. You shared his thoughts and plans. You deceived us over the wreck. Do not say you did not, for I will not believe you.'

'You are right that I have always been in Redmond's service. I am his kin and he has my loyalty as they have given me a place, and raised my standing amongst all. We were accepted with kindness. You must know why they are bitter towards the Crown. In the last rebellion in '80, the Lady Medb was taken to see her sons' heads impaled, alongside many others known to us, on stakes lining the path to the Lord Grey De Wilton's tent. Thomas looked on. Redmond's mother had been raped and killed for a basket of fish.' He added, his eyes cold, 'Atrocities do not only belong to one side you know. We have dreams of liberty, mistress, and governing ourselves.'

Thomas began mumbling, but no clear words were heard. Niko then pleaded, as she turned and leaned over her brother and wiped his brow, 'It was all I could do to keep the peace as long as we did, Alice. I doubt if Redmond was involved, but Thomas should have given my brother a greater share of his wealth so that he could obey and pay the increasing tithes to his Overlord and still provide well for his people. Neither he nor the Lord Deputies have ever tried to understand how we govern ourselves and how we live, even after much explanation. Song and dance yes – they are universal in their appeal. As religion should be but, sadly is not…'

Alice turned round, interrupting.

'Mercy is in all faiths and should be in every heart. Go, Niko. I cannot believe that you or your people knew nothing of this. Did you come back to gloat over the ruin that is Thomas? I do not want to see you again.'

'I had nothing to do with the attack of which you speak. You accuse us falsely. Tyrone is emerging victorious, so I came back to see you- to ask you, now that peace terms are likely to be agreed, to return to Ireland with me and Matthew and continue your good works there in the aftermath of war. Also we can find out what truly happened at Hurst Place and seek justice.'

She answered, contemptuous.

'Our Queen considers that Lord Essex's campaign in Ireland has failed. She has appointed another General. Tyrone will be defeated, you will see. The war is not over. Go! I deny you my home and household. Also to your squire should he be with you, as he has caused havoc amongst my women.'

There was a silence. Niko's mind and stomach were churning. From condescension, he knew that they had both moved to admiration and desire. He could hardly believe that he was fated to care so much for one whose interests were so opposed to his own. The goodwill of this woman had never seemed so important. He remembered how her hands had caressed his swarthy frame, and how they had laughed together at the waving arms and gurgles of Susannah's babe. And now, the one he now admitted was his love, was squirming with the knowledge of what she thought was betrayal.

Deciding he had nothing to lose, he said, 'Very well, but you must give me the child. Redmond's rightful son and heir- Rory MacFeagh not Matthew Breydel.'

'He will be brought up in a civilised way here in fosterage. Go now. There is no chance you will have him. He shall be well guarded.'

Niko's face turned red with anger and he stalked to the door.

'You should ask Redmond what "civilised fosterage amongst the English" means. He was beaten more times than he was spoken to. Perhaps his revenge was sweet!'

As he went through the door Alice sat, crying more bitterly than she had done for many years.

Niko swiftly left the city, fearing that, in her rage, Alice would declare him a traitor, and arrest would follow. He decided that the best way to ensure that Matthew returned to the sept was to do everything in his power to ensure the rebels were victorious.

His journey to Dover was dangerous due to increasing panic over Spanish invasion; his accent betrayed him. When stopping at a way station and an ale-house on his way, he was obliged to leave hurriedly or fight. But he was jeeringly informed that the Crown would still prevail as a new English Commander was already on his way to Ireland.

At the great back entrance to her courtyard, Alice and her friend Hope, wrapped in furs, indulgently watched the two children who were perched on large, slow mares and being led around, waving as they passed nearby. The chained guard dogs had barked until they were shown the whip, but now stood attentively by. She longed for some cheering prattle as Thomas was irrevocably weakening, his breathing more laboured and his mind wandering. As she watched the children riding, in her mind's eye she remembered with what ease Niko had sat his horse and how, for amusement, in the selfsame courtyard, he had trained the strongest horse in her stable to prance and dance for her delight. She squeezed her handkerchief tightly and forced his dark gaze from her thoughts.

Like many in the city, Hope Polsted, her abundant hair neatly covered by a woollen scarf under a wide-brimmed hat, was keen to discuss the possible invasion and the news of Ireland.

'It seems that Lord Essex's promises have come to naught and he and many of our people out there in savage Ireland have suffered. You know, of course, that he is now called traitor. The Queen is not accepting his explanations as to why the two Earls met, without observers or her permission, and agreed a truce. She has said that we are harbouring "snakes in our bosom." There will be a trial. The Irish Lord is known to have made overtures to the Pope to support his war. It looks as though Lord Tyrone and Lord Essex are in league with the Catholic powers to overthrow our monarch and our Faith. Her Majesty's advisors thinks Tyrone wants to govern Ireland, and Essex wants to govern England, and that they will stop at nothing to do it.'

'My steward says that on the streets they speak publicly and angrily of the lies and untrustworthiness of these nobles,' said Alice. 'But it seems that the Lord Essex has been, almost since his departure with his army, and in common with many of his men, laid low by debilitating illness, brought on by the incessant heavy grey fogs, dampness and downpours that have dogged his campaign. I suppose he may have sought a truce to rest himself and his troops.'

'The gossips at Court say that Lord Essex has always had ambitious rivals, such as the Cecil faction, and many clerics as enemies. These denounce him now and turn the Queen's heart against him,' replied Hope. 'I would be surprised if it really was his intention to take the throne. He has long been one of her particular favourites.'

Alice was thinking that, like the Queen, she had also been betrayed and cozened. She wondered at this conjunction in their lives and whether, had she consulted Astrologers, as had some of her acqualntance, it could have been foretold.

Hope had noted that Alice had been depressed since the departure from her life of the handsome Irishman, and now asked, 'Have you had messages from your friend Niko about this turn in the Irish war?'

'I have told him I do not wish any further contact with him.' said Alice shortly. 'Since Thomas arrived in such a parlous state, Niko is no longer in my thoughts.' She suddenly dissolved into tears. 'Hope, I think some of his people burnt Thomas's manor. My brother's lands and fortune are in the balance and may be utterly lost now.'

'Another great General has been given the task of containing the rebellion. Do not despair.' Hope put an arm around her friend's shoulders.

'Thomas's will to survive is weak. His life's work is undone.'

'Are you sure Niko's kin were involved?'

'Thomas said he heard shouts that confirmed this.' Alice clutched her damp handkerchief. 'After what has happened, I cannot give house or heart-room to an Irishman, especially one named MacFeagh.'

CHAPTER EIGHTEEN

The French port was full of bustle, with porters scurrying hither and thither, shouting in many different tongues whilst sacks and chests were being piled high. Dermot and Niko repaired to their usual ale-house, filled with traders and seamen, the air thick with pipe smoke and the smell of ale and damp frieze clothing.

'Master Niko MacFeagh, isn't it? I have been seeking you. I heard you were in Le Havre, but have not had cause until now to dock here.' The captain of the vessel that had carried Susannah and Pieter to Flushing, named Norris, called from near the door. 'They said I would find you here.' He beckoned Niko over to the bench where he sat smoking a long pipe.

His lined face was grim as he said, 'You were the one who came with the Dutchman, Pieter Heyden and his fair young countrywoman, to Harwich?'

Niko nodded.

'Do you know their final destination? I remember I was told that she is niece to a merchant who traded in Leiden before the embargo. What else do you know of her?'

Niko frowned, as the captain continued,

'The man died of a sweating sickness on board which came on suddenly. It was not plague-there were no buboes- but the fever was violent and deadly. We had to consign him to the deeps without delay in case he had a spreading contagion. The girl was prostrate during the crossing, which was slow and at times stormy, but she was not fever-ridden. My men were restless and she almost went overboard as well. We did not tell her about the man's death until we disembarked. Then she shrieked like one possessed, fell on her knees praying, trying to rend her clothes. A crowd soon gathered so, as the man had a purse with silver and many documents in a satchel with him, I lodged her, and their belongings, with an honest widow in Flushing where I had a cargo to bring and where I heard that you could often be found in Le Havre. I gave her the purse – minus my expenses of course- and the satchel. I called on her before coming here. She said that the girl had lost her wits and did not speak. I can do no more.'

A shocked Niko thanked him for his charity and ordered a servant to fetch them another tankard of ale. The misfortunes of the Dutch couple took his mind to Lady Medb and also impelled him later into prayer and confession for the anger he had felt towards them. His penance was to escort Susannah to her uncle, and he arranged a passage back to Flushing with Captain Norris, then resolving to journey on to Amsterdam.

The Captain took them to the widow's tenement. This was clean and well-kept. Susannah sat in the parlour staring fixedly into the distance. Her hair had escaped from her cap and hung, dirty, and lifeless. Food had spilled on her bodice and there was an unpleasant aroma about her. The room felt cold in spite of a large fire. Niko started, fancying there was a ball of light in the corner where there was no window or candle. No-one else seemed aware of it. The widow, shaking her head, encouraged the girl to take some of the bread and cheese she had left on a platter. Susannah stuffed a fistful of food into her mouth, her head down. She did not answer any questions and ignored them all. The widow made the sign of the Evil Eye.

'She does not take care of herself or her linen – although she will eat and drink. She says little, prays and moans in the night and only leaves the house with me when I insist upon it from time to time. She does nothing-even if politely asked. She just sits and eats. Although I am well paid, I shall be glad when she's gone. I think a devil tries to claim her.'

He stands tall and questions me…I will not answer ….he is kin to that witch…my sufferings are her doing. I have nothing to say to them. He says he will take me to my uncle… I care not… I care not what happens to me… I feel as if I am made of glass and am like to break. I am Chosen but Pieter disputed with the Calvinist pastors and he is not…. Oh my God, do not forsake him now….

Dermot said, as they left to prepare to travel to Amsterdam, 'The Morrigu has hovered. I wonder if she hovers still.'

Susannah remained either sullen or prone to fitful crying throughout their journey, which was lengthy and delayed by poor weather and rutted carriageways. She had shrieked in distress and refusal at the suggestion that they sail north to the Zuider Zee. They were forced to make the journey by road, during which she tried their patience on many occasions. Fortunately, they were able to glean much information from Ireland, London and other major cities, from other travellers, or from harbour pilots and sailors in the alehouses. They also came across huddles of distressed English refugees from Ireland. Many more devastating attacks had been made on the settlers there.

Niko and Dermot were gratified that men from Munster had joined the rebellion, and, longing for victory, hoped that the Irish forces would ally and unite. To their joy, the Spanish planned, now that that they had Papal dispensation, to open another front on the religious war, and sail to Ireland to support the Earl of Tyrone.

My aunt and uncle receive me warmly. I cannot return this. I am as cold as glass. I believe that I am one of the Elect, the Chosen, and so must give all my heart to my God. He has not intended that I should give my love to man or woman as all those that I loved have been destroyed. They say that working with the loom and the designs will comfort me, and say, as Pieter did, that my soul will be saved through prayer and faith. They cleave to the Lutherans rather than the Calvinists, but I cannot believe that all that has happened to me has not been predestined. The De Hems do not seem overly concerned that Mathieu is not with me….they are charmed by that heathen

Niko. They do not believe that my life amongst the savages was unbearable. He tells them that my husband was of high rank and gave me every courtesy…. that half- Mahommedan is as silver-tongued as a serpent…..

Susannah had greeted her relatives dully, rather to their surprise. Surveying her, her Aunt thought she had filled out but looked wan. Niko told them privately that she had become attached to Pieter Heyden and was still mourning her mother and leaving her son in England.'

'Ah Pieter! Such an inconvenient loss! Perhaps it was just as well. Attachment or no, I would never have consented to a marriage. His rank was too low. But his loyalty, contacts and diligence are greatly missed. I doubt if I will ever find another like him.'

The De Hems were respectful and pleased at Niko's civilised manners as well as his knowledge of their tongue, albeit this being somewhat rough. He praised his foster-brother Redmond, speaking of a noble demeanour and connections, consummate Generalship and skill at arms. They shared knowledge of trading markets, the Spice Islands and discussed new reports on discoveries in the East. After a sumptuous meal they were offered rooms for a few days before they departed. This Niko politely refused, wishing to rid himself of Susannah as soon as possible, and as Alfonso was waiting for them at the port. Before they left, M. De Hem gave them gold for their expenses and Susannah's safe arrival.

'You understand, Niko MacFeagh, this is not for the rebels, or for a dowry, but for you, for your escort and your good offices to me and my niece. Any marriage portion I may give must be discussed with Lord Redmond in person.'

Niko smiled winningly and did not comment. De Hem did not confide that the marriage to a Catholic may not now be legal in the Protestant Dutch Republic, or could be annulled. He also suspected that Lord Redmond could be dead or proscribed.

Niko then frowned as De Hem added, 'My niece tells me that Pieter compensated Alice Plymmiswoode well for looking after Susannah and that this Englishwoman fosters her son Matthew. She hopes that when he is more grown she will send him to us.'

Susannah stayed in the household of M. De Hem rather than returning to Leiden, and settled into what remained of her old life. Although loath to take her from her work, about which she was gratifyingly obsessive, the family did try to bring her out into company. All found her lack of response tedious. She grew bulky, dressed only in voluminous black, covered her hair in an old-fashioned Venetian filet, spoke little, ate silently, as much as a man and more, and volunteered no conversation at suppers except to answer questions. She invariably quoted from the Bible in her replies, and once asked if could enter a religious house for women. M. De Hem scorned this, accusing her of picking up Popish ways from the Irish. Many more orders had come in from other markets he had developed and also from England, including the Court. Susannah had found a new way of weaving, using two looms, featuring fantastical shapes and swirls and influenced by Venetian style. She also incorporated delicately embroidered transparent and mirrored motifs which had not been seen on fabrics before. The opulent cushion designs on linen canvas dyed in golds and greens with silk, wool and silver thread depicting lions, hounds, hawks and heraldic escutcheons, had become highly fashionable.

The preachers tell me that my misery is the key to the life in Heaven hereafter. Did He not say "whosoever doth not bear my cross, cannot be my disciple?"

Niko exchanged the Dutch gold for the hire of some mercenary troops to join him and the Spanish fleet when it sailed. He bought Dermot a modern, well-made musket delicately engraved with silver plaques. His cloak and doublets being somewhat worn, Niko bought himself accoutrements and clothing, so he could fight alongside his brother and their people with dignity as Irish gentry. Pushing aside thoughts of Alice, he convinced himself that his heart and mind were now one.

CHAPTER NINETEEN

That summer, Redmond's warrior band had managed to escape Cahir before the looting and massacre of the inhabitants after the surrender of the town to the Earl of Essex. It was subsequently garrisoned. He and his remaining men then furiously ambushed, skirmished and harried their enemy wherever they could find them. Now, in September, at the rath of the Gathering they shared ale and bread with other southern army officers. The rath's fires were barely alight, its stores depleted, and only boys were retained there as ostlers and servants.

Richard Keohane, a grizzled nephew of an earl, had recently arrived, having ridden hard from the north. He talked of the Earl of Essex's recent dramatic meeting with the Earl of Tyrone.

'I observed it all. The O'Neill was arrayed in a fine sleeved quilted doublet and fur cloak. And the pair were on horseback in the middle of a river throughout. They parleyed alone and refused to allow any to accompany them. They agreed a truce of at least six weeks over the coming winter. Arrangements are being made for it to be formally ratified with witnesses. It is said that Lord Deputy Essex has agreed that Irish nobles and the 'Old English,' such as my uncle, if they support the Crown, can continue to make tithes and own lands.'

'It seems they showed each other respect,' said his squire.

Redmond opined, 'The O'Neill has long had enemies in the English Court, as indeed does the Earl of Essex. For instance, we heard that last year, Tyrone's entreaties for more parleying and a milder proceeding against him were intercepted by spies and were delayed by his enemies, not being delivered until he had been proclaimed a traitor.'

'Perhaps The English Devereux is weary of war,' suggested Ronan. 'We heard he has been ill with fevers for many weeks.'

Richard Keohane's squire added, 'It is true that after the parley, Essex went down to Drogheda to take physic.'

Brian, a younger son of Chief O'Byrne, with a disfiguring scar across his chin and neck, shook his head.

'They may have spoken on equal terms but I have heard that supplies, and more troops for the English commanders, have been requisitioned from England, but have not yet arrived. A pause in the fighting will allow Lord Essex time to repair his decimated army.'

His squire agreed, murmuring 'Lord Essex has to pause. At present, because he has garrisoned so many towns, and because we constantly raid his defences, he can spare few reinforcements for battle engagements.'

Many round the fire were pleased at the prospect of a truce, optimistic that either the course of the war would remain in their favour, or that a settlement would soon be reached. They were already thinking that they could go back to help gather their harvests and ensure that their homesteads were safe and protected.

'This parley and truce may be a real opportunity to achieve more liberty. Even now, when the war is in his favour, The O'Neill makes no unreasonable demands of the Crown. It is believed that he asked for more toleration for us and the Catholic Church, who would be asked to found a University.' Richard Keohane ticked off points on his fingers. 'It also seems that he would gladly submit, quench the fire of rebellion, and renounce his title if his captured relatives could be pardoned, there could be freedom from garrisons and sheriffs - and of travel - and that all important officials, and all clerics appointed by the Crown, must be Irish-born.'

A young O'Byrne asked, 'Will the Governor then be English? If so, we will never be allowed us to determine our own succession and affairs.'

Redmond said to Richard Keohane, 'There will surely be further parleying on the details before ratification. Had you heard of any specific concessions to the Vassals, as well as those given to their Overlords?'

'I understand that Lord Essex insisted that we cannot assume that our children will inherit titles and lands.'

'Then this could mean that, even if so elected, our kin could not govern our people!'

'It was also said that the castle at Blackwater, which we destroyed at the outset, must be re-built by us – and huge fines paid, which we, no doubt, will have to pay for – and we must not intrigue with Scottish Lords or with Spain, even if others do.'

'A promise many would find hard to keep,' said a Munster officer, to general nodding.

Redmond still longed to be free of English domination, but welcomed the truce, partly because of Lady Orlaith's poor health and partly because, although used to death and violence, the bloodbaths of innocents he had witnessed sickened him. He said nothing else, but was inclined to agree with those who said that the Earl of Tyrone, as well as the Earl of Essex, were both playing for time, Essex to get re-inforcements and Tyrone so that more pledges of faith from the southern Irish Chiefs could be gathered.

'Whatever happened at the parleying,' he said later to Ronan, 'I doubt if the truce will hold beyond the halt in winter campaigning. More fighting is inevitable. The sticking points have always been the Crown's power to appoint judges and the clergy, over which our overlord nobles want control.'

The regiments dispersed soon after. Redmond's troop of gallowglass and kern left the camp the next day and travelled to a sheltered bay in the south-east, taking a circuitous route away from the river valleys to avoid other armed men. Once there, they were welcomed by Orlaith and a large company of women, children, the ailing, and very old, who were settling into winter lodgings.

Orlaith's long hair was still glossy, but her skin was almost white and translucent except for high red spots over her taut cheekbones. Her nose was sharp and, because of her pallor, her eyes unusually protuberant. He had never seen her so thin. He remembered the look of others dying, and realised sadly that the 'white death' would eventually claim her. He held her cold fingers, the nails brittle and pale and looked desperately at Oonagh standing by her side. But the warmth of Orlaith's smile as they embraced, cheered his shocked spirit. They walked to the low-slung clachans built around a clearing and surrounded by trees. They exchanged news. Redmond told her of their military victories, and she told him of the cyphers received from Niko that Rory called Matthew by the English was safe in London.

'I long to see your son,' she whispered. He remembered her voice which used to ripple alongside the Irish harp like the waters reaching the lakes' pebble beach.

'Do you know anything of the destruction of Thomas's manor?' she then asked carefully.

'What destruction? What are you saying?'

Orlaith sighed with relief.

'I didn't think it was you – in spite of your anger at the killing of Medb. Many related to our clan, still working in his household, were burnt to death,' she said, 'including, we think but do not know for certain, his catamite and steward Walter. Thomas had sent most of his armed men to join the Constable's troops in The Pale, together with some provisions for the garrison. Those remaining to guard were betrayed and cut to pieces. Fintan heard from those who saw the burning from afar. He rode speedily there. The next day he found Thomas, and some women, barely alive amongst the lake reeds. He took them to the Glendalough Hospice. I don't know if Thomas still lives.'

Redmond looked hard at his mother, thinking again how much she had changed, and turned away, heartsick.

'Is Fintan now back with the defences at our tower?' he then asked.

'Yes. He said that Hurst demesne was most violently destroyed,' answered Oonagh, who had joined them. 'The horses, the livestock, even the chickens, had all been taken. There were deep ruts on the cinder paths to the great barns, so their wagons had been filled with stores, grain and hay. What was left was burnt. The stripped bodies of the men in the guardpost had been left. Those blackened corpses from within the house that were found could not be recognised – some would have been our people. Other manors in Leinster and Munster have also been attacked and pillaged.'

Redmond paced around, even more restless than usual. The light was failing and the charcoal mound near the river glowed red and black like a devil's eye. The cauldron of hot water suspended over it was being poured into barrels.

'Rough men in the country always join in the mayhem, but we will be blamed for this. Just when a truce until Spring has been agreed! Tyrone's troops have been successfully pushing south and this has given the Earl of Essex pause. The burning of Hurst Place will not help peace negotiations. As you know, settler Thomas was respected and trusted by the Crown for peacefully holding some Marcher lands, and we and other local clans tolerated him as at times he could be bought, and his tithes were not excessive. At other times he defended our interests. This attack will confirm their view of us as faithless and savage.'

'Maybe it was deserters and mercenaries come through The Pale,' said Oonagh. 'Fintan says there are many sleeping in the forests, and roaming around for gain or wherewithal. They may have seen his gallowglass troops leaving.'

Orlaith said, 'Thomas was wrong to think that his lands would not be too much affected, and that the arrival of England's Great Army would tip the balance for the Crown with those wavering about joining the rebellion. He had been away from war too long.'

Redmond added thoughtfully, 'Perhaps it was the O'Byrnes. Old Seamus, for example, is bitter at the bribes, coigne and livery[6] he pays which he has said beggars him. He keeps an extravagant house and has a costly wife and two married daughters whose portions were more than generous. He resented having to send Nuala and others to work as servants for Thomas in lieu of his unpaid tithes to the Crown. He has had no Niko to smooth his path with the Occupiers, and get licenses for trading hides and linen.'

Orlaith said, 'I thought Seamus was fighting with you.'

'He sent a son and others of his kin instead. They say he is now blind and keeps to his rath. Perhaps he incited some of the youths left behind to burn and loot Hurst Place.'

Oonagh said,'Niko's latest cyphers also said that there are alarums in London about invasion. Queen Elizabeth has ordered complete submission of Ireland in every respect. He, Niko, is now in Le Havre, seeking news of whether a Spanish fleet will sail to us again.'

'Did he give a time or a place for their coming?'

'Niko thinks that when they come, it will be to the south. The western seas have too often been their undoing. But I doubt if they will come soon, even if this latest truce does not hold. Storms in the south could drive them back again.'

Oonagh then took Redmond to one side. Her expression, for once, was serious as she said,

'She coughs blood and sweats at night and wants little sustenance, Redmond. She has picked up the contagion. Others too have it.'

Then Redmond knelt and took Orlaith's face in his hands.

'You cannot spend the winter in our land,' he said. 'It is likely that soon we will move from woods through bogs to uplands, and rocky moorland paths, perhaps not just staying at allied raths, towers and homesteads, but to fastnesses or caves to avoid troops and mercenaries, and to drive cattle beyond their reach. You must go to Niko in Le Havre, who will find physicians to help you.'

'What if I just stayed with Fintan in the tower house – it is well-defended and is my home,' she cried.

Redmond swallowed hard.

'But can you be kept warm and have good nourishment? Provisions in the tower will be sparse and have to last many months if it is besieged. The chambers there will be needed for extra guards and weapons and to succour those in extremity. I need you to be well to take care of my son Rory when this is over. It will ease my heart to know you are with Niko.'

Orlaith looked straight at him.

'There is no physic that I know, and I am known for my knowledge of salves and simples, that can cure me.' She turned to Oonagh who was blinking away tears.' Will you come with me?'

'You know my place is with Fintan. I and the other young

wives are strong, but we will have to care for many wounded. You know this, Orlaith. Now, you must take the sick, the old clanspeople and care for each other – those who wish it and can manage to travel – and,' she looked at Redmond and took a deep breath. 'And take my children and the small infants to safety in Le Havre. We will send for them when we can.'

There was a long silence during which he paced restlessly. His hounds whined.

'Start preparations for departure then, Oonagh.'

'Come, Redmond, there is little we can do now this minute. I have oysters, salmon, boiled rabbit, and pottage for all, but first get you to the washing tubs – you all stink like a midden and, to be sure, we'll soon be pushing past the fleas they are so big!'

'Salmon, Oonagh! How did you manage that?'

'Well, we crept by night into the Earl's deer park, and, as we passed the river, this big salmon just jumped into my pan, quicker than a nun's kiss,' she replied, desperately wanting to make Redmond and Orlaith smile.

Some days later, Redmond and his followers escorted Orlaith and her column on sheltered silent leaf-strewn forest by-ways which followed a line from a cleft in the mountain to standing stones near to the harbour cliffs. The smell of mushrooms, damp bracken, fallen logs and slow decay had accompanied them. They all parted, their eyes heavy with unshed tears, whilst gulls wheeled and called in a farewell.

Redmond and the remaining people turned their pretty, hardy ponies onto faster roads. Eventually, through a soft pall of rain, they reached Castle MacFeagh where Fintan was ensconced with their guard, pleased to be re-united with Oonagh but desolate that his children were gone. On arriving at the stronghold, Redmond was concerned at the large number of people now living in it, even though it had been extended and ringed with a high stockade. As he moved through, Redmond saw over-crowded cabins and whole families round fires, either slumped or fevered outside their damp makeshift shelters near the lake shore. Other refugees, from the fighting and homesteads, were living alongside men-at-arms in the fortress. Both food and warm clothing were now in short supply. The shaking sickness and the' white death' that was claiming Orlaith was everywhere amongst the folk.

'We have had to turn many away,' said the sentry at the guardpost on the bridge. The man was scrawny, his face pitted with lesions. 'Although some linger here or by our walls. It is heart-breaking.'

Later, from a slit in an upper chamber, Redmond, holding a puppy, stared at the skeletal trees etched against a bright early morning sun. He wondered if he would see the hauntingly peaceful vista again. A haze of frost had sent the last leaves of summer earthwards. A thick shaft of light struck the stacked piles of cut peat and the clumps of brown shrivelled shrubbery hiding the still, misty grey-green lake. He fondled his dog's ears. He heard Medb's distant mutterings and counsels in the core of his mind. The brutality of the campaign so far, the condition of his people, the de facto exile of his loved ones, the Overlords and fighting men whose thoughts were only of gain and not of their country's liberty, were all considerations which were turning his mind against going again to war.

CHAPTER TWENTY
Anno Domini 1600–1603

Back in Le Havre, Niko, in his new black taffeta quilted waistcoat and grogram clocks on his stockings, sat with Alfonso, equally resplendent, in a harbourside inn. Rattling spits could be heard turning in the kitchen adjacent to them, and the smell of the roasting meats blended with the pipe smoke filling the ale-house area.

The two men regarded the chess set found for them from a large oaken cupboard, and arranged the small wooden square blocks painted with letters that represented the various pieces.

'I heard that last year the Crown insisted that the terms of the truce made with Lord Tyrone be rejected, and that the Earl of Essex and his advisors be recalled from their duties in Ireland. It seems, now that the Lord Essex has fallen from the Queen's grace, that another General has been appointed Lord Deputy of Ireland in his stead.'

'I know this, but not who she has chosen.'

'Sir Charles Blount. He has been commanded to suppress the rebellion once and for all,' said Alfonso solemnly, taking tobacco abundantly and then moving a knight square as an opening. 'Although Lord Essex has remarked that the man is "drowned in book-learning" I hear he makes steady progress against your people.'

'General Mountjoy! God's Teeth! I had not heard that. He is

a master tactician. I fought in one of his campaigns in the Low Countries.'

Niko had been quite affable and contented until this information was imparted. He remembered this hard, frugal, bookish man who spoke many tongues, as a clever and competent soldier who had the respect of all his men. Recovering himself he said, aloud and triumphantly, 'Although Mountjoy is to be feared, remember that Robert Devereux, the Earl of Essex, was also an experienced and successful general, now outmanoevred both by Tyrone, and how it is in our Irish land. The heavens sent deluges to support us. Spain will tip the balance in our favour next year when campaigning starts again in Spring – of this, I am sure.'

Niko continued to be tossed between hope and fear as he moved his knight. This was quickly followed by a similar move from Alfonso.

'It's a pity that this conflict could not have been avoided,' said Alfonso. 'From what I have seen of Ireland, it is beautiful, and rich in nature's bounty, unlike the dry coasts and uplands which cover so much of my land. Your people should not take "civilisation" so hard. Foolishly, in spite of many of your nobles and gentry having been schooled in the English way, they seem to praise or celebrate bloodthirsty legends and take much pride in self-sacrifice, retribution and revenge… do not protest – I know they are pious too but…'

'You do not know what tyranny we endure! We do not bear a light yoke. When Tyrone has petitioned for pardon, which he has done many times in past years, he has been judged insolent by the Crown's Commissioners – including when he offered his kin as pledge! All this fires his wrath, and that of his neighbour Lord O'Donnell and their allies.'

Niko banged a chess piece on the table and then made a foolhardy move in the game. It had suddenly occurred to him that once the previous officials of past Lord Deputies, many of whom were 'Old English' and familiar with the culture of Ireland, were recalled, there would be a hiatus. He feared that ruthless and bigoted hardline clerks and justices were likely to be sent in their stead.

'Well, whatever, we are here now, and, like this game, must be played out,' said Alfonso, taking Niko's bishop. 'I await instructions from the Court of the King of Spain before we can all sail. The catastrophe of the Armada is still fresh. Ships meeting storms again en route will be turned back. Timing is all, as well as the size of the fleet and number of footsoldiers.'

'Many Scots support The O'Neill, rather than the old Queen, and are part of his army,' Niko said, considering his next move. 'Their Freebooters have been driven from their own country, much of which is barren and mountainous and does not provide much living, whilst their borderlands are lawless and dangerous. They are hardened and violent men who hope to be given fertile acreage or liveries in return for protection from the swaggering English troops and militias.'

'I suspect the Protestant Scots are more likely to be recruited and settled in Ireland by the English than the Catholic Scots given lands by the Irish! Much depends on who becomes victorious or the terms on which peace is made,' replied Alfonso with a knowing smile, puffing on his pipe.

Dermot then arrived at the Inn. He had not been expected so early. He was breathless and tousled, having run through the cold wind. His face was intense, his voice flecked with anticipation.

'The Lady Orlaith has disembarked with a company of elderly freemen and women, churls and a number of infants. Will you come ? We can escort them to our lodgings.'

Niko quickly excused himself, bowing farewell. Alfonso acknowledged this wryly, his nostrils flaring.

He said, 'This game was soon over. May the one in Ireland be equally swift! You know where to find me.'

Holding fast to his brimmed hat, Niko walked rapidly and eagerly with Dermot to join the crowd of porters and passengers. Their heads jangled from the fierce gusts from the south-east which swept across the harbour mouth. White-bellied gulls wheeled and screeched above the gathering surf, fluorescent in a livid winter sky. Oak barrels and chests, suspended on lines over a large bobbing barque waiting to be unloaded, swayed alarmingly. Observing Orlaith, waiting with others, he stopped, aghast at her appearance. She had pushed back the hood of her dark green cloak with its jewelled clasp. Niko saw that her marriage ring of twisted gold ropes was loose on her gloved knuckles. Her russet hair, now streaked with grey, was fringed around a close fitting black cap. Her extreme pallor enlarged her dark grey-green eyes and the square outline of her chin. He found he could not speak at this worst moment of his life. The hoots of recognition from Fintan and Oonagh's children were a welcome distraction.

Later, in the spacious parlour of the house that had been leased in St Francois, up an incline but overlooking the stormy harbour, they ate a light supper and talked of all that had befallen. They pondered whether The O'Neill could truly unite the clans. Both they and the Irish community in Le Havre had some sympathy with the Earl of Essex who had, after all, tried to make terms with them. They wondered that such a man, known to be brave, thoughtful and diplomatic, and indeed who they thought may well have eventually brought peace, could be so brought down. It was as though, in Ireland, or somehow through being in Ireland, knowledge of the poisonous realities of the Court had left him. They thought that the long shadow of Medb and the power of the Morrigu had turned him mad.

An elderly dulcimer player and a thin young boy with an apple-shaped face whistled and strummed a lute in the corner, whilst women, carrying infants or candles aloft, slowly climbed the oaken stairs to upstairs chambers. All finally retired and slept. On a fur-covered pallet downstairs, Orlaith closed her eyes, wanting oblivion without dreaming. After a painful coughing fit, she hid a blood-stained linen kerchief in her cloak and fell into a reverie. These were much more common now.

She thought she felt Medb's arms around her shoulders clawing at her spirit whilst she dozed. Then Medb pointed a long finger at Hugh O'Neill, the Earl of Tyrone, dressed in velvet and gold lace like an English gentleman, and with the powerful body, saturnine face, and the hard, almost cruel and visionary gaze of a true leader, if not king.

Orlaith sighed, and turned her thoughts to her half-Irish son. Although he had never opened his heart completely to her, from their conversation that night, she guessed of his love for the settler's sister and Redmond's son. She felt for Niko's hurt that Alice had jumped to the conclusion that their people had been responsible for the burning of Thomas's manor.

'Settler Thomas did his best,' she thought. 'I did my best. No doubt, Alice Plymmiswoode must have become deeply attached to little Rory or Matthew, as he had seemingly been christened. Under the ancient clan laws of inheritance, he would not be allowed to rule until he was a man and even then, another, more keen and active, may be chosen. As her eyes closed, she knew she had no energy to consider or advise what could and should happen now.

Orlaith died soon after in Le Havre, to great grieving. Her people longed to take her remains to be laid to rest in the place of her ancestors, but Ireland was alight and increasingly desperate. The religious houses in the English, Dutch, French and Spanish coastal towns, with camps mushrooming around them, gave alms to those fleeing the country although many of their residents turned their backs. Those who could pay their passage even set sail across the dangerous ocean to distant and largely unknown lands. Even Cecilia's remote Abbey was crowded with the families of settlers, causing her to bring her devotions into the real world, a circumstance which gave her a degree of satisfaction she had not expected.

As soon as his appointment was confirmed, the Lord Deputy, General Charles Blount, had quickly set out for Ireland. Hearing that the Spanish had fortified some townlands in County Sligo in the north-west, and that the re-building of their Armada was nearly complete and may head for the south of the British Isles, he had sent more troops to the garrisoned towns there. In the City of London, fears of invasion reached fever-pitch. The old prophecy was on many lips:

> 'If you England wish to win
> Then with Ireland you must begin.'

By the time that snows settled on the mountain tops, Redmond and his people had learned of the Earl of Essex's downfall, that the truce would not hold and that Thomas Hurst's, as well as Orlaith's, painful lingering on earth had finally come to an end.

He and some kerns, all now having grown winter beards, were out guarding those folk foraging, breaking ice pools or gathering wandering goats, pigs and cows from deserted homesteads, when Ronan, hair flying, galloped anxiously from afar towards them.

'Word had come that the new Lord Deputy continues campaigning even though it is still deep winter!' he gasped. 'He is everywhere at once- even at this moment in the Marcher lands- systematically building and garrisoning forts in places where an army could pass. His troops are being re-supplied with weaponry. He spends days on end on horseback, no matter rain, wind or snows. He makes long journeys to places where he is not expected. Worst of all, his armies are clearing forests to prevent ambush and everywhere living off the land.'

Redmond tensed in fear and disappointment. He knew that the Earls of Tyrone and O'Donnell would be fully occupied in trying to hold the north, so that now the southern chiefs must again muster their men – but this time in the depths of winter with more foreign mercenaries arriving. He knew that some would not hear the call, being stuck in snowy fastnesses, others would be widely dispersed and vulnerable when travelling to the Muster, and yet others too sick or unwilling to fight in the conditions that would prevail.

*

Campaigning throughout the country continued all the following months and the next year. Slowly the tide of war turned against the Irishmen, not least because of the General's tactics and widespread famine. Mountjoy had commanded that all flocks and cattle other than for themselves, should be kept on the move, all the provisions and stores they came across should be burnt, millwheels destroyed and thrown into rivers, wells poisoned and that all fields should be laid waste around the advancing army. Large quantities of shot and cheese were sent over from England to arm and provision his troops. The General had forbidden all parleying, and was severe in administering what, it was said bitterly, he termed 'justice'. They discovered that more and more of their cottagers had been killed, like annoying insects, by the Freebooters, rogues and vagrants that had been conscripted into their soldiery.

Redmond and Fintan watched their wealth and provender, the horses, goats, sheep and cattle, normally visible nibbling or grazing on the lower hills, disappearing or wasted from being driven. Instead of going to the Muster, they ambushed where they could do so safely, but mainly guarded and protected the stores, fields and townlands.

Castle MacFeagh was spared a siege because of its daunting and hidden position, allowing the inhabitants to fend off approaching marauders and make skirmishing and foraging expeditions. But all suffered from sickness, cold and insufficient food. Then, disastrously, new long distance cannon were launched from lakeshores and river banks everywhere, directed at the isles and old crannogs, which held provisions and arms. The storehouses were then looted and the buildings burned with any defenders put to the sword.

It became essential that the MacFeaghs broached the mountains in hard weather to drive any remaining animals back again on to remote tops and escarpments. Many beasts and their young had been, and would be, lost. The steep hidden valleys and moorlands contained little pasture on the tops, and what was there became buried in ice or snow. The survival of any of the herds remained in doubt.

As Sir Charles Blount's reputation for piety, study and discourse with the Jesuits was well-known, Fintan, Oonagh, Father Ignatius and Redmond could hardly believe that he countenanced such widespread famine and hardship, and raged that he must surely have realised what would follow such tactics.

'This is a shameful war,' Ignatius said fiercely. 'Our people are seeing their livelihoods pouring away as if from a bad barrel of wine. The Good Book says that "there is a time to kill, but a time to heal." Only devastation will be left for the victor.'

Refugees multiplied. Although promised, the Spanish troops did not arrive when expected. The famine became more acute. General Mountjoy's army did not leave at all during even the coldest weather, but remained, fighting in both the north and the south at the same time, rapidly re-building and garrisoning the forts that had been previously destroyed. The northern Earls-in-Arms continued to be confined to their region. Then they heard that Lord Essex had been declared traitor for agreeing terms with Earl Tyrone without the consent of the Queen and the Irish Council, and of his execution.

Eventually, except for Fintan who was to hold the castle, the MacFeagh fighting men, increasingly hemmed in, but lean and even more hardened, prepared to re-join the rebel army. This was now mustering in the south-west, awaiting the Spanish fleet which had now sailed and whose confirmed arrival would be the signal for the northern Earls' army to forcemarch south and join them.

First they stocked the cold undercroft of the stronghold's tower with the meagre carcasses of deer and small game they had hunted. Fintan and the young churls remaining, resolved not to advance far from the stronghold, to keep it as impregnable as possible, and try to divert any sustained siege if they could. They were ordered to make sallies, attacking any invading troops they found taking livestock or firing homesteads. The womenfolk were included in the defence of the stronghold, and also continued to guide the weakest folk into the deep forest and caves, and supply them with as much as could be spared. Friar Ignatius led prayers that the Spanish army would be prodigious, with many soldiers in many ships, and that this would, at the very least, cause the Crown to parley, and another truce to be declared.

Before leaving for the Muster, Redmond said to Fintan and Oonagh, 'As you know, my son is being fostered in London by Thomas's sister, Alice Plymmiswoode. Niko thinks she will not harm him, but he is, in effect, a hostage to the English. I, and you, must dispute any claim that my wife Gile makes on him, although I doubt if she will ever come here again. Remember, if I should die, that Rory's true home and his birthright is here, until he is a man. Send for him when the time is right – and stand with each other.'

Having been provided with healthy ponies, preserved meats and oats for their saddlebags, fur cloaks and woollen stockings, Redmond's little troop took their leave. As they travelled, their mood was despondent. Redmond, although dispirited himself, he tried to lift their hearts and keep their aggression focussed.

'The Spanish will arrive in the south-west – they will come. I know it. Niko's cyphers say this is certain. Remember – we did not live much better for the Overlordship of the English Crown! It was mainly we who protected their holdings from foreign brigands. In return we were punished for our religion and our best pastures taken. Earl Tyrone in the north still has not been subdued. We must pray he continues to hold out and meets the Spanish when they come.'

CHAPTER TWENTY-ONE

usannah, invariably morose, did become animated and loquacious at the news of the Earl of Essex's despair and pleadings, house arrest, trial and execution. This had become the talk of Britain and the Holy Roman Empire. Her response was always sour.

'He should have defeated the savages. He was a traitor. He did not deserve life.'

'But one of such high rank! Who fought the Turks and the Catholic Empire for his Queen!'

One evening, her uncle spoke of the progress of the Irish war, commenting that although Sir Charles Blount's campaign was proving increasingly successful, he was laying waste to all around, and her husband's people could be in difficulty.

Her aunt said, 'There is unnecessary death. When this happened in France years ago many lands have still not recovered. Inhuman slaughter is bad. And to starve pious peasant folk! That is surely not God's Will!'

Susannah had then commented viciously,' Has our God smitten that Redmond MacFeagh yet? He calls himself Lord, but he looks and behaves like an animal, frequenting lurking dens. You think not? I pray that He will smite him soon. "If thy right eye offend thee, cast it out!" That foster brother of his, they call him Niko, is a sly cozener. You should have given him your boot, not your gold. Mark my words, he will slither out of any danger!'

The depth of her loathing had startled the De Hems.

'You are harsh, niece,' her uncle said. 'Lord Redmond MacFeagh is Irish gentry, kin to nobles. Master Niko MacFeagh is his foster-brother and civilised. Lord Redmond rescued you. And he honoured you with marriage and you have given him a son and heir. Niko MacFeagh brought you to safety here as he had promised and deserved reward.'

His wife added, 'My brother-in-law and many of their household have not survived like you. My sister's death was hastened by her grief. You have reason to thank our God. You should cast the bitterness from your heart!'

At these rebukes, Susannah began to weep copiously, which her uncle could not abide.

With Alice, Niko MacFeagh oozed with beguiling charm, but my beloved Pieter liked him not… he said he was close in his secrets and valued none but himself. My aunt says that Niko and his long-haired squire were given gold for returning me to them. But Pieter and Mistress Alice were my saviours. Groats only were what those men deserved. For that I shall not speak to my uncle unless I must. Now he dares to reprimand me. I should have died with my family – I am like the detritus floating on that fog-laden sea. In my dreams, fingers of mist swirl and writhe like those of that hag who clutched at my gown…my uncle does not allow me to live with other Chosen women in a religious house as he says I am wed. I repudiate my marriage to Redmond but I think sometimes on my little Matthew… I know Mistress Alice dotes upon him… I wonder whether he will broaden and whether his burnished red hair will darken, so he will look like my brothers, dead, all dead. I see them reflected in my glass clogs. I do not out for fear I should break them. My aunt insists they are wooden, but I know she lies. That Calvet could not have been of our Faith…. he was a devil incarnate..may he be damned for eternity.'

After Orlaith's death, whilst waiting impatiently for the Spanish invasion fleet and troops to be mustered, Niko and Dermot had sold their swords to standing mercenary armies as the Protestant Republics and the Spanish regions were still frequently engaged in hostilities. The payments the Irishmen received helped to maintain their growing community in Le Havre and allowed them to harden themselves for war. Through their loyal pilots, they sent cyphers on the Spanish plans to Ireland, but many were intercepted.

His resentment towards her petering out, Niko did his best to ensure that Alice knew the truth of the burning of Thomas's manor. He received no reply.

Eventually towns and villages in Ireland gradually submitted, as not only had harvests been bad, but also corn and other seed could not be sown on the poisoned land and cattle had been driven off for the armies. Starvation was omnipresent.

To the Irish commanders' relief, six thousand Spanish troops received Indulgences from the Pope and, after being turned back once, did finally arrive in the south-west of Ireland. Alfonso was with them, captaining a two hundred ton fly-boat, accompanied by Niko, Dermot, mercenaries and a large contingent of Spanish troops. The southern Irish rebel army was mustered shoreside, and quite quickly took the town of Kinsale, forming a garrison in the castle at the Head of Kinsale, protected by more supporting Spanish navy, carrying more troops.

Dermot managed to bring Redmond and Niko together, during one of the lulls which had interspersed the nerve-wracking, intense and brutal engagement. The brothers talked far into the evening. Niko, wearing the livery badges of a Spanish duke, was as spruce as ever with a padded doublet under light armour, in contrast to the wild-looking Redmond in his faded leather jerkin, long boots and vast woollen cloak. Gulls swung above them in glittering arcs in a largely clear September sky, ornamented with puffs of cloud.

Niko said with some emotion, 'I had hoped to carry Lady Orlaith home to be at rest with her beloved aunt. At least she was shrived and is now with God. When this is over perhaps we can make some memorial.'

Redmond was relieved that he had not seen Orlaith at the end. He remembered his Uncle Fergus's deathly looks. He nodded sagely.

'A strange pale mist draped Medb's body as she was interred. It then moved off towards the sea. She is in Tir-Na-Nog, and away from this. I pray that she and Orlaith will meet again.' He paused and eventually said, ' It warms my heart that you want to fight our cause Niko, but you have disobeyed me. You should not have come to fight. Someone may betray you for the price of a meal.'

'I have only just removed the visor I wear in battle. It's uncomfortable and ancient, but hides my face. I doubt in the melee, or even now, whether I have been or will be recognised. And how could I not join you? Dermot and I, so far away and fighting for whoever will pay, have been chafing to return.' He paused. 'I am losing my honour. I redeem it by coming here with you.'

Whilst the war in Ireland was heading to resolution, there had been uncertainty and disquiet at Court. Queen Elizabeth was ailing and had not yet named a successor. Previously Niko had found his foster-brother's dreams of victory boring and unrealistic. Now, bloodied in new battles and having bitterly experienced the good soft lives of the successful London traders compared with the hardships of their people, he was pushing for glory and the return of their lands and wealth. His vengefulness was fuelled hearing of the atrocities committed by enemy troops. His optimism was fuelled by the comparative ease with which Kinsale town had been taken by the Spanish and Irish armies.

Now it was Redmond who was tired of the bloodshed, the condition of his people after the many defeats. He found himself longing for peace.

'We are at the tipping point, my brother,' he said quietly. 'The country, including Ulster, is in a sorry state.'

He had told an increasingly depressed and angry Niko of how the policy of laying waste the lands had utterly decimated the populace, and that large numbers were submitting as they spoke.

'It will take at least a generation to put all to rights. The Irish people will lose, whoever wins this battle. The kin of the Old English loyal to our cause who, if we fail, are able to keep their heads from the block, will still have the wealth of the monasteries they sacked and kept hidden in other lands years ago. This will keep them from starvation, but we will have nothing left, even for an unlikely victory feast. The enemy has cleared many of our woods and other ambush places and holds the passes and supply lines. They can now avoid our watery sucking mires. Tyrone comes now to join us from the north, but he must fight, and fight hard, to make his way through. Please God he will succeed. Our people will need your honeyed words and smooth speech if this fails. We have to keep what lands we can. I will be proscribed, with our Overlord, if I live.'

Niko was silent, and then to cheer himself as much as Redmond, he said, 'I am using this new pistolle –' Niko handed the weapon to his brother, 'made in Liege. I can obtain one for you.'

'I have seen them in action,' replied Redmond, squinting through the sight, 'against our forces. We have little powder – unlike the English troops.'

'If we can get near enough, we can deal with the cannon crews before their mortars are lit! And the Spanish also have plenty of muskets and powder - which they know how to use. We have taken the town of Kinsale and can hold it. We hold a garrison at The Head. We can do it. If the clans are united, we can do it! Many of our allies are the Old English. And we can prise reparations from the Queen when we are victorious – indeed this war may be her downfall!'

'Some of those Old English are now fighting with the Crown.' Redmond gave him back the pistolle.

'From my time in England and in France, I know there are many of the Catholic Faith who will help us. And most refugees will return to their homesteads and re-build. The Old Queen will be busy fending off the Spanish who, once successful here, will no doubt move on to England – and London.'

'You are certain that Rory thrives? Did you hear from Alice Plymmiswoode?' asked Redmond.

'I have not been able to see your son and heir for some time, but have often thought on him and Alice with whom I spent much time in London. I have had no word from her,' replied Niko stiffly, 'but she grew to love the boy and he will have been well protected.'

Redmond had already been talking with Dermot and guessed his foster-brother's mind.

He now suggested, 'Woo and marry the woman. She is wealthy and well-regarded and has courage. If we succeed, you can bring her and Rory here. If we do not, you will perhaps be in a position to help us.'

'That will be impossible. She blames me – us – for the death of Thomas Hurst and the ruination of his manor and demesne. She will have nothing to do with me.'

'I am sorry Thomas perished as he did. His sister has courage and sense. Go to her – say the truth and with your suave ways and politic talk, she will not be able to resist your charms.'

Niko just smiled and shook his head, but remembered some of Orlaith's last words to him in Le Havre, 'Find that English-woman. You know she is our only hope. If you love her, keep her. If you do not, still keep her and you will not regret it.'

The two brothers clasped each other in farewell and left, both with the easy loose-limbed gait of those accustomed to spending much time in the open. They were grim, knowing that they were not to meet again for some time, if at all.

Niko's optimism proved unfounded. The English commanders had pinned Tyrone and his forces down in the north just when the Spanish fleet arrived in Kinsale and took Kinsale town. The Ulstermen broke out eventually and moved south-west, but were not in time to prevent the English army, with batteries, siege engines and extra battalions, arriving before them and besieging the town. Not only were the counties that Tyrone's troops passed through, already in desperate straits, uncooperative because his army was allowed to live off those lands where the people did not support or join them, but also there were insufficient horses and saddles for their own use, let alone the cavalry.

When the host of Spanish ships discovered that Queen Elizabeth's navy was on its way to harry them, and that a siege of the town had been mounted by the English, they returned to their home ports saying that September storms threatened. They left only twelve ships in Kinsale harbour, which either fled or were destroyed by the incoming English fleet. Under fierce bombardment, the Spanish captain surrendered the castle at the Head and he and its garrison were captured and imprisoned there.

Finally approaching Kinsale, Tyrone and his allies' attacks and engagements on the fortifications held by their enemy were fierce and bloody, but Mountjoy's forces quickly began to have the advantage, and the Irish lines broke. Eventually, bombarded by six well-placed demi-cannon, the town's defences were thoroughly breached and it surrendered. Niko and the survivors said later that they could have won, were it not for the Spanish ships leaving, and some tactical mistakes made by the Irish generals.

A massacre ensued in and around Kinsale, which included the priest carrying the white flag of surrender and the Spanish Captain and his troops in the garrison. Horrific reprisals were burned again into the memories of the folk in that region. In 1603, just before Queen Elizabeth of England died, the insurgent Irish and 'Old English' nobles sued for peace, as even the Earl of Tyrone and his main ally, the Earl of O'Donnell, realised the rebellion had failed. They went back to the north, hoping to still keep their lands.

General Mountjoy was recalled. The terms of the Peace were crushing. New English Protestant officials were sent to replace Irish ones and enforce a condition that all those nobles, gentry, clerics and officials who refused 'in lowly and reverent form' to sign the Oath of Supremacy, would, to all intents and purposes, be deprived of all their temporal and spiritual power, estates and wealth.

Niko, exhausted, slightly wounded and smarting from defeat, eventually found his way back to the beleaguered MacFeagh stronghold which was still holding out. After the Earls' submission, as he feared, avaricious clergy, justices, carpetbaggers and adventurers moved in. Dermot managed to elude pursuers and join him after another week or so. With Fintan and survivors, they tried to draw together their scattered folk from the high clachans and hide-outs in caves and bogs. Then, as their people became increasingly weakened and starving, Niko and Dermot volunteered to ride into Dublin to submit to the Crown and plead on their behalf.

Separated from his companions, it was believed that Redmond had perished, until word was received that, helm under his arm, russet hair flying in the wind, he had been seen at a hidden cove, standing in the prow of a currach made of hides and hazel rods skimming across the water to a waiting ship moored off the cliffs.

CHAPTER
TWENTY-TWO

uring the final phase of the war, Alice continued to work with her stepsons who were reaching agreements with the London Muscovy Company. Clothing, fleeces, tin, hides and as many requested goods as could be acquired were traded for furs, Eastern silks and gemstones. The Plymmiswoodes also invested heavily in the newly formed East India Company.

Alice had provided a fine carved headstone for her brother. The Crown sent written appreciations of his loyalty and sent courtly representatives to his burial. Privately, Alice would have preferred Thomas to have a memorial in Leinster, where he had kept the peace for so long.

Feeling depressed, as there was still a section of her heart that wanted Niko, whatever he had done, she spent some of her profit on a finely worked jewelled fob for the little gilded timepiece left to her by her husband. This glimmered richly when she hung it from her brocaded girdle. It pained her when little Matthew, often hugged close on her lap, asked for Niko. She could hardly bring herself to listen to the progress of the fighting in Ireland. Once she had received a garbled message that the MacFeaghs were not responsible for the fire at Hurst Place. She did not trust the source and decided not to reply. She suspected that Niko had gone to fight for his Overlord and may now be killed and agreed with Hope Polsted that Redmond's people had either perished, or sought refuge in another land. She was also disheartened when the messenger from M. De Hem, informing her of Susannah's safe arrival, told of the demise of Pieter Heyden. She could hardly believe that the Dutch woman could be the victim of so many misfortunes.

Here they say that I need good air and must venture out as I will sicken if I sit all hours at the loom. They take me to walk along the dyke but the flat grey sea gives me no comfort. I step slowly even though,grumbling, they have glued new leather to my clogs they say are not glass, although in them I know. I see Pieter passing in those waves and the seas that roll and break in my dreams…

When the London plagues again raised their ugly head, Alice travelled as usual to Somerset Abbey. Cecilia could not help but be charmed by Matthew's high tuneful singing of a Psalmody she found time to teach him. Most of all, she noticed how much softer and more patient Alice had become through her devotion to the child. She did not even object to Cecilia's teaching him the Roman Catechism and telling the boy of the Catholic tenet that it was good conduct, and not just studying the Scriptures, that would keep his soul from harm. Various vessels mysteriously appeared in the chapel. Alice merely commented that they should be hidden, and was pleased that the 'Egiptian' women were given alms or allowed to stay until they could be re-settled.

But Cecilia had said sharply, 'Donations have decreased Alice. Although Lady Templeton has received us graciously and has kept us informed of developments in the Irish war, in which Lord Edmund served with honour, she has given us nothing since taking Susannah to Plymmiswoode Hall. Previously she gave generously to our Abbey. Indeed you surely must feel obliged to make up the deficit!'

To her surprise, Alice had agreed, taking from her reticule some pieces of eight, bright and new-minted from the Spanish treasure ships.

'We must visit Lady Ann again. We can tell her that Susannah is in Amsterdam but not that I am fostering her child.'

Cecilia was not aware that Alice had just been distracted by the further piece of information Cecilia had imparted. She had said 'Our Abbey's resources have been stretched by the numerous refugees from Ireland. One family had a desmesne in Munster –one Theobald Netherton –he said he knew Thomas -'

Alice interrupted. 'God Be Praised they escaped. I know them. A good pious couple.'

'They were fortunate that they had prior intelligence that a band was on its way to kill them and burn their manor. As it was, on the road, they were attacked by a group of beggars who stopped their horses - a frightful sight it seemed, as one was a leper with no nose and another a giant wielding a long pole. They threw them money and some belongings and, whilst the wretches scrabbled for the goods, they rode quickly away. They also told me of the burning of Hurst Place and that Thomas's neighbour Chief Redmond MacFeagh was disloyal but has not yet been found. His foster-brother however <u>was</u> captured and imprisoned as a traitor, and indeed may be hanged by now. I asked if it was the MacFeaghs who had betrayed you and Thomas, their benefactors, and looted Hurst Place, but it seems it was some youthful O'Byrnes, with renegades, turncoats and foreigners who had foolishly gloated over their deeds. They were discovered and are now hanged. May God forgive them.'

'May they burn in hell!' said Alice with unusual vehemence and considerable distress.

Following the submission of the northern Earls and the publishing of the draconian terms for peace, a messenger from a Clerk of the Court informed her that an official in Dublin had written to say that Thomas had willed her his Irish desmesne and the ruins of the manor. An excited Alice could hardly wait to tell Hope Polsted.

'He said that M. De Hem has sent some gold to the Crown for their assistance to Susannah and her board and lodgings in Dublin in '97. No doubt he wants to be on the winning side, and hopes for some lucrative orders. It seems that Susannah is well and that her work is now in demand by courtiers here and in France. A Crown official – he is titled Vice-Treasurer and named Master

Gideon Goodyear – has invited me to travel to Dublin, saying that the country is now quiet under the Crown's rule. He has offered an escort for me to see Thomas's estate and manor, mostly ruined, and has said that the entire adjacent lands – including the MacFeagh lands – were also up for sale having been annexed.'

'Shall you go?' Hope looked concerned. 'I worry at what might happen to you in that benighted country. You told me you would never go there again.'

'I want to go and see Hurst Place and what has happened to his desmesne. I owe it to Thomas. As for Matthew, I heard that Constable Porter was killed in the Battle at Yellow Ford in '98. There have been no further instructions as to the boy's future. I shall be escorted and take Matthew. He should begin to know something of his Irish, if not his Dutch, heritage.'

'What will his mother think of you going back there?'

'She shows little interest in the boy. She just sends religious homilies through the Dutch Church pastors who constantly urge me to go to Preachings. She has not asked for his return yet, and I pray that she will not until he is more grown. Hope, I have been thinking. Perhaps I could obtain some of the neighbouring lands now annexed by the Crown, including those of the MacFeaghs. The accessible forests could be made to flourish again, giving valuable timber, and mines were being opened when I left. There could be profits to be made. No-one wants to go there. The land could cost little.'

'You really want those wasted lands?'

'I really don't know yet,' said Alice impatiently. 'I must go and see.' She had realised she also wanted to find out what had happened to Niko. 'I shall do what I can for the MacFeaghs – on the whole, they largely kept their faith with Thomas.'

'Be sure to take many guards to Ireland! Come back safely, Alice,' replied Hope, hugging her.

Alice's journey out of London was delayed by the crowds greeting General Mountjoy's triumphant arrival. Whilst some cheered, others, including many of the women whose fathers and brothers had been killed or died from disease during the war, shouted at him angrily, and had to be kept at bay by his escort.

'God did his will most vehemently here,' thought Alice as she, with Nat Gibson and a heavily-armed escort, travelled from Dublin to Hurst Place on a new fast road, laid for the English army to pass through. Her entourage, including Matthew on a small palfrey with guards each side, carried small ale and provisions on mules, as the wells on their route were still poisoned.

The rutted highway she remembered had been bordered with thick forest, settlements and small fields of crops and stoops. Laden carts and peasant folk had meandered or trotted along its fringes, doffing caps when in the fields, or passing the time of day when she lingered at way stations. Now she stared with deep emotion at the desolation. Alongside roofless cottages and mills were now rough stone defensive bivouacs or towers. The bones or remains of beasts littered the black stubble on the fields. There was no birdsong or sign of the plough. Millwheels lodged haphazardly in the middle of rivers, whose banks were now denuded of their shaggy willow trees. There was no food and little fresh water at the halts, except at one of the remaining monastic houses, where they paid for some sparse provisions. Matthew was lifted into her wagon, silent and afraid as half-starved refugees thronged here. Her column was mobbed and kept at bay by her guard. The women and children in the mob cried piteously in lilting English for the thrown bread and skins of ale.

'Give us bread, for the love of God!'

'Truly,' thought Alice, 'The Court poet who said "calamity is our true touchstone" was indeed correct.'

Occasionally, figures could be seen looming on misty islands in the lakes, otherwise only small groups of liveried kerns, or pairs of armed travellers and packs of wild dogs, scattering at their approach, passed them on the road. On the high tops, there were few grazing animals. Soberly, she contrasted the condition of the people with her stay in Dublin where, at the Crown's residence, comfortable beds, well-lit rooms, meats, cheeses and good wines were offered for her and her entourage.

She had been glad to get away from Gideon Goodyear in Dublin. He was an Anglican, given to some devotional excesses, a small, spare man with a narrow face, a widower, invariably attired in an old-fashioned cap and fur-trimmed robes. Chains of office hung about him and his lips glistened wetly under his long grizzled beard. She squirmed at his pompous gallantry.

Goodyear had been given wide powers in this part of Ireland as Vice-Treasurer. Goodyear was thought to be experienced in Irish affairs. For many years, he had served the Crown in East Anglia. But before that, he had been a junior clerk to an official in The Pale and had known of Thomas Hurst. Alice had silently fumed at his comment that although the Crown then had profited from the tithes paid by Thomas, her brother's leniency to the hill clans and deviation from tough military policy had allowed the rebellion to gain momentum.

Goodyear's eulogies on the manners, strategy and piety of General, now ennobled as Earl of Devonshire, were extreme. His opinion of the rebel Earls and Niko MacFeagh was quite the opposite.

He had harrumphed, 'That smooth-talking half- Ottoman scoundrel and traitor who sells his sword to the highest bidder insists he was never with the rebels at the battle of Kinsale although reliable information has been laid against him. He languishes in our dungeons at present. He came with his Squire, submitting the sept MacFeagh and seeking to sue for peace and reparations, as if he had anything with which to bargain! A medallion showing his loyalty to the Mahommedans was found on his person. He will be sent to the Devil that spawned him. They are due to be hanged at a public cross with other traitors next week.'

She had profoundly thanked God that she had come to Dublin and had intervened to save Niko's life.

Visiting Niko and Dermot in the bowels of the castle, smelling of ordure and decay, had been the worst experience of her life. Stick thin, bootless, with bedraggled hair and beards, they had been divested of much of their clothing. Breathing in with shock, she saw that even Niko's gold earring had been torn off. He rose in surprise as she peered in the grating in the oaken door, but Dermot stayed sitting on his haunches like an animal at bay. Water globules dripped and draped the stone walls and the only light and air came from two other gratings high above them. She had found it hard to look at him. Niko's black eyes, although bleary and red, still had a sparkle and his smile was wide, if sardonic.

'So,' he had said, bowing. 'You see how low I am now, mistress. Your revenge will soon be complete.' He showed his teeth. 'And how does little Matthew – or Rory as I think of him?'

She had taken another deep breath and had spoken in a low voice, quickly.

'When you left, Matthew cried out for many a night. He does well and is now with me and his nurse Benedicta here in Dublin. I am sorry Niko. I now know it wasn't the MacFeaghs who devastated Hurst Place, although some Irishmen did the thing. My – how you stink! What would you have me do? I can speak for you – I have already – but I might not be able to save you from the gallows. Why did you come here – into the lion's den? I cannot abide seeing you like this, Niko!'

'I could not abide seeing how many of our women and children were violated, starved or killed. We had to submit or all would have been killed. If you can, save us from the gallows. If not, I beg you to help our people.' He had added, not meeting her gaze.' I have often thought of you and Rory, Alice Plymmiswoode.'

'You say this because you are here in this foul prison!' she had accused. Then he had just looked at her and she had flushed. She had left soon, giving money to the warder to improve the Irishmens' conditions. Then, whatever he had done, or would do, she had decided it was God's will that she forgive him.

Trotting slowly along the road to Thomas's demesne, she recalled the difficult negotiations for Niko's release. The Vice-Treasurer had been unyielding for several interviews, loath to reverse his previous decision about the two men. She had to argue, threaten, wheedle and explain, saying that Niko had most likely been fighting in France or the Dutch Republic for the Protestant cause, and that he was definitely in London for many months when the Lord Essex was campaigning in Ireland. She assured him that the Spymaster's men would corroborate this.

Fortunately for her pleadings on Niko's behalf, Goodyear wanted to conciliate her. He was determined to now flood the land with Protestant pastors and Settlers. So far there had been no rush to come. In fact, he was having increasing difficulty in finding purchasers for the ravaged Irish lands, although he hoped that this would change in years to come. Gideon Goodyear had been surprised when she offered, as well as restoring Thomas's acreage and pastures, to purchase those bleak annexed MacFeagh lands bordering Thomas's which were for sale. She gave her reasons.

'As many of their former lands neighbour mine, the goodwill of the MacFeaghs is essential for my enterprises. I will put their people to hard work. Executing their leaders will delay full cooperation. Remember too that I am fostering their little heir, Matthew MacFeagh, who will, under my care, become civilised and keep them loyal. It is possible too that I can negotiate trade links for the Crown with the boy's kin in Amsterdam.'

'You do not have my experience of how often the degenerate Old English and Irish and particularly that devil Tyrone turned their coats, treated their churls with contempt, betrayed us and each other or made innumerable false promises,' Goodyear had insisted.

She paid more than she wanted to for the annexed lands, strongly suspecting that part of this would be taken as a bribe.

Agreeing at last, he jeered, 'Chief Redmond MacFeagh's corpse has never been found and it is believed he has fled to safety, leaving his people and his brother to fend for themselves. He is now proscribed –an outlaw- and can be taken dead or alive.'

Niko and Dermot were released, first having to abjure Catholicism and swear allegiance to the Crown. This was harder for Dermot than Niko, but, persuaded he was in extremis, he finally agreed. She thought it wise not to see the Irishmen depart, which they did hastily, but ensured that they were given horses and provisions before she set out later for the Marches of Leinster.

'If I had been the fainting sort,' she thought, now walking around the ruins of Thomas's previous home and clutching the prayer book hanging from her girdle, 'I would be prone by now.'

Its remaining bricks were blackened, its gates and stone

walls plundered for fortifications.

'Look, Benedicta, Aunt Alice – look at the old woman!'

Matthew had suddenly shouted. Nat Gibson beside them frowned and then caught sight of what looked like the back of a form in a long cloak with grey hair lurking beneath the remains of a tower. He ran forward, but all he found was a thin horned and bearded goat, which trotted off at his approach.

'It wasn't a goat. It was a woman, it was,' insisted Rory. 'She hailed me.'

The guards, inclined to garrulity, fell further into conversation on the topic until stopped by Alice. She said it was a trick of the light. She removed an uncomfortable memory from her mind.

The mill, lake and fish ponds were clogged with weed and detritus, including the bloated carcass of a sow. Bones and pieces of cloth could be seen in the ground in places, and also some mounds clothed in stones and marked with crude crosses.

Her surveyor made measurements and dictated notes to a minion at his side and made drawings on a slate as they traversed the site. Looking up at the surrounding hills, she remembered that, in Thomas's time, the clans complained that the bare moorland tops, extensive lakes and thick forest, re-granted to them in the previous century, provided poor grazing and a hard living.

'There is even less living now,'she thought.'What have I done? I have a fine London house, an interest in a steady business and good rents from the estates. I have paid far more for all this than it is worth. Restoring the manor, buying enough seed, cattle and pigs, clearing fields – all this could beggar me. And how will I find churls to labour? All the locals I've seen so far look as though they could not lift a brick!'

After leaving the ruins of Hurst Place, they moved on to the nearest garrison town where some stanchions of horse chestnut trees were still standing and where lodgings had been arranged. She had little appetite for the good bread and pies prepared for supper, remembering the wounded or destitute people to whom they had thrown coins and bread. At one point there had been a short-lived attempt at an ambush, easily fended off. The ragged men, armed with wooden staves, desperately crept back into the boggy furze.

The young guard captain, Master Francis Hay, seemed pleased to have her company at supper. He glowed with health, was elegantly dressed and tall with curly hair, trimmed beard and polite manners. He queried her mood, as she sipped at her sweet wine.

She decided to reply honestly.

'I know that war on land is, as often as not, pitched battles in strategic positions between seasoned armies, or that war at sea is conducted by conscripted navies – yes – and that sieges and bombardments cause slaughter and hardship which lead to surrender. But, although I had vaguely heard of the policy of laying waste to all, I never properly knew of its effect or that this conflict would so devastate this fair land. To see the suffering of the women and children, the sick and wounded and the old... my heart sickens and my Faith rocks. When I was here with my brother, these river meadows were green pastures, the fields waved with ripening barley and oats, and the bordering forests were thick with game. The nobles and landed gentry's orchards were full of blossom, and the granaries full of seed, with the animals fat and contented. The Irish folk Thomas talked of, and most of those I met, were hard-working and free spirits with character and life – acting and speaking beyond their station often, but engaging nonetheless, but now...'
She paused, fearing she would weep.' I remember the words of the prophet Malachi "Why do we deal treacherously, every man against his brother, profaning the covenant of our forefathers?"

'The nobles and the Church are giving considerable alms. Dreadful atrocities accompany war and insurrection,' Francis acknowledged, spearing a morsel with his pearl-handled knife, 'but on both sides. Remember that with all that plenty, the people did not have to rebel. Remember they are Papists, and that they also wanted the freedom to bear arms at will – even and often raiding and attacking each other as well as settlers like Thomas and other officials. The Crown's governance, had they properly accepted its authority, would have protected them and civilised them, and they would not have been subject to the dynastic ambitions of the likes of the Earl of Tyrone. You have to admit that they brought all this upon themselves.'

Battle-hardened, he had come to regard Ireland as a hopeless case. But he was also still young and had been more touched by the hardship he had witnessed than he was prepared to normally openly acknowledge.

'Sometimes I think that terror is the nobility's only occupation, and violence and dogmatic preachings, the Church's,' Alice continued, somewhat recklessly. 'When Generals and the Bishops have dragged so many into misery, it is a poor triumph indeed.'

He looked sharply at her. He replied carefully.

'Preachers can, and have been, executed for declaring that the Scriptures should govern us not our Rulers. But I believe that our Queen has ever wished to preserve her kingdom and punishes those Catholics that rise against her for this reason, rather than to save their souls.'

'In future,' said Alice, 'I hope all will see that trade and commerce is the better way. Our dear Queen encouraged our Merchant Adventurers. Perhaps the nobles – or King James - will follow her lead and then can Britannia and the Holy Roman Empire prosper.'

'I have a fancy, when I am released from army duties here, to go to the Americas where I hear there are opportunities for enterprise.' He added, 'I'm surprised you do not wish to sell your ruined inheritance. There is much to do for a woman alone – even one with your reputation and contacts. Do your kin support you in this?'

'Perhaps. They will want to know that it will be worthwhile and I am not sure of that myself quite yet. It will take much money and the goodwill of the people. I have the one, but am not sure about the last!' She glanced hopefully at him. 'I need strong labourers, and ones with building skill. Can you spare any troops from the garrison?'

'Unfortunately not – although in future, it might be easier. I hear that the rebel northern earls may well flee in exile to the Catholic nations to try and gain further support for their cause. If so, then we can at least stand some of the garrisons down. But at the moment, the danger of attack is still not past and desperate bands of brigands are everywhere.' He paused. 'I did hear that on a desmesne near to you some valuable metals have been discovered. Its owner is digging mines. It might be worth you investing in some prospecting on your new lands.'

She thanked him for the information, and gave him her London address, saying that her stepsons had recently had dealings in the Americas and could be of assistance.

As she rose to retire, he said, 'I recently met an envoy from the sept called MacFeagh. He was a man of tawny complexion. Since the acceptance of their submission I keep a small garrison of loyal Old English troops at their stronghold, whose supplies indeed have helped to reduce their impending starvation. He is a pleasant clean-looking fellow who somehow has managed to avoid the gallows. By some miracle, he had found some cattle and goats to sell us – rather thin but we can fatten them. He may be able to help you find churls. I'll send a messenger to say you are here, and to meet you, if interested, at the ruins of Hurst Place.'

It was nearing noon when she, in her wagon, approached the manor again on the way back to Dublin. A vestigial seeded spring forest canopy was beginning to surround some of the remaining stone buildings but all was still and silent. Matthew was mounted with her retinue. Whilst riding along, she had reminded the boy of his friend Niko.

'I see him!' Matthew knee'd his pony, trotted to a weatherbeaten Niko, greeting him with a bow and a broad smile, his guard following hesitantly behind.

'I lost you, uncle. I lost you but now I've found you again. But you are changed. Where is your earring?'

'I've found you too, Matthew. God Be Praised. You too have changed. You are now a fine little man!'

Niko, thin, his patched English garb and a voluminous Irish cloak hanging loosely on him, was waiting with a number of unarmed churls. He was the only mounted one. Alice could not help smiling as Niko approached her carriage, followed by the boy. He then climbed down from his horse, bowed deeply and kissed her hand, then holding her gaze until her stomach seemed to liquefy under the beating of her heart. Then he turned and lifted the boy from his palfrey and held him in the air, turning and showing him to his companions.

'Matthew, you must meet some of your father's people, who

will know you as Rory.' He added in Gaelic, 'Hail Redmond's heir, MacFeaghs!'

There were cheers and bows from everyone. Alice ordered food to be given to the churls, her retinue, Matthew, his guard and Benedicta who went to sit on the remains of a wall from what had been the Manor's kitchen garden. Bread, cheese and ale was then brought to her, Niko and the surveyor, placed on makeshift stools alongside her carriage. After eating, they discussed the drawings of the new manor and the plans were finally agreed.

The house was to be raised again, more modestly with cross wings, of mostly red-brick and stone. It would have tall chimneys, leaded glass windows, bedchambers, kitchens and pantries. A small chapel would be built in the north-east corner. The manor would be defensible with look-out towers. Handsome stables would have vented bricks and little timber, and new barns and stores would also be added. Niko agreed to find and choose the workmen and artisans. Alice agreed that he could employ drovers to bring the remaining livestock in the mountain fastnesses bordering Thomas's desmesne to be fattened on any new pasture that could be found.

Slowly, the ease and enjoyment she had experienced when with Niko in London was returning. He found himself remembering his lust for her and how they had laughed together at the waving arms and gurgles of Susannah's baby in that brightly-lit chamber. They both wanted to find that closeness again.

'Is it your intention to live here when it is finished?' asked Niko. 'I can find you a good steward.'

She was silent for a while.

'I will be away now but will return with Matthew from time to time and see how all progresses. Be aware that there may be much that cannot be done. As a 'femme sole,' I have one third of my departed husband's wealth, but when our Lord takes me, it will revert to his family. If Matthew's mother makes no provision for him- she has not yet asked for his return, but it may happen- then I will ensure that Thomas's wealth passes to Matthew on my death.'

'What will you do if she asks that the boy goes to her in Amsterdam?'

'I do not know Niko. I hope that time never comes.'

Alice then prepared to depart for Dublin and then on to London to buy and ship materials and to persuade her stepsons to invest in the works, and possibly sell some of her other assets. Before leaving, she agreed that Matthew could explore the ruins, followed by Benedicta and a guard. They were joined by a thin bearded churl with a voluminous cap and a scrawny hound who showed Matthew some of the dog's tricks causing the child to exclaim in delight.

When all except Alice were mounted, Niko approached for the farewells. Although recognising his love for her, and now resigned to the supremacy of the Crown in Ireland, there remained a slow burning in his heart at all that Alice's countrymen had visited upon this land.

'When I am stronger,' he found himself thinking,' and have hired the artisans, I will leave here and make money by selling my sword or travelling to distant shores once again, perhaps never return.'

'Niko, you have seen enough of war and pestilence.' She seemed to have almost divined his thoughts. 'I know you for a master trader. Would you help trade my wool and fleeces when the flocks increase? And in time sell linen, salt and hides on the continent as you did in partnership with my brother-returning with silks and perfumes from the Levant and elsewhere? This will provide Matthew with means of his own and employment for all here. Ores and pitch may be discovered in the barren mountains here as well. I will send you some wherewithal to travel as a trader not a soldier. You may take a knowledgeable member of my household, and instructions where to obtain the goods I will initially send soon to be traded. Will you do this and make profits for Matthew, the MacFeaghs and me?'

He looked hard at Alice, wondering whether to say more and if she knew that she had not left his heart. He said, 'yes - for Rory's future – the success of these lands is his birthright. Redmond would want this. I thank you Alice. I am glad that our regard for each other remains. Let it not be dimmed again.'

Dropping his eyes, he took her hand and kissed her palm.

Black clouds advanced above them and the ruins glowed in a sudden strong shaft of light. Soon they were doused with rain. Without further conversation, he shrouded her in his cloak, and hurried her to the covered wagon where he wished her God-speed. Heedless of the downpour, he watched it and its following guard and horses roll onwards into a blueish mist.

Sadly turning back to the company, he saw a black pony he had not noticed before, tethered amongst some shrubbery. He heard hounds barking and some shouts where a number of his people had crowded into an enclosed, roofed space in the ruins. Hurrying into this, he saw the churl who had played with Matthew, now hoodless and smiling broadly, surrounded by jubilant faces and cries.

'Redmond? Can it be you?'

'I saw and spoke to him in Gaelic whilst you looked on,' chuckled Redmond. 'He did not understand but showed no fear. He is a fine lad with much of the look of my father.'

Later, when the rain had stopped, they talked of what had happened since they last met whilst taking the long mountain road to their battered stronghold.

'Our home and its surroundings have suffered from years of grief, neglect and overcrowding,' said Niko. 'Now at least the garrison shares some of its supplies with us and we hunt and poach as much as we can. Fintan and I had to submit, or all would have been killed, ransacked and violated. He and those still surviving are trying to hunt, herd and breed horses, although these animals, and all game are scarce and scattered. Crows only thrive and make poor eating. Living off this spoiled land has been exhausting us.'

Niko then told Redmond of his imprisonment and also of Alice's plans for the Hurst desmesne.

'God be praised that Thomas's sister saved you from a hanging, my brother. You would have sacrificed yourself in pleading for our people in Dublin. I thank you for it. I cannot stay at the castle because of the garrison. But I collected Fintan's children in Le Havre and have sent them to our castle with my new squire. He is not known to people here but is swift with the dagger and adept at foreign tongues. Ronan died bravely in a battle in Ulster. I have his sword for you to give to his family. After dark tomorrow, meet me at the place of the cross with Fintan and Oonagh.'

As they journeyed part of the high little known route back together, the day was still overcast, but the air less oppressive. They stopped to rest the horses and dogs at a point where they could see the promontory, on whose peak the ruins of the ancestral square keep were silhouetted. Here had emerged a large disc of indigo sky, crossed by one half of a rainbow. They both said 'Medb!' together and hailed her.

A thin and haggard Oonagh greeted Niko when he returned.

'Look at our great lubberly children,' she cried pointing to the somewhat bewildered boy and girl, Finn and Fionnuala. 'Dear Redmond has brought them back to us. He has had them looked after well. I thank God for it. They will have to get used to meagre fare now – the deer are well-guarded and fire has swept away the stacks of oats, but they still have stories and the love of parents. Children, did you hear the story of the Bald Man and Finn McCumhail and the litter of pigs?' And she walked off, one in each hand.

The next night, Niko, Father Ignatius, and a gaunt smiling Fintan, his legs before him in his little wheeled cart, gathered at the place of the cross; Redmond, followed as ever by hounds, being greeted with joy. They settled on their cloaks and talked at length of the defeat, and of the clan loyalties which had undermined the military command structure, as well as of those who had died and of Alice's plans. They were fortified with the contents of a small barrel of brandowine which had mysteriously appeared with Redmond. It seemed that, after the defeat at Kinsale, he had first joined those holding out in the north and fought in Ulster with them until all seemed hopeless.

'Tyrone and O'Donnell know that the country will not now fight on. I fear that the clans will never again unite. You were right to submit, Fintan. The northerners are not my people and there was word that in time they intend to leave Ireland and to try to gain support again from Spain and Rome. Rather than remain on their charge with little to do, I decided to find and spend time with whoever of our people are still in Le Havre, and then secretly come back and see how things had transpired here. I've missed you all.'

Fintan said sadly, 'There has been so much death. Deaths celebrated, disregarded and countless deaths unknown. And betrayal. English against Irish, Scots against Irish, Irish against Irish, rough men – adventurers – against all, brutality, disease, suffering...'

'Perhaps I was wrong,' opined Redmond, 'perhaps we should not have joined this conflict...'

'It would have happened anyway, Redmond,' Niko said robustly.'You were in honour bound to follow our Overlord... and see, some at least of us have survived to re-build our lives.'

'God and maybe you Niko,' Redmond glanced sidelong at him, 'having touched the heart of Thomas's sister, may provide a better future for us all.'

Redmond got up, turned away and then suddenly back again. He said at last, 'Maybe you have more choice than you think. I have a place known only to me and where I shelter now – a cave – where I hid Gile when I first found her after that wreck on the shore in '97 – you recall that wreck? I confess I stashed away valuables and gold that I did not share. I went back there to get gold to buy weapons, but the remainder is still undiscovered. You must all now have most of this wealth, although I will keep some for my exile. As you did for us those many years ago, Niko, now will I do this for you. Re-building the manor and demesne for Rory will be quicker and be my contribution to his patrimony. Mind now, that hiding places are built within the new manor somewhere, for the friars, should they be persecuted, and for vessels and the Host to be kept.'

They all gazed at him fondly, overwhelmed at what they had heard.

Oonagh said, 'Do not part with gold too quickly or the English will have it off you quicker than a twitch of a nanny goat's eyebrow.'

There was laughter.

'Now that Alice has asked me to trade and add to her means, this gold will certainly help that endeavour. Having gold leads to yet more gold, and we can build more quickly and give a living to our churls, rather than hiring English and Scottish rogues,' said Niko, adding, 'You sly dog! I always wondered where you managed to succour Gile for so long.'

'What is your wish, Fintan? You have nobly held this place for us all against all odds. What is your wish?' asked Redmond. 'You have a right to be Lord in my stead should you wish it.'

'I must talk to Oonagh. But release me from command now, Redmond. I have found it onerous and feel my age and my wounds tell more on me. I want my Oonagh to eat and be fat again and the children to be tutored and have an easier life than can be found here now. Fionn tells me they like Le Havre, find it hard to always speak our tongue and have become somewhat accustomed to different ways. They may not settle here.'

'You must go to Le Havre if you wish it,' said Redmond, clasping his uncle's shoulder in understanding, 'but I cannot for some time, if ever, lead the sept as I am intended for the gallows as an example if I am caught. Prepare yourselves and I will guide you and your family over the sea. Niko, it is you who must stay, and, in between your trading trips, let Dermot take more responsibility here, until my son can claim his birthright. Messages can still pass between us. '

'Yes,' agreed Niko. 'Dermot has learned much and is held in respect. He is loyal and true. But Redmond, what will you do, after escorting Fintan and Oonagh to France? Do you not want to come back when the dust settles? The old Queen has died and King James of Scotland is on the English throne. In time I may be able to obtain a pardon for you.'

'I must make much penance. There is a restlessness in my soul. Father Ignatius, come with me to make a pilgrimage, and say masses for Orlaith and all our dead !'

'I long to do this and may stay in Rome,' said Ignatius. 'These

Protestant pastors, full of fire and brimstone, will have me disembowelled if they find me.'

Now I am settled here, and living with pious women is forbidden me, our Lord guides me to think more and more on my Mathieu, who should have some part of my comfort here. God forgive me for leaving him so young, but I could do naught else...I knew Mistress Alice would care for him. I wonder if he now has more of the countenance of my brothers? I doubt if he can speak our tongue. That father of his will by now be hanged as a traitor or slain in battle. I will send to Mistress Alice and ask for tokens of my Mathieu's thriving. Perhaps she would bring him to visit us here...I do not wish to cross the sea...

'After the pilgrimage, what then Redmond?' insisted Niko.

'Well now,' said Redmond, looking as wolfish as his thin-shanked hound. 'I will get me to my wife's lodging in Amsterdam. And maybe sire me another son!'

That night, the wind sang mournfully in the mountains.

I curse thee Gile.
Disgorged by the brimming sea,
Found by the glint of gain,
I curse thee Gile.

Be ever the scourge and bane
Of thy loved and noble swain.
I curse thee Gile.
Return to the rippling tide
And never in Ireland bide!

About the author

S.R. Nicholls grew up in south London and was educated at Manchester and Bristol Universities. She lives and works in Birmingham. This is her first novel.

GLOSSARY

Arquebus – firearm in use from the 15th to 17th centuries
Brandowine – archaic word for spirit distilled from wine
Buannacht – archaic Irish: a tax or tithe paid to landlords
Children of Lir – mythical people in an Irish folktale.
Churching – Archaic word for a Christening
Churls – farm workers, peasants and servants
Clachan – village or small hamlet
Crannog – lake forts
Currach – an ancient river and coastal boat
Desmesne – a piece of land belonging to a manor
Egiptians – this is the spelling used in 16th-century documents
Erin – archaic word for Ireland
1598 Edict of Nantes – a French law granting religious and civil
liberties to Protestants in France
Freebooters – pirates or lawless adventurers who may also wage
Ad Hoc war on other nations
Freemen and kerns – retainers of a Lord who were trained and
armed soldiers but could also have their own homesteads
Indigent – destitute, needy
In Extremis – a latin religious phrase giving dispensation to
desperate acts where one is on the point of dying or in extreme
difficulty
Gallowglass – 16th century soldiers
Lemures – spirits from Irish myth

Pistolles – muskets

Place of Easement – archaic phrase for lavatory

Prie-Dieu – a french word for prayer furniture with a kneeling surface and ledge for elbows and religious books

Rath – ancient Irish stronghold

Royals – Tudor continental currency, widely accepted

Salves and Simples – Simples - herbal medicines made from flowers, barks or the whole plant. Salves- herbal ointments or creams for external use

Sept – the branch of a clan, often used interchangeably with clan

Spitle Fields – this is the spelling in old documents of an area of London now referred to as Spitalfields

'Stranger' – Tudor word for immigrant

The Pale – a region around Dublin colonised and garrisoned by the English

Tir-Na-Nog – Celtic heaven

To 'civilise' – This referred in Elizabethan Tudor times to change or pacify so as to promote or enforce the English way of life. Other, not understood, behaviours or cultures were seen as 'savage.' 'Civility' meant more than politeness and good manners i.e. it included 'not savage'.

Recusant – person who refused to attend Anglican services in Tudor times

Vassal – in this context a person bound in honour to serve and obey one of higher rank

Footnotes

[1] In theTudor period, this included the Netherlands, Belgium and parts of Northern France

[2] A male demon believed to have sexual intercourse with a sleeping woman.

[3] Tudor spelling

[4] causey-an archaic word for a paved way (cf.causeway)

[5] This was named after the Minchins or Nuns of St. Helen's in Bishopsgate. The name survives now as Mincing Lane in the City of London.

[6] The quartering and maintenance of troops in a district ostensibly for protection.

Printed in Great Britain
by Amazon